D0410859

THE HOURGLASS

Beyond high gates fastened with chain lies stark, beautiful Trawbawn. Here, haunted by the past, lives the frail Lydia Beauchamp, whose private existence is interrupted when a young man called Adam wanders into the vast grounds and becomes her confidant. Lydia sets him a challenge – Adam must travel to Dublin to find her estranged daughter, but this is a task tainted by menace, for what has driven a daughter from her mother? Soon the unlikely friends are entwined in a deadly game, as an old lady's desire for peace mutates into a terrible, relentless need for revenge...

THE HOURGLASS

THE HOURGLASS

by

Julie Parsons

Magna Large Print Books
Long Preston, North Yorkshire,
BD23 4ND, England.

Gloucestershire County Council Library

British Libr

Parsons, Juli
The I

A cat
avail:

ISBN
ISBN   978-0-7505-2627-2

First published in Great Britain in 2006 by Macmillan
an imprint of Pan Macmillan Ltd.

Copyright © Julie Parsons 2005

Cover illustration © Anthony Monaghan

The right of Julie Parsons to be identified as the author of this work
has been asserted by her in accordance with the Copyright, Designs
and Patents Act, 1988

Published in Large Print 2006 by arrangement with
Pan Macmillan Publishers Limited

Magna Large Print is an imprint of Library Magna Books Ltd.

Printed and bound in Great Britain by
T.J. (International) Ltd., Cornwall, PL28 8RW

Grateful acknowledgment is made for permission to reprint lines from 'An Arundel Tomb' from *The Whitsun Weddings* by Philip Larkin, published by Faber and Faber Ltd.

'I Whistle a Happy Tune', words by Oscar Hammerstein II and music by Richard Rodgers © 1951, Williamson Music International, USA, reproduced by permission of EMI Music Publishing Ltd. London WC2H 0QY.

'You Got It', words and music by Jeff Lynne, Roy Orbison and Tom Petty © 1989, EMI April Music Inc, USA, reproduced by permission of EMI Music Publishing Ltd, London WC2H 0QY.

To my father,
Andy Parsons.
Rest in peace wherever you are.

ACKNOWLEDGEMENTS

My grateful thanks to

Liam Cotter, Baltimore, Co. Cork
for his knowledge of Cape Clear

Gov. John Lonergan and Gov. William Connolly
and the men I spoke to in Mountjoy gaol

Alison Dye, Joan O'Neill, Phil MacCarthy,
Renate Ahrens-Kramer, Sheila Barrett and
Cecilia McGovern for their unfailing support
and helpful criticisms

Maria Rejt and Sarah Turner for their
thoroughness and editorial rigour

my husband, John Caden,
for his creativity and inspirational love

and Harriet Parsons and John Moriarity
for their extraordinary gift of Emily

With the dawn came the light. And with the light came the pain. The light shone into the house. The pain throbbed through her body. The light brightened the dried blood on her hands and her face. It glanced across her swollen eyes so she winced and her eyelids closed of their own volition. She tried to sit up, to move towards the window, to draw the curtains to keep out the light, but she couldn't lift her legs. Not even to crawl on her hands and knees over the polished floorboards. She could do nothing. Nothing to protect herself. Nothing to save herself. Nothing except lie as still and as quietly as she could. And hope that he had satisfied himself. And that he was gone.

She wrapped her arms around her body. And she listened. The house was quiet. Perhaps she could sleep for a few minutes. And when she woke she would feel better. Stronger. Braver. And she could pick herself up and tiptoe to the door. And open it. And creep out onto the landing. And listen. Always listen. For the sound of his footsteps in the hall below. For the sound of his fist. For the sound of his voice. And if she waited quietly and heard nothing she could put one hand on the banister and begin to walk downstairs. And maybe then he would not be there any longer. He would have decided that enough was enough for one day. That he had got everything that he could. And he would leave her and her daughter in peace.

But as she lay on the floor she heard him. Not his fist, not his footsteps. Just his voice. He was shouting. She lifted her head and held it up. She tried to twist

13

around towards the door, but her neck was stiff and so sore that she could not move it. She laid her head down again. Tears dribbled from the corners of her swollen eyes. They stung as they slid down into the cuts on her face. She could hear what he was saying.

'I have the hourglass, Lydia. And you know what that means. I have all the time in the world. Time means nothing any longer, nothing for you, and everything for me.'

But it didn't matter what he said. All that mattered was how he said it. And what he was going to do. And she knew from the tremors that rose up through the house. She knew what he was going to do. He was coming back for her. And this time there would be no way out.

ONE

The first time Adam saw the house was from the river. He'd come in from a couple of days' fishing off the Fastnet. The weather was breaking. Storm-force winds were forecast. They were heading for the safety of their mooring upstream. He was sorting nets, tidying up the deck. But the sight of the house made him stop what he was doing. Lean back against the wheelhouse, push his cap out of his eyes and stare at its slated roof and long windows as they slipped past just visible through the trees.

'Nice, eh?' Pat Jordan, the skipper, grinned at him. 'Nice one, don't you think?'

And all he could do was nod and grin back.

And afterwards, when they'd washed out the fish holds and left the boat tied up at the pier and were sitting in the pub, a pint and a plate of cheese and ham sandwiches on the counter in front of them, he asked Pat, asked him about the house.

'That's Trawbawn. Where old Ma Beauchamp lives.'

'Beauchamp.' Adam savoured the name. 'That's a funny one. Not what you'd expect around here. A blow-in, is she? Like me?'

And Pat laughed as he supped his pint.

'You could say that. Cuckoos in the nest more like, Lydia and that useless husband of hers. Got the place when Daniel Chamberlain died. Now,' he paused, and took a deep drag of his cigarette, 'there's a story.'

'Yeah? Tell us, tell us all.'

But Pat just smiled and shook his head and called for another round. While outside the rain began to lash against the windows and the wind roared like a bad-tempered bull.

Later, when the storm had passed over and the skies had cleared and the sun had come out and cast its sparkling sheen across the newly washed countryside, Adam drove along the river road. There were more gates than he'd noticed before. The first couple he tried brought him into farmyards, modern houses built next to tumbledown cottages, tractors parked beside heaps of manure and dogs who barked with a frenzy that made him disinclined to get out of the car. The next one led to a small slip with a couple of punts tied up on running moorings and a jumble of nets

15

and lobster pots. And then half a mile further on, just where the road bent and straightened again, there were high wrought-iron gates set in an ivy-swagged stone wall, closed and locked with a length of chain wrapped around them.

He slowed and pulled the car onto the verge. He got out and put his face to the bars. A long gravelled drive stretched away in front of him, an avenue of trees on either side, smooth grey trunks with branches that spread to form a canopy. He bent to examine the chain and the padlock. The padlock was hanging open and the chain was loose, so it was easy to reach in and lift the rusty latch and push the gates apart. He stepped back to get a better look at the wall. Then noticed the door to one side, sagging on its hinges, standing half open, the ivy pulled roughly away from it. He looked around. No one or nothing, just the low rumble of a tractor somewhere over the hill and the sudden silence as the sound of the last passing car died away. Nothing but a fresh breeze that made the stiff leaves of the ivy rattle.

Adam pushed through the door and walked slowly down the drive. His shoes raised little puffs of dust from beneath the gravel. It was so quiet here. Just the soft murmuring of the leaves from the ash trees. And the sudden loud shriek of a sea-gull as it glided above him. He followed the wide sweep of the drive and there, in front of him, was the house. It wasn't particularly huge or grand. Not awe inspiring. Not the kind of house that would make you gasp or shrink back or marvel at its opulence. It was just very beautiful. Three storeys with a curved bay from roof to basement.

Windows of perfect proportions. A roof slated in blues and greys. Tall chimneys. A front door with an elegant fanlight. And as he stood on the lawn that surrounded it on three sides, he could see through the windows that its rooms were of perfect proportions too.

The front door stood open. A canvas deckchair was outside it on the wide stone step. A book lay face down on the seat. Beside it was a glass, half full. He picked it up and sniffed. Gin, he thought. He held the glass to the light. There was a deep red smear on its rim. He swirled it around. Ice cubes tinkled. He dipped his finger into it and licked it carefully. It was gin all right. He fitted his mouth to the shape of the red lower lip and drank. The cold liquid danced on his tongue and snatched at the back of his throat. He bent down and placed the glass where he had found it, then straightened up and moved slowly away.

Colm had told him about the house. He had told him about the river, the bay, the islands, the sea, the rocks, the birds and the fish. He had lain on his bunk and talked and talked. Through those long nights when the landing lights burned holes in their eyelids. And the prison noises kept them ever on the alert.

'You go there when you get out of here. It's a good place. There's more than one living to be made over there. There's fishing, there's farming, there's always building work. There's bar work, there's plenty there, plenty for a lad like you. With a busy brain and a willing body. Isn't that right, Adam, isn't that right?' As he reached up to take his hand and hold it against his face. Hold it, stroke it, smooth down the tight young skin, then turn it over and press his lips against the soft palm.

Now Adam walked across the lawn, watching the house as he moved away from it. From a distance the windows looked black and empty. No sign of life within. When he reached the trees he turned. He followed the path that wound through the wood, down to the riverbank. It was low tide. Sticky black mud, criss-crossed with runnels of murky water, stretched away towards the river's sluggish flow. He leaned on the low wall. It was warm to the touch. Above his head a gull banked, drifted, flapped its white wings, and banked and drifted again. He began to walk along the margin of the riverbank, running his hand lightly across the top of the wall. A smell of salty mud rose up and filled his nostrils. There was flax planted here, exotic among the briars and brambles, the bracken, the twisted shoots of wild rose. And here ahead was a clearing among the trees. Gravestones, some fallen and scattered. Others still upright. Slabs of limestone, carved and decorated. He stopped and stood and leaned down to trace the names. Thomas, Rebecca, William, Judith, Margaret, Jane, David and Daniel. Plain, no-nonsense Christian names and all with the same surname. Chamberlain. Except for the newest of the lot. *Alexander Beauchamp. Born 1933, died 1995. Beloved husband and father. Rest in Peace.* He leaned over the smooth grey stone and pressed his index finger into the carved shapes. It was warm to the touch. He climbed onto it, then turned over and lay with his back pressed flat, feeling the hardness against his shoulder blades,

18

his ribs, his hip bones. Hard and unyielding, like the floor of the punishment cell. But here, when he opened his eyes wide and gazed upwards, the sky was the blue of a baby's blue eyes, and the smell was of the sea and the earth, not the stench of the overflowing piss pot in the corner.

He took a deep breath, sucked in the air, felt it push his lungs up into his chest. He was hungry. He felt empty. When he lifted his head to look out at the river the movement made him feel sick. He hadn't quite adjusted. To meals at irregular hours. Seven years of eating at 8.30, 12.30 and 5.30 had trained his body, given it expectations. Needs that had to be satisfied. But it wasn't like that any longer. Now that he could eat whenever he felt like it, half the time he didn't feel like it at all. Except now. Now he wanted food. And quickly.

He swung his feet to the ground and stood up. It was cooler than before, the sun beginning to dip beneath the trees on the far bank of the river. He moved away from the small graveyard, and took the path again. The growth was more dense here. Rhododendrons towered above his head and pressed in against him. He recognized their huge shiny leaves, so bright and glossy that they looked almost good enough to eat. The ground under his shoes was carpeted thickly with last year's leaves. His feet scuffed through them and he wondered for a moment what might lie beneath. For a moment he felt as if he might vomit. He could feel his toes curling up away from the thick rubber soles of his shoes. He couldn't bear the thought that there might be a mouse or a rat hiding somewhere, watching him,

19

waiting for him to slip and fall. Then he remembered what Colm had said to him once, one Sunday afternoon, when they were shut in together and he'd woken out of a nightmare, the same one, the one that always came back to him. The rats running over his body, their tails flicking across his mouth. The fear that he might catch something from them. The shame that anyone might know. That a rat had sat on his chest and reached out its delicate little paw and touched his chin, touched his cheek, crawled up to kiss him on the lips. Woke screaming, sweat streaming down his face, his back, his chest, feeling the warmth of the piss as it flooded down his legs. And the smell, the sweet, sickly smell.

But Colm was there beside him. Holding him, soothing him, speaking to him in a language he didn't understand. *Mo chroí, mo chroí, a ghrá, a ghrá,* over and over again until his heart slowed and his sobs ceased. And Colm stripped him and washed him, wrapped him in a dry blanket and soothed him and said to him,

'Don't mind those rats. Aren't they even more scared of you than you are of them? Aren't they even more determined to stay out of your way than you are out of theirs? Sure, don't you know that? Aren't you a great big fella who's well able to look after yourself? Aren't you, Adam? Aren't you?'

But still and all, even though he could hear Colm's words and Colm's voice, still he walked more and more quickly until, breaking almost into a jog, he saw that he had come to the walled garden, its wooden gate closed, but a rope handle to pull and a latch to open. And here was safety. Rows and ordered rows of vegetables, and against the wall, warmed by the afternoon sun, a greenhouse filled with strange flowers, great hanging trumpets of yellow and orange, pots of tomatoes still to ripen, and cucumbers and peppers, and a vine too, grapes, small and round and green, hanging down above his head, not yet ready for his mouth.

But canes of raspberries, luscious and red, the juice dripping from his fingers as he stripped the cone-shaped fruit, leaving behind the white pointed centre they clung to. And burrowing into the beds of straw for the strawberries, sweeter than the raspberries, feeling the indentations in the skin as he crushed them to the roof of his mouth with his tongue. Then turning on a tap that stood by the side of the compost bins and sluicing cold water over his face, bending his mouth to it, feeling it drip down onto his T-shirt, as he closed his eyes and felt the stickiness, the cloying sweetness washed away by the chill of the drenching stream. His eyes closed so he did not see the hand that reached out to turn off the tap. Did not hear the quick steps on the brick path behind him. Heard and saw nothing, until the voice saying, loudly, angrily without fear.

'Who are you? What do you want? What on earth makes you think you can come into my garden and help yourself to my fruit? Answer me, answer me, do you hear? Before I kick you out of here. Answer me.'

21

TWO

Lydia had seen the top of his head, his hair
bright, almost golden in the afternoon sunlight.
Not golden now as the water from the tap sluiced
over his face and dripped down onto his clothes.
Now in the sudden shade of the walled garden
his hair looked dull and mousy rather than
blond. But as he looked up at her, surprise and
anxiety distorting his features, and he moved
quickly away from her into a patch of sun, she
saw how it gleamed again. Fine, pure, yellow. Her
daughter's hair. Grace's hair. And a smile to
match. A smile that stopped her in her tracks and
slowed the angry flood of words from her mouth.
So they stood, the old woman and the young
man, face to face. Silence, then birdsong suddenly loud in their ears.

She had been upstairs when she saw him first.
Called from her chair and her drink and her book
by the phone ringing, a sudden sense of urgency
as she hurried into the hall to answer it. But it was
nothing of any great moment. An enquiry from
the local hotel as to when the gardens would be
opening to the public. They had an American
couple staying who had heard of the Beau-
champs' collection of tender perennials. They had
seen the photographs in an in-flight magazine.

'Tomorrow,' she said. 'Tomorrow morning. Tell

them to come at eleven. I'll have coffee and freshly baked scones for them after we've done the tour.'

But as she stood in the drawing room, the phone in her hand, listening to the voice at the other end, she felt such a pang of loneliness, of isolation, that when the call ended she walked out into the hall and quickly up the stairs and into her bedroom at the front of the house and sat down for a moment on the chair by the window and looked at herself in the long gilt-framed mirror on the far wall. Just to reassure herself that she was still the woman she had always been. Small, lithe, strong. Hair which had once been black, now streaked with grey, but still thick, curly, springing back from her forehead. And still her own face, the familiar bones beneath the betraying skin. And she still had the full lips of her young days. And she stood and picked the lipstick up from her dressing table and dabbed at her mouth, filling in the gaps in the colour, pressing her lips together firmly, as her eyes drifted from her reflection across to the treetops, beyond them the river, above them the sky. And saw movement down there, unfamiliar movement. And as she stepped across to the window to get a better view, she saw the head, fair and bright, pushing through the trees and the shrubs away from the house.

And the thought came slithering into her mind, the joyful thought that the fair head bobbing through the garden was Grace. Her beautiful Grace. Her daughter, Grace.

She pressed her hands against the glass and

23

leaned her forehead against it too. Her breath fogged the window. She moved back and wiped it clean. But she had lost sight of the head now. Whoever it was had gone beyond her view, disappeared behind the tallest of the trees, the beeches which stood in a tight grove between the house and the water's edge. She walked to the door. The landing was bright, lit by the afternoon sunshine. The doors to the other bedrooms were open as always. She passed by them, her footsteps still light and quick, although she felt as if she might need to lean against the wall to catch her breath, such was the pain that flooded through her as she glanced to right and to left. At the rooms, their beds made, their floors swept, their shelves dusted. Ready for those for whom they waited.

Outside it was still warm. She leaned down to pick up her drink. The ice had melted. She bent her head to it, then raised it to her mouth and drank. And stood for a moment, the glass in her hand, looking out across the lawn towards the trees which stood between the house and the river. Saw Grace climbing the monkey puzzle, her bare legs scratched by its scaly branches. And Alex holding out his arms to catch her as she jumped. His hands sliding up her thighs. Alex with his hair bleached by the summer sun and his wide smile and his bright blue eyes crinkled up against the light. Closed her eyes against the memory. And opened them and thought: Alex dead, Grace gone. Just me here now, all on my own. She spread out her hands, gnarled, spotted with age, wrinkled, reddened. And turned them over, looked at the thick blue vein that travelled down each wrist. And

24

the lines scored deeply into her palms. Turned them back again and clenched them into fists. Walked away from the house, along the path that led to the small shed to the back and side of it. Stepped inside, picked up a spade and swung it as she walked back to the lawn, across it and into the trees.

And now as she walked she could see the young man who had invaded her garden. He was making no attempt to hide. He moved with ease and sureness ahead of her. She hung back and watched him. She saw him in the little graveyard, saw the way he lay down on her husband's tomb. Waited to see what he would do next. Watched him as he walked on ahead, sensed an urgency and anxiety in his movements, a sudden tension and lack of ease in the way his shoulders hunched, his hands clenched. Hung back and watched as he pushed open the door to the kitchen garden. Saw the way he plunged into the raspberry canes, his hands and face red with their juice, scrabbled on his hands and knees for the strawberries. And realized he reminded her of whom, of what? His hair like Grace, but there was something else in him too. An elegant sense of glee, as he roamed through the garden. That reminded her of whom? She couldn't put a name or a face to it. But it was there. Somewhere in her memory.

She struck the ground with her spade, but he did not hear her. She watched as he reached for the tap, watched his hand twist it, and waited. For just a couple of minutes until he had drunk his fill, and then she began to move as quickly as she could, along the brick path, straightening her shoulders, filling her lungs with air, feeling a sense of righteous anger puff her up, so by the time she was close enough to touch him she was ready. To shout out loud.

'Who are you? What do you want? What on earth makes you think you can come into my garden and help yourself to my fruit? Answer me, answer me, do you hear? Before I kick you out of here. Answer me.'

Saw the sudden panic in his face. Then the smile, that slow movement of his mouth that stopped her words. Turned them off. Rendered her, like him, dumb.

They sat in the large basement kitchen. She poured tea from a flowered china pot. She offered biscuits, half-covered in dark chocolate. He took one, then on her insistence he took another. A small tabby cat drowsed on her lap. He wanted to drowse too. Put his head down on the table and drift off.

He had used his smile. His granny always told him: never forget your smile. It's your greatest asset. And she was right. Right about so many things. He had smiled at the old lady with the wild black hair streaked with grey and the spade held in her hand like some kind of a weapon, and she had smiled back, then leaned the spade against the wall and looked away.

And he had held out his hand. And said, 'Sorry for upsetting you. I didn't mean to. I didn't mean to trespass. It's just this place,' he gestured around him, 'it's so beautiful.' And he smiled again and said, 'My name is Adam, Adam Smyth.'

26

And she smiled back at him and took his hand. Her grip was firm, her palm was cool and her voice when she spoke was clear and strong.

'And my name is Lydia Beauchamp. How do you do?'

It was cool here in the half darkness. But not cold. He shifted on his chair and its legs grated on the tiled floor. He grinned apologetically. She nodded but said nothing. A clock chimed somewhere in the house. It was a pretty, musical sound. He sipped his tea and ate another biscuit. She watched him closely. He had the strangest eyes. The left was a frosty greeny blue, like water beneath ice, and the right was light hazel with dark flecks like a piece of Russian amber. He returned her gaze. She held out the plate of chocolate biscuits. Her hands still had a certain elegant grace. She wore a ring with a dark red seal on the little finger of her left hand. The finger next to it bore a wedding ring, a wide circle of buttery yellow gold. As she moved her hand it slipped up as far as her knuckle then slipped back again. Around her wrist was a plain gold bracelet and around her withered neck a heavy chain of the same colour and weight as her wedding ring.

'So how did you find us? Was it chance?'

The first lie. 'Chance, that's right. By chance. I saw the house from the river and wanted to get a closer look. I'm sorry for trespassing. But I couldn't resist it.' He smiled at her as he bit into his biscuit.

'Not good with temptation, no?'

'No.' He shook his head. 'Not good at all. Always in trouble when I was in school. Always

27

getting into mischief, always getting sent home with a note. Always driving my mother crazy.'

'Girls?'

'Girls, fun, parties, horses, dogs, cars, you name it.'

'And now, what about now? How old would you be now?'

'Twenty-eight. Not quite the big three-oh yet.'

'Big three-oh, that's nothing, that's barely out of infanthood. Wait till you get to my age.'

'And what would that be?'

She smiled and showed her teeth. They were still white, still straight, with a small gap between the front two.

'That'd be telling, wouldn't it? Did no one ever warn you that it's not good manners to ask a lady her age?'

'That's what I mean.' He reached for another biscuit. 'Can't resist doing what I've been told not to. Can't resist it at all.'

The clock in the hall began to chime. It was six. She stood up. He half-rose with her.

'No, no, you stay where you are. It's not often I get the opportunity to entertain such a young and handsome man, even if you are a trespasser and a thief.' She smiled at him again to take the sting out of her words. 'Let's have a drink. I always have a drink at six. And it will make a change not to be drinking on my own.' She reached into a cupboard and brought out a bottle. 'Gin OK?'

The thought of the drink snatched at his throat and he felt again the stickiness of her lipstick on the glass.

'Of course,' she said, 'gin wouldn't really be

28

your drink, would it? Young men like you drink all those fancy beers. Straight from the neck, isn't that what they call it?'

'Not me, I like wine best. But gin is pretty good too.'

The second lie. Just a little one, not as big as the first. It slipped out so easily. It lay between them on the kitchen table as his gaze shifted to the box of empties by the back door and the rack of full bottles in the corner.

'Wine. I see. That's a good vice to cultivate. My husband, my late husband, was a wine drinker. He thought for a while that we might be able to grow grapes here. Make our own. But, you know, the weather, too unpredictable.' She paused. The gin splashed into the glasses.

'Your husband, when did he die?'

She looked at him. She lifted her glass and drank. She set her glass back down on the table.

'You know,' she said. 'You saw his grave, didn't you?'

'His grave? That one there...'

'That one, there. The most recent one. The one with his name on it. Alexander Beauchamp. The one you saw down by the river.' Her smile was gone.

'Of course,' he began to stammer, 'of course, of course, your husband.' He could feel the cold of the stone against his back, its hardness against his ribs and his hips, against the back of his head.

'So it was chance, was it?' She raised her glass again and drained it. She stood up and walked to the fridge. She opened it, pulled out the ice tray, and the bottle of tonic. She turned her back on him as she poured herself another measure. 'I'm never quite sure about chance, coincidence, happenstance, serendipity, call it what you will. I'm never quite sure that there isn't someone, somewhere, who rolls the dice, or lets loose the golden thread, then raises the scissors and cuts it, just,' she gestured with her right hand, 'just like that. And just like that it all begins, or alternatively it all ends. Depending on which way you look at it.' She turned towards him and held out her hand for his glass. He lifted it, drained it and handed it back to her. She turned away again and he heard the tinkle of the ice, the splash of the gin, the fizz of the tonic. She moved towards him and put out her index finger and pushed it beneath his chin. Her bone met his bone. He could feel the sharp tip of her nail, pressing into his skin as she forced him to look up at her. He wanted to wrench his face away but somehow he couldn't. He tried to look down but he could not escape.

'So.' She raised her glass with her free hand. 'What's it to be, Adam? Chance or fate? Which one do you pick?'

He smiled again, but this time it didn't seem to have the same effect. She didn't move away from him. He lifted his arm and caught her, quickly before she had time to react, around her wrist. He could feel how fragile she was, how little flesh covered her bones. He held her gently and eased her hand away from his face.

'I'd go for fate. If I had to choose, that is,' he said, and he lifted his glass, drained it, put it back on the table and stood. He saluted her, index finger resting for a moment just above his eyebrow as he turned and walked away down the corridor, up the stairs, along the hall and out into the evening sunshine.

THREE

It was quiet in the ward on the top floor of the hospital. So quiet that it seemed to Johnny Bradshaw as he sat beside his mother's bed that he and she were the only two people in the building. There were others. But they were all, like his mother, terminally ill. There was none of the bustle and clatter of the usual hospital ward. No medicine trolleys rattling, no bang and crash of food trays, no visitors bearing bunches of garish flowers or boxes of chocolates. There were no get-well cards propped up on bedside lockers. There was just a quiet air of resignation and acceptance.

Or so it seemed to Johnny. He didn't know what his mother thought or felt. She was in a deep coma. She had been like that for the last two days. Another stroke had sent her far from his reach. Now she lay, motionless, pale, silent. Her breath was irregular. Sometimes it seemed to have stopped altogether. But when he leaned forward to scrutinize her mouth and nose, she would breathe again, a deep, sudden sucking in of air as if she was telling him that she was still in the room with him.

From time to time a nurse would appear. She would rest her fingers on his mother's wrist,

31

checking her pulse against her watch. Then she would smile and nod and leave him alone. He didn't mind. He liked it here with his mother. She had always been a quiet woman. Not one for sparkling conversation or quick-fire witticisms. She kept her own counsel and only spoke when she had something important to say. When his father had been alive she had left most of the talking to him. And after he died, three years ago, she had become even more silent. Sometimes she would phone Johnny and when he lifted the receiver and said hello, there would be no response. So he would tell her about his day, how he was getting on with his class of sixth-formers, what films he had been to see with his girlfriend. He would chatter on and on, until he would hear her sigh. And then she would hang up.

Which was why he was so surprised when she phoned him and told him she wanted to talk to him. It was a couple of weeks after she had first become ill. A stroke which had paralysed her left side, made her face droop and her speech slur. She was still living at home, just about managing with the help of a few kind neighbours, but he could see as he made her tea and sat with her in the sitting room, that soon she would not be able to manage on her own.

'Johnny,' she said, then stopped.

'Yes?' He waited.

'You know, don't you, that you're adopted?'

'Yes, you and Dad told me when I was a kid.'

'We did, didn't we?' She looked up at him and smiled as best she could with her poor, distorted face.

He didn't remember when or how they had told him. He just knew. He had always known. He hadn't minded. He had boasted about it at school. He liked that it made him seem different. And sometimes it was useful. When he looked at his mother and father and saw that they were older than the other kids' parents. That they didn't care about money or possessions or package holidays to Spain. That they were happy with their dusty old second-hand bookshop in a back street in Chichester. He could dismiss them with a wave of his hand. He felt guilty now when he thought of it.

'Well, there's something I want you to have. It's up in the attic and I can't climb the stairs now to get it. I want you to go up for me. Just on the left of the trapdoor there's a bag. It's what they used to call a vanity case. Bring it down to me, will you?' She sat back against the cushions, exhausted, the cup and saucer rattling on her knee.

The bag was where she had said it would be. He'd noticed it before, the last time he had gone up there. When he was finally moving into a flat of his own, and he'd packed up all his old junk from his bedroom. School books and pictures that he had drawn in art class, that he'd once thought were good enough to stick up on the wall. His collection of model aeroplanes and battleships, and the little silver cups he'd won for swimming. He'd thought the bag looked out of place, not the sort of thing either his mother or father would have owned. Now he put it on her lap and sat down again. She clicked open the shiny gold clasp with her one good hand.

'Here.' She gestured to him. 'You take it. You

see what's in it.'

He reached over and pulled it towards him. He reached inside. His fingers felt the softness of wool. He looked down. It was a baby's cardigan. White, with a decorative trim of blue sailing boats. He looked up at his mother. Tears were running down her cheeks.

'You were wearing it when we got you. There's a little bonnet and bootees to match. They're hand knitted. Your mother had made them for you.'

'My mother? You're my mother.' His voice broke as he spoke.

'No, darling. Not really. I'm not going to be here for much longer. I know it. You'll need someone. You should go and look for her.'

He looked down at the tiny clothes.

'No,' he said. 'She gave me up for adoption. You and Dad took care of me. You're my mother. You'll always be my mother. Not some woman who I don't know and who doesn't know me.'

'Johnny, listen to me.' She leaned forward. 'I know you feel like this now, but when I'm gone you may feel differently. She was very young when she gave birth to you. Only a child really. She was from Ireland. Things were different there, then. She must have loved you to make these clothes. Take them and keep them. And if you change your mind, remember that you have my blessing.' She sank back against the cushions and closed her eyes. He reached over and took her cup from her.

'It's all right, Mum, really. It's all right,' he said and kissed her on the cheek.

But it wasn't all right. A week later she had another stroke and another. He went with her in the ambulance to hospital. And sat and watched as she slipped further and further away. And every night when he went home he opened the little bag with its heart-shaped mirror on the inside of the lid, and looked at the tiny white cardigan. Decorated with the blue sailing boats and the blue bonnet and the blue bootees to match. And he began to wonder. As he looked in the mirror at his thick, black curly hair, and his dark brown eyes. At his small, lithe body. At his hands with their square fingers and jointed thumbs. At the space between his front teeth. And when his mother died, when he heard the last breath come from deep within her chest. And felt the last traces of warmth go from her body, he remembered what she had said.

'You'll need someone. You should go and look for her.'

FOUR

Adam could take to this life. It was one great big bowl of cherries. He lay in the large bed, in the brand-new holiday home beside the pretty blonde he had met three nights ago in the local hotel. She snored rhythmically, a little puff of alcohol-scented breath popping from between her full lips. He pushed himself up on his shoulder and looked down at her. He drew his index finger down the hollow between her large pale breasts.

Colm had been right, he thought. There was

plenty going on here. Plenty for a bright lad like him. The weather was perfect for a start. The fishing was good. He had as much work as he wanted on a variety of boats. There was Pat's trawler, heading out past the Fastnet every three or four days. He was always happy to have Adam on board.

'You're a lucky lad,' he'd said to him, pinching his cheek with an oily hand. 'A very lucky lad.'

And if he didn't feel like a trip out of the sight of land, there was work on the mussel beds off the island. It was harvest time, hard work out in the punt with the outboard idling as they hauled in the strings of shellfish. But after the heavy stuff was over, they'd head back to the island for a few pints. Sometimes Adam would stay overnight, find a floor to sleep on or a warm bed and an even warmer embrace. Those were great nights. Darkness hardly seemed to fall at all. The light would stay in the sky long after the blood-orange ball of the sun had dropped beneath the horizon. Was it light? he wondered. He didn't really think you could call it light. It was more like an absence of darkness. It was an in-between kind of state, neither one thing nor the other. But whatever it was it was fucking wonderful. It was a great scene. He'd never known people drink so much. And there were drugs for every occasion. Mostly draw, hash, but also Ecstasy for the weekends and word had it that as the summer season got going and more and more visitors came down from Dublin and over from London and even, so he was told, all points west, there'd be coke too.

Anything you want,
You got it,
Anything you need,
You got it.
Anything at all.
You got it.
Baby!

Sort of the way the song went. He sighed and rolled over on his back. The sun slanted through the skylight above his head. It shone down into his eyes. It would soon be time to go. He shifted his weight and the bed beneath him creaked. The woman lying beside him, her arms thrown over her head, groaned and turned away from the light.

'What time is it?' she whispered.

'Time I was going, Maria, that's what time it is.' He sat up straight and leaned back for a moment against the wall behind him.

'Christ.' Her voice was hoarse. 'What did we do last night?'

'Too much of everything, that's what.'

'Oh, God.' She reached out for the glass of water on the bedside cabinet and gulped it thirstily, then scrabbled for her watch among the pile of discarded jewellery. She pushed her hair from her eyes and squinted at the dial. 'Oh, God, they'll be here in less than four hours. How am I going to get myself together?'

'Good question.' He swung his legs out of the bed. She reached out and touched the tattoo on his shoulder blade. The skin was puckered and ridged beneath her finger tip.

'I like that,' she said. 'Where did you get it done? I'd like to get one.'

He didn't reply. He stood up. He bent down and pulled on his underpants and jeans. Picked his shirt and his jacket from the chair by the door. Felt in his pockets for his wallet and his keys.

'Hey.' She sat up straight.

He opened the door, his back to her.

'Hey, when am I going to see you again?'

He didn't answer. There was no need. He was surprised she even asked the question. He walked from the bedroom onto the landing and took the wooden stairs two at a time. He paused in the hall. Light flooded in from the huge picture windows. The view of the sea was overwhelming. It filled the space from edge to edge, a shining, glinting blueness. He could taste the salt on his lips. He stepped over the pile of toys on the floor. Her name was Maria Grimes. She was thirty-five. She'd told him about her family, her husband and her three children. They were expected to arrive sometime this afternoon. She had come down from Dublin a few days earlier to get the house ready after the winter.

'I always do it,' she told him that first night in the bar after she'd introduced herself. 'I leave the kids at home with the au pair and I come down and get everything sorted. My husband is very particular. I clean the house and air it, and do the shopping – do everything.'

'And he doesn't help you with it?'

'No.' She shook her head slowly. 'No, he's very busy. You know the way it is. He always likes to

38

invite some of his colleagues from his company to stay. It's part of the whole business thing. It pisses me off. I never get a break. As soon as he and the kids arrive it's work, work, work. Everything has to be just right. Food and drink served up all the time, to this boss and that boss and sometimes the bosses' shagging wives too. So,' she finished her drink with a large gulp, 'I kind of deserve this time on my own. I get so little of it. And sometimes I can make the most of it.' She gestured towards his glass. 'It's a pint, isn't it?'

'Wait.' Now he heard her bare feet on the floor above. 'Wait, hold on, just a minute.'

He picked up a bunch of keys from the hall table and unlocked the front door. He stepped out into the early morning sunshine, then closed the door quietly behind him. He walked quickly towards his van. She wouldn't follow him outside. She wouldn't want to attract her neighbours' attention. He put the keys into his jacket pocket. Just in case he might want to pay her a visit again. Then he pulled out his phone. He punched in a number.

'Hey, Pat, how's it going? Yeah, that'd be great. See you in a few minutes. How long will we be out for? Fine, terrific. Cheers, mate.'

Just what he needed. A couple of days' fishing. Get him away from any messy scenes. And when he came back he'd have money in his pocket. And she would have her husband and her children to keep her busy. She'd be out of his hair.

FIVE

The boy called Adam reminded Lydia so much of Grace. Stupid, she chided herself. You're a stupid old woman. You're imagining things. You're a prey to wishful thinking. He's just another charmer. A boy who thinks he's a man. With his golden hair and those unmatched eyes.

And what was Grace? She pondered the question as she sat in the walled garden in the midday sunshine. A butterfly, a painted lady, passed before her, hung in the still, warm air, then drifted off towards a patch of nettles and perched, wings languidly opening and closing, absorbing the heat, the light, the energy. Lydia watched it. Held out her hand. Wondered if it would be trusting enough or stupid enough to think her finger was a branch or a twig, if it would rest its slight body on her wrinkled skin.

But of course it didn't. It landed gently on a clump of nettles, then as a soft breeze stirred, lifted itself up, and fluttered off. She watched it as it went. She remembered. It was a butterfly, probably a painted lady too, that Grace had been chasing all those years ago, when she had fallen just here on this same brick path. A three-year-old who wanted to be a thirteen-year-old. Bossy, aggressive, loud. Rushing ahead of them, her sandals noisy in the hushed stillness of the late afternoon. Tripped and landed heavily on her bare knees.

Lifted her head, her mouth open, silence for what seemed like forever, then a scream of pain and rage, her cheeks suddenly scarlet and a torrent of tears starting from her eyes.

And who had picked her up? Risen unsteadily from the same wooden bench on which she now sat, one hand clutching his stick, the other reaching down to the child? Daniel Chamberlain, that was who. They'd heard all the stories about him since they'd left Dublin and come to live here. He was eccentric at the best, mad at the worst. His only son had died in a boating accident years ago. Bereft and grieving, Daniel and his wife had taken solace in their garden. And when she became ill with cancer he had nursed her by himself at home, wouldn't allow her to go into hospital. Now he lived alone in the house. And the house? People threw their eyes up to heaven when it was mentioned. What a state. The roof leaks. The basement is awash. He's letting it fall down around his ears. And what about the rest of the family? The cousins, the second cousins, the first cousins once removed who live nearby? He hates them, haven't you heard? He's sworn they'll never get the estate, that he'll let it slide into the sea before he'll leave them a blade of grass or a single brick.

But here he was, bending over, bending down, holding out his free hand to Grace. A stick of barley sugar in its cellophane wrapper in his thin white fingers, the sun glinting on its spiralled, gleaming surface. And somehow Grace had stopped crying, had pulled herself up, clutching at his faded flannel trousers, pointing at her scraped and bloody knee. And he had put his balding, age-

41

spotted head close to her soft fair curls and whispered something to her, so she stood still, reached out for the barley sugar, waited patiently while he untwisted the cellophane, then took it from his hand and put it to her mouth.

Was that how it all began, that bright spring day in the garden? The old man and the child, head to head over the barley sugar and the bloody knee? If Grace hadn't fallen, if she hadn't cried. If Alex hadn't said that he wanted to see the gardens and the house. That his mother had been there once years ago. That she had told him about the gaff-rigged fishing boats which were sailed on the river. He was sure it was the same place. And he wanted to go and find it. Although Grace had sulked and whined and said she wanted to make a sandcastle and go for a paddle.

'And you promised, Mummy, you promised we would, and now he says we're going to a house and a garden, and I hate him,' her face turning red and her bottom lip quivering. While Lydia tried to placate Grace, her daughter, and support Alex, her new husband, and make them both happy. But if she had taken Grace's side, and they had gone to the beach that day, they'd still have met Daniel. Lydia was sure of it. Daniel Chamberlain was always going to come into their world. If it hadn't been that Sunday it would have been the next or the next or the next.

Now she got to her feet. She was nearly as unsteady as Daniel had been all those years ago. He used a stick. She wouldn't. I'm fine, I can manage, she said to all who tried to help, or interfere as she thought of it. She steadied herself then began to walk slowly down the brick path towards the flower borders. She gathered together a bouquet. There were tall stems of campanula, blue and white. The yellow daisy-like heads of rudbeckia. Hollyhocks, taller than she was, in pale pink and white. She cut an arching branch of philadelphus. The cream flowers gave off the heady scent of orange ice cream. It reminded her of the ice pops Grace used to suck as a child, the coloured rivulets of melting ice water running down her chin. Daniel had told her the philadelphus was his wife's favourite. Darling Elsie, he had called her. Always darling Elsie. The long mahogany table in the dining room was always laid for two, even though she had been dead for years. Until Lydia and Alex and Grace had come to live, first of all in the gate lodge, and then in the big house. After that first afternoon when they had met in the garden and he had walked with them to the boathouse and showed them all that was left of the fishing boats' rotted hulls. And he and Alex had stood and talked while Lydia and Grace had roamed the gardens together. And as they were leaving to go back to their damp rented cottage, with the outside toilet, Daniel had asked Alex if he needed some work. And Lydia's heart had nearly stopped. As she waited for Alex to pretend. That he was working already. That money wasn't a problem. To smile his friendly grin which hid all his fears. And shake his head.

But he didn't. He told the truth. That he and his wife and his stepdaughter, Grace, had come from Dublin with nothing.

A cloud glanced across the sun and for a

moment it was dark. And she remembered. The first winter they had spent at Trawbawn. Living in the gate lodge at the top of the long drive. Alex working in the gardens. Lydia working in the house. Thankful for the roof over their heads. And the night of their first storm. When their relationship with Daniel suddenly changed. There had been thunderclaps over the house like giant hands breaking giant paper bags against their ears. A sudden flash of lightning made even brighter as all the lights in the house went out at once. Candles casting a buttery glow over the kitchen. Lighting up Grace's small face as she demanded to be allowed to hold one of the light sticks, as she called them. A sudden sense of gaiety as they clustered around the Aga for warmth and Daniel felt his way to the wine cupboard under the stairs and emerged with cobwebs in his hair and a bottle in each hand. And insisted.

'You'll all stay here and eat with me tonight.'

She remembered it so clearly. That night in the kitchen when the lights went out. They drank the bottles of wine and then Daniel went again to the cupboard and came back with Calvados and she made coffee and Grace stood on a chair and stirred the egg custard on the top of the cooker and they ate it hot and creamy poured over the apple pie that had been warming in the bottom oven.

And Alex sang all his favourite songs. 'The Foggy Dew' and 'The Mountains of Mourne' and 'Trotting to the Fair' and 'My Bonny Lies Over the Ocean'. And Daniel told ghost stories and Grace fell asleep on his knee. And when Lydia had done the washing up and tidied everything in readiness for the morning, and they had made as if to wrap Grace in a blanket to take her out into the storm and up the drive to the lodge, Daniel had insisted,

'You'll stay here in the house. Make up the bedrooms on the top floor, Lydia. You won't go out in this weather.'

The first time they slept there.

And the next day he said to her, 'I want you to move in. Too much room for me. Can't possibly find a use for all this space. Makes me feel guilty. And please, you will eat with me, won't you? Darling Elsie would want it. I know she would.'

And he showed Grace where all the boxes of silver cutlery were kept, and gave her the polish and a rag.

'A penny a piece, dearie. Your job now, to keep them clean.'

The cloud moved and the garden was sunlit again. Lydia bound the flowers tightly with a piece of plastic twine, then moved quickly along the margin of the curving pond towards the woodland by the river. She pushed through the rusty gate and into the small graveyard. Today was the last day of July, the same day that Daniel had died. She laid the flowers on his slab of stone. She stood for a moment, her head bent. Then she opened her eyes and stepped back from the grave. A shadow fell across the grass. She looked up. A heron flew with stately sweeps of its huge wings above her head towards the river. She stopped and watched its slow, elegant progress. It looked prehistoric, its long neck stretched to its fullness, its thin legs moving as if paddling through the air. They had watched the herons together, she and Daniel, on those long days when he had lain in bed, too weak to get up, and she had sat with him, watching over him.

'They look like me, don't you think, Lydia?' he had said.

'No,' she protested, slipping her fingers beneath his wrist to find his pulse. 'Of course they don't.'

But she smiled as she said it and noted the long beak of a nose, the angular face, the bones barely concealed beneath his white skin.

The last day of July, the day that Daniel had died. It was very early in the morning. Four thirty-eight to be precise. Lydia heard the breath come from his mouth and then the silence that followed. She waited. She sat down beside him and reached for his hand. It was warm and pliant, soft to the touch. She kissed it, then held it to her cheek.

'Goodbye, Daniel,' she whispered. 'Goodbye and thank you.'

She had nursed Daniel, washed him, fed him, stayed with him until that morning. She had used her skills, learned when she was in her twenties in the hospital in London. Kept him hydrated, kept him clean, tried to keep him pain free. The local doctor who was young and new to the practice wanted him to go into hospital, but Daniel wouldn't hear of it. He had cried, tears trickling down his thin face, like a small child instead of a man in his eighties. The doctor shrugged his shoulders and swung his stethoscope from one hand to the other, then looked at her for support.

But she just stared out of the window, at the river beyond the treetops, then said, 'Well, you know, I am a registered nurse. I have all my papers. I can look after Daniel here, if you just prescribe whatever drugs are necessary and whatever equipment I'll need. I can do it. It's no problem.'

Now she turned and followed the heron's course towards the river. Nestled beneath the overhanging pines was the stone boathouse. She pushed open the slatted door. Inside it was dark and cool. She waited until her eyes had adjusted to the gloom, then she took a couple of halting steps forward on the wooden decking. The boats were clustered together, their bows nudging each other. They reminded her of young horses at a gate, waiting to be fed. There was a sudden ripple of movement on the water outside and the boats began to rock, their gunwales gently rubbing. She could hear the noise of an outboard. Its mosquito whine buzzed in her head. She waited until the sounds outside had retreated. Then she stepped carefully down into the wooden punt that was tied closest to the water gate. She loosed it from its neighbour and pushed gently with the boat hook until it began to slip away. The boat floated free of the boathouse, its prow rising up on top of a long, low wave, the wake from another craft which had passed a few minutes before, she thought. She and the boat rocked gently up and down.

Alex had loved the river. He had been so happy here, for those first few years when Daniel had been alive. During the day he worked in the garden. He got stronger and healthier. Gone was the pallor of the city. At night she watched him undress. His back and chest were brown. His muscles flexed and the hairs on his upper body shone in the lamplight. They lay together in the old iron bed and he told her about his dream, his project. He had gone out to the islands and spoken to the fishermen about the rotting timbers in the boathouse. He explained it all to her. He was going to rebuild one of the boats. He drew a diagram with a stub of a pencil on a scrap of paper.

'I can do it, I know I can,' he said. She had never heard such conviction in his voice. 'I've spoken to Daniel. He's going to pay for the wood. You wait, Lydia. This time next year we'll be sailing. You've no idea what it will be like. It will be wonderful.'

Now she watched the ripples widen and spread out across the broad expanse of the river. In the distance above the crowns of the trees the slated roof of the house gleamed as the light stroked it. She bent down and trailed her fingers through the cold water. There was a strong smell of salty mud. Beneath her she knew the mud was thick and black. At low tide it gleamed, its smooth oiliness pocked with shells, with worms, with the tracks of birds and other small amphibious creatures. Sometimes the carcass of a cow or a sheep would be revealed by the outgoing tide. Sometimes it would be something else that lay, curled foetus-like or sprawled, limbs in an exaggerated cross, half-submerged beneath the mud's blue-black coating.

Still the boat rocked. She heard the sound of another engine. Diesel, inboard. Something that would take a trawler all the way to the middle of the Atlantic. It was still a good distance away, further down the river, nearer the sea. It would have to be careful. Even at high tide the river was treacherous. Filled with sandbanks and rocks. The skipper, whoever he was, would have to have his wits about him. Not that that was of concern to her. Her boat was almost flat-bottomed. Just the smallest amount of keel to keep her steady.

Alex had done what he said he would. All that winter he had worked by himself down in the boathouse. He had come home late every evening with wood shavings in his hair and down the back of his trousers. His hands were calloused and scarred with the cuts he had given himself as he struggled to control the chisels and saws. But he didn't care. His sleep was deep and dreamless. And he was up every morning before she stirred, barely able to wait to get in a couple of hours more before he began his work outside. Sometimes she wondered, as she heard the sound his boots on the stairs, if he was hoping that some elves would have done their magic in the night and the boat would be finished by the time he got there. But she could see how much he loved the process. He brought home little presents he had made for them. A crude wooden doll with hair of coiled shavings for Grace and a bowl and spoon for Lydia.

'I hate dolls,' Grace shouted and dropped it on the floor. Lydia waited for Alex's temper to flare, but he just picked it up and put it on the dresser and carried on discussing with Daniel what colour to paint the hull.

She reached down and picked up a single oar. She fitted it into the slot in the stern and began to scull. Lazy sweeps to left and right just to keep the boat from drifting on the incoming tide back to its place of shelter. She moved slowly forward. She stopped and then drifted back again. She could just about see the drawing-room windows through the trees. She turned the boat around in a wide slow arc, so her back was now to the house. She leaned over and looked down into the river's murk. Along its margin the heron stood, its pointed beak extended, its eyes alert to the slightest ripple beneath. She picked up the oar and sculled again, propelling herself further out into the middle of the channel. The boat's engine was louder now. She could feel its throb reverberating back from the riverbed. She wasn't sure. They had never told her exactly where Alex had been found. She hadn't asked. She hadn't wanted to know. She knew they had brought his body into the boathouse. He had been dead for three days. He hadn't been found right away.

She gripped the oar tightly and began to jerk it from left to right as quickly as she could. Her arm hurt. She cursed it out loud. Fucking body. Falling to pieces. She jerked the oar again and again and the boat slewed from side to side. She stood up, planting her feet, one on either side of the boat's centre of gravity. It would be so easy. To let herself slip and slide out of the boat and into the river, just like Alex. Had it been in this boat that he had taken his last trip? They had never told her. She hadn't asked. But he had done what she was doing now. He had sculled out into the river and sat for a while. He hadn't been seen. He had chosen a night when there was no moon, when there were thick clouds obscuring the stars. When the only light on the river was the flicker from his cigarette lighter, as he smoked his last cigarette before he went over the side.

'How do you know he smoked before he died?' she asked them.

'He was holding his lighter in his hand. It was clenched in his fist. And there were three cigarette butts in the boat when we found it.'

That would be Alex. He never did anything without having a cigarette first.

'His blood alcohol level was very high. We found a bottle of whiskey in the boat too. There was hardly any left. I suppose he might not have known what he was doing. It might have been an accident, but there was a note, you see.'

She had tried to understand it. She had sat in her hotel room in the Holiday Inn just south of Rhinebeck, New York, the same hotel she always stayed in when she was invited by Spencer Wright and his wife Betty to give her series of talks to the Federated Garden Clubs of New York State. She sat surrounded by her lecture notes, and tried to grasp what was being said to her. She didn't want to picture it. All the way home in the plane she had tried not to think of how it had been when the tide went out and his body was revealed. He must have known. He must have planned it. Taken the tide tables from the shelf in the study and worked out how and when he should do it. So he would be found. But not immediately. He had gone out in the boat. Drunk the whiskey. Smoked the cigarettes, then swung his legs over the gunwales and dropped carefully into the water. Hung onto the

51

side for a few moments. Maybe his nerve was failing him. Maybe he was suddenly terrified, didn't want to go through with it, wanted to change his mind. But the alcohol would have kicked in. He wouldn't have been able to concentrate, wouldn't have been able to organize his thoughts, his movements. And perhaps the cold would have started to get to him. His fingers numb and a fearsome numbness creeping up through his legs. He was always so thin, she thought. He could never stand the cold. He would never join her for a swim, even on the hottest day when they would take the boat and go out into the sea, and she would flop over the side and swim around in circles.

'Come in, come in,' she'd say, waving to him and calling him. But he'd never risk it.

So why did he drown himself? It didn't make sense. He would never have chosen water. A gun maybe, pills perhaps. He had tried to hang himself once. All those years ago. When they first met. When he had been brought into the psychiatric hospital where she was working. A red raw mark around his neck, a deep bruise that lasted for weeks. He had talked to her about it, those dreadful seconds of choking and then the dense blackness that pressed in on his eyelids. He had talked of it again and again and she had encouraged him. All part of the healing process, she had thought. And he had confessed that he had tried it a number of times before. But his family had covered up for him. Called his uncle who was a well-known doctor in Dublin. Sent him to a private nursing home to recover. Until this last time. When he had been too close to death. He had promised her he would never do it again. And his mother, a small, pretty woman with her hair neatly permed, had seen how Alex had come to trust Lydia and had asked to meet her. Befriended her, took pity on her, the poor unmarried mother with the baby and no family to help her. Found her a better flat. Encouraged the relationship between the nurse and her son. Gave her presents of money. Took her shopping for clothes. Supported their decision to marry. And said to her, 'Take him out of the city. Take him away. I know he'll be better away from here.'

And he had been. For all those years. So the police must have got it wrong. It wasn't suicide. It was an accident. But he had left a note. It was absolutely clear and simple.

The police hadn't wanted her to see him when eventually, after six hours in the air and another couple of hours in the car, she had got home. He was in the mortuary of the local hospital. The Garda inspector had taken her aside and told her bluntly. It wouldn't be a good idea. Her husband had been dead for three days when he was found. The water had speeded up the body's decomposition.

'It's, um, not a pretty sight,' he said, his nose wrinkling with a distaste he couldn't hide.

'I don't care,' she replied. 'He's my husband.'

The sound of the boat's engine was much louder now. She used the oar to push her further out into the centre of the channel, where there was a view down the wide sweep of the river towards the next big bend. She could feel the trawler before she

53

saw it. The vibrations shook through her body. She sat still and waited. It came around the bend, travelling swiftly towards her. Its bow wave curved out on either side, its frill of white bright against the dark green river. She felt the punt beneath her begin to rock. She held the oar steady. The trawler's engine drummed in her ears. She could see a figure in the wheelhouse. She sat still. The trawler altered its course. It turned towards her. She heard a shout from the deck. She waited. There was a row of men now, lined up watching her. The boat began to rock violently from side to side. She straightened her back. She lifted one thin arm into the air and saluted them. She heard whistles and shouts. For an instant she thought the trawler would swamp her, but at the last moment it veered away. She watched as its crew stood at mock attention. And saw among them the bright golden hair that was Adam's.

'Yahoo.' He raised his hand, his fist clenched. 'Yahoo,' he shouted and she heard the crew's laughter and catcalls drift across the water. The trawler's wake charged towards her, a huge foaming wave. She gripped the punt's gunwales and then grabbed the oar again and turned it as quickly as she could. The bow swung around, and cut through the water's white head. She looked up at the trawler's stern as it moved away. Adam was leaning out. A wide smile split his face in two.

'Yahoo,' he yelled and waved his arm around above his head. 'Ride 'em, cowboy.'

She held on tightly, bracing her legs against the violent movement. Water slopped over and into the boat. It soaked her trousers, filling her shoes, and left dark splotches across her white shirt. She pushed her hair back from her face with one wet hand and tasted salt on her lips.

Adam watched her as the distance between the two boats increased.

'What the fuck does she think she's doing out there in that old tub of a thing?' He turned to Pat Jordan. 'What's wrong with her? Has she got a death wish or something?'

Pat shrugged. 'Like her old man. He went in somewhere round here.'

'Oh yeah? Is that what happened to him?'

'It is. It's a few years ago now.'

'An accident, was it?'

'Not really, not unless you call suicide accidental. We found him at low tide. It was a spring tide. There was a tree, just about there. Came down in Hurricane Charlie. Got washed out into the river.' He pointed towards a mudbank on which a couple of seagulls had taken their place. 'Bloody dangerous it was too. I was always meaning to get at it with a chainsaw. Anyway, he'd got caught in its branches. He was hanging by the neck. He'd been in the water for a few days.'

Adam said nothing. He closed his eyes. He tried not to see it.

'Wouldn't wish it on your worst,' Pat grunted. 'Although there wasn't much sympathy for him from anyone around here.' He paused. 'Or for her either. Not much sympathy at all.'

'Is that so?' Adam turned to face him. 'And why was that? I've met her. She's nice enough. Lonely, I'd say. Finding it hard to manage on her own.'

'Well, there was a lot of talk about the note he

55

left behind.'

'A note?'

'Yeah, it was particularly interesting for our old friend Colm O Laoire. You wouldn't know him. He's been away in England for years. Got himself into trouble over there.'

'Trouble?'

'Yeah, woman trouble. Killed his wife. He's been in prison for a long while.'

'And what's that got to do with our friend back there?' Adam jerked his head towards the punt, now bobbing peacefully in the sunshine.

'Ah.' Pat moved away towards the wheelhouse. 'It's a long story. Remind me to tell you some night when the telly's on the blink.' He pulled his cigarettes from his coat pocket and offered them around. 'But I'll tell you one thing. Colm, now, he knows more about your woman than the rest of us put together. And not only her, but her old man and her daughter. Colm's the one with all the dirt on them. But Colm was never one for telling.'

Adam turned away and moved forward. Up ahead he could see the pier and the boatyard, and the pub beyond it. There were tables out on the lawn, and groups of people sitting in the sunshine. He could taste the beer on his tongue and his palate. He had a plan for the afternoon. There would be alcohol and food to begin with. And then he'd take the river road, turn off down the long avenue to the house among the trees. And then, he wiped his mouth with the back of his hand, and then, who knows? He'd have to get his inspiration from Colm. Colm would have all the answers. He always had in the past and he would now.

SIX

Lydia sat in the punt and waited until the trawler's wake had lost its momentum. It broke in a small neat wave against the narrow strip of shingle that fringed the river's edge so that the heron moved at last, its curiosity pricked by the sudden swirl of movement around its long thin legs. Then she picked up the oar and began to scull back towards the boathouse. She was tired now. Her hip burned with pain and her shoulders and arms ached. The sharp light which sparked from the water dazzled her eyes. She wanted to close them tightly and slip into the welcoming darkness. But she knew she couldn't. She was an idiot to go out in the boat like this, she thought. No life jacket, not even a buoyancy aid. Nothing to protect her from the downward drag of the water. It would never have been tolerated back in the days when Alex ran the sailing school here. After Daniel died and she inherited the house and the gardens and all that went with it. And set about making it into a business. A sailing school from mid-May to mid-September, the river filled with small boats, and Alex in his baggy shorts and faded sweater, his long, thin legs the colour of polished leather, and a cheerful smile permanently on his face.

She reached the stone entrance to the boathouse and pulled herself inside. She took the painter from the punt's pointed bow and tied it through the iron hoop on the wall. Twisted the rope into a loop, twisted it around and back on itself, pulled it tight. The simple bowline. Alex's favourite knot. Drummed into her and Grace. Over and over again. A length of rope hanging from a chair in the kitchen. For practising, Alex said.

'Now do it, and do it and do it again. Now, let's switch off the light. Do it in the dark. You never know when you're going to need to be able to tie that knot without light.'

'Oh come on, Alex, don't be ridiculous.' Grace's whine, 'You're just being silly, obsessive. Who'd ever need to know such a stupid thing?'

And Alex's face stiffening. His voice rising.

'Do as I say, Grace. For once don't argue with me. Just do it.'

And Lydia, intervening as always, 'Come on, Grace, sweetheart; it's a game, imagine. It's a game. You're out on the boat one night and you forget what time it is and the next thing you need to be able to tie yourself up.'

'Oh yeah.' The sneer in her voice. 'And you don't have a torch or a box of matches or anything. And there's no moon. Or stars. Come on.'

Silence in the kitchen. Until Grace picked up the rope and effortlessly, easily, her eyes closed, tied the knot, then let it loose, then dropped the rope on the floor at Alex's feet.

Now Lydia sat still in the boat. She didn't have the energy to pull herself up and out of it. Her hip hurt, her knees hurt, her arms ached. She sat with her head in her hands and she waited. For the rise and fall of the river's swell to leave her.

She sat and waited. This, she thought, is what old age is all about. Waiting. Forever waiting. She tried to stand, but the boat moved as her weight shifted and it rocked, so her feet slid beneath her on the wooden slats. She sat down again, heavily. She looked at her watch. It was getting late. She had another group of tourists coming for lunch with Jackie, the usual tour guide.

'What on earth did you think you were doing,' she said out loud, 'making a fool of yourself in a small boat on the river when you've work to do?'

She ran through the list of preparations in her mind. There was cold meat in the fridge, and smoked salmon. She could pick everything for the salads from the garden, and gather raspberries and strawberries for dessert. There was cream to be whipped, the table in the dining room to be laid, glasses to be polished, but the white wine was already chilling and the red wine just needed to be opened. If only she could get her balance and get out of this damn boat and damn boathouse. She was getting cold here. It was damp, dark and miserable. A narrow blade of sunlight eased through a gap in the slates above her head. She held out her hand and felt its warmth. It shone on her wedding ring, bringing out the brightness of the gold. She craned her neck and looked up at the roof. She would have to get it fixed before the winter gales shuffled the slates like a pack of cards. So much to do here, always another problem, another task. If only Grace had stayed. If only.

'Shut up.' Her voice was loud again. 'Just shut the fuck up, Lydia. Stop being so self-pitying. You're on your own. And that's the way it is.'

There were voices now coming along the path. Laughter too. It was the Polish boys. Pavel and Sebastian were their names. They had arrived at the door one rainy Monday morning. Said they would do anything.

'No job too small,' Pavel repeated slowly over and over again, his English hesitant and imperfect, his smile nervous. She put them to work weeding in the vegetable garden. They didn't mind getting their hands dirty. They didn't want to cut corners, use chemicals. She brought them into the house and they cleaned the windows, washed the paintwork, polished all the silver in the dining room, stood on a stepladder and dismantled the glass chandeliers that hung from the high ceilings, and washed the crystals in soapy water. Climbed into the attic and sorted through the bags of old clothes, piles of newspapers, brittle with age, and boxes of books. No job too small. Pavel's mantra. She didn't ask about their work permits. They arrived promptly at nine every morning and left at six every evening. She paid them in cash and they thanked her, folding the notes carefully and zipping them into their plastic purses.

Now she called out again.

'Pavel, over here. Hey, Pavel, can you give me a hand? I'm here in the boathouse.' She waited. 'Pavel, can you help me? I can't quite make it on my own.'

Saw the thin face with the spiky brown hair, the old-fashioned blue dungarees with the VW logo on the breast pocket as Pavel pushed through the door. And behind him at his shoulder, Sebastian's round brown face, his expression anxious, concerned as he came forward and encircled her thin wrists with his large hands and pulled her carefully to standing. The boat swayed and rocked and she reached out and grasped his upper arm and hung on while he half-lifted her out onto the decking.

'Thank you, thank you.' Her voice was hoarse. 'You're very good to come and help me.'

'And you, you should not be in that boat, Mrs Beauchamp. It is not safe for you; you know your legs are not as strong as they once were.'

He stood back and let go of her and wagged his finger primly in her face. And she smiled and pushed past him, out into the sunshine again.

'Nonsense, I'm perfectly all right. I just felt a little bit unsteady, that's all. It's time for a cup of tea, I think, boys, don't you? Will you join me?'

But they wouldn't. They escorted her to the back door and held it open for her. Refused the tea as always, but took two slices of chocolate cake.

'Please,' she pressed them, 'I love to make it, but there's no one to eat it. I can't eat it all by myself, can I?' Watched them as they disappeared back into the walled garden again. Saw how they reached out and grasped each other's hands, swinging their arms backwards and forwards like small children in the playground. Knew they would eat their sandwiches and the pieces of cake in the sheltered corner out of the wind where the dahlias nodded their spiky heads and after their lunch they would sit on the wooden bench, Sebastian's dark head leaning on Pavel's thin shoulder, their fingers entwined.

She switched on the radio in the kitchen, turned the volume up loud as she busied herself with her preparations. Just enough time to get everything ready. Time was when she had help in the house. Cáit O Laoire from Cape. She had come as a teenager and stayed on. Suggested that they employ her brother, Colm. When they were booked out all summer long. When they were all working from six in the morning until the long shadow from the monkey puzzle tree slid across the lawn just after ten o'clock at night.

'Sure he's doing nothing much at the moment. He's a great sailor,' Cáit said. 'He knows all about those old fishing boats, like the one that Alex restored. He learned it all from our grandfather. He taught Colm all about the currents in Roaring Water Bay, the hidden rocks, the reefs. The way the wind works. I'll give him a ring, get him to come in and see you.'

That summer. When everything had been right. And good. And wonderful. And they had all been so happy. For the first time ever Alex and Grace had stopped fighting and seemed to like each other. After so many years of trying to get Grace to see how kind and good and sweet Alex was, she seemed to have accepted him. She had been so jealous as a small girl. So resentful. And everything Lydia tried had made it worse. Until that summer when she was nearly sixteen. And Colm had worked out so well too. Until it had all gone wrong. And Colm had left. And the next summer the weather had been so bad. Gale-force winds in July and torrential rain in August. Complaints from the tourist board about the quality of the food and the service. One couple threatened to sue because their son capsized and was in the water for an hour before the rescue boat picked him up. Alex trying to manage the sailing school on his own. While Lydia tried to cope with the house and the guests and the garden.

Now she washed the soil from the Pink Fir Apple potatoes. The Polish boys had dug her a bucketful. The potatoes' skins were knobbly but their flesh would be waxy, flushed with colour and delicious. She would steam them, cool them and dress them with olive oil and lemon juice. The Polish boys had picked a selection of lettuces too. And handfuls of rocket to be mixed into the salad. And there was a punnet of fresh raspberries, and a smaller one of loganberries. Her mouth watered as she washed them and trimmed off the stalks.

She walked up the stairs from the kitchen in the basement. Sunlight lay in blocks of gold on the polished floorboards of the hall. The Persian rugs were worn but their colours were still vivid. She stood in the doorway of the dining room. Daniel's old silver shone against the darkness of the mahogany table. She opened the sideboard and took out wine glasses and heavy Mason's Iron-stone plates. She laid the table. She opened a drawer and counted out the linen table napkins. She slipped the silver napkin rings over them and placed them beside each mat. She hummed as she worked. She had looked after the house well, she thought. Daniel would have been pleased. She stepped back from the table. She moved around it, stroking the smooth shiny wood with her fingertip. Then she turned away. She would sit outside and wait for the visitors. Another group of Americans. This time they were from California. San Francisco, she thought. The Pacific Ocean on their doorstep. She tried to remember everything she knew about the moderating influence of ocean currents. She wanted them to enjoy their visit, to feel they had learned something useful from her.

But today they had learned more than she wanted to reveal. She had known there was something strangely familiar about the small middle-aged man with the jutting goatee beard and the bright blue eyes behind gold-rimmed glasses. He had bided his time, lagging behind the others as she shepherded them through the gardens. He had taken his own route, turning away from the usual path, then appearing in front of her again. That was fine. She had no objection. She liked her visitors to feel at ease. But what was it about him that made her uneasy? He waited until lunch was served and their glasses had been filled, emptied and filled again. She had taken her place as she always did at the head of the table. Her back was pressed into the carved chair where Daniel had always sat. Her fingers fiddled with the silver napkin ring with the Chamberlain family crest engraved upon it. The volume of the voices in the room was rising. A good sign, she thought. They were enjoying themselves. She began to relax, drank some more of her wine. The ache in her hip had dulled. She crossed her legs and pushed herself away from the table. At first she didn't realize what he was saying. She didn't even realize that he was speaking to her. He reached over and took the napkin ring from her fingers. He rubbed the silver on his sleeve and held it up to the light.

'Yes,' he said loudly, 'that's the right one.' He tossed it lightly from hand to hand. She looked at him quizzically. 'The hourglass, the Chamberlain crest.' He pushed up his glasses and held the napkin ring close to his eyes. *Veritatem dies aperit.* The family motto. Time reveals the truth.' Then he slipped it into his jacket pocket. 'You want it back?' His tone was loud and aggressive.

'Well,' she shrugged, 'we don't usually encourage our guests to make off with the silver.' She smiled.

'You don't?' He took the ring from his pocket and dropped it on the table. It bounced and rang with a loud unmusical sound. 'You don't encourage them to be like you, in that case.'

'Sorry?' She leaned closer to him, suddenly anxious. 'I'm not quite sure I understand you.'

'Don't you?' He picked the ring up again and slipped it over his index finger. He spun it around and around, then let it drop again onto the table. 'You obviously didn't catch my name, Mrs Beauchamp. I am Peter Wilkinson. My aunt was Elsie Wilkinson. Of course you never knew my aunt, did you? You only knew her widowed husband, Daniel.'

Lydia said nothing. She looked down the table to where Jackie, the tour guide, was sitting with the other guests. They had all turned towards her. Eight pairs of eyes, curious.

'Elsie was my mother's favourite sister. My mother often used to come and stay here during the summer. We came here too on holidays from

65

the States.' He paused and swallowed the last of his wine, then helped himself from the bottle open on the table. 'My mother always thought that when Daniel died we would inherit some part of this place. Elsie had promised her. And so we waited. We kept in touch with Daniel, we sent Christmas cards and birthday cards, called him up for a chat from time to time. Invited him to come visit us in New York. And then, do you know what happened?' He turned to the others and waved his glass in Lydia's direction. 'Can you guess what happened?'

'Just a minute, please. Is this really necessary? Jackie?' Lydia leaned forward, her expression supplicating.

'Oh I think this is very necessary, very necessary indeed.' He stood up, swaying gently from side to side. How much had he drunk, Lydia wondered. 'You see, our good lady host here, well somehow or another she and her husband managed to convince my uncle Daniel that he should leave everything to her. Every single thing. Every brick, tile and blade of grass. And we, well we got sweet fuck all.'

'Mr Wilkinson.' Jackie stood up. 'Really I think that's enough. In fact I think it's time we were leaving.'

'Leaving, not at all. We've only just begun.' He turned towards Lydia again and now she saw the resemblance. He was very like the photographs of Ben, Daniel and Elsie's son. An older version, but a version all right.

'How did Daniel die, Mrs Beauchamp? He was ill, there was no doubt about that. My mother spoke to his doctor. He told her he had end-stage cancer. But how exactly did he die?'

'Mr Wilkinson,' Lydia stood and faced him, 'I have no intention of having this conversation with you now. If there is something you want to ask me, phone and make an appointment and I will answer any of your questions then. But I will not discuss my private affairs in this public manner.'

She watched the minibus until it had disappeared through the gates. Behind it wobbled the Polish boys on their old bicycles. They turned back towards her and waved, their hands fluttering as if synchronized. She didn't respond. She turned away and faced the house again. It looked the way it always looked at this time of the evening when the low sun was reflected in the long windows. The glass gleamed and shone as if burnished and polished. She moved closer and the light shifted with her. Suddenly the windows were dark as if there was an emptiness within. The leaves of the tall oaks and sycamores rustled and a tremor of cool air ran through the garden. She stopped and listened. In the distance beyond the high wall she could hear traffic sounds, a horn blowing, the bang of a backfire. Then silence. She took another step and felt the pain in her hip. It made her shift her weight from one leg to the other and she stumbled, losing her balance. She reached out for support and fell forwards. Her hands hit the ground first, sharp pieces of gravel slicing through the thin skin, so she cried out and fell further, her knees sinking onto the hard surface, and the rest of her body collapsing too. The pain cut through her. Tears started into her eyes. She lay helpless, her legs twisted beneath her. She could not bring herself to try to move. She was terrified that she had broken something. Dirt clung to her lips. She could feel its dryness on her tongue. She lay still, sobs catching in her throat. She would wait; she would lie where she was and when she was feeling more calm she would test her body, see if she could push herself up onto her hands. But for the moment she was fine. She could fall no further, hurt herself no more. She closed her eyes and sobbed and felt the tears drip down the side of her nose and into her mouth. She would wait and when the pain had lessened she would get herself to her feet again. She could, she knew; it was just a matter of time. She had to be patient and wait. She lay still. Time passed. It was beginning to get dark. She could feel a sudden urgent pressure on her bladder.

'Help me,' she called out. 'Please someone help me.'

The birds in the ash tree called out in response.

'Please, please,' she shouted again. Again the harsh response from above her head. She laid her head back down on the gravel and closed her eyes. And then she heard, slowly coming towards her, the sound of footsteps on the gravel. She opened her eyes and squinted upwards towards the sun. The feet stopped beside her head. She tried to lift herself to turn in the direction of the sound. She made as if to push herself up onto her hands, but the pain in the palms made her cry out.

She twisted around to look up at him. Such a

head of golden hair in the evening sunlight. As yellow as butter, as yellow as buttercups. She felt him come around behind her and his hands slip beneath her armpits. She leaned back and felt his warmth and his strength. She closed her eyes and the tears once again slid from beneath her lids. She bowed her head and let him pull her to her feet.

'Thank you,' she said. 'Thank you.'

And felt the rush of wetness, warm at first then cold, so very cold as it ran down her legs and dribbled onto the gravel at her feet.

SEVEN

They'd come in from the boat, tired and dirty. Hungry and thirsty. Pat had called for the first round. And before Adam knew what had happened he'd downed that pint and then another and another. He tried to hold onto some kind of control. He still couldn't really cope with it all. The freedom, the open space, the alcohol. He pushed himself back from the bar. The room was moving, rocking gently, up and down, up and down. What was it? he wondered. Was it the alcohol or was it the swell from the Atlantic? He turned away towards the toilets in the far corner.

'Hey, Adam, where you off to?' Pat let out a roar. 'Your round, your round next.'

The girl behind the bar grinned at him. She was so pretty with her curly dark hair and her white teeth and her long legs, bare and brown beneath her short denim skirt.

'Same again, sweetheart, same again,' he shouted as he turned and lurched towards the toilet. He stood in front of the dirty urinals, then pushed into one of the stalls. He slammed the door shut behind him and sat down on the seat. He leaned his head against the cold white tiles. He closed his eyes.

'Colm,' he whispered, 'Colm, I wish you were here. You'd love this. I know you would.' And he smiled and rocked himself slowly from side to side. Until he heard the door crash open and Pat's voice, raucous, slurring.

'Get out here, you. Get out here and pay for this round, before I come in and get you.' And a surge of laughter from the bar. And Pat again. 'What do you think he's doing in there, lads? Having himself a good time all on his own, is that it? Will I bust down the door and have a look?' And more laughter and the sound of a fist slapping into a cupped hand. Adam stood then, flushed the toilet, straightened himself up and opened the door. Stepped out, laughing, pushed Pat out of the way and pulled his wallet from his back pocket.

'Here.' He waved a wad of notes. 'Here you go. Who's having what?'

It was late afternoon by the time he left. He'd had enough. He could still stand. Still drive his van. Not like the rest of them. They'd be in a sorry state come midnight. Fit for nothing. Barely able to crawl their way to bed. But he had plans. He drove along the river road, back towards the high wrought-iron gates. He turned the van off the road and stopped and got out. He pushed the gates open. He drove slowly through then got out again to close them behind him. To his right was the lodge, a small pretty cottage, with a yellow rose climbing up and over the front door. He stepped up to it, cupped his hands around his head and peered in through the small panes of glass. Then he moved away and back, stopped, looked around him, then slipped through the narrow passage between the cottage and the high garden wall. The back door stood half open. He pushed it, and it swung in, the hinges squeaking in a way that set his teeth on edge. He looked inside, into what once must have been a scullery. A brass tap dripped into a square white sink. Open shelves were piled high with dusty crockery. It was dark and cool, with a strong smell of damp.

He walked through into a small square sitting room. There was a sofa and two chairs, one on either side of the fireplace. The walls were covered with a flowered paper. Thick dust covered the mantelpiece. But not the penknife which lay on it. One blade was open. He picked it up, folded it back into its slot and put the knife in his pocket.

He moved to the stairs and took them quickly two at a time. The old wood creaked beneath his feet. He stepped carefully onto the landing. There were three rooms up here. He pushed open each door in turn and glanced in. There were two bedrooms, furnished with old iron bedsteads covered with eiderdowns and patchwork quilts, and a small bathroom. The bigger of the rooms ran from the front of the house to the back. He ducked his head beneath the low ceiling and sat down on the double bed. It shifted beneath his weight and the mattress sagged gently. His right foot knocked against something on the floor. He reached down. It was an empty cigarette packet. He picked it up. The brand name was unfamiliar. Caro. Like the brand of vodka that the bottle lying on its side against the skirting board had once contained. He spelled out the name. Z-u-b-r-o-w-k-a. The Polish boys, he thought. He'd seen them wobbling on their old bicycles along the river road. They looked so innocent in their cheap clothes with their big eyes and their halting English. He wondered what else they'd been getting up to here, away from prying eyes. He swung his legs up off the floor and lay back against the pillows. He stared up at the ceiling, at the water marks that decorated it. A swirling pattern of brown and cream. He turned over on his side and closed his eyes. He yawned loudly and settled his hands beneath his cheek. He'd have a rest here for a few minutes. He was in no rush. He lay, breathing quietly. If he kept his eyes closed he could almost be back in his cell with Colm. He felt so close to him here, where his name kept on coming up all the time.

Even this afternoon in the pub, they'd been talking about him. When he came out of the toilet and sat down with his pint, they'd all been looking at a magazine. He'd craned his neck to see what had them so interested. And Pat said to him,

'Hey, Adam, take a look at this. The old bird in the boat, it's her lovely daughter.'

He handed it across to him, folded open at the page. There was a photograph, a tall woman standing with a group of teenagers in school uniform. The surroundings were dark and depressing. A school yard and behind it a building that loomed forbiddingly over them. But somehow the woman's presence shone out. Her hair was fair and waved around her face. She was looking straight at the camera and smiling. The kids were smiling too.

'"Grace under Pressure, the story of Grace McNicholas and her amazing students".' He looked up at Pat. 'McNicholas?'

'Her married name, I guess. But that's definitely her, no mistaking.'

'You wouldn't know it. She doesn't look a bit like her mother.'

'Well, she takes after her father, whoever he was.' Pat took the magazine back from his hands. 'A pity Colm isn't here to see this. It would drive him fucking mad.'

'Yeah?'

'Yeah, he winds up in prison in England and she's become a fucking saint. Listen to this. "Grace McNicholas turns the base metal of the school kids others reject into the gold of university entrants. With a mixture of charm, charisma and down-to-earth discipline, McNicholas's last year had a record that would put most fee-paying schools to shame. A true original in her attitude and teaching methods, Grace McNicholas is one in a million."' He dropped the magazine back on the table and lifted his pint.

'Yeah?' Adam looked down at the picture again. 'What's the connection? Were they friends?'

Pat finished his pint and held out the glass to him.

'Get me another and I'll tell you the whole sad story.'

Adam sighed and rolled over on his stomach. He didn't need to be told. Colm had told him often enough. But there was no stopping Pat now.

'Well, you see, it was like this. Ma Beauchamp accused him of sticking one on the daughter.'

'And she, what did she say?'

'She denied it. Said it wasn't Colm. But the mother wouldn't buy that. She insisted it was Colm. She fired him. Threw him out.'

'So he left?'

'Didn't have much choice. Things were bad then. No work anywhere. Everyone was emigrating. So he went too.'

Adam picked up the magazine again and turned the pages. There were more photographs. The woman called Grace in a tracksuit running the Dublin marathon, in a suit with her hair swept up on the top of her head greeting the President. Standing on a podium, making a speech at some kind of a public meeting.

'So, what happened to the baby?' He pointed at the pictures. 'No happy kiddy snaps here.'

'No, no way. Ma Beauchamp wasn't having it. She packed Grace off to England to get her out of the way and, as far as we all know, the baby was adopted. No one ever spoke about it again. The old witch waved her magic wand, and hey presto, no more baby.'

Colm had told him. All about Grace. One of Colm's favourite stories. Something to get them through the long nights. When Colm would talk and he would listen. How he was with her the day the social worker came and took the kid. Colm could even remember what the baby was wearing. He'd told him over and over again. He could hear Colm's voice. Soft, crooning, like a kind of a lullaby. He had on a white cardigan, what Colm called a gansey, with blue boats on the ribbing. He had a blue babygro. He had a blue hat and blue bootees to match. And he was wrapped in a crocheted blanket.

'Why did I leave Ireland?' Colm would say. 'If I'd stayed at home none of this would have happened. I wouldn't have ended up in this stinking, foul place.'

And he'd ball his fists and beat them against the wall until his knuckles bled. And then he'd retreat into a sullen state, turn his face to his pillow and lie without speaking for hours at a time. Until eventually Adam would hear him stirring and he would reach up and find his hand and entwine his fingers.

'How will I manage without you when I leave here?' he had said to Colm a week or so before he was due to be released. Colm had just smiled and stroked his hair and handed him the joint that he was smoking. 'I won't forget you, you know that. I'll be waiting for you when you come out.' Adam let the smoke drift from his mouth as he spoke, but Colm just shook his head, then lay back, pulling him close.

'Don't be an eejit,' he said as he slipped his hand under Adam's sweatshirt. 'They'll never let me out of here, never. And it would be a pity for you to waste your time on me. No, you go off and have fun. Just think of me, won't you?'

Adam rolled over onto his side and opened his eyes. He sat up. The sun was gone from the room. He stood up and moved into the bathroom. The walls were panelled with rough tongue-and-groove timber. He took out the penknife and slid it in behind a loose board, pulling it away from its neighbour. He put his hand in his pocket. He felt the smooth plastic of the small bag. His stash for later on. He slipped it into the cavity and pushed the board back into place. Later on tonight there was a woman he wanted to see. She'd been at the pub too, sitting at the next table. He'd leaned across to speak to her. Friendly, interested. Asked her where she was from. She was Dutch, she said. From The Hague. Her English was perfect. She was with a group of girl friends from school that she'd met up with through a reunion website. She shrugged her shoulders and edged closer to him.

'Not really my scene,' she muttered. 'All women together.'

He felt her thigh press against his and her large soft breasts brush his upper arm as she reached past him to pick up her glass.

'Where are you staying?' he asked.

She gestured towards the pub. 'In the B and B upstairs,' she replied and smiled.

'So you'll be here later on?' He drained his glass. She nodded.

'Easy to find,' she said and smiled again, her small pink tongue delicately licking the froth of beer from the corners of her mouth.

'Excuse me, folks.' The waitress pushed between them and dumped down plates of fresh prawns.

'Have one,' the Dutch woman offered. She

picked over them carefully with her long-nailed fingers, and selected the largest. 'Here.' She broke its jointed neck and separated its tail from its head. He opened his mouth and she dropped the pink flesh onto his tongue.

'Truly delicious,' she said as she pushed her finger up into the prawn's head cavity and scooped out its brains. 'The best, this bit.'

He looked at himself in the small mildew-spotted mirror hanging from a nail. He smoothed down his hair. This place would do. Much better than the room he was renting in Pat Jordan's house. Much more privacy. He liked this little house. It made him feel safe and secure, with its small rooms and low ceilings. He could imagine Colm here. He could see him on the floor in the corner by the low window. He would be sitting cross-legged, his knees almost flat to the ground. He would be rolling himself a cigarette as he talked. He would stop and lean forward, cupping the match flame with his hands so the light would shine up into his lined face. He would look for a moment like a bird with a long pointed beak, all the planes of his face angular and sharp. As if there were no width or breadth to him. And the hair on his head shaved close to his skull, so there was a dark shadow that came to a point just where a twisted vein showed through the skin of his forehead. And his eyes that were small and bright, and would stare out at him, not blinking. Just like a bird. Like the crows that he could hear now, their song harsh and unmusical. He could imagine them, perched on the tall ash near the house, dark shadows against the evening sky.

'Caw, caw, caw,' he shouted out loud. And listened and heard an answering cry. And heard it again. He walked to the window and opened the catch so the top pane slipped down. He stuck his head out into the evening light and listened again. There was something about that cry that wasn't quite right. He turned from the window, hurried down the stairs and outside. The birds flew up in a great fright of black wings as he ran towards the trees and the house behind it. And saw the old woman on the ground, her legs twisted beneath her body, her arms flung out, and her head lifting and turning towards him. He slowed his pace. Stopped, saw the look on her face. Moved again towards her and this time bent down and began to lift her up. Heard her voice, thanking him, felt the bird-like, boneless nature of her body as she folded against him. Then heard her sob and felt her try to pull away, and looked down and saw the dark stain, and the way her linen trousers clung wetly to her thin legs.

He walked with her back into the house, holding her tightly under the elbow, so she wouldn't fall over. He sat her down at the kitchen table. He made her a cup of tea with sugar in it.

'For the shock, that's what my gran always said. Sweet tea is for shock.'

But she pushed it away.

'Pour me some whiskey. That's what I need,' she said, her face the colour of milk. He stayed with her until she had drunk it. And another glass and another one too. He had offered to make her something to eat, but she refused. Shook her head so hard he thought it would snap off her thin neck.

'Let me help you,' he said. 'Will I get a doctor? Is there someone I can call to come and sit with you?'

But she just shook her head even harder and sipped her drink. Then looked around at the mess in the kitchen. And he piled the plates and saucepans, the cutlery and the glasses into the sink and began to wash up. Moving up- and downstairs between kitchen and dining room, carrying plates of left-over food. Washed and dried and swept the floor and put everything away. Chatted away to her. Told her about his gran, who died of breast cancer and his mother, who didn't love him. Entertained her with stories of his father, who was a gambler and a drinker and a womanizer. Watched her as she sank down into her chair, her eyes half-closing. Then when she began to droop to one side, he helped her upstairs to her bedroom. The big room with the long bay window looking across the lawn to the river beyond. He laid her on the bed. He took off her shoes. Then he opened her zip and pulled off her trousers, still damp, the pungent scent of urine catching in the back of his nose. Her thighs were skin and bone, but her skin was still white and smooth. He stood and looked down at her. He covered her with a blanket. He pulled the curtains. He walked slowly down through the silent house and out the front door. Stopped in the twilight and looked back. Then he turned and walked away.

Later, much later, that night it came back to

him. The way the old woman had looked. The Dutch woman had had something of the same expression in her face. A mixture of fear and panic. And a sudden realization that she was helpless. That she'd been brought to this pretty little gate lodge with its yellow rose around the door and the lavender bushes outside the window. And it wasn't quite what she had thought it was. And that the man who earlier in the evening had been a handsome boy with a nice smile, was now something much more frightening. Much more dangerous. As he straddled her body and crushed her face into the pillow. As he forced open her legs. As he shouted out his glee and his pleasure as she sobbed and moaned and tried to push him away. And knew that whatever control she had thought she had over the situation was gone.

EIGHT

Lydia woke with a start. She was in bed. She was lying on her side. She moved gingerly and felt the softness of a blanket across her bare legs. She tried to turn over onto her back but as she began to move her arms there was a sudden sharp pain in her left wrist and she shrank back from it. She lay still for a few minutes, then slowly, carefully, lifted her head from the pillow. The curtains had been drawn, but light was beginning to seep around their edges. And in the half light she saw that there was someone sitting on the chair by her dressing table. His head was slumped to one side and his legs were stretched out in front of him. She pulled herself up to sitting. She didn't remember how she had got to bed. She didn't remember taking off her trousers. She didn't remember much. Except that she had fallen, outside on the gravel. That she had lain on the ground unable to move. And that the English boy with the fine, blond hair and the eyes that were two different colours had found her and picked her up. That she had wet herself.

The figure in the chair stirred and sighed. She pushed herself upright, cradling her aching wrist against her body. She leaned forward and pushed the blanket from her. She swung her legs off the bed and felt the cool of the floorboards beneath her feet. She looked down at herself. At her thin shapeless thighs and her flabby calves. Once they had been muscled and strong. They had helped her to dig the garden, and mow the grass. To climb ladders, to paint the house and fix the roof. To haul boats in and out of the river. Now they barely held her upright. She picked her dressing gown from the chair beside the bed. She man-oeuvred her arms into the sleeves, wincing at the pain, then held it tightly closed around her body. She shuffled awkwardly towards the windows. She grasped the curtains and pulled them apart. And turned. Adam opened his eyes, blinked quickly, yawned and stretched.

'So,' his voice was hoarse with sleep, 'how are you feeling today?'

It had been very late when he left the gate lodge. The Dutch woman had got into her rented car and driven away. She had seemed fine. She had made a bit of a fuss earlier. Screamed, protested. Said she didn't want what he was offering. But she'd calmed down by the time she left. They'd finished the bottle of whiskey she'd brought and he'd told her he'd give her a call sometime. He watched her drive off. Waited until he could no longer see the red of her tail lights, then he closed the gates behind him. He was hungry. Starving. Ravenous. He began to walk down the drive towards the house. His mouth was filling with saliva and his stomach was cramping. He broke into a jog. His feet sounded loudly on the gravel. He lifted his head. The sky was bright with starlight and a crescent moon was rising just above the roof. He wanted to shout out with the beauty of it all and the joy of what had passed and what was still to come.

The kitchen was warm and welcoming. He opened the fridge. He took out a plate of cold salmon. And there was home-made mayonnaise too. He tore off a hunk of bread from a large white loaf. He stuffed it into his mouth, then sat down at the table, dipping a knife into the bowl of mayonnaise and smearing it over the fish. He ate and ate until he could eat no more. He opened the fridge again. There was a half-empty bottle of white wine in the door compartment. He pulled out the cork and lifted it to his mouth. It poured coldly down his chin and onto his shirt. It tasted better than anything he had ever tasted before. He moved to the sink and turned on the tap. He sluiced water over his face and hands. Then he walked up the stairs to the hall. The light was on outside the front door. It poured in through the fanlight. It glanced off the crystal chandelier above his head. He shifted from one foot to the other and the glass droplets above his head tinkled. He could feel the breath of the house on his cheek. Squeaks, creaks, sighs. He put one foot on the bottom stair. It gave beneath his weight. He moved his foot to the next one. And the next. And the next. The stairs curved away above him. He rested his hand on the polished mahogany banister. He moved quietly up and onto the landing. The long window looked out onto the lawn. He stood and gazed down. Then he turned to the first door on his left. He pushed it and it swung noiselessly inwards. Lydia lay where he had left her. She hadn't moved. He stepped back and away. He walked from room to room, switching on and off the lights. They were all spotlessly clean. Polished furniture, beds, chests of drawers, wardrobes, all smelt of beeswax. Clean, white sheets were turned down over thick eiderdowns. Floors were strewn with rugs with patterns, in vivid colours of birds, flowers, animals. The walls were hung with paintings. None of them was familiar to him, but he could tell that they were all valuable. They had that look, that ring of authenticity. Like the paintings in his gran's house. She had been a collector. She had visited auction rooms and small dealers. She had bought and sold shrewdly. She had told him she would leave him everything. But his father had poisoned her against him. Spread lies about him. So she had refused to see him when he came out of prison. Wouldn't answer his letters, or speak to him on the phone. Even though he swore to her that he was innocent of all the charges against him. That the girl who said he had raped her had been lying. He had been vindicated when the charges were reduced to sexual assault. And even that had been a mistake. A misunderstanding. She had led him on. They had got drunk together. That was all.

But she wouldn't believe him. And he had been so sad and sorry. Because he loved his gran. Much more than he loved anyone else in his family. He loved her soft white hair and her wrinkled skin. He loved her knotted hands and stiff fingers. He loved her stooped back and her slow stumbling steps. Her eyes that were just like his. One the colour of sea water, and the other the colour of dried grass. And he couldn't believe that she didn't love him too. It was all his father's fault. And one day he would make him sorry for what he had done.

He walked into the bathroom. He opened the cabinet above the mirror. There was the usual collection of pill bottles. Tranquillizers, he noticed, and he put them in his pocket. And on the bottom shelf, tubes of foundation, mascara and lipsticks. He picked them up in turn, twisting down the barrels and checking the colours on the back of his hand. One of them was the colour of dried blood. He held the tip to the middle point of his upper lip. It left a dark mark, like an old scab. He touched it with his tongue. It tasted musky, fermented. He screwed it up again and put it in his pocket. He was tired now. So tired. He wanted to sleep. He walked from bedroom to bedroom, trying out each of the beds in turn. Goldilocks, that's what I am, he thought. He caught sight of himself in a long mirror. He smiled and bowed. The boy in the mirror smiled and bowed in response. Then he backed away and moved once again towards Lydia's room. She looked so comfortable. He was tempted to lie down beside her. He could curl himself into a little ball and snuggle up against her. And maybe she would sing to him the way his gran used to. But then he remembered. She had wet herself. She didn't smell nice the way gran smelt. Of lemon soap and apple blossom talcum powder. He sat down in the chair by the dressing table. He stretched his legs out in front of him. He leaned back. He closed his eyes. He listened to the sound of Lydia's breath. And he breathed with her. And slept.

'Will you drive me to the hospital? It's my wrist. I think it must be broken. Look.' Lydia pushed up her sleeve. Her forearm was swollen and bruised. It looked misshapen and ugly. She sat on the end of the bed. Adam leaned forward.

'Of course, of course I will. But first I'll make some breakfast for us. Would you like that?' He rested his fingertip on her hand.

She nodded. 'Thank you for putting me to bed. It can't have been the most pleasant task.' Her face reddened as she spoke. 'And thank you for staying with me. It's not often a woman of my age gets to wake up in the same room as a good-looking young man like you.' She forced a smile.

He stood and picked his jacket from the back of the chair.

'No problem, Lydia. Anything I can do to help.'

He left her at the front entrance of the hospital.

'You're sure you don't want me to come with you?' He held her door open for her.

'No, really, I'm fine now.' She held herself straight.

'Well, if you need anything, you've got my mobile number.'

'Really, I'm fine. You go now.' She moved away from his van. She didn't wait for him to leave. She walked slowly and carefully through the automatic doors and into the reception area.

The X-ray showed the damage.

'You've a Colles' fracture,' the doctor grunted. 'The bone is osteoporotic.' He glanced at her chart, then looked at her again. 'At your age it's pretty much inevitable.'

'At my age. What on earth do you mean?' She shifted in her seat.

'Well.' He looked speculatively at her, then down at her chart. 'What age are you? Seventy-five? Post-menopausal for how many years, twenty, twenty-five? It's all part of the ageing process.'

She looked hard at him.

'I thought we'd gone beyond inevitability,' she said. 'I thought as a race we'd conquered all before us and were almost super human.' She smiled. 'I thought I'd never get old.'

He looked at her again, one of those scans which started at the grey in her hair, passed over the wrinkles and lines in her face and neck and ended with the blue jeans that he was sure he had seen his daughter wearing and her small feet in their runners that would have suited a fifteen-year-old. He smiled, this time with ruefulness rather than condescension.

'Sorry to disappoint you. Osteoporosis, like the poor, will always be with us.'

She would need surgery, pins to hold the bones together. She sat in the dingy waiting room while the nurse made the arrangements to admit her. It was crowded, busy. Most of the other patients were old. Most of them were women. She recognized herself in their slumped shoulders and misshapen hands and feet. The downward turn of their mouths and the lines in their faces, isobars of despair and unhappiness that charted their lives. There were younger women there too. Daughters, she reckoned. She could read the nature of their relationships in their varying degrees of indifference. And she could see their genetic inheritance. Fine hair that would become sparse in the years to come. Thick hair that would coarsen and bush out. Fair skin that would turn to chalkiness, and sallow skin that would become pitted with open pores and soft, sagging lines. There was comfort though, in their presence. She saw the whispered words of support. The hand on the arm, the little squeezes of affection. The giggles over the shared magazine articles and the unspoken agreements and disagreements. Loneliness weighed down on her, and grief made her, for a moment, breathless.

'Are you all right, dear?' A nurse passing by stopped. Her expression was of carefully modulated concern.

'The pain is very bad. Can you give me something?'

'When we admit you we'll deal with that. Not too long now. Here.' She reached over to the low table between the seats and pulled a bundle of magazines towards her. 'Have a read. It'll take your mind off it all.'

Lydia glanced down at the magazines. She sighed. She hardly ever read anything like this any longer. She flicked through them, looking for any gardening magazines. She had once, years ago, stolen a packet of poppy seeds from a supplement from one of the Sunday papers she found at the dentist. They had turned out to be beautiful, those poppies, a wonderful plant. Delicate pale pink, dark pink, light blue to purple flowers with a corona of stamens that had a greenish hue. They flowered all summer from early June until mid-September, then set seed and flowered again the next year, migrating around the garden, appearing here and there in the most unexpected places. She still came across them, even now thirty-odd years later, their beautiful heads nodding their greeting at her through the grass as she approached. But there was no such comfort in any of these. She pulled one randomly from the pile. The pain in her wrist was becoming more and more intense. She peered down at the pictures and text, trying hard to concentrate on what was in front of her.

And then she saw the photograph. A tall, blonde woman in a schoolyard. She was surrounded by girls all in uniform. Lydia stared hard at her. Her heart had begun to race. She felt breathless. Her mouth was suddenly dry, but her fingers were slippery with sweat so the paper stuck to them. Her eyes scanned down through the text. Grace McNicholas was the woman's name. She was the headmistress of a school in Dublin. She was described as a wonderful teacher, dedicated to her pupils. Lydia mouthed the words, half out loud. Spittle dropped onto the magazine's shiny pages.

Born in London, brought up in West Cork, left home when she was a teenager. Went back to London, put herself through university, began teaching in the East End, found she loved it, realized she was good at it. The more disadvantaged the area, the tougher the kids, the more she liked it. Had never thought she'd come back to Ireland but her husband had got a job at Trinity College and had persuaded her to return.

Married, so she was married. Of course, that explained her name. Lydia scanned the rest of the article quickly but there were no more details about Grace's husband. Just a couple of terse sentences.

'If you don't mind, I'd prefer not to go into the details of my marriage. We're separated now. That's all I'll say. It's a private matter and doesn't have anything to do with my work.'

Now Lydia was reading out loud, oblivious to the curious stares of the others in the waiting room. Her lips, tongue and teeth formed themselves around her daughter's words.

'"Yes, I am a mother as well as a teacher. My daughter, Amelia, is fifteen. She's like all kids of her age. An angel one minute and something less than an angel the next." McNicholas abruptly signalled that this part of the interview was over.

She stood up, pulled her coat from the back of her chair and said firmly, "Now, let's go and find someone interesting for you to talk to."'

Lydia carefully placed the magazine back on her knees. She smoothed the pages down with the flat of her hands. She was trembling, her legs moving uncontrollably beneath the chair. She could hear her daughter's voice. Cool, indifferent, confident. She had always been like that. Even when she was a small child in a pushchair. She had fixed people with her blue stare, her eyes that were round and the colour of cornflowers, that should have signalled warmth and softness, but instead gave off an alien hostility.

Lydia stood up quickly. She swayed awkwardly on her feet, cradling her arm protectively.

'Are you feeling OK?' The young woman next to her put out her hand and touched her gently. 'Shall I call the nurse?'

Lydia tucked the magazine under her arm. She shook her head. Tears were prickling at the back of her eyes, and there was a solid lump in her throat that made her feel like vomiting. She swallowed hard.

'I'm fine; I just need some fresh air. It's the pain, in my wrist, you know. If they come looking for me will you tell them I've gone outside for a minute.'

Outside it was a beautiful day, fine wisps of cloud trailing high across the sky. She sat on the low wall that surrounded the hospital garden. Cars passed slowly up and down the drive. This was the hospital where Alex's body had been brought. Where the post-mortem had taken place.

Where she had come to identify him. She could still smell him. They had waited for her to gag and retch. But she had stayed calm, in control, always in control. But she wasn't in control now. She opened the magazine again, and again began to read. This time she was looking for some reference to her. Something about Grace's childhood, her family. But there was nothing more than a brief comment about a childhood spent by the sea.

'"And what about school? What kind of school did you attend?" McNicholas laughed. "Oh I went to a few. The local national school was my first one. I loved that. Then I was sent to boarding school when I was nine. It was a Church of Ireland girls' school in Dublin. Very prim and proper. But then my mother decided I'd do just as well at the local school in Skibbereen. And actually she was right. I worked very hard and I did really well in my Leaving Cert. And I decided I wanted to study in England, London actually, so I went to the University of London and that was when I decided I wanted to be a teacher."'

Lydia held up the pages and angled them to the light as if she might sense something extra beneath the harsh black and white of words on paper. She scrutinized the photograph. Grace had changed, of course she had changed in the nearly twenty-five years since Lydia had last seen her. But she was unmistakably and simultaneously the same small girl, same teenager, same adult she had always been. There was the familiar expression in her eyes. Her brows were slightly furrowed and her mouth was smiling. But her eyes were cool and distant. Her arms were held out wide, encircling the shoulders of the group of teenage girls who pressed in close about her. But it wasn't a comforting embrace. It was a demonstration of support, but one which said, 'I will provide a structure for you, but I am not your mother. I am here to catch you if you fall, but only in order to send you back into the world again.'

Lydia got up and began to walk slowly towards the hospital gates. The sounds of children's voices came to her through the mutter of the morning traffic. There was a school playground just across the road. It must be break time, she thought. A group of girls were playing with a long skipping rope. She leaned against the railings and watched them. Six of them were skipping together, their feet drumming on the tarmac surface. They were chanting in unison,

All in together girls,
This fine weather girls.
When is your birthday,
Please run out.

As they chanted the names of the months of the year, each girl in turn would dodge out of the rope and take her turn swinging it for the others. She remembered Grace's first day at the school. She had driven her in Daniel's Land Rover half a mile up the road.

'Stop here,' Grace had commanded. 'Now, stop now.'

'No, it's all right; it's raining. I'll take you all the way.'

'No, I want to get out now.' Grace's small fingers reached for the door handle. 'Now.'

'OK, fine, if that's what you want.'

'And you don't come with me, you go home this minute.'

Lydia had sat and watched her. The wind was blowing long streams of water vertically across the narrow country road. But Grace didn't look back. When Lydia went to collect her at lunchtime, the child was already walking down the road. She was with a group of boys. As Lydia came near she slowed down, but Grace ignored her. She stopped the car. Still Grace ignored her and kept on walking. She passed right by her without stopping. Lydia sat in the Land Rover and watched her daughter. Her blonde hair was slicked to her skull by the rain which had fallen without cease all that cold September day. She swung her heavy schoolbag in one hand as if it weighed nothing. And when the boys began to run, she ran with them, keeping pace all the way, only stopping when they got to the main road and the boys turned towards the village and she to Trawbawn House.

Lydia had waited, until they were out of sight, then she had driven slowly after them all, catching up with her just as Grace opened the side gate into the avenue. She had sat and watched her small figure, the set of her shoulders, the swing of her bag, then put the car in gear and followed her down to the house. She had put the Land Rover away in the garage then gone into the greenhouses and checked the temperature gauges. By the time Lydia returned to the house Grace was seated at the kitchen table, a large bowl of soup in front of her. She was spooning it greedily into her mouth and talking loudly.

'It was great, Daniel. I sat at the back of the class with the big boys. Then Mrs O'Farrell said because I was in junior infants I had to sit at the front. But I said no. But she said I had to and she made me. But at break time when we all went out into the yard I played with the big boys again. I didn't play with the girls. They are all silly; they only wanted to play skipping and mess around with their Barbies and things. I wanted to play football.'

Lydia met Daniel's eyes over Grace's head. He smiled, then cut some more bread for her.

'That's my girl,' he said as he sat down beside her. 'That's my girl.'

Her hair had been so wet that day that it had turned almost black. She sat in the warm kitchen with her exercise books spread out in front of her and as her hair dried so it became as fair as fair could be. She gripped the pencil and copied out the letters, laboriously, with much rubbing out of her mistakes.

'See.' She held the book up triumphantly. 'See.'

Lydia had to admit. Grace had made a good job of it. No one would ever have known that she could already write with ease and fluency. That she could read virtually anything that was put in front of her. That she had already grasped addition and subtraction and would soon be capable of multiplication and division. She turned to Lydia, the book in her hands and said,

'Mrs O'Farrell said that mammies have to be shown what kids can do. Here.' She dropped it

94

into Lydia's lap, and turned away. 'I'm going to look for Daniel. We're going on a rabbit hunt.'

Bye, baby bunting,
Daddy's gone a-hunting,
To catch a little rabbit skin.
To wrap his baby bunting in.

She chanted it under her breath. Bunting, hunting, skin, in. Bunting, hunting, skin, in. The stamp of Grace's rubber boots on the flagged floor. The slam of the door. That hard blue stare. That hard blue stare that dragged her back. To the operating theatre in the teaching hospital in London where she had been a theatre nurse. That hard blue stare over the surgical mask. The gloved hands slick with blood. The glint of the scalpel, the fine red line as its sharp edge peeled back the skin, the fat, the muscle. His name was Jonas. He was from Stockholm. He was older, in his forties. He was divorced with an ex-wife and children in Sweden. She had been seeing him for months. She had thought he was going to ask her to marry him. They had kept it a secret from their colleagues in the hospital. She thought it was for professional reasons. But when she told him she was pregnant he had told her the truth. He had no intention of marrying her. He was seeing another woman, another doctor. The only person he intended marrying was her. They were going to New York. They'd both got great jobs there. He was sorry. It would never have worked with Lydia.

'And now this. Well, I'll take care of it for you. I'll arrange an abortion. Perhaps you'd like to go on holiday for a few weeks. The south of Spain, Italy, to recuperate. And afterwards, well, I'll give you something towards your living expenses.'

He was so blond, so perfect. His skin glowed and shone. It looked burnished. She had nodded her head, unable to speak. He gave her a phone number. He told her who to ask for, what to say. She had nodded her head again.

'Did you love me at all?' she asked him. 'Tell me the truth.'

'Love you? Well,' he cocked his head on one side and looked her up and down, 'I did love, do love, aspects of you, Lydia. Many aspects of you.'

'But my essence, my essential being, do you love that?'

'You've become very philosophical all of a sudden. Why?'

She shrugged.

'Well, if you can't become philosophical when you're contemplating birth and death, when can you?'

She had left him then. Torn up the phone number. Handed in her notice at the hospital and moved to another. Less prestigious. A local asylum. A place where the homeless and helpless, the crazed and the handicapped were locked up. It was an asylum for her too. She hid her pregnancy for months beneath the shapeless uniform. And when she could hide it no longer the matron took pity on her and kept her on, working in the office until she gave birth to Grace. Suddenly, unexpectedly, on the black and white tiles of the staff lavatory one morning just after breakfast.

She picked up the magazine again and scrutinized the photograph of her daughter. She could see the signs of ageing. Lines around her mouth and eyes. A slight thickness under her chin. Her body looked bigger, not fatter exactly, just more substantial than Lydia remembered. It had as much to do with her posture, Lydia thought. She stood with her body square on to the camera, her shoulders straight. She looked so confident, sure of her place in the world. And what of her daughter? Again Lydia scanned the pages looking for some other details of her. But there was nothing else. She was called Amelia and she was fifteen. That was it.

How could Grace not have told me that I was a grandmother? she wondered. How could she have been so cruel? She must have known I would want to know. It would have been an opportunity for her to get in touch. After all those years of silence. She could have phoned. Told me her good news. We could have arranged to meet. If she didn't want to come back here, I could have gone to Dublin. Met her husband. Stayed for a few days. Not too long. Not overstayed my welcome. Then we could have had phone calls throughout the pregnancy, and then when the baby was born I could have gone to stay again and helped her through all those difficult first weeks. And to call the child Amelia, of all names. Like the Amelia rock, just outside Schull harbour. They had sailed past it so often when Grace was a child. And she had made up stories about why the rock had been given its name. And Grace had called her own sailing dinghy *Amelia*. The Enterprise dinghy that Alex had taught her to sail and to race.

Alex and Grace, they both loved racing. Alex, who was competitive about nothing else in his life, was a changed man when he took the helm of the dinghy. His mother had told her. He could have sailed in the Olympics, he was so good.

'But he doesn't have the temperament. He's weak,' she had said. 'He has no backbone. He needs someone like you. And you, I would imagine, could do with someone like him. I take it, Lydia, that you are not a Roman Catholic. As you know, neither are we. People like us should stick together. We have money, Lydia. We will give you an allowance. He need never know. We will pay you monthly. Take him away from the city. You can give up your job. Make a new life for yourself and your little girl. Alex will be a good father to her. He's a kind man. Too kind, really, for his own good.'

Lydia sat in the sunshine. She was weeping now. She stared down at the photographs, blurred now by her tears. A grandmother, twice over, she thought. That first baby. A boy. She had never seen him. She had never even asked Grace about him. She had wished him away. How old would he be now, she wondered. Twenty-eight maybe, an adult. He might even have children of his own. Her own flesh and blood. And she had sent him away. She watched the people passing. Two women got out of a taxi. One was crying quietly. The other was holding her by the arm. They stopped at the hospital gate. They seemed to be having a row. Lydia watched them. They weren't speaking English. German maybe, or perhaps it was Dutch. The one who was crying had a bruised face. She was limping. The other one grasped her firmly, then pushed her towards the entrance to the casualty department.

'Mrs Beauchamp, Mrs Beauchamp, come here.' A nurse was standing by the door. The two women stopped beside her. The nurse bent her head to hear what they were saying. Her expression changed from impatience to sympathy. She held the swing doors open and gestured towards the reception desk. Then she turned back towards Lydia.

'What on earth are you doing out here, Mrs Beauchamp?' Her tone was irritated. 'We've been looking for you all over. We're ready to admit you. Come on inside. Now, this minute.'

Chastised. Scolded. She bowed her head, feeling the pain in her wrist overwhelm her. She closed the magazine and slipped it underneath her jacket. She began to walk slowly back into the hospital. A wheelchair was waiting just inside the automatic doors. I am helpless now, she thought, I am old. She allowed herself to be seated, her feet slipped onto the metal rests, and a pale blue cotton blanket placed over her knees. She could feel the magazine close to her heart. She would keep it safe. The lift doors closed with a gentle sigh and they began to move up towards the ward.

NINE

Grace McNicholas was dreaming. It was the same dream. Always the same dream. She had lost a leg. She didn't know where it had gone. She had no pain. No sense of physical discomfort. But she knew her leg was missing. When she tried to move it there was no response. When she lifted herself up from the pillows and looked at the bed there was only one raised ridge of quilt where there should have been two. When she reached down and felt for it there was nothing beyond her kneecap. She was trying not to panic. She knew somehow that this was a dream, that she would wake and when she did her leg would be restored to her. But at the same time she also knew that her leg was no longer part of her body. She could see it. Detached, separate, blood oozing from the cut. It looked so pathetic. The skin of her shin was very white and her foot was twisted and out of shape. There was scarlet nail polish on the toes. It was chipped, flaking. She tried to sit up to get a better look. It wasn't her nail polish. She never wore anything on her toenails. But she recognized the colour. It was the same as her mother always wore. The reddest it was possible to find. Applied carefully, wodges of cotton wool keeping each toe away from the next. The top of the bottle blotted with a piece of newspaper so it wouldn't clog and stick when the little brush was screwed back in.

She could smell the sickly tang of acetone. Nail-polish remover wiping away the old colour. It made her want to gag. She could feel the bile rising in her throat, pouring into her nose, her eyes watering as she choked.

And sat up. Coughing, gagging, gasping for breath. She reached out for the glass of water beside the bed and gulped it down. She pushed back the quilt. Two legs, two feet, ten toes and toenails, bare and unadorned. She lay back on the pillow, relief making her light-headed. She looked at the clock. It was 8.30. Time to get up. Time to get moving.

She would cycle across town to the women's prison. The exercise would clear her head. Give her time to prepare herself. She had volunteered. A two-week course. 'Telling Your Own Story', she called it. She did it every summer. When the school was closed. And Amelia was away. Some-times on holiday with her father. This year at Irish college in the Connemara Gaeltacht.

'You're crazy, you know. Why don't you just have a break, have a rest? Why do you have to take on more work?' All the other teachers said it to her as they packed up and prepared for their summer break. And muttered behind her back, 'Bloody woman. Who does she think she is? Mother Teresa?'

But she liked it. Enjoyed the women and their openness, the rawness of their emotions. The way they would say anything without fear of dis-approval. This year there were five in the class. Lisa O'Reilly from Dublin, Lyuba Sakharova, originally from Russia, Marcia Ecclestone, from

101

London, Honey Whitewater, from Trinidad, and another Dubliner, Mags Kelly. She knew that some of them would drop out. They would plead illness. Headaches, stomach problems, menstrual problems, emotional stress. They wouldn't be able to cope with the ten o'clock start. Getting out of bed would become impossible. Sometimes it would be the arrival of a quantity of drugs that would finish them off. They were supposed to be clean, the women who signed up for the course.

'But, you know the way it is,' Tanya O'Brien, the principal of the prison school said. 'Not much we can do about it. If the rest of society is saturated with drugs, why should the prison be any different?'

Grace liked Tanya. They had met years ago when Tanya had been doing a PhD in Criminology. Jack, Grace's husband, was her supervisor. They had all become friends. And when Grace and Jack had separated, Tanya had kept up the relationship.

Grace sat now in the classroom in the new purpose-built school block within the new purpose-built prison. It was well equipped, clean and bright, but even so it smelt. Of despair, dejection, depression, hatred, sorrow. She looked around the table. Five pairs of eyes looked back at her. She cleared her throat.

'You know who I am. You know why I'm here. I'm here to make it possible for you, if you want, to begin to write about your lives. So–' she smiled – 'who wants to go first?'

There was silence.

'I don't know what everyone else thinks, but I think you should show us the way. You should go

102

first.' The woman who spoke was large and round. Her jowls wobbled as she opened her mouth. Her arms folded across her belly were white and freckled. Her accent was English, upper class. It belied her appearance. Her hair was a dull, bleached blonde with two inches of black roots showing.

'And why is that?' Grace looked down at the sheet in front of her. 'Marcia, you are Marcia?'

The woman nodded. She picked up her pen and twirled it through her stubby fingers like a small cheerleader's baton.

'Because you're the teacher. We're just the pupils. We need to learn by example and what better example than your life, eh? Isn't that so, missy teacher?'

Grace waited. She didn't reply immediately. The woman reminded her of a pushy five-year-old. The kind who thinks she can rule the world and all in it.

'Well,' she said, 'an interesting idea but not one I'm about to entertain.'

'Not fair, not fair, not fair,' Marcia began to chant, clapping her hands in time. The two Dublin women joined in, giggling and laughing. The others stayed quiet. Grace waited. She said nothing. The noise was getting louder. Now the women were banging their palms on the tabletop. Grace stood up. She gathered together her books.

'OK, that's it. If you don't want to do this my way, then we'll call it a day. Pity really.' She looked around her, then let her gaze move to the frosted-glass windows. 'There's not much going on in this place in the summer, is there? Time must hang heavy.' She turned towards the door. The chanting stopped as abruptly as it had begun.

'Please, miss, don't go.' The Russian girl spoke. 'We keep our mouths shut now. We do what you want. Please stay.'

Grace turned back. The woman was small and slight. Her short hair was a bright, improbable red. She stood up and pulled out Grace's chair. She sank into a deep dancer's curtsey. Her feet were turned out and her back was flat. Her arms and hands made graceful semicircles. Grace looked from face to face.

'Lyuba, am I right?'

The woman nodded.

'So you want me to stay. What about the rest of you? Honey, what do you think?'

'I think there's fuck all to do in this place. We'd be mad to let you go.' Honey's skin was the colour of a polished conker. Her hair was shorn close to her skull. She held out her hand. Her palm was scored with lines that showed up pale pink. 'Anything to pass a few days. Take a seat, teacher, and we'll all shut the fuck up and be good little girls.'

She waited at reception for the officer to let her out. She was hungry, light-headed. They had offered her lunch in the canteen. She could have joined the queue, taken her tray of burger and chips, sat down at one of the moulded plastic tables and sat on a plastic chair. There were plenty of faces that she recognized. Plenty of women who would have welcomed her company. But she had had enough of the prison for one day. She made her excuses. Got to go and take my daughter to the dentist, she lied. Of course, they all smiled and nodded. Of course she should do that. The gulf yawned between them. She, with her daughter and her dental appointment. They with their convictions for drug trafficking, for assault, for robbery, for murder.

She waited for the officer to press the button and release the heavy metal door. Outside the sun was shining. A stiff breeze swirled dust in tiny tornadoes across the road. She stepped into the light.

'See you tomorrow, Grace,' the officer in charge called after her. She lifted a hand in acknowledgement. She unlocked her bike from the railings, slung her bag over her shoulder and began to walk down the incline towards the main road. A row of vans was parked, waiting to be admitted to the men's prison, the big Victorian building just opposite. She looked up at their mesh-covered windows. What tragedies lay behind them, she wondered. Stories to match the ones she had begun to hear this morning, she was sure. She had asked them to begin at the beginning. To write about their childhood. They hadn't got far with the writing. They had begun to talk. Each in turn had spoken of her mother. And each in turn had cried. She had listened in silence to their stories. Of neglect, of abuse, of abandonment.

'Tomorrow,' she said, 'tomorrow we stop crying and we start writing. Agreed?'

Five heads had nodded. She sat on in the classroom after they left. She gathered together her books and her notes. She tidied up the pieces of scrap paper the women had been using. There were doodles and scribbles. Initials intertwined and embellished. And one woman, the girl from Ballymun with the scar along her jaw from chin to ear, had drawn a baby. The drawing was careful and precise. The baby was tiny and perfectly formed. It was a boy. He was sucking his thumb. The girl had taken the trouble to get the details right. The baby's penis was wrinkled and soft. His toes and fingers had knuckle joints and nails. His navel protruded. And she had even shaded the diamond shape of the baby's fontanel on his hairless head. Grace slid the piece of paper into her folder and put it carefully into her bag. She would give it back to the girl tomorrow and she would ask her. Tell me, she would say, tell me who he is.

Now she slipped into the stream of traffic heading for the city centre. She was hot and tired. She would be home in half an hour. She would make tea, then she would go out into the garden. She would sit and watch the shadows move across the grass. And she would allow herself the luxury of memory. Of her own baby boy. Born prematurely nearly twenty-eight years ago. Taken from her when he was six weeks old. When he was moved from the incubator. When he could breathe on his own. Drink from a bottle. When he could open his milky blue eyes and stare up at her, the faintest hint of a smile hovering around his soft little lips. Tonight, with Amelia away and the house to herself, she would look at the drawing of the baby and she would let herself cry.

TEN

So she was from Ireland, this woman who had given birth to him. Very young, not much more than a child herself. So his mother had told him. Johnny Bradshaw couldn't imagine her at all. He sat in the crematorium chapel watching the curtains close in front of his mother's coffin. He couldn't feel anything. He suddenly wished he had buried her himself. Dug a grave and filled it in. Shovelling the heavy clay, hearing it drop noisily onto the wooden lid. Smelling the cloying wetness of the earth. Feeling the sweat drip down his forehead and the skin of his hands burn with the unaccustomed physical effort. He should have buried her. She hadn't left instructions. But the undertakers had assumed. She would be cremated. It would be quick and simple. It would be easy.

But this didn't seem enough. This plain service with no music. He was sure she would have wanted something more. She wasn't a churchgoer. But they always went to the carol service in the cathedral at Christmas. She surprised him. She knew all the hymns, all the verses off by heart and all the readings too.

'It was the way I was brought up,' she said when he questioned her. 'My grandfather was a clergyman. And we lived with him when I was a child. I went to church twice on Sundays. Morning and evening.'

'And do you believe in God?'

She shook her head.

'No, not really. I try, but I have no faith. But I love the ritual, the liturgy. And my knowledge was useful when we adopted you.'

'Oh?'

'Yes, you see we had tried so many times before and hadn't succeeded. But this time we went through a C of E adoption society. My grandfather had been involved in setting it up. They looked kindly upon your father and me.'

He didn't ask her anything else. He was sure she would have told him more. But he didn't want to know. She loved the cathedral and so had his father. Loved the twelfth-century carved stone panels that showed the story of the raising of Lazarus, loved the portraits done in Tudor times of the Kings and Queens of England, loved most of all the tomb of Richard and Eleanor of Arundel, lying, hands clasped in death.

Now he sat in the front pew in the crematorium chapel. It was plain and unadorned. Impersonal. His girlfriend, Lucy, sat beside him. She held his hand. She wiped her eyes with a damp tissue. Lucy was his first real girlfriend. The first woman he had ever brought home to meet his mother. He hadn't had much luck with relationships before Lucy. There had been a time when he wondered if he might be gay. He just didn't seem to be able to get it right. But he wasn't interested in men sexually at all. He had lots of friends, men and women. When he went to Sussex University in Brighton, he'd had a great time. But there was no one special until he met Lucy. She was a teacher too in the same school where he worked. He taught English and she taught French and Spanish.

'She's so pretty, Johnny,' his mother often said to him. 'So pretty. Such a sweet face and that lovely long black hair. If you ever have children,' she began, then stopped herself. He could see she was close to tears. He waited. 'If you ever have children, they will be lovely to look at.'

Scattered around the chapel were his mother and father's neighbours. And a few old friends. There weren't many. The Bradshaws didn't socialize much. They kept themselves to themselves. They were readers. They didn't play bridge or golf or tennis. They didn't join clubs or societies. They liked each other's company, and a stack of books to share and discuss. They loved each other's company, he corrected himself. They should have been buried together like Richard and Eleanor. Side by side, hand in hand. The way Philip Larkin described them in his poem. His mother had loved it. She knew the first verse off by heart. She would murmur it to herself as they sat in the congregation waiting for the organist to strike up the first notes of 'Once in Royal David's City'.

Side by side, their faces blurred,
The earl and countess lie in stone,
Their proper habits vaguely shown
As jointed armour, stiffened pleat,
And that faint hint of the absurd–
The little dogs under their feet.

After the ceremony the mourners waited in an orderly queue to shake his hand. He and Lucy

109

went to the pub across the road. They sat by themselves at a table in the corner.

'She was nice, your mum,' Lucy said.

'Yes, she was.' He stared down into his pint of lager.

'She wasn't your real mum though, was she?'

Johnny looked up at her. He wanted to slap her face. He could feel himself going red with the effort of not hitting her.

'I mean, well, you know.' Lucy's face had gone red, too.

'No, I don't know. She was my mother in every way except one.'

'But that one was important. She told me about it. The last time I saw her, before she got really sick. She told me I was to make you go and find her, you know, your, um...'

'My birth mother, you mean? That's what they call it now.' His voice had turned into a sneer.

'Yeah, whatever. Look,' Lucy put down her glass, 'don't be so cross with me. I'm just saying what she said. It's up to you. But you must be curious at least. At the very least. She, your mum, she said if we ever thought about having children ourselves then you'd want to know who your birth mother was. She said that was when you'd be really curious and that it might be better to do it before all that.' She took a sip of her glass of wine. 'Not that I'm saying that we would want to have children.' She smiled nervously. 'I wouldn't want to make any assumptions about, you know, about the future, but if we, if you ever did, well, maybe your mum is right about it.'

He lay in bed that night. He couldn't sleep.

110

Lucy breathed deeply beside him. Was he curious? He stared at the ceiling. Then he got out of bed and walked across the room to the wardrobe. He reached up and into the shelf at the back. He pulled down the little bag. He sat cross-legged on the floor and pushed open the metal clasp. His fingers touched the soft wool of the white cardigan. He lifted it to his face. He inhaled its musty smell. He closed his eyes. He tried to imagine this other mother. Irish, young, desperate. He got back into bed. He put the baby clothes under his pillow. He'd sleep on it. Wasn't that what his father always used to say? Sleep on a problem and in the morning there'd be a solution. He closed his eyes. He rolled over and buried his face in Lucy's hair. But sleep wouldn't come.

ELEVEN

Adam decided. He wouldn't bring her flowers. There was no point. Her garden already had more flowers than the average florist's shop. Should he bring her chocolates? He pondered the question. She had fed him with chocolate biscuits the first time they had met. He had eaten them. She had looked at them, licked the tip of her index finger, then reached out and picked up a few crumbs that had dropped onto the table. She had appeared to savour the flavour, but when he had pushed the plate towards her, she had shaken her head and pushed them back towards him. He'd bring her champagne, that's what he'd do. Maybe oysters. But perhaps that wouldn't be such a good idea. With one arm in a sling, she might find the whole business of extracting the oyster from its shell, lifting it into her mouth and swallowing it down in one movement a bit too difficult. He had decided. Champagne would be the best. He'd take a trip into the off-licence in Skibbereen and see what they had on offer.

He should have realized she'd hurt herself when she fell on the drive. When he'd pulled her to her feet she had winced as he took her by the arm. Those old bones, not as strong as they used to be. His gran had always been breaking things. It started with wrists. She'd needed a lot of help then. He'd helped her. He liked helping his gran. And sometimes, the odd time, he'd help himself too. There was always money lying around. In her purse and in her bag. She never knew what she had. Could never remember when she'd last gone to the bank. When she'd last got her pension. When she'd last paid the milkman or the guy who came to cut her grass and trim her hedge. She didn't mind him helping himself anyway. He knew that. He was her favourite. Her first grandchild. She'd told him once that she loved him more than she had ever loved his father, her son. But that was then. Before he went to prison. Before his father ruined it all for him.

He drove down the avenue to Trawbawn House, the bottle wrapped in tissue paper on the seat beside him. Lydia would be surprised to see him. She wouldn't know that word had travelled fast from the casualty department to the pub. They'd all been talking about it. He didn't quite understand the fascination that Lydia Beauchamp had for everyone locally. It was a strange mixture of loving and loathing. Colm had it too. He could while away hour after hour talking about her. In the gym in the prison, as Adam lifted weights and worked on his upper-body strength. And Colm pounded the treadmill, his words coming in gasps as the sweat dripped down his face and spread in dark patches across his T-shirt. As he told him again and again how that woman, Lydia, had destroyed his life, sent him off to England, blamed him for something that was nothing to do with him. How everything had gone wrong for him from that moment to this.

He could see Colm here so clearly. See how he belonged, how he fitted in. He could see him on the boats. He could see him in a force ten south of the Fastnet. His legs planted on the deck, his body leaning into the wind. He could see him in the pub sitting at the bar, his long legs wrapped around the legs of a stool, one arm reaching up behind his head, a cigarette hanging from between his index and second fingers. He could even see him in the gardens at Trawbawn. Lolling on the bench beneath the apple trees in the orchard or walking across the lawn, following the path through the trees, down to the boathouse on the river's edge. He could see him out in one of the wooden punts, his hands resting on the oars, a gentle flick of his wrist propelling the boat out into midstream, where the water swirled in eddies of bubbles as the fresh and the salt mixed and mingled as the tide ebbed and flooded. He could see him too, in the kitchen of the house, a mug of tea on the wooden table, his muddy boots left at the back door, his legs stretched out, his feet in thick hand-knitted socks. Could he see him with Lydia? He wondered as he parked the car at the end of the avenue and walked quickly around to the kitchen. He paused before he knocked. He could see her through the window. She was standing at the stove, one arm in a sling, held tightly against her body. As she turned, he could see that she was very pale. She wasn't wearing any make-up. No lipstick to define her mouth, no powder to cover up the wrinkles. Her hair needed to be brushed. It was flattened against the back of her skull, the natural curl pushed into an unsightly fizz. She was wearing what looked like a man's cardigan slung around her hunched shoulders and there was an old pair of slippers on her feet.

As he stood at the door watching, she lifted a milk pan from the stove and turned to pour from it into a mug. But her hand trembled and milk began to splash down onto the floor. He watched her face, her mouth trembling, the loose skin around her chin and neck crumpling. She tried to control the flow of liquid, but the pan slipped from her grasp and dropped. Milk poured over her slippers and spread in a smooth white puddle around her feet. As she turned towards the sink, she saw him. A slow smile spread across her face and for a moment she looked almost beautiful. But the moment passed. And she was just an old woman with her arm in a sling and a puddle of spilt milk on the floor.

'Hey,' he pushed open the door, 'let me do that.'

She stepped back. He put the bottle of champagne down on the draining board and reached into the sink. He picked up a J-cloth, wrung it out and dropped down into a squat. He carefully wiped up the milk, squeezing it into the basin, and rinsing the floor clean. Then he stood, washed his hands and dried them.

'Now,' he said, 'all better.'

She nodded and smiled at him again.

'You sit down, and I'm going to make you something to eat. But first,' he unwrapped the bottle, 'I'm going to put this in the freezer to get nice and cold. Doesn't do to drink champagne lukewarm, does it?'

They sat together in the kitchen, the afternoon sun slanting through the windows. She was very quiet. She sipped her glass of champagne, but barely touched the plate of bread and cheese he had laid before her.

'Does it hurt?' he asked.

She nodded.

'They put in pins to hold the ends of the bone together.'

'And did they give you anything for the pain?'

Again she nodded.

'Yes, I have a prescription somewhere. I'll have to get to the chemist soon. They gave me some to bring home but I've nearly used them all.'

'Give it to me; I'll sort it for you.'

She raised her head and looked at him.

'Thanks, I appreciate it.'

He reached over and rested his forefinger against her hand.

'Anything you want. You've got my mobile

number. You just call me. OK?'

She nodded again.

'You're very kind.' She looked hard at him. 'You never did tell me what brought you here, did you? We never did get to the end of the fate-versus-chance conversation.'

He lifted the bottle and refilled her glass.

'No?'

'No.' She sipped carefully. 'But I wonder about you, Adam. A young man of your, how will I put it in these politically correct days, of your background. Shouldn't you be doing something a bit more rewarding than working on a fishing boat or helping out a daft old lady who was stupid enough to break her wrist?'

He shrugged.

'Should I? Maybe I'm downsizing or whatever they call it in these politically correct days. Maybe I just don't like city life and all that goes with it. Maybe I didn't want to be a doctor, or a lawyer, or someone who had to wear a suit all the time.'

'But why here? Why Ireland? Why not, I don't know, Wales or the West Country or the Scottish Highlands.'

He shrugged again.

'Well, there's no mystery to it. I have a friend who comes from around here. He talked so much about it, I decided I had to come and see it for myself. So here I am.'

'And this friend, who is he? Would I know him?'

'Would you know him? Now, there's a question.' He leaned back in his chair and smiled at her. But she had begun to cry, tears welling up silently and spilling down her face. 'Hey, what is

116

it, Lydia? What's wrong?'

She bowed her head.

'Don't pay any attention to me. It's just the pain in my wrist.' She drained her glass. 'Get me my painkillers from my bag and pour me a whiskey, will you? Champagne is lovely, but it's no good as anaesthetic.'

He watched her as the alcohol and the analgesic kicked in. Her eyelids drooped and her body sagged.

'Do you want to go to bed, Lydia? Will I help you upstairs?'

She shook her head, a faint trace of a smile hovering around her mouth.

'I'm fine where I am. You've done quite enough putting old ladies to bed to last a lifetime. Anyway, I don't want to move. I don't want the pain to come back.' She sighed. 'You go. I can manage. I'll call if I need anything.' She reached out and picked up his phone. 'Handy little things, aren't they? I'll have to get one.'

She scrutinized its display. Her mouth trembled. And then it rang. A loud chirruping sound. She dropped it onto the table. It lay there, vibrating. He reached over and picked it up. He pressed the answer button.

'Hello,' he said.

He left her slumped in the chair at the kitchen table. He had promised he would come back with more pills. She thanked him and waved her hand towards her bag. He took the prescription and helped himself from her purse. He hummed as he drove the van out through the gates and onto the

117

main road. She didn't seem to have noticed his phone conversation. She didn't pay any attention to what he was saying.

'Hello,' he had said. There was silence. 'Hello,' he said again. This time there was an intake of breath. In the background he could hear the sound of doors banging, footsteps and loud voices. He waited.

'Hello?' He looked over at Lydia. She was staring vacantly out the window.

'Adam.' The voice was unmistakable. 'Adam.'

Adam got up from the table and moved towards the door. He turned his back on her.

'It's you.' His voice dropped almost to a whisper.

'Yes.'

'Where are you?'

'I'm in Mountjoy Prison, in Dublin. My transfer came through.'

'How is it?'

He could hear the sound of the smoke from the cigarette being drawn into Colm's mouth. He could smell it.

'It's fine. It's better than the other place. And you, where are you?'

He turned around and looked at Lydia. Her head had dropped forward onto her breast. Her eyes were closed. Her breathing was deep and regular.

'Guess.'

'You're not.'

'I am. I'm here.'

There was silence again. The fridge motor clicked on. It was loud in the quiet sunny kitchen.

'I want to see you. Give me your address so I

can get a visiting order to you. I want to know what you're up to. How you're getting on. I want to know all about it.'

'You will, don't you worry. I'll tell you everything. But send it to the local post office at Trawbawn. Do you know it?'

'I do. You've done well. Very well.' There was a sound of loud voices. 'I've got to go, Adam. There's a queue for this phone. You'll hear from me again very soon. OK?'

'OK, mind yourself. I'll be thinking about you.'

'And you, and you.'

He drove slowly into town, parked the van and headed for the chemist. He handed in the prescription. The woman behind the counter looked suspiciously at him. She read out the name of the drugs and the recipient.

'They're not for you. Where did you get this?' She dangled the piece of paper between her thumb and index fingers. Light gleamed on the hard red surface of her nails.

He smiled.

'I do some work for Mrs Beauchamp. She's in a bad way. She broke her wrist. She's in terrible pain. She asked me if I'd pick these up for her.'

'Well.' The pharmacist scrutinized the prescription again. 'DF 118. These should sort her out. They're very strong. Make sure she doesn't have any alcohol while she's taking them. They don't mix.'

He smiled again.

'Don't worry. I'll look after her. It's bad news seeing someone in pain like that. It really tears your heart out.'

119

The pharmacist smiled at him and pushed her glasses back on her head.

'She's lucky to have you around. A lot of people of her age are on their own. Here.' She took a tin of barley sugars from behind the counter and offered them to him. He nodded his thanks, picked one out, carefully unscrewed the wrapping and dropped it into his mouth.

'Yum.' He crunched down hard and felt the sugar rush on his tongue. 'Nice.' She nodded and smiled.

'Can you come back for them? Say about fifteen minutes or so?'

Outside, the sun was hot on the top of his head. Crowds jostled past on the narrow footpath. He pushed through the swing doors into the pub next door. It was packed with tourists. A guy with long white hair scraped away on a fiddle while a girl with a concertina tried in vain to keep up with him. He stood at the bar and ordered a pint. He looked around. There were a few people he recognized. Lads in from the boats for a break. A couple of local girls he'd seen around the place. And one very, very familiar face. And the rest of her too. Maria Grimes was sitting with a group of women by the door which led to the beer garden outside. They were sharing a bottle of wine. The table was cluttered with empties and overflowing ashtrays. He stood at the bar and watched her, waiting for her to see him. She was laughing loudly, too loudly. She swung around on her stool. She straightened her back and lifted a hand to push her hair from her face. He sipped his pint and waited. The waiting was good. The waiting was part of it. He knew he wouldn't have to wait too long.

She didn't acknowledge him when she came up to order another bottle of wine. But she stood close to him, so close that he could smell the rose oil that she always put behind her ears and on her wrists.

'My husband likes it,' she had told him. 'It reminds him of his mother. He loves his mother very much.'

'And do you?'

'I love the fact that she is a very wealthy woman. With just the one son. I love that.'

'Where have you been?' She leaned on her hand. Her voice was muffled.

'Oh here and there. Around. You know the way it is.'

'You haven't been to see me.'

'But you've been busy. Husband, kids, friends from Dublin. Nice ladies like those ones over there.' He nodded in the direction of the table.

'Don't rub it in. The boredom is killing me.'

'Killing you, eh? Killing you, is it?'

'Yeah, driving me crazy. Got a solution?'

He finished his pint and set the glass back down on the smeared counter top.

'Tell you what. I've an errand to run. A mission of mercy. Why don't you come with me? One good turn deserves another after all.'

She gestured towards the women at the table.

'What'll I do about them?'

'Do nothing. Tell them you've a headache and you're going home. Tell them it's the time of the month and you're feeling bad. Tell them whatever.' He picked up his jacket. 'My van's parked at the end of the road. The back doors are open. I've something to collect. I'll be a couple of minutes. It's up to you; take it or leave it.'

It was early evening by the time he got to deliver the prescription to Lydia. She was sitting where he had left her. Her face was the colour of flour and water paste.

'Sorry,' he said, 'I got sidetracked. A bit of business I had to take care of.' He took the packet from his pocket. He read the instructions aloud.

'Two twice daily. To be taken with water. Avoid alcohol. Here.' He filled a glass from the tap and broke the tablets from their foil cocoons. He dropped them into her hand. She swallowed them down in one gulp. He sat down beside her.

'How are you doing?'

She shook her head.

'Not well.' Her good hand rested on the pages of a magazine that was spread out on the table. He twisted his head around to have a look. And recognized the woman in the photographs.

'Who's that?' he asked. She hesitated.

'It's,' she sipped more water from the glass, 'it's my daughter. It's Grace. The first time I've seen her in years.'

There were tears in her eyes. Her mouth shook.

'She looks nice.' He pretended to read the text. 'She sounds great.'

Lydia nodded.

'Yes, she does. No help from me, I have to say. I haven't seen her for, let's see,' she paused, 'it must be twenty-five years at least.' She held out her glass. 'Pour me some whiskey, will you?'

'Hey, weren't you listening?' He tapped the packet of pills with his index finger. 'No alcohol.'

'I don't care. I don't give a damn. What's it going to do? Make me feel worse? I don't think so.'

He stood up.

'OK, if that's what you want.'

'That's what I want. But it's not all I want. I want you to do something for me, Adam. Will you?'

'Well, I don't know. Maybe, depends.'

'On what? How much I'll pay you? Is that it?'

'No, Lydia.' He sat down beside her. 'It depends on what it is you want me to do.'

'Well, it's like this. I want you to go to Dublin and find my daughter. I want you to talk to her. Tell her about me. Get her to come and see me. Will you do that, Adam? I'll give you plenty of money. You can take my car. I've no use for it while my wrist is in plaster. And if you get Grace to come back to me, I'll give you a bonus. OK? What do you say?'

He pulled a face, scrutinized the magazine article, fiddled with his phone and his keys.

'Well, I don't know Dublin.'

'What's there to know? It's a small place. She'll be easy to find.'

'Are you sure about this, Lydia? Are you sure this is what you want? Twenty-five years is a long time. Maybe it won't work out. Are you prepared for that?'

She didn't reply. He waited.

'I am prepared for it. I've had years to prepare

myself. I need to see her again. Even if it's just one more time. I need to talk to her. There are things I need to say.'

She reached out and touched his hand.

'But surely she'd be on the phone or something. These days it's dead simple. Here.' He held out his mobile. 'Call directory enquiries.'

She looked away.

'It's not simple,' she said. 'It's anything but simple. I've tried phoning her before. She just hung up on me.' She sipped her drink. 'You see, something terrible happened between us. I can barely bring myself to think of it. It ruined our relationship. It was my fault. She'd always been a difficult child. But she had a difficult childhood. My husband, you know, he was her stepfather. She didn't like him. She was very jealous. I sent her away. I sent her to boarding school. She never forgave me.' She paused and fiddled with the plaster fraying around her thumb. 'I need someone to intercede on my behalf. Please, Adam, if there was any other way I wouldn't ask you. But I need someone who she doesn't know. Who's not part of–' she stopped –'not part of here and all that here means to her. Please, will you do this for an old woman?'

It was dark by the time he left her. The gravel crunched underfoot as he picked his way towards the van. He put it in gear and drove slowly down the track towards the boathouse. Everything he needed was there, he reckoned. An old anchor and a length of chain, and the punt. That was enough. The anchor and chain would weigh down the body which lolled, swathed in a sheet in the back of the van. And the punt would carry them both out into the middle of the river. To the spot which Pat had pointed out to him. The deep hole where Alex Beauchamp had wanted to end up.

Maria Grimes seemed heavier dead than alive. He grunted with the effort as he heaved her over his shoulder. She was still warm. She was still pliant to his touch. He was tempted to lay her down and look at her one more time. But he didn't want to hang about too long. He didn't like it down here by the river. Especially in the dark when he couldn't see what was beneath his feet. But it had to be now. When there was no one around. No one moving up and down on the stretch of water. No one to see him and what he was doing.

It was easy getting her into the boat. Easy to wrap the chain around her and use a couple of big shackles to keep it in place. Just as easy as it had been to kill her. He hadn't set out to kill her. He had driven in through the gates and parked the van beside the lodge. Then he had gone around to the back and opened it. She had barely got into the sitting room before she had stripped off her clothes. He could see she was more drunk than he had realized. She had gone upstairs and lain down on the bed, on her stomach, with her head hanging over the side. He had taken off his own clothes and straddled her the way he had the Dutch woman. But somehow it wasn't enough. He wasn't getting the same blast of excitement, even though she was screaming and crying. But then he realized she was screaming for more. She wanted more and more. He had stopped then, and gone into the bathroom and pulled back the panel of wood and found the plastic bag. He had snorted the last of the cocaine, waited for the sensation as it rushed through his body. And then he had gone back to her.

'I thought you'd given up,' she said, a sneer on her face. 'I thought you'd gone soft on me, in a manner of speaking.' And she laughed out loud.

He hadn't realized that it was so simple and that it could happen so quickly. One minute he was on top of her, his hands around her throat, her body arching beneath him. And the next her eyes had glazed over and she was floppy and still. He had thought she was pretending. That it was part of the game. He called out her name and slapped her. But she was dead all right. He was fascinated. He'd never seen a dead body before. She looked very beautiful. The sweat was shimmering on her breasts and stomach. He pushed himself into her again. She still felt good. Better than before. He pushed and pushed, in and out, in and out, and her body moved with him. He felt dizzy, exhilarated, out of control. He called out her name as he collapsed forward. He lay still, his heart banging, struggling to breathe. Then he slept. Suddenly, instantly. For how long, he wasn't sure. Only minutes probably, but it seemed longer.

When he woke he slipped off the condom, went into the little bathroom and flushed it away. Stood in the bath and washed himself. Dried himself with the old roller towel hanging on the back of the door. This place had been a gift, he thought.

This little gate lodge had made it all possible. He walked back into the bedroom and got dressed. Then he went downstairs and picked up her clothes and her shoes. Opened her bag. Took out her lipstick. Unscrewed it. Walked to the window. Looked at his reflection. Then outlined his lips with the bright red. Filled them in and smacked them tightly together. Just the way his gran always used to do. Put the lipstick in his pocket. Went back upstairs and dragged her body off the bed and wrapped her in the sheet. Dragged her down behind him, hearing the heavy thump of her head on each step. Was glad then that he had done all that work with weights in the prison. It had stood him in good stead. He'd never have been able to manage her if his own body hadn't been so strong. He dumped her clothes, her shoes, her bag in the sheet with her. Tied it in a knot at her head and her feet. Carried her out and pushed her in the van. Drove down to the house and parked in the shade. Felt the packet of pills in his jacket. The old lady would be wanting them. He couldn't keep her waiting any longer.

Now he laid Maria's shrouded body on the slatted boards in the punt and rowed out into the river. It was a dark night. No moon. But he could see the outline of the low hills on either side. There were bright points of light at intervals. He remembered the sight lines Pat had told him about. He lined up the house on the hill with the grove of trees on the other shore. He stood up. The boat rocked beneath him. He bent down and rolled her to the gunwale. The boat slewed to one side and water slopped in. He carefully manoeuvred her head and then her feet and slowly, carefully lowered her down. The boat jerked and he staggered, nearly lost his balance and sat down quickly. He looked over the side. The white of the sheet was just about visible. But only for a moment. The blackness of the water had swallowed it up. She was gone. A ring of bubbles was all that remained.

He picked up the oars and began to row back towards the boathouse. It had been her idea. The whole thing. She had wanted it. She liked it rough. She liked it painful. She liked it frightening. He had given her what she liked. Even cut her with the penknife. Cut the hourglass tattoo into her shoulder. It was her idea. All of it. Colm would understand. He'd always told him. Give them what they want. It's the best way in the end.

He tied up the punt and got back into the van. He drove it to its sheltered spot behind the house. He'd sleep here tonight. And in the morning he'd go and see the old lady again. He'd take her money. He'd take her car. He'd take her trust. And he'd be gone.

TWELVE

'So tell me about the baby,' Grace pulled the drawing from her bag and laid it on the table. The girl called Lisa stared down at it, then pushed it away with the tip of her finger.

'I dunno.' Her voice was a monotone. 'It's just

some kid. I dunno.'

'Well, it's a bit more than just some kid, isn't it? You took the time and the trouble to draw him. There's a lot of detail here.' Grace tapped the piece of paper. 'You've given him a face and an expression. You've given him fingers and toes.'

'And a micky,' one of the other women shouted, and they all laughed.

'Yeah, you've given him a micky.' Grace smiled too. 'A pretty good one by the look of it. And I really like this.' She gently touched the baby's fontanel. 'It's that real baby thing, isn't it? You know the way when they're tiny, how you can see the pulse, their little heart beating.'

There was silence in the room. No one spoke. Even Marcia was quiet. Her large white hands lay motionless in her lap.

'Do you want to write about him? Write the story of your son and what happened?'

The girl nodded. Tears slid down her cheeks.

'OK, well let's see now.' Grace looked at her watch. 'You've all got half an hour. I want you to write something for me about a child. It can be fact or it can be fiction. It can be about yourself or someone else. But I want you to write it. OK? No more talking.'

She got up from the table and walked to the door. She stopped and looked back. Five heads were bent over their sheets of paper. Five hands were moving. She closed the door quietly behind her. There was a coffee machine in the staff-room. She would sit and wait until their time was up. She filled a mug and sat down. She pulled a crumpled envelope from her pocket. A letter had come from Amelia this morning. She read it quickly. It was full of complaints. The food was bad. The *bean a' tí* was cranky. The other girls were boring. The classes were a drag. Her phone had run out of credit. She needed more money. Was Grace coming to see her at the weekend? Would she bring her some more clothes? They were having a *céilí* soon. She needed her new short red skirt and the top that went with it. And would Grace phone Jack and tell him to write to her. She hadn't had any letters and the other girls were getting hundreds.

'Anyway, Mumma, I love you and I miss you. Hope you're all right all on your own at home. And hope your prison girls are being good. Next year let's go to Spain. Wouldn't that be fun? Lots of love, Amelia.'

The end of the letter was decorated with kisses and hugs and little cartoon drawings of the two of them, wearing bikinis and straw hats. Grace folded the letter and put it away. She sipped her coffee. Such a lucky life Amelia had had so far. She was safe, secure, protected, loved. The only bad thing that had ever happened to her was her parents separating, five years ago when she was ten. And somehow she seemed to have survived that.

'It's OK, Mumma,' she had said when Grace had told her Jack was moving out. 'I'll look after you. I can make tea for you on Sunday mornings and bring it up to you in bed, can't I?'

The novelty of the Sunday morning tea-making had soon worn off, but Amelia had quickly adjusted to two homes and her life shared between them. For the first couple of years there had been a formal arrangement. Days of the week and weekends spent in Jack's new apartment on the Quays or with Grace in their house in Rathmines. But Amelia had soon begun to decide for herself. She had keys to both places. And she came and went as she wanted, leaving a trail of discarded clothes and the other debris of her teenage life. Lucky, lucky child, Grace thought as she washed out her mug and put it back on the shelf. She was never going to end up here. Never going to carry heroin or cocaine in plastic bags in her stomach or hidden in the lining of her suitcase. Never going to be convicted of assault and robbery to feed a drug habit. Never going to find a knife in her hand and her pimp lying on the floor, blood pumping from a wound in his chest. Have her children taken away from her and see them once a month in the prison visiting room. None of that would ever happen to Amelia, Grace thought as she walked back to the classroom. She pushed open the door. The women were all still at work. It was hot in the room. Oppressive. Stuffy. Grace sat down. She looked from face to face.

'OK. Time's up,' she said. 'Now, who wants to go first?'

It was hot even within the thick stone walls of the men's prison. Colm O Laoire lay on his bunk and stared through the small barred window at the sky beyond. It had a different quality this sky than the sky above Manchester. Even though he could see so little of it, he knew it wasn't the same. There was a depth, a quality, a different kind of pigmentation to it. It must be the light, he thought, or the angle of the earth to the sun, something that made it so much more beautiful than any of the patches of blue that he had seen through the thick reinforced glass of the cell windows in England. Even on what passed for a fine day, the sky was murky and miserable, hanging down low just above the heads of the prisoners as they slouched around the exercise yard. Not that the inmates here were any better off than they were in England. If anything, he reckoned they had it worse. He couldn't believe they still had to slop out. Carry their pots to the toilets every morning to empty them. It made him want to throw up. But he supposed he'd get used to it. He'd have to. Everyone else seemed to handle it. A lot of them were a pretty miserable bunch. More deprived, more illiterate, more desperate, more hung up on junk than their English counterparts. But the way they were treated. It was incredible. He'd been asked at reception if he wanted methadone.

'Do I look like a fucking junkie?' he said. But the screw just smiled and told him if he wanted to go on the methadone maintenance programme he could. He was amazed. In the prisons in England they were put on a withdrawal programme. Five days in all. Sweating it out on their own. And the methadone didn't stop the amount of drug use in the prison. It was everywhere. It was the currency of the prison. First and foremost, with mobile phones a close-run second. Phones were in constant circulation. He'd already got hold of one. But he'd have to build up a bit of credit if he wanted more access. He'd have to work on that a bit more. Then he'd be free from the tyranny of the phonecard and the three official phone numbers. He could phone anyone, anywhere, anytime.

He noticed as he watched the other prisoners, as their faces became more familiar, as he was better able to distinguish one individual from the other, how many of them were HIV positive. But here there was no separation. No isolation from the rest of the prison population. He'd have to be careful. He had enough problems without picking up the virus. He'd have to be very select-ive about who he was going to get to keep him happy. He'd spotted a few likely candidates, nice-looking boys with friendly smiles and welcoming body language. And he'd heard that sex was no problem here. As long as it was consensual, the screws didn't give a monkeys.

One of the older guys had told him, 'You can shag all you like. No one will interfere. Just as long as there's no violence. No coercion.'

But he'd take his time before he made his choice. He'd more on his mind than a quick blow job from some skinny teenager. He'd forgotten how close Mountjoy was to the city centre. Just a couple of miles from O'Connell Bridge, and just a few miles more from Rathmines where he now knew that Grace Beauchamp, or McNicholas, her married name, apparently, was living. His sister had told him. When she'd come to see him yesterday. He'd sent her a visiting order, but he didn't think she'd take it up so quickly. But sure enough he got the call just after lunch. She was waiting for him in the Portakabin, the visitors' centre as they called it. There she was. All sixteen stone of her. Squeezed onto a hard plastic chair. When he saw her he was tempted to turn on his heel and walk away. But she spotted him and stood up and waved and called out his name. Shouted at him. In Irish of all things. So every head in the place turned to have a gawk.

They got through the niceties pretty quickly. He asked after the health of his mother. It was bad. He asked after the weather. It was good. He asked after the state of Cape. It was mixed. There was silence then while both tried to think of what to talk about next. He stared at the floor. The linoleum was stained and scuffed. He had a sudden longing for carpet. Soft, deep pile. His toes twitched inside his shoes. He wanted to feel that stubbled texture of wool. He knew how it would be beneath the soles of his feet. He stared again at the linoleum. He didn't want to see cream or grey or washed-out green. He wanted dark indigo, rich navy, glowing emeralds, acid yellows, red, the colour of blood. And white, the pure white of the caps of breaking waves. He wanted all that suddenly, violently. He wanted it to so much he thought he would faint.

'Hey, Colm.' Cáit's plump hand took his. 'Hey, here's a bit of gossip for you.'

He didn't respond.

'Listen. It's about Grace.'

He lifted his head.

'Grace?'

'Yeah, Grace Beauchamp. Remember her?'

'What about her?'

'She's here. In Dublin. There was a big article

about her in one of the magazines. She's running some school. She's the head teacher.'

'Here, in Dublin? Are you sure?'

'Yeah.' Cáit sat back, a satisfied expression on her face. 'She got married. She's got a teenage daughter. She's separated from her husband. There were loads of pictures of her. It's Grace all right. Not Beauchamp any longer. She's Mc-Nicholas.'

Colm said nothing.

'D'ye hear me, Colm? Isn't that a quare one? The two of so near to each other after all this time. You liked Grace, didn't you? Before old Ma Beauchamp threw you out.' Cáit's expression was knowing. Her small eyes gleamed with pleasure. 'I'd say you liked her enough to, you know,' she made a small ugly gesture, 'you know.'

'Liked her, didn't like her. What does it matter? Between them that family fucked me over big time.'

If only, he thought, if only he'd been able to hurt them the way they had hurt him. The fucking bitch of a mother who threw him out. Her husband, the bollocks who thought he knew how to handle a boat, but could do nothing without Colm's help. And even Grace. If she'd come out with it. Said who the baby's father was, none of it would have happened. He'd never have gone to England. Never have grovelled for shit jobs on building sites. Never have been so lonely that he got involved with that slag of a cow and married her. Never have felt so lonely and betrayed. And so much an outsider. Irish in England in the eighties, when the Provos were

135

planting bombs. It was bad news.

And Grace had betrayed him. He'd thought she was on his side. She said she trusted him. She cared about him. She had let him hold her baby boy, wait with her until the social worker came to take him away. But she had rejected him then. He had asked her to stay in England with him. But she had ambitions. She went back to her mother even though she hated her. Had to finish school, she said. The only way to escape was to get an education. And when she came back to London as a student she hadn't wanted him around. He had gone to see her in that squat where she lived with her all student friends. She was polite and friendly. She invited him in for a cup of tea. She had to search through the cupboards for some real tea. It was all that herbal muck that they drank. She asked him to stay for dinner. Brown rice and some kind of lentil stew. A big pot of it on the filthy old gas cooker. People walking in and out, helping themselves, laughing and joking, speaking a different language from him. He tried talking to her in Irish. She responded. Her Irish was good. Not the Irish of a native speaker, but pretty near fluent. One of the lads, a tall, thin guy called Jack with an earring in his left ear lobe, got narked. He kept on butting in, getting her to translate. Colm could see how it was between them. When she suggested they go to the pub he pushed between them as they walked down the road together. Grace had looked embarrassed, apologetic. But it didn't stop her from putting her arm around the guy as they squeezed together into a seat. And soon she'd stopped talking to

Colm at all. She had nothing to say to him really, once they'd covered all the old ground. And she got nervous when he mentioned anything to do with her other time in England. He realized then. The boyfriend didn't know about the baby. Colm was sorely tempted to tell him. Especially as the night drew on and the boyfriend became more and more hostile. There was going to be a fight. He knew it. He waited and bided his time. Then he leaned over and put his hand on Grace's hand. He picked it up, squeezed it. She turned and smiled at him. The old Grace, the child Grace. The sailor and swimmer, the rider of ponies bare back. The Grace who was fleet of foot, whose white feet became as seal's flippers in the cold sea. Whose smile had made him smile, made him feel welcome and wanted, made him feel that he belonged. That he was no longer the lad from the islands with his face pressed to the window. That he had a right to be on the inside, sharing the spoils.

His eyes had slid past her flushed face. The boyfriend, Jack, was staring at him. Colm grinned. The boyfriend stood up. Colm stood too. The boyfriend leaned forward. His forehead cracked into Colm's. There were screams and the sound of glasses breaking. Well, he had to retaliate. He couldn't let it go. He had the boyfriend's head in an armlock before he knew what was happening. He dragged him down to the floor. He wanted to stamp on him, feel the bones of his skull crumple beneath the sole of his shoe. Hear the same sound that shells make when they are crushed beneath a boot. The way it was on the shell beaches of the Catalogue islands just to the northern tip of Sherkin. Centuries of sea creatures who had died on those little outcrops of rock. And left behind their legacy. Cream and white and bands of pale blue. An iridescent sparkle here and there as the sea washed over and back, and the hushing and shushing of water trickling through them.

'Are you listening, Colm, are you listening? Did you hear what I said?' Cáit's voice was petulant.

Instead he had reached down and grabbed hold of the earring, twisted it and jerked it hard, so it came away in his hands. Drops of blood smeared his fingers. He wiped them down on his jeans as he walked away. Paused at the door and looked back. Grace was on her knees. She was holding Jack's head up. She turned and looked at him. She was saying something but the noise in the pub was deafening. It was that kind of roar that he had heard before whenever he was in a fight. It surged through his head and filled him with joy. He pushed open the pub door, stepped through it and out into the cold, wet night, then stopped and looked back. She had taken a half-step towards him. She was holding out her hands. They were bloodstained. He couldn't hear what she was saying, but he could read her lips. 'Why?' she was asking. 'Why, why?'

'Colm, Colm,' Cáit banged on the table, 'Colm, are you listening to me? Are you listening? I told Mammy I'd ask you. Will they let you out now you've come back here? Haven't you been in prison for long enough? Mammy says we want you to come home. We need you. Mammy says she knows you're in for life. But what's life these days? Sure it's not much more than seven years for most people. And you've been in for ten already.'

But he wasn't listening. He stood up, his face pale and blank. He walked away from her. His shoes squeaked on the shiny hard surface of the floor. He gestured to the screw that he wanted to leave the visitors' room. He waited, his head slumped, his eyes fixed on his shoes until the door was unlocked and opened. Then he pushed past him. Didn't look back. Didn't want to be near her any longer. Wanted to be on his own, with his own thoughts, his own desires and his own needs. Didn't want to remember what the governor of the prison in Manchester had said to him as he was telling him his transfer request had been granted. He'd stood in his office with the picture of the Queen on the wall above his head. It reminded him of the Virgin Mary that his mother had in the front parlour above the fireplace. Same blue cloak, same pose, half-turned towards the viewer, same blue eyes that followed you wherever you moved.

'And just one thing, 357682. I know you'll have heard that the sentencing policy in Ireland is more lenient than ours. But don't get too excited about it. Your life sentence is going to mean the same there as it does here. You've a tariff of fifteen years. What does that mean?'

Colm cleared his throat.

'Fifteen years before I can be considered for parole,' he muttered.

'Say again, 357682. Say it louder so we can all

hear you.'

Colm stared at the Queen. He kept his eyes fixed on her eyes. 'Fifteen years before I can be considered for parole,' he said, trying to keep his voice as neutral as possible.

'Well done, 357682, well done. Got it through that thick Irish skull of yours. Fifteen years before the parole board will even consider your application and then God knows how many more before you get a sniff of fresh air. Now, if you'd committed a political offence, if the woman you'd killed had been a policewoman or a prison officer or a soldier, or even a census taker, well, you'd be onto a winner there. You'd be out on the terms of the Good Friday Agreement. But a domestic? I don't think so.'

A domestic. That was what he called it. Colm closed his eyes. Didn't want to think back to that night in London. When he had found out that his wife was screwing someone else. And she'd jeered at him and laughed at him. Said she'd found a real man at last. That he was nothing but an old Irish queer. Couldn't get a hard on. Couldn't keep it up long enough to make her feel good.

'Fucking chip on the shoulder, and a huge fucking pain in the arse. Aren't you? Fucking Irish fairy, that's what you are. A leprechaun, isn't that what they call you in the old country?' She was shouting and laughing and doing some kind of a mad Irish jig, lifting her skirt as she kicked her feet up high. So he caught her leg and twisted it and she fell. Banged her head on the washing machine as she went down. But even that didn't stop her. She opened her mouth and began to howl. So he'd hit her hard, to shut her up. But she wouldn't shut up. She just kept on and on and he kept on hitting her, first with his fists, then with the iron. There was blood everywhere. It was a terrible mess. So he picked her up and carried her into the bedroom. He tied her to the bed. Doused the sheets and the duvet with white spirit and set fire to it all. Stood and watched her burn and suffer, the way she had made him suffer.

He lay on his bed in his cell and stared at the ceiling. There was a stain, just above his head. It was a regular shape. A bulge at top and bottom with a neat waist in the middle. The shape of an hourglass, like the hourglass fob that Grace had given him to thank him for helping her when she had the baby. He closed his eyes. He needed to talk to Adam. He would be able to help him. He would make him better. He would make him whole again.

The girl called Lisa read slowly, stumbling over her words. They all listened in silence.

'I brung him home from the hospital. He had been born early. He was very small. They wouldn't let me take him for a good few weeks. He had to be in the special unit in the hospital. He had to be on a ventilator because his lungs were too small. He had to have a tube in his tummy so he could feed. But then they said he was big enough. So I came to get him with me mam. We got a lift from her fella. We went back to the flat. It was great. I was so happy to have my baby home. I got a new cot and new everything for him. And Christy was happy too to see his little boy. At first it was all great. We called him Liam after me daddy. But then he wouldn't stop crying. It was bad at night. I was up to him all the time. Christy was getting mad. He wanted me to go back to work. But I told him I couldn't, the baby needed me. He said he'd mind him, then I could go out at night the way I used to. I didn't want to, but I needed the money. I'd gone off the gear when I was pregnant but I was soon back on it again. So I started going out just for a couple of hours and Christy would stay in with him. But then Christy made me stay out for longer and longer. And I could see that the baby wasn't OK. He wouldn't wake up. He wouldn't take his bottle. And I noticed he had bruises all over his tummy. Christy said he'd fallen out of the cot. But I knew that couldn't happen. Christy said he'd be more careful with him. And I believed him. But when I came home that night the baby was on the floor and his head was smashed in. Just where you could see his heart beating. And Christy was pissed and he was passed out on the sofa. So I picked up the poker and I beat the shit out of him. And then I called the guards and the ambulance and they took them both away. And now I'm in here. I got life for murder because they said Christy was asleep when I hit him and there was no way he could have defended himself. So now I've no babby and I've no fella. I've nothing.'

The girl lit a cigarette. Her hands were trembling. Her small face was the colour of milk.

'Thank you, Lisa,' Grace said. 'Thank you for

142

being so honest with us all. It must have been hard for you.'

'Harder than beating the shit out of that fucker.' Marcia's voice was loud. 'Men, fucking useless and worse than useless.'

There would be no more work done today. Grace stood up

'OK, that's enough for now. I'll take your pieces and read them this evening. And we'll talk about them all tomorrow. How's that?'

But none of them were listening to her. They were back in their own world. She gathered together the sheets of paper. Her hands were trembling. She hurried from the room, down the stairs, out into the open area between the high brick walls where there was a basketball court. Into reception, to wait until the steel door rumbled back and she could escape. And now the memories were with her again. The neonatal unit in the hospital in Birmingham where she had given birth. The curve of his cheek as he lay on his side. His starfish hands and arched feet. The almost transparent skin of his eyelids. The whorl of fine hair which spiralled around his head. His pulse throbbing beneath the fontanel's fine membrane. The cold plastic of the breast pump as she expressed her milk for him. Her nipples tingled and leaked when she heard him cry. And one night when he was big enough to breathe on his own, and suck from the bottle and the nurses were busy with an emergency, she had lifted him out of his cot and fed him herself. Even now she could feel the sensation of the milk pouring into her breasts. She had fed Amelia too. But it had been different. Amelia's birth had been simple and straightforward. It was virtually pain free. The epidural saw to that. Amelia was a week overdue. She was round and fat, sleek with amniotic fluid. She had opened her eyes and shrieked.

Jack had looked from her face to Grace and said, 'She's so beautiful. She's just like you.'

And Grace had turned her face away and wept. When her baby boy had been born, a month too soon, violently and painfully as if he knew she wanted rid of him, she had been on her own. There was no one with her to place him in a recognized line of descent. But she had whispered to him, told him how beautiful he was, how he looked like his father. Then thought of how his father had abandoned her. And had said nothing more to him.

She was home from the prison almost before she knew it. She wheeled her bike into the small garden at the front of the house. Unlocked the door and let herself into the cool dark hall. Walked into the kitchen and opened the fridge. Poured herself a glass of white wine and drank it down in one gulp. Refilled her glass, then went out into the garden. Sat down on the wooden bench that Jack had bought her one birthday and buried her head in her hands. It still hurt so much. So many years later and the pain had not left her. She had never told Jack about him. Never told Amelia that she had a half-brother. Never shared him with any of her friends. That baby boy who would now be an adult. She lifted her head and looked around her. Then she stood up and walked back into the house.

'Go away,' she said out loud. 'Go away and leave me alone.'

But this time she knew he wouldn't.

THIRTEEN

Adam had never been to Dublin before. As a rule he tried to stay out of cities. They made him feel nervous and edgy. He had tried London once. After his father threw him out of the house and his grandmother wouldn't have anything to do with him. But although he could see the potential and the advantage of anonymity that the city's huge population gave him, he couldn't stick it for more than a few weeks. He couldn't sleep for the fears that dogged him, that followed him around, that sat on his shoulder nibbling at the nape of his neck.

The memories kept on surfacing as he drove north from Cork. But, he comforted himself, Dublin was hardly in the same league as London. It was small, barely as big as an English provincial town. It wouldn't be a problem. He was just going to have a bit of fun. And there was Colm. He would go and see him tomorrow. He had the visiting order in his pocket. And in the meantime he would book himself into a good hotel, and decide what he would do. Would he do what Lydia had asked him? Would he go and find her daughter? She'd given him enough money to stay in the city for a month at least, longer if he was careful. So he wouldn't have to steal the way he had before. Not that he minded stealing. Stealing was the best. And not just stealing tangibles, like money or jewellery. But stealing the things that people cared most about. Their identity, their reputation, their self-esteem. Adam had done plenty of that in the past. There was that nice young teacher at his boarding school. Henry Jackson was his name. Such a trusting guy. Adam had used Henry's credit card to buy child pornography. Then he'd sat back and watched as he was fired from his job, destroyed, ruined. And then there was the time when he'd done something similar with one of his father's cards. He'd bought stuff from a mail order company in Birmingham. Whips and chains and rubber clothing. Hoods and helmets and gags. Had them delivered to his mother. Heard the row between his parents. Heard his father's loud protestations of denial. Knew she didn't believe him. Because she knew about his visits to prostitutes. In particular the women who specialize in humiliation, sadism, punishment of all kinds. Knew that she knew he had betrayed her already.

And then there was rape. The best theft of all. He'd talked about this with Colm. Tried to explain it to him. Colm had never raped anyone. Not really. He'd threatened a few with it inside. And he'd sometimes made assumptions that he shouldn't have. But he didn't feel about it the way Adam did. The sex was the end result for Colm. Not the power. Adam tried to make him understand.

'You see, Colm, it's the ability to be able to do it. To control someone else completely. And it's

146

the ultimate theft too. Because it takes away self-respect and it replaces it with self-loathing. And it leaves behind all those pretty pictures. It's like they're tattooed inside your head. You can never get rid of them. And the best thing about it all is that you know there's another person in the world who has the same memories. The exact same memories. And it's the person who made it all happen.'

He laughed when he thought about it and he sang as he accelerated onto the Port Laoise bypass. The song was one his gran's favourites. It was from *The King and I*.

'Whenever I feel afraid,
I hold my head erect,
And whistle a happy tune,
So no one will suspect,
I'm afraid.'

She used to sing it to him all the time when he was little. And he would sing it back to her. Such a pity that she wasn't around to see him. Driving this big old car, money in his pocket, and so many choices to make. Maybe he wouldn't stay in Dublin at all. Maybe he'd go and see Colm and then he'd head for the airport and get a plane somewhere, anywhere. After all, he had left that bit of rubbish behind him in the river by the house. Sooner or later it was bound to surface. Or was it? He pondered the chances. He had weighed her down well. He didn't think the chains would slip. The place in the river where he had dumped her was deep, and even at low tide there was still plenty of water. It wouldn't be long before she'd be reported missing. He supposed someone would have seen him talking to her in the pub. Maybe she would have been seen getting into the van, but he didn't think so. He'd left it parked in a narrow lane, a quiet spot out of the way. She'd been out of sight in the back of it. Wouldn't have been spotted as he drove to Trawbawn. And no one had seen her go into the gate lodge with him. And after that? Well he was absolutely certain that no one had seen anything then.

Anyway, no need to make any decisions for the time being. It was a beautiful hot day. He had nothing to fear. He had it all ahead of him. And he was going to make the most of it for as long as he possibly could. He put his foot on the accelerator and watched the needle on the speedometer climb. Lydia's car was a pleasure to drive. It was a lot better than Pat Jordan's old van. Up ahead the stretch of motorway was coming to an end. He cut across into the inside lane, narrowly missing clipping the front of a huge articulated lorry. The driver leant on the horn and as Adam looked at him in his rear-view mirror he could see the expression of fury on the guy's face.

'Fuck you, mate,' Adam yelled, and pounded the steering wheel with the heels of his hands. 'Fuck you.' And he accelerated again, as soon as the road ahead was clear.

He had to slow as he approached the outskirts of the city. He wasn't sure where he was going. Lydia had given him a list of places to stay. She had even given him a map and marked her daughter's school with a big red X.

She had told him, 'It's a small place, Dublin. You'll have no difficulty finding her.'

'And what do I do then?'

'Tell her, Adam, tell her I want to see her. Persuade her, convince her. Just tell her how things are with me.'

So what was a guy to do? Make her beg? Make the poor old girl get down on her arthritic knees and bow her grey head and clasp her knotted hands together? He contemplated her kneeling before him, contemplated what might come next. Then banished the thought from his mind. Wouldn't do to have those kind of ideas about a woman like Lydia Beauchamp. Better to hold off. There was bound to be more coming his way if he kept her sweet.

The traffic was slow and congested now. He fiddled with the car radio, switching from station to station until he found some music he liked. He tried to change lanes to give him a bit of an advantage, but he was hemmed in. He glanced out and up. The truck to his left was the one he had passed twenty miles back. The driver was staring down at him. He was smiling. He began to speak. Adam couldn't hear him. He tried to lip-read his words. But he didn't need to know exactly what they were. The man's intent was plain to see.

'I'll get you, you little fucker. Watch your back, I'm on to you.'

Adam lifted his hand from the wheel. The lights ahead were just turning orange. The traffic at the intersection was slowing. But he wasn't. He shot across the junction and held up his hand, gesticulating with his middle finger so it formed a defiant 'fuck you'. The truck driver tried to follow him, but the lights had now turned red. He was stranded, halfway across the road. Adam watched in his mirror as a cop on a motorbike slowed beside the lorry and signalled to the driver to open his window. Serve the fucker right. He was getting just what he deserved. Now Adam joined the rest of the queue for the turn-off for the city centre. He was tired. He needed to get out of the car, stretch his legs, have a shower and something to eat and, even more desperately, something to drink. He needed to prepare himself for his visit to Colm next day. That was what he needed to do.

Lydia was cold. She stood at her bedroom window and looked out, across the tops of the trees to the river beyond. Bright points of light flashed from the small white crests that marked where the river flow met the incoming tide. A small trawler was hurrying downstream. Coming upstream was a yacht. She reached for her binoculars and lifted them to her eyes. There were two girls crewing the sailing boat. They were wearing shorts and tight T-shirts. Their skin gleamed. She let her gaze dwell on them, their legs, their breasts, their smooth, tanned arms. The lads in the trawler waved and shouted. Lydia watched the exchange. Once that would have been her. She would have been the object of their desire. But not now. She stepped back from the window and put the binoculars down on the dressing table. Now she was old, ugly, helpless. Her body no longer functioned with the careless ease of youth.

She walked to the wardrobe and opened it. She

150

pulled out a long, woollen shawl and wrapped it around her shoulders, hiding the plaster cast beneath it. Her wrist ached and every now and then a dart of pain shot up towards her elbow, making her catch her breath and bringing sudden hot tears to her eyes. She needed to get out of the house. She needed some exercise. Anything to take her mind off the pain in her arm.

Outside she stepped from beneath the over-hanging beech trees and into the brightness of the morning. Ahead was the drive, and beyond it the road. She began to move towards it, her steps hesitant at first on the gravel. There were weeds springing up between the small stones. Dandelion and dock and buttercup with its long tendrils taking root. Another job to be added to the list. She would have to speak to Pavel. She wondered where he was. He had said something about going to the city to meet up with his other Polish friends. She would have to get the weeding done. It wouldn't do if Grace and her daughter were to come and visit. Everything must be in order for them. Grace would be expecting the house and the garden to be as beautiful as ever.

She took a deep breath and began to walk again, slowly, her step careful on the loose stones. Light poured down on her in shafts of pure gold. She raised her head towards the sky. It was a perfect day today, the kind of day that would make a believer fall to their knees to give thanks. But Lydia wasn't a believer. Not like Alex. He had prayed every evening without fail. He gave thanks constantly. For meeting Lydia. For leaving the city. For finding Trawbawn. She couldn't tell him. About the money that was paid into her bank account every month.

She walked slowly up the drive. Off to the right was Alex's favourite herbaceous border. He had planted it, choosing the cranesbills and poppies, the rudbeckia and agapanthus, the penstemons and delphiniums, the peonies with their glossy green leaves and extravagant dark red blooms, and the row of arum lilies whose creamy flowers gradually unfurled as the spring turned to summer. She stopped to rest beside it, sinking down on the low retaining wall. She could smell the scent of cloves from the tiny pinks he had planted between the slabs of limestone. They were so lovely, their delicate petals like butterflies' wings. Alex was a good gardener. Like his mother before him. He had grown up in a big house on Killiney Hill, the oldest son, expected to follow his father into the family firm of solicitors. But he didn't do well at school. Now he'd be diagnosed as dyslexic. Then he was classed as a fool. But he was good with his hands. Took over the gardens that stretched down towards the sea. Took refuge there. He'd told Lydia all about it.

'I had a really bad stammer. I couldn't string more than two words together. They were always having parties. I was expected to be sociable. It was agony. My father was so disappointed in me. I couldn't handle his disapproval.'

'But what about all the things you could do? You could sail, you could garden. Did none of that count?' Lydia tried to comfort him.

'No, none of it counted. The only thing that mattered was the family business. My father was a man obsessed with class and tradition. I was named Alexander after my father, my grand-father and his father before him. It was unthink-able that I wouldn't be able to take his place. He just couldn't understand why I wasn't like him.' And his eyes had filled with tears, and she had kissed him and held him tightly. And thought. It's not so bad that I'm doing what I'm doing. I'm not really using him. I'm making him happy.

She sat on the wall and looked out across the fields. Cattle grazed it now as they had then. That year there had been a bull in the field, as there was now. He was lying on the ground, his front legs tucked neatly underneath him. He was a beauty, a Charolais, his coat a glossy silvery gilt. The bull then was a Friesian, smaller than this monster, but no less dangerous. At the end of that summer he had been destroyed. He had got into a fight with a neighbouring animal and turned on the men who tried to separate them. Chased them back across the field, then stood and roared his triumph at the top of his voice. They had got their human revenge. They had shot him, dragged him with the tractor to the meat truck, rendered his magnificent body into offal and bone meal. Talked about him in the pub that night. Sneered at his presumption of invincibility. Bragged how they had faced him down and brought him low.

She had been sorry about the bull's miserable end. Better that he had crushed one of them, stamped on him with his hard black hooves. After all, they had bred him to be aggressive and full of power. She had complained to Daniel about it. She had thought he would agree with her. But he had listened while she ranted, then shrugged his shoulders and said,

'He's an animal, Lydia. For thousands of years bulls have been killed by the men who breed them and own them. That's the way it is. Don't make the mistake of giving him emotions he doesn't possess.'

But it didn't make her feel any better. This bull now made her heart beat faster and her palms sweat. She stood still, holding her breath and peered over the hedge. The bull had stopped chewing the cud. He turned his head so his small eyes met hers. He snorted loudly, and slowly pushed himself up from the grass. She moved away and he began to move too, keeping her in his sights. Around him, his herd grazed. But as he walked forward, so they began to follow him, at first in a casual streeling manner, but then forming into a neat, purposeful queue. Lydia began to walk more quickly, back towards the drive. The fence was barbed wire here, less resistant to the huge press of body weight that the bull and his followers would be capable of. As she turned onto the gravel, she looked back. He had stopped by the drinking trough, and lowered his mouth to the water. Around him, the other animals crowded closely. The bull drank, then raised his head. Water ran in crystal droplets from his fleshy black lips. His eyes shone in the bright sunlight. Then he lowered his mouth and drank again. As she walked past the gate and the water trough she felt the cold again and the weight of the plaster cast shielding her shattered wrist.

'Silly old woman,' she chided herself out loud.

'Frightened of a stupid animal that has no interest in you at all.'

But she could feel the imprint of the bull's eyes as she walked slowly away. They made the tiny hairs on her back prickle and her shoulder blades twitch.

Ahead was the gate lodge. It had been months since she had gone inside. She pushed open the door. It grated on the doorstep. She stood in the small sitting room. It smelt of damp and soot from the chimney. She sat down on the sofa. She had made the covers out of material that Daniel had given her. It was left over from the last time his wife had re-covered the chairs in the drawing room, he said. Lydia had invited him to afternoon tea when she had finished the job. Grace had helped make the cake. They had been happy then. Even Alex had come out of his shell. And for the years afterwards, while Daniel was still well and they had all lived together in the big house. But then he had got sick. Diagnosed with prostate cancer. And he had told her. He was going to leave Trawbawn to Grace. That she was more to him than anyone else. And Lydia had said that was wonderful. But she had thought about it and thought about it. Leaving it to Grace was a risk. It made her future with Alex insecure. Grace had never come to terms with Lydia's marriage to Alex. She had never accepted him. Life was intolerable with the two of them together. That was why Lydia had decided to send Grace to boarding school in Dublin. She had said it was because of the education that Grace would get there. But it was really because she couldn't cope with the tension and the rows. It was too risky. Who was to know what might happen? Alex wouldn't be able to cope if anything went wrong and they had to leave Trawbawn. He couldn't take his chances in the world beyond its high stone walls. So she went to Daniel and told him that it wouldn't be right for a child to inherit so much. It would be better if he left it to her. And after she died it would go to Grace. And he had agreed. But made her promise.

'Promise me, Lydia, you won't let me die in hospital. Elsie died there. It was a terrible death. You'll look after me, won't you?'

She had agreed. And everything was fine until that night, that last night when he had asked her to phone the solicitor, said he wanted to change his will. It wasn't that he didn't trust her. He just wanted the absolute security of knowing. That Trawbawn would go to Grace. And she had soothed and comforted him, left the room for a few minutes, then come back to his bedside and lied. Said the solicitor would come first thing in the morning, that it would be sorted out then. And because he was in such pain she had helped him. She had topped up his morphine drip, and then to make sure that the pain didn't sneak up on him and make him cry out and sob like Grace when she fell that day and grazed her knee, she gave him an injection as well. She separated his fourth and fifth toes. The skin between was soft and damp and almost webbed. She slipped the needle into the space and carefully punctured the flap. Then she let go of his toes and watched how they immediately sought each other out, the smaller of them folding itself back against the bigger. As Daniel folded his arms around his body, turned on his side and closed his eyes.

There were no questions asked about the nature of his death. She sat beside him and waited for his last breath. Kissed him goodbye, then let herself fall asleep too. She did not wake until the morning sun had risen high above the trees. She shouldn't have slept so long, but she was exhausted, she told the doctor when he came. It was her fault, she said. She should have been awake to check his pulse, but he seemed so peaceful. It was such a relief after all he had been through. And the doctor had reassured her. Told her not to be silly. That she had done everything that anyone could possibly want.

She had done everything, that much was true. Everything to ensure that she and Alex would be secure. There had been no post-mortem. No one had scrutinized his wasted body for puncture wounds, for signs or symptoms of anything out of the ordinary. No one had asked any questions. She had washed him and prepared him for burial. Dressed him carefully in his favourite suit. Put his signet ring back on his little finger and his gold watch in his waistcoat pocket. But she had taken the fob in the shape of the hourglass from the gold chain. It was so pretty. It was a pity to think of it going into the grave with him. She had given it to Alex. He had attached it to his watch chain and worn it for years. But it had not been found with his body. Buried, she had thought, in the mud. Fitting really. She should have let it go with Daniel where it belonged. It was bad luck to

157

have taken it, she could see that now.

She stood up. She moved towards the narrow stairs. Sunlight poured down from the skylight in the landing ceiling. Dust rose from beneath her feet and hung, shimmering, before her as she moved carefully from step to step. She stopped at the bedroom door. She pushed it and it swung open. The iron bedstead was neatly made with the old-fashioned quilted eiderdown pulled up over it. The small pine wardrobe stood open and as she walked forward her reflection swung towards her from the mirror inside it. She stopped and put her hand to her face. Was this what she had become? This old woman with the stooped back and the grey hair standing up in a tangled fizz around her lined face. A sob caught in her throat, and a wave of pain washed through her arm. And a sudden noise startled her so she jumped and had to reach out to catch hold of the end of the bed. It was a butterfly, a red admiral, clinging to the bottom pane in the small window which looked out onto the drive. Its wings twitched and fluttered, beating in vain. It bobbed up and down, pressing itself close to the smeared glass. Lydia giggled, sudden relief making her light-headed.

She sat down on the bed. She felt something hard against her foot. She bent down and reached for it. Her hand touched something cold and metallic. She pulled it out and looked at it. It was a penknife. Bright red. Heavy. A number of different blades all tucked away inside it. She had seen it before. It belonged to the Polish boys. She had seen them using it in the garden. Cutting lengths of twine. Peeling apples. Slicing up the

Polish sausage they brought with them for their lunch. She would have to speak to them. She didn't want them using the lodge. It was private.

The mattress gave beneath her body. She leaned back against the pillows. It had always been comfortable. She and Alex had slept well here. They had been so exhausted by the fresh air, the physical exercise, the overwhelming beauty of the place. Every evening she remembered they had gone to bed early, even though the sun was still in the sky and the birds were still singing in the branches of the apple trees behind the house. Alex had wanted to have a child with her. She had humoured him. But she had made sure it wasn't going to happen. Another secret. Like the money in the bank account. Her running-away money. Her mother had told her. Every woman should have it. Keep a suitcase packed. Keep your options open. She closed her eyes and rolled over, pulling the shawl tightly around her. And smelt the faintest hint of perfume. It was on the pillow, beneath her face. She got up quickly. She pulled the quilt from the bed. There was no sheet. Just the old striped mattress, stained and worn.

She turned away. She pushed open the door to the bathroom. A stub of a candle still stuck in its bed of wax was on the ledge beneath the window. Another butterfly in here too. A tortoiseshell. Its wings beat frantically as her shadow loomed over it. She undid the catch on the window. But the butterfly would not fly out. It clung onto the glass, until she shouted at it, and waved her fingers, then bent down and scooped it into her palm, closing her hand into a fist, as she leaned out of the window and opened her hand into the soft breeze from the sea. The butterfly hesitated, its wings slowly opening and closing. Then it lifted from her, hovered for a moment, then caught an up-draught and floated away, up towards the sun. Her gaze followed its flight path. It had been joined by others, three, four, five of them, all fluttering together in the warm air that rose up from the heated tarmac surface of the road.

There was a lot of traffic passing now. Cars with roof racks laden with luggage, four-wheel drives pulling dinghies, a couple of horseboxes, and even a group of cyclists, all wearing match-ing gear, orange jackets, orange helmets, sleek black glasses and skin-tight shorts with an orange stripe down the thigh. And a Garda car, slowing, indicating, then pulling in and stopping at the gate. She drew back from the window. One of the officers got out. He looked around him, then tried the handle. She turned away, hurried down the stairs and out onto the drive.

'Hello, can I help you?' Her voice was polite.

The guard smiled at her through the bars. 'Mrs Beauchamp. Good afternoon.'

She knew him. His grandfather had once worked for Daniel. He had looked after the horses. A nice man. He had often brought his grandson to work with him. A boy with freckles and a bullet head. The kind of kid that was always climbing trees and falling into the river.

'It's Liam, isn't it? Liam O'Regan? Jim's grand-son?'

'That's right Mrs Beauchamp.' He waved towards the guard in the driver's seat. 'And this is

Bill McCarthy. He's a jackeen. Come down from the big city to show us what's what.'

She smiled in acknowledgement, then turned back to him again. 'I was sorry to hear that Jim had died. He lived to a good age, didn't he?'

He nodded.

'A good age. He was just short of his hundredth year. Just about to get the telegram from the President.'

'He'd have enjoyed that.' She stepped closer to the gate. 'I remember he loved a good party.' There was silence for a moment. 'Now, what can I do for you? I don't expect you've come to see me to talk about your grandfather, have you?'

He shook his head, then pushed open the gate.

'We're asking around. We've a missing woman. Owns one of the holiday cottages in Baltimore. Hasn't been seen for the last three days. We're just doing a routine check.'

'Oh, I see.' Lydia paused. 'Who is she? Would I know her?'

He leaned back into the car and pulled out a file. He opened it, and held out a small colour photograph.

'That's why I'm here. We're asking everyone. This is her. Maria Grimes, aged thirty-five, married with three children. She's from Dublin.'

Lydia gazed down at the picture.

'Pretty, very pretty.'

'Yeah, so she is.'

'And you think something's happened to her? Around here? Hardly likely.'

He shrugged.

'Hardly likely. But who knows? These days

everything's different.'

'Well, I haven't seen her. But the gardens are only open by appointment at the moment.' She lifted her arm. 'Broke my wrist.'

'Nasty. My mother did the same last year.' He paused. 'We're also interested to know if you've seen anyone around, any strangers, anyone out of the ordinary.'

She shook her head again.

'No, I haven't. I have a couple of Polish lads doing some work in the garden for me. Nice boys. Not sure if they have work permits.'

'Yeah, we know them. Funny isn't it,' he smiled ruefully, 'who would have thought the day would come when we'd be getting illegal immigrants here? There must be a good fifteen nationalities living in the Skibbereen area. Half the time we have to have an interpreter on call. Hard to believe.'

She smiled at him again.

'So that's it: the Poles, no one else?'

'Well, of course, there's Adam,' she said.

'Adam? Who would that be?'

'Oh, a nice young Englishman I've got to know recently. Very nice. Very thoughtful.'

Liam took out his notebook and opened it.

'That would be Adam who?'

'Smyth is his name. Spelt with a "y" he told me.'

'And where does he live?'

'I'm not sure, but I think he's been staying with Pat Jordan from the boatyard. He's very interested in the gardens. And he's been so good to me since I did this: he spent the whole day with me when I came out of hospital. Went into town to get my prescription filled, then came back with my pills and kept me company. So nice to have someone around. I hadn't realized how lonely it is when you're ill.' She felt as if she was babbling. As if she was saying too much.

'So, where would we find this young man now?'

'Actually he's gone to Dublin. I'm not sure when he'll be back.'

'Dublin, eh? And why's that?'

She opened her mouth to tell him. Then she stopped herself. It was none of his business. Too many gossips in this place. She had never forgiven the guards who had found Alex, who had found the note he left behind for her. They had opened it and read it. And made sure that everyone knew what was in it.

'Mrs Beauchamp?' Liam put his hand on her shoulder. 'Are you all right? You look very pale.'

She shook her head.

'I'm fine.' She straightened herself up. 'Adam has gone to Dublin to meet some friends from England, I think. I think that's what he said. But you know young people. They're always rushing around, having adventures. Half the time you wouldn't know what they were up to.' She forced herself to smile.

'Well, if you happen to be talking to him you might ask him to give us a ring.' He handed her a card. She nodded. She watched them drive away, then she tore up the card and scattered it on the ground. She turned and began to walk slowly down the drive. She hadn't recognized the woman in the photo. But she knew the type. She had the kind of face that brought trouble with it wherever she went. Narrow, heavy-lidded eyes, and a broad mouth. High cheekbones and an expression that was just short of a sneer. She reached the front door. She sat down on the bench and closed her eyes. She was so tired. She would sit for a while. And maybe Adam would phone her and he would have news. Good news for a change.

'She's a nice old thing,' Bill McCarthy said.

Liam snorted.

'You wouldn't say that if you were a local. She has quite a reputation.'

'Well, that's the country for you. In Dublin we've too many real villains to bother about old ladies in big houses with broken wrists. Next you'll be telling me she's a witch with her broomstick by the back door.'

'Wish it was that simple, Bill. You haven't heard the half of it.' Liam leaned back in his seat. 'Now, who's next on our list?'

Adam lay on his bed with his arms stretched out behind him. His eyes were closed and his mouth was slack and open. The room was huge and ornate. Long windows, curtained with heavy brocade, shut out the glare from the street lights and muffled the sound of traffic. A soft glow came from the bathroom. He had already tried the bath. It had a built-in jacuzzi and he had lain in the bubbles until the skin on his fingers was white and ridged. Then he had pulled himself upright, wrapped himself in the luxurious towelling robe hanging on the back of the door and checked out the minibar. He had opened one of the small bottles of champagne, drunk it down in one gulp and opened another. Turned on the television, flicking through the channels, then collapsed onto the bed. He was tired after all that driving. He had fallen asleep almost immediately. But now he was in trouble. The rats were lined up in a row by the door. They were sitting back on their haunches with their little paws held up in front of their faces. They were cleaning between their claws, their small, pink tongues delicately searching for traces of food. Their red eyes gleamed in the light from the bedside lamp. He counted them. There were ten that he could see. But he knew there were others. He could hear them and smell them. Sense their warmth. They were somewhere very close by. He lay as still as he could. He tried not to move his head. His eyes swivelled from side to side. He was sure, he was almost certain, there was something, a shadow, a dark movement on the white pillow. It was just beyond his peripheral vision. He was sweating, drops rolling down from his hairline, dribbling into his ears. A little puddle of moisture forming beside his cheek. And he knew. He could sense. He could just about feel the tickling of the long whiskers, hear the snuffling from the delicate, pointed nose as the creatures began to mass on the pillow beside him. See the lapping of their tongues, the glisten of their teeth as they drank his sweat. He opened his mouth to scream. But no sound would come, and he had a sudden terrifying sense that, instead of something coming out of his mouth, something would go into it. A paw, a claw, the swish of the end of a long tail. And he might bite down on it. Involuntarily, instinctively. And then what would he find in his mouth? A scream forced its way up his throat, out into the room. It hung there, echoing from wall to wall.

He sat bolt upright. Awake. What had woken him? Was it the noise of his own raucous cry? Was it his heart beating so fast that when he looked down at his chest he could see it leaping around just beneath his skin? Was it the fear that gripped him so tightly that he could feel the ache in his testicles? His eyes swivelled, his gaze darting around the room. He was alone. There were no small creatures lined up against the wooden panelled door. No dark shapes slithering along the cream carpet. No smells but the stench of his sweat and no taste but the sourness on his tongue and the fur that coated his teeth. He stood up and staggered into the bathroom. He turned on the cold tap and filled his hands with water, dipping his face down and pouring it all over his head and his neck. He dried himself and walked back into the bedroom. There was whiskey in the minibar and he twisted open a small bottle, dumped it into a glass, then drank it quickly. He needed to get out of here. The place had become tainted. He wouldn't feel safe here any longer.

He pulled on his clothes, grabbed his jacket from the chair. Checked his wallet. He had all the cash that Lydia had given him. She had told him he was to spend whatever he needed. And she'd arrange for more whenever he wanted. He walked quickly down the corridor to the lift. There was already one waiting for him, its metal doors open.

He stepped into it and pushed the buttons. Soft music flowed from speakers in the ceiling. He lifted his eyes. Mirrored glass, a smoky pink, surrounded him. He smoothed down his hair with one hand and straightened his collar and cuffs with the other. He looked good in the dusky reflection. The lift slowed and stopped. There was a faint hiss as the doors opened. He stepped out into the lobby. It was busy, noisy. He could smell alcohol and perfume. He looked into the bar, but it was all couples, too cosy for his liking. Outside, warm air drifted up from the pavement. He hesitated for a moment, then turned to his left. A group of girls passed him. They were dressed up, swaying on their stilettos, their stomachs bare, their skirts and jeans low cut. They were singing, loudly and out of tune. One of them saw him, caught his eye and turned back.

'Hey, fella, are you on your own?' she shouted.

'You're right there.' He hurried to catch them up.

'Not any longer.' She reached out and took his hand. 'Hey, girls, look what the cat dragged in.'

Her accent was English, Yorkshire he reckoned. The girls were already very drunk. They swept along the street, and he swept with them.

'Here, have some of this.' The girl held out a joint. He took it from her, inhaled, felt the drug rushing into his blood vessels, spreading out through the tributaries of his veins, reaching into every part of his body. His legs felt soft and malleable. A sudden smile split his face in two.

'Wow, fucking brilliant,' he said and passed it back to her.

'Yeah, that's right and there's plenty more where that came from.' She grinned. 'Stick with us, fella, and we'll see you right.'

Easy, nothing to it. He'd stick with them for as long as it suited him. Then he'd be off. There was a long night ahead of him. And the way he felt, he'd do anything rather than go back to that room. Anything at all.

FOURTEEN

It seemed to Johnny Bradshaw that every time he turned on the TV or opened a newspaper he would see or read something about Ireland. The booming Irish economy, more discussion about whatever was going on in Northern Ireland. And the travel supplements of all the Sunday papers were stuffed with articles and photographs of white beaches and purple mountains and green fields.

Lucy kept on at him too.

'It's easy,' she said. 'There's a government website that tells you all about how to find your natural mother. It's not the way it used to be. Here.' She waved a sheaf of pages at him. 'Read this and it'll tell you what you have to do.'

But he didn't want to. He wasn't ready.

'I have a mother for Christ's sake. She may be dead but she's still all I want. I don't need another one,' he said to her, barely able to conceal his irritation.

'But aren't you curious? At the very least, don't you want to know what she looks like? And what about your birth father? What about him?'

What about him? He pondered this as he walked along the High Street towards the book-shop that his father had owned since before he was born. Bradshaw Antiquarian Books. It still bore the family name even though his mother had sold the business after his father died. She had been fortunate to find a buyer. His father had run the shop as an extension of their home. Piles of second-hand books all over the floor and mugs of cold tea on every surface. Not that the biblio-philes who whiled away their afternoons in the shop's snug warmth cared. The new owner hadn't changed too much. He had smartened the place up and barred some of the least savoury of the old hands. And he had expanded the antiques side of the business. Now he sold china, porcelain and silver as well as the beautiful leather volumes that his father had hoarded for years.

Johnny pushed open the door and the little bell tinkled, as it always had. James Nesbitt, the new owner, looked up from his newspaper and smiled a welcome.

'Johnny, how are you? I was so sorry to hear about your mother.' He waved a hand towards the leather armchair that had been Johnny's father's favourite. 'Tea? I've some delicious gun-powder I got last time I was in the city.'

They sipped slowly. The cups were Spode now, not mugs from Tesco.

'Something on your mind?' James pushed a plate of custard creams towards him.

169

Johnny didn't answer. He nibbled his biscuit and sipped his tea.

'You knew my father well, didn't you, James?' he asked.

'Mmm, well, I'm not sure I'd say well. He was a hard man to get to know. He didn't talk much.'

'Did he ever say anything about me?'

James looked away.

'Not really. Except occasionally he'd say how pleased he was that you had become a teacher. He thought it was a worthwhile occupation. Why do you ask?'

Johnny put down his cup.

'You know I'm adopted.'

James nodded.

'Well, I've been wondering whether I should try and find out where I came from. My mother told me a few things before she died. Apparently my birth mother was Irish. I just don't know. It all seems so strange. Lucy keeps on about it all the time. She thinks I should.'

'But you're not so sure?'

'No, I'm not. It seems like a betrayal. Bob and Sally were good to me. They gave me a good home and education. They looked after me.' He stopped and stared down at the faded rug beneath his shoes.

'But? Is there a "but" there?'

'I just don't know, James. I didn't look like them. Sometimes I felt very different from them. And now that they've both gone, I feel there must be more to my life. But, to be honest, I'm scared. Who knows what I'll find?'

'Well you know, Johnny, you're on a winner

really. Even if it doesn't work out, you won't lose Bob and Sally. You'll always have the legacy of their love and protection. When I was clearing out your father's desk I found this.' He got up and began to rummage in the cubbyholes of Johnny's father's old roll-top desk. 'Ah, here it is.' He pulled out a brown envelope. 'Here, have a look.'

Johnny walked home. As he passed the cathedral he turned and went inside. He moved slowly up the aisle and slipped into a pew. The afternoon sun angled through the stained-glass windows, casting lozenges of red and orange light across the stone floor. Someone was playing the organ. Practising. Bursts of music followed by silence. Then repeated phrases, over and over again. He put his hand in his pocket and pulled out the envelope. He opened it. Inside was a letter and three small colour pictures. A baby with a screwed-up face. He was lying in a cot with metal bars. He was wearing a white cardigan with blue sailing boats around the trim. He had blue bootees on his feet and a matching blue knitted cap. Johnny turned the photographs over. Printed neatly on the back were the words, 'Daniel, 3 weeks old'. He unfolded the letter. It was written on stationery with the name 'The Fannin Institute' embossed in red at the top. He began to read.

Dear Bob,

I am delighted to tell you that at last we have a baby for you and Sally to adopt. He is a two-month-old

171

boy. He was born prematurely and was quite ill for a couple of weeks, but he is now healthy and has put on enough weight, so the doctor considers it time that he goes home. I am enclosing a few photographs that were taken a couple of days ago. As you will see, he is healthy and quite bonny.

Usually adopting parents would not be given any information about the circumstances of their child's birth, but as Sally has such a strong family connection with the Fannin Institute I thought it appropriate that you should both know something about this child's origins. His mother, Grace Beauchamp, is a sixteen-year-old girl from West Cork in Southern Ireland. She comes from a good family. Her local Church of Ireland rector put her mother in touch with us. It was considered advisable, for obvious reasons, that she should come to England to give birth. We have no information as to the baby's natural father. The girl has consistently refused to name him. Grace is an intelligent, pretty girl and I am sure she will quickly put this behind her and resume her life. She has no hereditary illnesses, as far as we know, or anything else that would suggest that the baby will need special care in the future.

Please phone the matron, Miss Briggs, at your convenience and make an appointment to come and collect him.

With best wishes to Sally,

Yours sincerely,
Geoffrey Furlong

Johnny turned the letter over and over again in his hands. He picked up the photographs and stared at them. He sank down onto his knees and covered his face with his hands. And he began to cry.

FIFTEEN

Hot this morning. A bright blueness outside the windows. The grass in the back garden looking parched and singed. Grace stood in her night-gown on the terrace outside the kitchen, a cup of coffee in one hand and a piece of toast in the other. She sat down on a slatted wooden chair and stretched out her legs. A robin ventured close. He hopped on springy legs across the paving. She broke a piece from the crust of her toast and crumbled it between her fingers. She scattered it in a wide semicircle and sat back and watched him. His red breast swelled as he contemplated this sudden treat. He turned so he could keep his bright eyes fixed on her, then quickly hopped forward. He paused. She sat very still. He moved again, this time lowering his beak and picking up as much of the bread as he could. She bit down hard on her slice. The crunch was loud in the stillness of the garden. The bird stopped. Lifted his head. Waited. She bit again. This time he ignored the noise and carried on with his feeding. Then, when he had satisfied himself that there was no more to be foraged from between the cracks in the paving, he flew up and away and perched in the branches of the next-door neighbour's apple tree.

Lucky bird, Grace thought, as she took the last bite of toast and licked the remnants of melted butter from her fingers. Such a nice simple life here in this suburban garden. She picked up her mug of coffee and sipped from it. Leaned back, closing her eyes. Sunbursts flashed. Sparks of brightness, like the light leaping from the surface of the sea. She braced her feet against the warmth of the paving stones. The murmur of the traffic was a soft sound today. Soft and constant. Just like that other sound that had been a constant of her childhood. The sea and the river, the fresh and the salt, mixing and mingling, one flowing upstream, the other downstream, and meeting in the great swirl of current just below the house.

She sat up straight and opened her eyes.

'Don't remember,' she warned herself. 'It's the past. It's far away now. Only think of the present. That person, that child, that girl, doesn't exist any longer. She is not you. She has gone. She is buried in the ruins of her relationship with her mother.'

She stood up quickly. The garden shone and glistened in the morning sun. Jack had created it when they had first moved into this house when Amelia was a baby.

'I don't want a house with a garden,' she had insisted. 'Let's live in an apartment. There are plenty of nice ones on the market.'

But he had got his way.

'That's one of the great things about living in Dublin,' he had said. 'Lots of Victorian houses with big back gardens.'

He bought all the gardening books. He began to plan. She tried to ignore the pile on his desk. She looked sideways at the titles and the authors. She couldn't help but see Lydia's books. *Planning an Irish Garden. Gardening the Trawbawn Way. Organic Gardening Made Easy.* They all had a distinctive red cover with the title embossed in gold.

'She is your mother, isn't she?' he asked. She nodded. He turned to the photograph on the jacket flap.

'You don't have her colouring, but you do look like her. There's an expression that you share.'

She shrugged and turned away.

'It must be a beautiful place. We should go and visit sometime. Take Amelia. She'd love to see her, I'm sure, wouldn't she?'

'Not everyone is like your mother, Jack. Not everyone embraces being a grandmother.'

'Oh come on, whatever happened between you was years ago. You should be able to put it behind you.'

But she cut across him.

'I don't want to. I have no interest in my mother. I've told you the way I feel about her.'

'But I don't understand, surely there's a way to repair whatever went wrong. And what about your father? You've never told me anything about him? Is that him?' And he opened one of the books at a photograph of Lydia and Alex, sitting on a bench together, glasses of wine in their hands. 'He looks a bit like you, more like you than she does.'

She didn't answer him. She just turned away. Then turned back.

'He's not my father. He's my stepfather. He's dead now anyway. My biological father was just a guy that my mother had some kind of a relationship with years ago. I don't know anything about him. And I don't want to know. Look, Jack, please, I don't talk about it because it hurts me. I made a decision to leave it all behind. And now,' she raised her voice, 'I don't need counselling or therapy or a few sessions on the couch. I just need to forget about it. I don't want to see my mother. I don't want to have anything to do with her. And most of all, I don't want her near Amelia. Is that understood?'

She hadn't told him about the phone call. It was years ago. Just after she had seen the death notice for Alex in the *Irish Times*. 'Suddenly' it said. She had gone to the newsagent and bought the *West Cork Advertiser*. There had been a short piece on the front page. It had announced the death, by drowning, of Alexander Beauchamp of Trawbawn House. It was obvious from the article that the drowning was not an accident. It was obvious it was suicide. She had waited for the phone call and it had come. Her mother's voice loud in her ear.

'Darling, is that you? Grace, I need to see you. I need to talk to you. There's something I have to say to you. Please, darling, please.'

She had hung up quickly, then taken the phone off the hook for the rest of the day. Lydia didn't phone again. And Grace had felt suddenly bereft. She had sat down with a pen and a piece of paper and tried to write something. A quick note, just a few lines. But the words wouldn't come. How to make it all better after so many years, so many bitter memories. But every time she looked at the garden that Jack had created she could see her mother's handiwork. It had that distinctive Trawbawn look. Even in the confines of suburban Dublin, he had managed to contrive her sense of wilderness.

When she had separated from Jack she had told him she would leave the house and he could have it. But he insisted that it was Amelia's home.

'So, you stay here,' she reasoned. 'Amelia comes to you for half of every week. I'll get an apartment. She'll be happy with that.'

But he wouldn't hear of it.

'I couldn't live here without you, Grace,' he said. 'I did all this to make you happy. But it didn't work. I couldn't live here now. It would be a constant reproach to me that I had failed.'

'Don't be ridiculous,' she had snarled at him. 'You didn't fail me. I failed you. I failed to have a proper relationship with you. But that's not your fault. It's mine. It's my lack not yours.'

But he left anyway. Moved into rooms in the university for a few months then into a shiny new flat in a block by the river. Came to tend the garden every week to begin with, then once a month, then stopped completely. She had watched it deteriorate: the weeds take over, the grass become spongy with moss, the roses blighted with black spot and mildew. Even Amelia had noticed. She had come into the kitchen one morning with a handful of dandelions and dropped them on the floor. Said, 'Not so nice these flowers. Don't smell nice like the ones that Daddy grows.'

So Grace had begun to work on it. At the weekends and during the long summer evenings. Found herself on her knees with her hands in the warm soil. A hobby, she told the other teachers. Always good to have a hobby. Something to take your mind off work. Heard them laughing about her behind her back.

'A hobby? Are you mad? She's so competitive she'll be winning prizes for her dahlias yet.'

She got up from the bench and walked forward onto the lawn. The grass tickled her bare feet. It needed mowing and there were weeds now pushing up through it. Alex would not have approved. He was the lawn expert. He loved the wide sweep in front of the house. He would roll it and cut it, weed it by hand, sprinkle sand to improve the drainage. Walk up and down, up and down, behind the big mower, his sleeves rolled up, a cigarette hanging from his mouth, and his big straw hat shading his face from the sun.

'Stop it,' she said out loud. 'Stop it.'

Where had these memories come from? She had fought so hard to keep them away and for the most part she had won. But now, for some reason that she couldn't fathom, they had risen from the depths again. The time signal for eight o'clock sounded loudly from the radio in the kitchen. She walked back inside and piled her dishes into the sink. The newsreader intoned the headlines. The usual summer stories. Road deaths were on the increase. The number of tourists had decreased. A boating tragedy off the Connemara coast. And finally: 'There is still no news as to the whereabouts of missing mother of three, Maria

Grimes. Mrs Grimes, from Dublin, was on holiday in the Skibbereen area of West Cork. Her husband has appealed for help.'

Grace reached over and turned up the volume. She listened to the man's voice.

'Please, if anyone has seen Maria or knows anything about where she is, will they please get in touch with the guards. Either in Skibbereen or any Garda station. Our children, Jodie, Declan and Ella are desperate for news of their mother and so am I.'

The newsreader continued.

'Garda Liam O'Regan had this to say.' She heard a voice she recognized. An accent she knew. She sat down at the kitchen table to listen.

'We have been searching the area between Baltimore and Skibbereen for Mrs Grimes. Anyone who knows the area, knows that it is a difficult job. It is open countryside with the river running through it. Mrs Grimes may have had an accident. We would ask all local landowners, fishermen, farmers to be on the alert for anything unusual or suspicious and to contact us immediately.'

Liam O'Regan had been a nice kid. He used to come in and swim from the jetty. He would help his father with Daniel's horses. A stocky boy with freckles, lugging a bucket of oats. And curious. Always asking questions. The names of plants and flowers. Wanting to get in under the bonnet of the tractor and fiddle around with it. Playing hide and seek in the garden down by the river. When she was a teenager and not interested.

She stood up. Time to get dressed. Time to go. As she began to walk upstairs the phone rang.

She turned to go back to the kitchen to answer it, then heard the answering machine come on. And the message. It was Jack.

'Grace, have you heard from Amelia? She phoned me last night. She sounded pretty miserable. I thought I'd go and see her this weekend. Do you want to come? Let me know. Hope you're OK on your own. Take care. Bye.'

The last thing she needed was a long car trip with Jack. He would try and persuade her yet again that they should give it another go. He would go over and over how good they had been together. How much they shared. How hard he found it on his own. And again, he would ask. Why did you end it? Why did you do it? What was wrong that we couldn't sort out? But she wouldn't be able to tell him. Because she would have to tell him about the baby. She just couldn't bring herself to do it.

She stood in the shower and turned the taps on full. Then she dried herself, dressed and hurried back downstairs. She would call him later. When she knew he'd be out. She would leave him a message. Friendly, polite, non-committal. She would tell him that being unhappy in your first week of Irish college was part of the whole experience. Amelia would get over it. Next week she'd be so happy she wouldn't want to come home. Sorry, she wasn't going down this weekend. But it would be great if he did.

'Just watch who you talk to down there, Jack. They eat Brits for breakfast. OK? See you.'

Hot outside. She'd stop along the way and buy a bottle of water and hope she wouldn't be too sweaty by the time she got to the prison.

It was a hot morning along by the river. The guards were in a bright orange inflatable. Easier to get to the sheds and barns and the old mill on the bank from the water rather than struggling through the thick summer hedgerows and undergrowth. It was hard to know. Had Maria left home because of a row? Or had something happened to her? The Super was inclined to the row scenario but he wasn't taking any chances. And they'd been keeping a check on her bank account and her mobile phone. Neither had been used. So they'd taken her husband in for a bit of a session. Not arrested him or anything so formal. Just asked him to come into the station for a chat. The guy was shattered. Red-eyed, unshaven, could barely speak.

'What do you want me for?' His voice was breaking and hoarse. 'I love her. I'm devastated, the kids are going crazy. Why aren't you out there looking for her?'

They'd told him then. What the neighbours in the holiday village had said. The drunken rows, the screaming in the middle of the night. The day that Maria came out wearing dark glasses even though it was raining. And there had been another call too. From a woman in Dublin who said she was Maria's sister. Had quite a story to tell. A litany of abuse. The bruises on Maria's upper arms, the deep scratches on her back. How she'd begged her to go to the doctor.

'Yes, I did hit her from time to time,' Maria's husband said. 'But she hit me too. We have that

181

kind of relationship. We're both very volatile. And I'm under a lot of stress. I got promoted a few months ago. I'm way up there now in the bank. I'm a player. And it's tough. And Maria, well she doesn't always understand. To be honest, she's selfish and very self-centred. But we always make it up. We never let the rows last too long. I'm mad about her. She's my wife. I'd never do anything to her.'

They let him leave. But they made sure that he knew he was under observation.

'Don't go anywhere,' they told him.

'And where would I go?' he replied. 'I've three kids who've lost their mother. I'm not going anywhere. And please. OK, I admit that things could be difficult between us, but you've got to believe me. I haven't done anything to her. Please don't stop looking for her.'

They hadn't. They had a team of guards in town, going from shop to shop, showing her photograph, handing out questionnaires and asking the usual questions. Anything out of the ordinary, anything suspicious, anyone who stood out. Everyone was trying to help. The problem would be, Liam O'Regan knew, not too little information, but probably too much. They would be swamped with details. He sat with a pile of paper on his desk, wondering when he was going to get the time to go through it all. He shuffled through the completed forms. The pharmacist in Sweetnam's chemist shop had been very thorough. She had attached a list of the names of people who had had prescriptions filled that day. He ran his eye down it. Lydia Beauchamp's name stood out. There was even the time it was dispensed: 3 p.m. He picked up the phone and called the chemist. Yes, she did remember that particular prescription. No, Mrs Beauchamp hadn't come in herself. A nice young man had got them for her. The pharmacist remembered him well. Very good-looking, very friendly. She had said to the rest of the girls after he had left that Ma Beauchamp hadn't lost her touch. She might be heading for the old folks' home but she still knew how to get a fella. Liam got out his notebook. Mrs Beauchamp had mentioned the 'nice young man' and she had said he had got her pills and then spent the rest of the day with her. Liam made a note in the margin of the questionnaire and filed it away. On the floor with the rest of the stuff.

Hot too in the room in which Adam woke. Light dazzling his eyes as he tried to sit up. Tried to remember where he was and how he had got there. A heavy weight across his legs, making it hard for him to move, so he began to struggle and to sweat, the panic from the night before returning. But then the weight began to shift, to change its shape, and he realized that it was soft, malleable, human. He pushed himself up on his elbows. Another hotel room, not as big or as grand as the one he'd checked into. A smaller version, a more modest double bed, but the same soft glow from the bathroom, thick curtains muffling traffic noise, cupboards standing open, a TV screen flickering, the sound muted. Clothes scattered across the floor and a woman's body lying at an angle across his legs.

She was from Bradford. Her name was Karen. Her sister was getting married and they'd come to Dublin for her hen party. There were ten of them. They all worked in the same office. He'd lost count of how many clubs they'd been to. How much alcohol they'd drunk, how much cocaine they'd snorted. The girls seemed to have an endless supply. Karen had explained. It was all part of the deal. When they'd booked the weekend, hotels, flights, all that stuff, they'd been told entertainment would be provided.

'Everyone does it. It's why we come to Dublin and not go to London. London's a drag. Dublin's a blast.'

He sat up and leaned back against the headboard. He ached all over. He eased himself slowly from beneath her sleeping body and carefully pulled himself from the bed. He quietly closed the bathroom door behind him. His body was covered in marks. Teeth, fingernails. He was bitten, scratched and bruised. Three of them had gone to sleep in the bed out there. Karen's friend, Michelle, had joined them. He looked down at his penis. It was red and sore. He turned on the shower. He winced and shuddered as rivulets of water trickled over his skin, flushing out the small puncture wounds and seeping into the damaged flesh. He reached out and picked up a sachet of shampoo from the ledge beside the shower head. He massaged it into his hair, closing his eyes as the suds coursed down his face and onto his neck and shoulders. And felt the sudden cold as the shower curtain flicked back, then the softness of a breast pressed up against his chest, and a thigh against his thigh and the sudden rush of sensation as she reached down and began to touch him. He took her head in both his hands and pushed her to her knees. He leaned back against the smoothness of the tiled wall and braced his legs. And gave himself up to her.

Afterwards they lay, wrapped in towels, together on the bed. His head lolled to one side on the pillows. Beside him the girl snored softly. He eased himself away from her and looked at his watch. It was after two. He would have to go soon. He had a date. He picked up his phone and checked his messages. There were two voicemails. The first was from Lydia. Just making sure he'd got to Dublin safely. Hoped he'd found a hotel and that everything was all right. If he needed anything he was to let her know. She was really grateful to him and she hoped she'd hear from him soon. He pressed the button and deleted the message. The next was from Colm. He stood at the window and looked out at the streets beyond. He listened to the message.

He dressed quickly. He picked up the girl's bag. He rummaged through its contents. There was the usual. Make-up, loose change, wallet. He pulled out a wad of notes. Bloody euros she'd called them. Can't tell one from the other. She and the other girls had spent them as if they were toy money. She had plenty left. He took half of them and folded them neatly. Then he unzipped the small inner pocket. His fingers felt the smoothness of plastic. He slid out a bag, half-full of white powder. He slipped it in between the notes and eased them into his jacket pocket. She stirred and her eyes flicked open. He held his breath. She yawned and stretched, turned over and began to snore. He tiptoed to the door. Nice girl. Good time had by all. He was glad he hadn't told her his real name. Or anything else about him. But then again she wouldn't have remembered even if he had. In a couple of hours' time the whole night and the morning that followed would just be a pleasant blur.

Outside, he stopped on the broad pavement and looked around. He had no idea where he was. He felt inside his jacket for the envelope that contained the visiting order. He'd get a taxi. A quick stop at his hotel to check out and get his car. Then he'd head for the prison. And after that, well, who knows? He'd let Colm make that decision for him.

SIXTEEN

A sudden fear as Colm waited for visiting time that he wouldn't recognize Adam. He could close his eyes and see the shape of his shoulders, the curve of his cheek, the gleam of fine hair across the base of his spine. He could feel the muscles in his thighs and his calves. The muscles of his buttocks as they tightened. He could taste the softness of his ear lobes and smell the oils that came out through the follicles of the hair on his head. But now, as he waited, he couldn't imagine him as a whole person. He could feel all those parts of him, smell and taste him, but he didn't know if he would be able to pick him out of a crowd.

But, of course, that was crazy because as he lifted his head and gazed at the visitors as they jostled and pushed through the doors into the big bright Portakabin where visits were held, he saw him immediately and immediately his heart began to bang loudly and his mouth was dry. He stood up. And he smiled. For the first time since Adam had left him, he smiled a real, involuntary smile.

They sat in silence. Colm had forgotten how beautiful Adam was. He looked so young and healthy. His skin gleamed and the whites of his eyes had that milky blueness of the newborn baby. He looked tall too, taller than Colm had remembered. Or perhaps it was just that everyone else in the room was so small. They were a stunted lot, the prison visitors. Bad food, too much alcohol, too many drugs. Not enough exercise. It was stamped into their sagging bellies and slouching frames. Not like Adam. Colm could see his biceps as he moved his arms, and catch a glimpse of his smooth, muscled stomach where one of his shirt buttons had come undone.

'So?' Eventually Adam broke the silence.

'So.' Colm leaned back in his chair.

'How is it?'

Colm shrugged and took out a packet of cigarettes.

'Got a light?'

Adam fiddled in his pocket. He put his lighter down on the table. Colm picked it up. He smiled as he looked at its smooth metal surface.

'You still have it then?'

Adam nodded.

Colm flicked back the hood and dragged his thumb quickly down the wheel. The flame flickered. He bent his head and drew hard on his cigarette. He held it up and inspected the glowing tip.

'And do you have anything else for me?'

'As a matter of fact I do.'

'Good.' Colm leaned back. 'Although this place is unbelievable. Do you know they give out methadone to whoever wants it? It's a fucking joke. And as for the rest of the gear, I've never been in a prison where it was all so easy.'

'Easy?'

'Yeah, fucking amazing. Remember what it was like in the other place? Searches, discipline, control, routine. Here it's like a fucking holiday camp. They let you out in the morning after breakfast and you're on the wing all day apart from mealtimes.'

'And the screws, what are they up to?'

'Earning a load of bread, that's what. You haven't a fucking clue how much they get paid. It's unreal. And they're always trying to be friendly. It'd do your fucking head in. It's Colm this and Colm that, and what can we do for you, Colm? How can we help you, Colm?'

'Colm? What about your number?'

'I said, it's fucking unreal. After twelve years of only answering to my number and my last name, now it's all so cosy. As I said, do your head in.'

Adam giggled.

'So, are you glad you made the move? Was all that waiting worth it?'

Colm giggled too.

'I don't know. I sometimes wonder. This place is a filthy kip. All this slopping out, and the state of it. The smell would get you. I said to them when they were checking me in, I said to them, "Hold on a minute, is this Bangkok or Dublin? Where the fuck am I?" And the other thing. It's dangerous here.'

'Dangerous? In what way dangerous?'

'Well, the downside of the no-control stuff. You remember the way in Manchester you couldn't fucking fart without a screw wrinkling his nose, well, here you could do anything and they wouldn't notice and half the time they wouldn't bother to intervene. So if you get on the wrong side of anyone, you're on your own.'

'And what about, you know, the other? How's that here?'

Colm smiled and spread his hands out flat on the worn surface of the table.

'That's fine and dandy. The screws don't care, they don't want to know. As long as it's what they call "consensual". Nice word that, isn't it, "cons being sensual",' he sniggered. 'But you know, you'd want to be careful, Adam. Everyone's got something. Hep C, HIV.'

'Don't they keep them all apart? Write "unclean" on their foreheads in red ink?'

'That's the problem: you don't know where you're putting yourself. What pile of shit you're getting yourself into.' Colm laughed again.

'And, have you seen any of your family?'

He nodded. The smile faded.

'Yeah, my useless sister was here last week. I'd

189

say it'll be a while before she comes back. She never came to see me in England, so she's no experience of prison visiting.'

'Bit different, isn't it? From Cape, that is.'

'Aah.' Colm smiled at him. 'So you've been.'

Adam nodded and looked over his head. The windows were covered with heavy metal mesh. He knew it was a fine bright day outside, but the light which came into the room was low and flecked with dust.

'Nice, isn't it? Specially at this time of year.'

How long Adam's eyelashes were. He'd never really noticed them before. They curled out from his eyelids. Thick, black, as if he were wearing mascara. When he looked down they cast a shadow across his cheek. And when he looked up again his eyes shone so brightly. The left the colour of green like shallow water in a rock pool, the right the colour of ripe wheat.

'Yeah, it's nice all right.'

'And where else have you been?'

'I've been everywhere, everywhere you asked me to go.'

'And you've met...?'

'I've met everyone. Everyone down there. And do you know why I've come to Dublin?'

'To see me?'

'Of course, to see you. But to see someone else as well. At least that's what I've been asked to do.'

'Asked to do?'

'That's right. Asked to do. And can you guess who asked me?'

'Her?'

'That's right, your old friend. And can you

guess what she wants from me?'

Colm ran his hands across the top of his shaved head and back down around his neck and over his mouth.

'Cut out the fucking twenty questions and just tell me.'

'She wants me to go and find her daughter. She's desperate to see her. She's all alone, on her own. She's got nothing left.'

'Well, not quite nothing. She's got that house and the garden and the land and everything that goes with it.'

'But that's not what she wants. She wants her daughter back. She wants her daughter to love her again. More than anything else.'

'And she's sent you, you of all people, to find her?' Colm's tone was incredulous. He began to laugh, a harsh, choking sound that drew looks from the other visitors.

'Yeah, she sent me.' Adam straightened himself up. 'What's so funny about that?'

'Well, if she knew about you and me. Imagine, Adam, imagine what she'd think. She'd never in a million years let you near her daughter. You, a thief, a rapist, a prisoner. You who's been fucked by me, the man she made an outcast, the man she kicked out, who she sent off with nothing.' He paused. 'She doesn't know, does she? This isn't some weird game of hers, some trap she's getting you into.'

'No.' Adam clenched his fists beneath the table. 'No, she likes me. She fancies me. She doesn't know what's going on in my head, and you know her, Colm. She likes to know what's going on in people's heads.'

'So, this is for real. She's sent you to Dublin to find Grace. And then what? What comes after the finding?'

'Well, that's what I've come to ask you. What does comes after the finding? You decide. You tell me. I'll do whatever makes you happy.'

They stared at each other.

'Time up now, lads and lassies. That's all for today. Say your goodbyes. Shed your tears.' The screws began to walk down between the tables.

'Hey.' Adam slid his hand from his trouser pocket along the flat grain of the table. The plastic bag was cold against his palm. 'Got this for you.'

'Thanks.' Colm grinned, his teeth showing. He placed his palm flat beside Adam's. 'Now.' He smiled again and began to stand up. 'Do it now.'

Adam was on his feet. He turned abruptly, banging into the screw.

'Sorry, mate, sorry about that. Wasn't looking where I was going.'

The prison officer pushed past him. He didn't speak. He just looked speculatively at Colm and shook his head.

Colm grinned at Adam, then rubbed his hand across his face. The bag slipped into the inside of his cheek.

'I'll come again.' Adam turned to go. 'Call me. Tell me what's next. OK?'

Colm nodded and lifted his hand.

'I'll ring you,' he said. 'Now I've got this, I've got the gold standard. I'll call you this evening. Have fun.'

Adam walked slowly down the incline towards

the main road. He stopped and looked back. The prison squatted above him. He could smell its filth on his skin. He felt tainted and dirty. He put his hand in his pocket and pulled out his car keys. He needed a place to stay, not a hotel or a guest house. He needed a place of his own. And he needed it soon. He got into the car. Everywhere he looked he could see police. Or prison officers. Police cars and prison vans. Prison visitors. The whole fucking world that follows the prison around. He opened the glove compartment and hunted for the map that Lydia had given him. She had marked all the pages he would need with yellow stickers. He opened them one by one. Outlined in red was the school where her daughter taught. Lydia had circled all the areas where she felt her daughter might live. There had been a reference in the article to her cycling to work. Something about enjoying the beauty of the Grand Canal, watching the swans hatching their chicks, watching the cygnets grow. Lydia had drawn a thick line along its curve.

'I know this area well,' she had said. 'I lived here when Grace was a baby. Before we moved to the country. It's all flats and bedsits. It's full of students. I suppose now it's full of immigrants. But a lot of the houses will have become owner-occupied.' She stopped and tapped her index-finger nail on the stiff paper. 'You'll find her, I know you will. Go to the public library in Rathmines. They'll have Thoms street directory. Search through it. If she owns her own house, she'll be in it.'

He hadn't paid much attention. His thoughts had been focused on the wad of cash she had taken from the top drawer of the desk in the study upstairs. If he had known she kept so much money in the house, he wouldn't have bothered with the small pieces of silver he had pocketed. The salt and pepper cellars, the mustard dish, the gravy boat, the spoons in the nice flat leather boxes. They reminded him of his gran's stuff. He had taken that and sold it all. But he'd been burned. He'd only got a fraction of its worth because he was in a hurry and he looked far too suspicious. This time he'd be much more careful and much more choosy about how he got rid of it.

Now he studied the map carefully. He was on the north side of the city. He worked out his route across the river to the south. He was tired. Strung out after his heavy night. He needed to rest, get himself together again. He put the car in gear and moved slowly into the traffic, down the North Circular towards the main Drumcondra Road. The traffic lights turned red just as he reached the junction. He pulled up sharply and sat, waiting for the lights to change. A stream of traffic passed him by slowly. He gazed idly at the drivers and passengers. Lots of women in big cars. He remembered. His father. His impatience. The term 'road rage' had been invented for him.

'You're a cliché, a dinosaur, do you know that?' Adam had laughed at him, made him even more angry. So he had thumped his fists on the steering wheel and shouted obscenities out the window. Women drivers were his particular hate.

'You're pathetic,' Adam had sneered, 'just pathetic. Give it up. Look at Mum, she's a perfectly good driver. Even Gran can drive pretty

194

well. Where do you get these ideas from?'

Cars passing slowly. His eyes flicked from driver to driver. The light turned to orange. He put the car into first gear. He could feel his heart pounding. He felt nervous, light-headed; he needed sleep. Just as his light turned green and he began to move forward, a woman on a bicycle appeared out of nowhere. She cut across in front of him. He jammed on his brakes and the car stalled.

'Stupid cunt,' he shouted.

The woman, blonde hair, dark glasses, half-turned, half-looked at him, then was gone into the traffic. His heart was banging. Its beat was irregular. He felt sick. He moved out into the junction, and turned right towards the city. He drove slowly and carefully. Sweat clung to his forehead. He glanced down at the map and tried to memorize his route. He just needed to concentrate for another half an hour or so, and then he could rest. Take stock. Then everything would be all right.

Colm had found the magazine article about Grace. He had gone to the prison library. The librarian couldn't have been more helpful. She had done an internet search. She had printed it out.

'It's only in black and white, I'm afraid. You don't get the colour pictures but the text is all there.' She handed him the pages. She was curious.

He thanked her, in Irish.

'*Go raibh math agat, a dhuine.*'

'You're a native speaker, is that right?' She smiled tentatively at him.

'That's right. It's a blessing to be back in my

own country with people who understand and love the language.'

'Of course.' Her Irish wasn't as fluent as his. She spoke it with a mechanical correctness. 'The teacher, in the article, do you know her?'

'I used to once, a long time ago. We grew up in the same place. I always liked her.'

'Is that right?' The librarian looked over his shoulder at the article again. 'It's a great school. I've heard her speak. About education, that sort of thing. In fact,' she smiled, 'she comes in here from time to time, to give classes on writing.'

'In here? To give classes?'

'Yes, she's doing one at the moment. Two weeks. Here, here's the leaflet.' She picked a piece of paper up from her desk and looked down at it. 'It's called "Telling Your Own Story". It's a pity it's already started. If you'd been interested you could have applied to join. Sometimes they let men go over for sessions in the school there.'

'In the school? Where is it?'

'In the new women's prison, just across the road.' She paused. 'You'd think a woman like her wouldn't be bothered, but I suppose it's because some of her pupils have been in here. She'd want to be a miracle worker to sort some of that lot out. There's generations of them in and out of this place. Mothers and fathers, brothers and sisters, sons and daughters. We even had a granny in at the same time as her oldest granddaughter.'

'Is that right? Isn't that sad?' His heart was pounding, but he smiled at her and moved a bit closer.

'Yes, terrible.' She was warming to her theme.

'That kind of criminality, it runs in families. You have to break the cultural cycle if you're going to do anything about it.'

He folded the pages and put them in the back pocket of his jeans.

'You'd be better off breaking their legs, don't you think?' His smile faded.

She laughed, nervously now, and glanced past him at the door. It was shut. He could smell her sweat coming through the synthetic fibres of her cardigan.

'It's getting late; I should be closing up now.' She backed away from him.

He took a step closer to her.

'Of course. Thanks again. I really appreciate it.' He held out his hand. She took it. Her palm was moist and fleshy. Her grip was weak. He squeezed her fingers tightly and she winced.

'Got to go,' he said in English, and stepped back. 'People to see, places to visit. You know the way it is.' He touched his forehead with his index finger. 'Missing you already.'

She watched him walk towards the door. She wasn't sure what his crime had been, what sentence he was serving. She was pretty certain he was a lifer. Transferred back from England. It was part of prison etiquette not to ask. Better not to know. But she wanted to know about him. There was the way he had looked at her. His body had been tensed, alert. He had made her more than nervous. She would ask the governor tomorrow morning. And she would make sure she was never alone with that man again. Never.

SEVENTEEN

The Polish boys were back. They had arrived on their bicycles, all smiles. Full of cheerful willingness. She had been so relieved to see them that tears had blurred her vision. They had been to Cork city, they said. They had friends from Warsaw there. They had brought her a present. A bottle of plum brandy. It had been made by their friend's mother. And they had decided they were going to cook her a special meal. They had sausage and sauerkraut, a jar of pickled mushrooms and cherry jam, home-made by the same woman who made the brandy. It was the best. But first they wanted to tell her. The police had come to question them about this woman who was missing. This Maria Grimes. They wanted to re-assure, Pavel repeated the word just to be certain that she would understand. They wanted to re-assure her that they had nothing at all to do with it. 'Nothing at all, missus, you understand me, when I say that we have nothing to do with the disappearance of the lady.'

'Of course.' She smiled at them both and reached out with her good hand and patted him on the arm. 'Of course, I didn't think you had. The police asked me about you and I said you were nice boys. There was one thing, though. I found something.'

She got up unsteadily from her chair and

walked to the dresser. She opened the drawer. Her fingers closed around the smooth metal of the penknife.

'Here.' She turned back to them. 'This is yours, isn't it?'

'Yes, yes, thank you, missus, very much.' Pavel stood and took it from her. 'I left it in garden somewhere? Where?'

'Not the garden, I'm afraid. I found it in the gate lodge. Now, I don't mind you going wherever you want around the grounds, but I would prefer it if you didn't go into the lodge. That place is private. Do you know what I mean?'

'But, missus, we never did. We have no reason to go in there. We just go past it every day when we come in and out of the gate.' Pavel's face had turned red.

'Well, whatever, boys. But that's where I found the knife.'

There was an awkward silence. Lydia could see she had upset them. They were both embarrassed.

'Look, it doesn't matter. I know you wouldn't do any damage or any harm or anything like that; it's just that place, well, I just don't like people going in there. OK?'

They both nodded, but the atmosphere had soured. Pavel put the knife away in the pocket of his overalls. He gestured to Sebastian.

'We go now, missus. We go to do the weeding. You tell us what more you want us to do? OK?' Sebastian moved towards the door. Pavel followed him silently.

'And at lunchtime, do you want me to bring

199

you tea?'

Pavel shook his head.

'No, we have our own. We don't need anything.'

She sat down again at the table. Her arm ached. The clock ticked. A tap dripped. Outside she could hear the call of the seagulls as they rose above the river and circled, looking for food. And there was the sound of a car, wheels on the gravel as it slowed, rounded the bend, then stopped. She stood up. Moved away from the table. Heard the slamming of doors and loud voices. Opened the back door and looked out. Saw two men in the yard. She recognized the older of them. Pat Jordan, the fisherman. He used to bring them boxes of prawns and lobsters. Used to take Alex out with him too. South of the Fastnet where the water was deep and the harvest was plentiful. Then bring him back a couple of days later and sit in the kitchen, drinking tea and telling stories. While Alex gutted and cleaned the fish they'd caught, the water in the sink running red and the draining board sparkling with scales. Now he nodded towards her.

'Mrs Beauchamp,' he said. The younger man put a cigarette into his mouth and fiddled with a box of matches.

'Pat, what can I do for you?' She shuffled outside. The pain in her arm had suddenly taken hold again.

'This, here.' He gestured towards the van, which Adam had left parked beside the house. 'I'll be taking it out of your way.' As he spoke, the younger man moved towards the back of the van and tried the door. 'I take it himself, young

Adam, isn't around?'

'No, he's gone to Dublin for a few days.' She leaned against the wall, unable to stand upright. It was Pat who had found Alex. Had seen his body hanging from the tree in the river. Had stopped the boat and got into a dinghy and rowed over to him. Tried to free him. Then, when he saw he was dead, he had phoned the guards.

'Keys, Pat,' the other guy shouted, and Pat took a bunch from his pocket and tossed them to him.

'Well, he won't be needing it then, will he? And I do,' Pat said. She heard the squeak as the doors were pulled open, saw the movement of the suspension as the younger man jumped inside. Now he poked out his head.

'There's a load of stuff in here, Pat. What'll I do with it?'

Pat turned around for a moment, then turned back.

'Fuck it out, Ronan. I'm sure Mrs Beauchamp won't mind.' He stared at her, then took a step forward. 'How's the arm?'

She shrugged and grimaced.

'Not great, but they tell me it'll heal. Eventually. What's that?' She nodded towards the pile of what looked like clothes on the ground.

Pat walked over to it and prodded it with the toe of his boot.

'Sleeping bag, wet gear, sports bag. Nothing worth anything, I'd say. I'd dump it all if your man, Adam, doesn't come back for it.'

He looked up at her.

'You and young Adam have been getting friendly, have you?'

She shrugged again.

'He's given me a bit of a hand. He found me when I fell and took me into the hospital. He's been decent like that.'

'Well, if you're talking to him, tell him I've taken back the van.' He stood aside to let the younger man into the driver's seat. 'Pity he didn't leave it in the boatyard the way I asked him to. Oh, and if you are talking to him, tell him the guards were asking about him too.'

'Really, why was that?'

'Oh, just to do with that woman who's missing. They've been in and out of the boatyard. Asking everyone if they knew her. Sure we all knew her. Anyway, I said I'd pass on the message. So I am. Doesn't do to get on the wrong side of the police. They can make your life misery.'

She watched them drive away, then bent down to look at what they had left behind. There was a sleeping bag, torn so that the stuffing was showing through. It was dirty, smears of brown on its faded check cover. Bright yellow waterproof leggings and a jacket lay beside it. And there was also a fleece, navy blue with an insignia of some kind on the front. She gathered it together with the rest into a bundle and shoved it into the sports bag. She carried it into the kitchen, opened the cupboard under the stairs and pushed it in. Her arm was so sore. She walked slowly to the sink and half-filled a glass of water. She would take some more of her pills. She sat down heavily at the table. It had been months since she had seen Pat Jordan. He didn't look so well. Overweight, red in the face, heavy bags under his eyes, his grey hair straggling over his shoulders and thinning on top. Too much drink, she thought. He had been a handsome young man. A friend of Colm O Laoire's. Always hanging around when Colm was working in the sailing school. Chatting up the girls. Taking them to the pub in the evenings. She'd even caught him sneaking out of one of the rooms early one morning. It had been their little secret. Alex had wanted him to come and work with them. When it looked as if the sailing school was going to take off and make their fortune. He'd had plans for Pat. Reckoned they could expand their range of classes. Move into power boats. Pat was good with engines. Anything mechanical.

'You should see him, Lydia,' Alex had said. 'He's incredible. A very talented kid. We should send him back to school. Pay him while he gets his qualifications. It would be worth it.'

That summer, that wonderful summer, when all had been right in the world. Lydia stood up. She was tired now. The pills were making her sleepy. She moved towards the steps up to the hall. She would go and lie down on the sofa in the drawing room. Maybe Adam would phone her. Maybe she would phone him. All she wanted now was to sleep.

There was a scattering of mail on the mat just inside the front door. She bent down and picked it up. Bills, junk, a few circulars from gardening organizations. And a brown padded envelope. An American stamp and that distinctive looped handwriting, the L of her first name, grandiose and exaggerated. She knew who it was from. She had met Spencer Wright when she first started going to America fifteen years ago. He was the secretary of the gardening club which had invited her. His handwriting wasn't as firm as it once had been. When Alex was still alive he had typed his letters to her. Then he had mastered the computer. His letters always looked official. He used the gardening club stationery and his language was guarded and careful. After Alex had died they had stopped writing for a while.

'You're not responsible,' she had said to him. 'He didn't know about you. There were other reasons for his suicide.' She didn't tell him that Alex had phoned her the day he died. She hadn't spoken to him because she had been with Spencer. On a boat. On the Hudson River. They had drunk cold white wine. Spencer had anchored the boat in a small bay and they had made love on a narrow bunk with the sound of the water slopping against the hull, and the breeze singing through the halyards and shrouds above.

Now she stood up and shuffled back to the kitchen. She sat down at the table. She manoeuvred the little clips from the envelope with one hand. She turned it upside down and shook it. A bundle of photographs and a letter dropped out on the table. She fanned them out in front of her. She recognized them. They were photographs of the two of them, taken over the past decade. She picked up the letter and began to read it slowly out loud.

'*Lydia, my sweetheart,*' it began. Her voice sounded through the empty house.

'*I've been thinking about you a lot recently. It's been*

such a long time since we've seen each other. I miss you, Lydia, you know I do, but I've decided that I should send these to you. Betty and I are moving to Florida. Neither of us has been too well recently. The usual ill health that comes with old age. I've had to have a stent put into one of my arteries and Betty's arthritis is making life in the cold winters of New York much harder to bear. You remember my son Jim? Well, he has a business associate who has sold us a condo in a retirement complex just outside of Fort Lauderdale. I know we always laughed at the kind of people who spent their dying days somewhere like that, but the truth is that the time comes for all of us. We've sold our house here, so we're getting rid of a lot of stuff, and when I was going through my desk, I found all these photos. They certainly brought back some wonderful memories, Lydia. But I can't take them with me. I didn't want to dump them, they're too special for that. So I thought it best if you had them. I'm sorry it has come to this, but I suppose we both knew that we had responsibilities to our families that would eventually come before our feelings for each other. I want you to know that I have no regrets about us. I have loved you since I first saw you standing in the arrivals hall in JFK that hot day fifteen years ago. I watched you for a few minutes before you saw me. All that noise and hustle and bustle, and there was a little pool of silence and control all around you. You looked scary, Lydia. And I liked that. For a small woman, you sure gave off big woman's vibes.'

He'd said that to her before. She could fit snugly under his arm. Unlike Betty, his wife. Betty was as tall as Spencer. Her flesh had spread. Rolls of fat around her waist, under her chin, around her wrists, like a chubby toddler. She had given birth

205

to four sons. They were all married with children. Spencer was an adoring grandfather.

'Those kids,' he had said to her, 'you've no idea how much I love those kids.'

She had been invited to parties and barbecues at Spencer's house. Betty was a wonderful hostess. The setting reminded Lydia of something from an old Doris Day film. She sat on the swing seat underneath the huge magnolia and sipped her drink. The garden was lit with lanterns. The air was warm and still. The smell of meat, grilling, drifted towards her. She sat and swung and sipped. The members of the gardening club came to chat. Spencer's sons paid court. They were handsome boys with pretty wives. Successful, wealthy, secure. Like Spencer. She toyed with the idea. She could get up and go and talk to Betty. She could destroy all this peace, serenity, security with a few well chosen words.

'You won't do anything, Lydia, will you?' Jimmy Wright, Spencer's oldest boy, sat down beside her.

'What do you mean "anything"?' She sipped her drink.

'Tell my mother what you and the old man are up to.'

'What do you mean?'

'Oh come on, Lydia, don't play games with me. We all know about you and Dad. It's so obvious. But you want to know something, Lydia. You're not the first.'

She looked at him now.

'If you've got something to say, Jimmy, just say it.'

'Well, how shall I put this? My old man has an appetite, like most men. My mother, for whatever reason, doesn't. So Spencer does what most men in those situations do. He gets his pleasure and he pays for it. What's he paying you?'

She handed him her glass.

'I'd like another drink please, Jimmy, if you'd be so kind. And I'd like you to understand one thing. My relationship with your father is none of your business. His relationship with me is similarly none of your business. So, I'll have that drink and then I'll have some of those delicious ribs that your mother has cooked. Your father doesn't pay me. He doesn't have to. You obviously don't understand the nature of the transaction that takes place between us. The currency is pleasure and love. Not money.'

She watched him walk across the lawn, threading through the groups of people, all eating, drinking, talking, laughing. She saw him hand her glass to Spencer, who was behind the make-shift bar. Spencer filled it up with chilled white wine. He took a sip from it, then handed it back to his son. She would slip her mouth over the imprint of his lips and drink it down. And taste him with her tongue.

*If anything should happen to me, I have asked my lawyer, Herb Sherman, you remember him I'm sure, the guy with the toupee and the pipe, to get in touch with you. I'll always love you, Lydia. I have often wondered if I should have been brave and left Betty when we still had the opportunity to have a life together. But there's no point in having regrets, is there? As ever, Spencer.'

207

She sat at the kitchen table. It was time to take her medication. The pain in her arm was excruciating. The tips of her fingers protruded from the end of the plaster. They were white and shrivelled. Like the rest of her body. That first time when she and Spencer ended up in bed together, they had gone to her hotel. They had sat in the bar on the twenty-first floor and looked out at the world beneath them. The air conditioning had sent a sudden chill down her spine. The hairs on her arms stood up. She had been wearing a white, long-sleeved T-shirt. She had pushed the sleeves up to her elbows. She knew Spencer was looking at her. She was acutely conscious of his gaze.

'You're too old for this,' she had thought. But when he suggested that they go to her room, she had nodded and followed him to the lift. He had undressed her slowly. Then taken his own clothes off quickly. She had wanted to cover herself immediately, but he had held her hands and stopped her.

'You're beautiful,' he said as he lay down beside her.

'So are you,' she had replied and rested her head on his chest, smoothing down the thick, curly grey hairs and listening to his beating heart.

The bottle of pills was on the dresser. Their effect was beginning to wear off. The last time she had gone to the hospital, the doctor had dismissed her complaints about the pain.

'It's not that bad, surely? You must have a low pain threshold. Make sure you take your tablets at regular intervals. That way, the dose will be constant in your system. All right?'

But it wasn't all right. It wasn't all right at all. She had insisted. It had nothing to do with pain thresholds. It was because of the pins holding her shattered bone together. But she could see she was making a nuisance of herself. The queue behind her was getting restless. She knew what she must look like. A mad old woman with frizzy hair and hollow eyes. Shuffling from chair to chair. But she was determined. She wasn't going to be fobbed off.

'Look, take the rest of these and if you're still in such pain when you come for your next check-up we'll try using a pain patch. You wear it on your back; it's very strong. It's not recommended for everyone. But maybe it will work for you. Finish up these before we take the next step though. OK, dear?'

She shook the pills from the bottle and swallowed them down with a glass of water. A sudden jealous pang resonated through her. Spencer had been ill. His wife wasn't well either. Their family were looking after them. They were making decisions for them. A new life was waiting for them in the heat and the sun of Florida. The children and grandchildren would visit for Thanksgiving and Christmas. They would play golf and swim, sit by the pool and drink cocktails. When the kids were out of school for the summer there would be picnics and barbecues and games of softball on the beach. The children would always be there for them.

'You've a daughter, haven't you? Does she live near you? Do you see her often? Does she have kids?' Spencer's interest was genuine.

She fobbed him off.

'Oh, you know. She's very independent. A bit of a rebel really. Does her own thing. I'm happy for her. It's so important to be able to stand on your own two feet in this day and age.'

Soon he stopped asking. They always talked about Spencer's boys, Spencer's grandchildren. Eventually she reckoned that he had forgotten that she had any family. She was glad. It suited her better that way. And she knew that, deep down, that was the way he wanted it.

He asked her about Alex. And she lied to him. Told him they had no contact, there was nothing physical left in their marriage. It was one of convenience, shared business interests. He didn't believe her. Not to begin with.

'Does he know about me?' he asked more than once. 'Surely he must wonder. You're a lovely woman, Lydia. He must know you're having sex. Doesn't he?'

But she convinced him. Said her husband had no interest in her. That he was like Betty. Age had taken its toll on him. And he accepted her assurances.

But it wasn't true. Alex still loved her and wanted her. He came to the airport to meet her when she returned from her trips. And he couldn't wait to get her home. To hold her tightly. Tell her how he felt. Ask her to forgive him for all his transgressions. She had never understood what he meant until after he was dead. And it was too late then to forgive him for anything.

Now the pills had begun to do their job. They had taken the edge off the pain. She felt exhausted and weak. She shuffled through the photographs. They both looked so happy. Spencer was so tall and good-looking. She looked stylish and elegant. Slim and suntanned with dark glasses hiding her eyes. She remembered all the times they had asked strangers, passers-by, people sitting at the next table, to take the photographs. They had told little white lies. They were celebrating their wedding anniversary; they were on holiday; they were visitors from some other part of America, from Europe. We didn't mean to hurt or deceive, they had told each other. And if no one else knew about it, what was the harm? She put the pictures and the letter back in the envelope and moved slowly from the kitchen, up the stairs and along the hall towards the front of the house. She opened Alex's desk and put it away in the top drawer. She was so tired now. She couldn't imagine that she had ever been that woman. She lay down on the sofa, covered herself with a rug and slept. And when she woke she would read Spencer's letter again. And remember what once had been, but would never be again.

EIGHTEEN

It had been easy to find the school. Adam had followed the main route from the north side to the south of the city. It had brought him into Rathmines. He had seen the school buildings just behind the large new shopping centre. He had stopped the car and consulted his map. He needed a place somewhere close by. He checked his phone for the time. It was just after four. He got out of the car and looked up and down. Shops, pubs, a bookie's, a few takeaways and restaurants. Everything anyone could need. And just in front of him, an estate agent and letting agency. He straightened himself up and ran his hands through his hair. Checked his wallet to make sure he had his ID and his credit card.

He was in luck. They specialized in short-term lets. They had any number of apartments on their books. He could take his pick. He could hand over his credit card, sign on the dotted line and, hey presto, two hours later he was lying on the king-size bed in the fully furnished, modern, fifth-floor apartment in a new block five minutes from the school.

He slept, showered, poured himself a beer and stepped out onto the balcony. There were chairs and a picnic table and even a small palm tree in a pot. Beneath him were red roofs and patches of garden. And beyond, the shimmer of the slow-moving water in the canal. It was quiet now. He could hear children playing, someone's radio, someone else's TV, even the call of the seagulls as they swooped down over the lock. It reminded him of Trawbawn. There were messages from Lydia on his phone. She sounded increasingly desperate. He should ring her, give her something to make her happy. He sat down and took out his phone. He was just about to punch in Lydia's number when it rang. He smiled.

'And how are you this fine evening?'

'All the better for talking to you.'

'And what can I do for you?'

'I've some news. About our friend.'

'Which one? The older or the younger?'

'The younger.'

'Yes?'

'Seems she's turned into a real do-gooder.'

'How do you mean?'

'She's teaching a class to the women here. Hold on a minute while I look at this.' Adam could hear the sound of paper rustling. 'A writing workshop. "Telling Your Own Story". Ten a.m. to twelve, Monday to Friday.'

'How convenient.'

'Isn't it?'

There was silence.

'Adam?'

'Yes?' Adam took a swallow from his beer. Cold drops ran down his chin and onto his hand. He licked them off.

'Are you listening?'

'I'm listening.'

'Now, you know how to find her. And when you find her give her a message. Not from her mother, but from me.'

'A message. What would that be?'

'Tell her she owes me. She owes me big time. And you're the debt collector. How does that feel?'

'Good, pretty good.'

'She has a daughter now, I hear.'

'She has.'

'Well.' There was a pause. 'What more do I have to say?'

Today it was Lyuba's turn to read. Her hair looked even redder this morning in comparison to the pallor of her face. She sat on the edge of her chair chewing the end of her biro.

'OK.' Grace smiled. 'Off you go.'

Lyuba looked down.

'My English not so good. It is better for me I write. In school we learned English, you know.'

'It's OK, girl, we don't care,' Honey, the woman from Trinidad, drawled and inspected her long red nails. 'You just go right ahead.'

'OK, I start.' She picked up the piece of paper. It trembled in her thin fingers.

'I born in Russia. I live in town called Perm. It is long way from Moscow. Near the mountains called Ural. My mother teach piano in the ballet school. My father is in Russian army. I entered ballet school when I am ten. I start classes. I am very happy. I love the classes even when the teacher gets mad and shouts at me. I live with my mother in one room in old apartment building. We are happy. All winter we go to ballet school. In summer for holiday we go to Black Sea. Then when I am twelve my father comes home. I am so happy to see him. He brings presents. Cakes and vodka, new leather bag for Mama and shawl for me. He stays with us and he sleeps in the big bed with Mama. I sleep on sofa. But one morning I wake up and he is in the bed with me. I think he wants to give me hugs, but it is more than that. I try stop him but he is too big. He put his hand over my mouth. He tell me not to say to Mama. He tell me this is our big secret. He stays for weeks. I hate him. He gives me money. Then he

214

goes. My mother is sad. I cannot dance any more. I want to leave home. I use the money he has given me to buy a ticket for train and I go to Moscow. I live on streets with other kids. I do bad things. I get into trouble. One day I hear it is possible to make a lot of money dancing in clubs here in Dublin. There is a man who will pay our ticket and give us job. My friend Oxana she wants to come, so we come together. The man who owns the club puts us in house and he wants us to be prostitutes. I say no. But he tells me I am illegal. I get sent back to Moscow. So I do what he wants, but I begin to steal from men. I get credit cards and I buy lots of stuff in the shops. I buy clothes, CDs, make-up, good things. These are presents to make me feel better. Then I get caught. I get put here. I like it here. It's safe. It's warm. I eat meals. I like the girls. I want to stay here when I get out. But I know they will send me back to Moscow, and I will die there.'

No one spoke when Lyuba had finished. She got up from the table and left the room. Honey followed her. Grace looked at the faces around the table.

'Anyone have anything to say?' she asked. There was no response.

'OK, we'll leave it at that. Who wants to read tomorrow?'

Marcia lifted her hand.

'I reckon it's my turn.'

'Fine. I'll see you all at ten. Mind yourselves.'

It was a relief to hear the rumble of the heavy door and watch it slide slowly open. To breathe

the air of the outside again. She slung her bag over her shoulder and began to wheel her bike towards the main road. There was a crowd milling around the entrance to the men's prison. A group of young men and a few women. Mothers, girl-friends, sisters maybe. Some had babies in buggies. A couple had small kids by the hand. She glanced across at them. She saw someone she recognized. Short blonde hair, thin face, long lanky body. A cigarette between his fingers. She began to walk towards him.

'Hi, how are you? How have you been?'

He looked at her, then looked away.

'I dunno,' he mumbled.

'How's Jackie? And the baby? Are they doing OK?'

He shrugged his shoulders.

'How should I know? What's it to do with me?'

Grace stared hard at him.

'Correct me if I'm wrong, Damien, but she is your girlfriend. And you are the baby's father. Isn't that so?'

He looked down at the footpath. He wiped his hand across his face.

'She's gone back to her ma's. I haven't seen her for a while.' He drew on his cigarette. There were tattoo marks across his knuckles.

'Oh, I see. Well, maybe she'll come back to school now. We could organize crèche facilities for her.' Grace could see his embarrassment, his discomfort, but she wasn't going to let it go. Jackie had been one of her brightest girls doing the Junior Certificate exams. Until she got preg-nant with Damien's baby and moved into his flat

216

with him.

'I don't know what she's doing. I told you. I haven't seen her.' His tone was hostile now.

'And the baby? Boy or a girl?'

'A boy.'

The door in the heavy wooden gate opened. A prison guard stepped out.

'Come on, now, let's be having you. Visiting time.'

Damien shrugged and moved away.

'Well, if you do see her, tell her I was asking after her, won't you?'

'Tell her yourself if you're that bothered.' He dropped his butt and ground it into the pavement. He turned away.

The crowd pushed past her. She walked down to the main road. It was always dark and gloomy here. The bulk of the Mater hospital blocked the sun on her right. It was so handy, the prison officers always said, that the casualty department was so close. Especially for suicides. Most of them became attempted rather than successful. Looked better on the yearly statistics.

She got onto her bike and began to cycle away as quickly as she could. She felt dirty. She would go home and have a shower and sit in the garden. She couldn't forget Lyuba's story. It was making her feel sick. The noise of the traffic filled her ears. The smell of the fumes clogged up her nostrils. She was breathless and nauseous. The road ahead seemed to shimmer in her vision. She swayed from side to side. And heard the beep of a car horn and a passing driver wagging his finger at her. She slowed down. Be careful, she thought.

217

Don't make an error of judgement. Hold on. Home was close now. Close and safe.

Adam watched her walk towards him. He recognized her from the photo in the magazine. He could see nothing of her mother in her. She was much taller. Broad shoulders and long legs. She had thick, fair hair, white blonde tendrils curling over her forehead and the rest of it pulled back into a low pony tail. She didn't look her age in her jeans and denim jacket. She looked strong and fit. He realized he had seen her yesterday. She was the woman on the bicycle who had overtaken him. She called out to someone in the crowd, and for a moment he thought that she was speaking to him, that somehow she knew who he was. He looked around for an escape route. But it was the guy standing in front of him that she knew. He could hear the exchange. Something to do with a girl and a baby. The guy didn't want to know. He wouldn't look at her. He kept on trying to back away. Adam could see that the girl standing behind him was the reason. She was small and pretty, with a tattoo on her upper arm and a bare belly pierced with a heart-shaped ring. He tried not to look at Grace. He knew he could draw her gaze to him if he wanted. The crowd carried him closer to her. He could have reached out and touched her. She might not even have noticed. But he kept his distance until the crowd began to move towards the prison gate and she turned away. He followed her down to the main road and got into his car. She was easy to track. There weren't many women like her riding through the city. She kept up a good speed and a couple of times he thought he'd lose her as she zigzagged through the traffic. But then she slowed right down. She looked unsteady. The car in front swerved to avoid her and the driver blew his horn at her. He stayed just behind her. He could see the direction she was taking. Towards the Grand Canal, turning left over the bridge at Portobello, then swinging to the right and along a narrow street with red-brick Victorian houses on either side. She had got off the bike and was wheeling it into the small, railed front garden of one of the bigger houses. He stopped and watched her. She opened the door beneath the long flight of granite steps that led up to the front of the house. She disappeared from view. He drove slowly into a narrow lane opposite. He picked up his phone and called directory enquiries. He made a note of her number. Then he checked his messages. There were three from Lydia. She sounded increasingly frantic. He pressed the button to reply. She didn't pick up. He wondered where the old bat might be. In the garden, down by the river, perhaps still in bed, or struggling to dress and feed herself. She'd be sorry she missed his call. Now if only she had an answering machine he could have told her where he was. He could have said, 'Hey, Lydia, I'm sitting in the car outside your daughter's house. I have her now. I have her. And this is where the fun begins.'

But he didn't. He slid the seat back and closed his eyes. She'd be tired after her morning's work. She'd want to have something to eat and a rest maybe. She'd want to catch up on her life. And he'd just have a kip too, and wait. He had plenty of time. He had all the time in the world.

A message from Amelia on the answering machine. She was fed up. She wanted to come home. The food was terrible. She'd had a row with Gemma. Gemma had gone off with some of the others and wasn't speaking to her. Why wasn't Grace coming to see her this weekend? She didn't want Jack to come.

'I'm warning you, Mummy. I'm going to run away.'

Grace stifled the urge to pick up the phone immediately. It would be good for Amelia to have a bit of privation in her life. She had it too easy most of the time. She was spoilt and indulged. She had refused to go to St Bridget's for her secondary education. Jack had backed her up. They'd had a terrible row about it. But he had insisted. Amelia was very bright. She deserved the best.

'I know Bridget's is a good school. It has a great record given the kind of girls that go there,' he said, his voice deliberately non-committal. 'But really, Grace, we can afford, at least I can afford, to pay for a top-class school for Amelia. Laurel Park is the best. I know. I see the intake every year. Laurel Park girls have it all.'

'Yeah, of course they do.' Her voice wasn't non-committal. 'They have one thing above everything else. They have money. They learn one great lesson. You can buy anything. You can buy status, position in society, and you can buy your future. That's what they learn.'

'Oh come on. Get a grip. We're not in Ken

Livingstone's London now. We're in the real world. Amelia wants to go to Laurel Park. Apart from anything else, do you think it's a good idea for her to go to a school where her mother is the Principal? Think how difficult that would be for her. In fact, Grace, while you're at it, why don't you think about what's best for your daughter, rather than what fits with your ideology?'

So Grace had given in. Watched her daughter acquire the mannerisms, the speech patterns, the spending habits of the wealthy. And remembered what Jack had said. 'Take a good look at yourself, Grace. You went to boarding school, didn't you? One of those elite schools of which you are so critical? Did it do you any harm?'

She opened her mouth to correct him. To tell him that she hadn't gone back to the boarding school after she had the baby. That she had gone to the local school with all the local kids. That she had slogged her way through her work with only one aim in mind. To leave Trawbawn behind. But she had said nothing. She hadn't told him before, when they were young and easy with each other. She hadn't told him when they were in that phase of their relationship where there were no secrets. So she wasn't going to tell him now, when there was nothing between them but secrets.

She dumped her bag in the kitchen and went upstairs to change. She pulled on a pair of Lycra leggings and a T-shirt and hunted in the bottom of the cupboard for her running shoes. She needed to move. She couldn't face the thought of staying in the house now. She hurried out the front door, dropping the keys in their usual hiding place beneath the large pot of lavender on the top step. The park was half a mile away. A handy run there, a few circuits of the grass and a run back. Her breath flowed easily in and out of her lungs. She could feel the sweat on her chest and between her shoulder blades. Her legs felt strong, her stride fluent and easy. Our secret, Lyuba's father had said. Our secret. They always said that. These abusers, these destroyers of childhood. Our secret. It makes us different and special. Beloved above all. The secret that was so powerful and terrifying that it was forgotten. And all that was left was the fear.

She reached the park now. She began to run faster along the narrow path that encircled the grass and trees. Her breathing was not so easy. Her chest was tight and sore. Her heart was beating too fast. Her knees and thigh muscles were aching. But she did not stop or slow down. This pain was more bearable than the other. The pain that had come from watching her baby asleep in the incubator. His tiny hands reaching out. His legs pulled up to his stomach. His mouth opening and the mew of a kitten coming from it. Lisa had killed the man who took her baby from her. Grace had wanted to kill the people who took her baby. The social worker with the bright smile and the neat suit and the briefcase. The matron in charge of the mother and baby home who had told her it was all for the best.

'You've no idea how quickly you'll get over this, dear. Within no time you'll be back home and back to normal, getting on with all the things that girls of your age do.'

And her mother. Who said to her when she came back to Trawbawn, 'We won't speak of this again. It's in the past. The future is all that matters.'

Grace could barely see now. Sweat hung in her eyes and trickled down her face. Air could no longer fill her lungs. She staggered, swayed, slowed and dropped to her knees. She slumped sideways and fell onto the grass. She lay there, her chest heaving, conscious of nothing but the need to breathe. He would be twenty-eight now, her baby boy. Old enough to come and find her. She read about it all the time in the newspapers and heard stories on the radio. Women of her age and older, and their children, reunited after decades.

She pushed herself up to sitting. The park was crowded. Children playing football. Young mothers pushing buggies. In the far corner, the sound of tennis balls hitting tennis rackets. She pulled her hair from its band and shook it out, then smoothed it back and slipped the band around it again. She stood up. She began to walk slowly back towards the gate, towards the road, towards home.

Adam sat on a bench and watched her. She looked exhausted. Her face was white. She was sweating. Her legs were shaking. It would be easy now. To follow her. To call out her name and when she turned, surprised, curious, to take her by the hair and drag her into his car. But it was the wrong time. Broad daylight. Wouldn't do. He closed his eyes and lifted his face to the sun. There was no rush. No hurry. He could take it slowly. He knew where she lived. He knew everything he needed to know about her. He put his hand in his pocket and pulled out the new set of keys. He had taken hers from behind the pot and driven to the shopping centre half a mile away. He had got the keys copied, then driven to the house and put the originals back where she had left them. He could never get over how trusting people could be. And now, when he was ready, he would make his move. Until then, he was just going to relax and enjoy himself.

NINETEEN

It was Marcia's turn to read. She was late arriving for the class. So were all the other women. Grace sat and waited. She wasn't surprised. It was always like this. They would start with a burst of energy and enthusiasm. Then it would wane and wither. Perhaps no one would come today.

Grace made herself coffee and flicked through the newspaper. She had a headache. She was tired. She had slept badly. She had dreamt again. The same dream about her missing leg. And another dream just before she woke. She had seen her baby. His eyes were open. He was calling out her name. His voice was the voice of an adult. His body was tiny and undeveloped. But he could speak.

'Where are you? Where are you?' he kept on repeating over and over again.

She had woken suddenly and had got out of bed

224

before she knew what she was doing. She had reached the bedroom door before she realized that she was awake. She had stood with her hand on the knob and the tears running down her face.

'No sign of them yet?' One of the prison guards put her head around the door. Hard sometimes to tell them apart from the prisoners. The policy was for them to wear their own clothes. If they wanted. Some of them did. Some of them didn't. The ones in the school all did. They were friendly, sympathetic.

'I'll send someone over to their rooms to get them out. Have another cup of coffee. I'll sort them for you.'

Grace refilled her cup and sat down. She looked at her watch. She'd give it another fifteen minutes. Then she'd leave. There was no point hanging around.

Adam was up too. Showered, shaved, had some breakfast. Sitting in the car in the little alleyway across from Grace's house. Takeaway cappuccino and a Danish pastry in a paper bag on his knee. He had seen her leave. Wheel her bike out from beneath the front steps. Cycle off, her bag banging on her back. He drank his coffee. He ate his pastry. He wiped his hands on a paper napkin. Then he got out of the car. Locked it. Crossed the road. Looked to left and to right. A quiet morning. No one around. Took out the bunch of keys. Slipped into the small front garden, to the door beneath the steps. Tried each key until he found the one that fitted the lock. Stepped inside. Closed the door behind him. Took a deep breath.

Stood still. Listening.

Silence. Nothing but the sound of a fridge motor ticking over. Moved through the small dark hall into the sunlit kitchen beyond. Big room, tiled floor, dresser, large rectangular pine table and chairs. All the usual kitchen stuff. Tap dripping into a washing-up bowl. Plunk, plunk, plunk. Moved towards it and tightened it. Turned around and looked through glass doors to the garden beyond. Reminded suddenly of the garden at Trawbawn. A pale pink rose arching over, what was it called? He searched for the word. A pergola, that was it. His gran had one in her old garden. He turned away. Saw the fridge. The door was covered with notes, photographs, all kinds of junk stuck to it with those corny old magnets. Pictures here must be of her daughter. Pretty girl, long brown hair, big mouth, white teeth, wearing a bikini. Very suntanned. Very cute. He reached out and pulled the photos off the door. He laid them out on the table. Then picked them up and shuffled them and laid them out again.

Another room next to the kitchen. Big TV and a sofa. Fireplace, mantelpiece. More photos. Daughter, mother, daughter and mother on horses. Vase of flowers. Pink roses. He leaned forward to smell them and some of the petals began to drop. They lay in a semicircle on the polished wooden floor. He shook the vase and more fell. He shook it again and again. A pale pink rug at his feet and just the naked flower heads and stems in the water.

He moved away, back through the kitchen, towards the stairs. Up and up and up. First floor, another sitting room. Formal, beautiful. Sofas and chairs in vivid covers. Deep red and dark blue. A huge abstract painting on the white wall. Shelves of books. He stood and looked at them. They were arranged carefully in alphabetical order. He reached up and pulled some out. He put them back in a random order. Haphazardly. Moved back towards the stairs and up again. Two bedrooms and a bathroom. Her bedroom. Quilt pulled back from white sheets. Cotton nightgown on a chair. More books heaped beside the bed. Cupboards with clothes and shoes and a row of drawers. He opened them. Underwear, T-shirts, sweaters. He buried his face in their softness. They smelt of sunshine and fresh air. He lay down on the bed. It was still warm. He rolled his face into her pillow and closed his eyes. Comfortable here. He could get used to it.

Grace looked at her watch again. Five more minutes then she was gone. She had things to do at home. An article she was writing for inclusion in a collection on young women and education. She stood up and put her books back in her bag. Just as the door opened and Marcia came in. Her eyes were red-rimmed and her face was even puffier than usual.

Behind her crowded Honey and Lisa.

'So you decided to come after all. I was just about to leave,' Grace said.

Marcia didn't reply. She took her place at the table.

'Sorry, miss.' Honey smiled. 'Marcia's not been too good. But she's here and so are we.'

227

'Is that it? Any more coming? Lyuba?'

Honey shook her head.

'No, maam. Lyuba isn't too good. Ate something that didn't agree with her. Up being sick all night. The others? Well.' She spread her hands in front of her. 'And Mags is in court today. Might be back, might not.'

They sat in a small circle. Marcia stared ahead of her. Then she picked up her exercise book and began to read.

'Once upon a time there was a little girl called Marcia. She lived in a big house way out in the countryside. She had everything a little girl could want. She had dolls and toys and books and pictures. She had a mummy and a daddy and she had a little brother. His name was Robert. Marcia's mummy and daddy were very busy all the time. Daddy had a job in the city and he left early every morning and didn't come home until late after Marcia had gone to bed. Marcia's mummy was very busy too. She always had lots of people to meet and lots of places to go. Marcia and Robert were looked after by a nanny. Her name was Ruth. She was very strict. Marcia didn't like her. She was rough with Marcia. Marcia had a bath every evening and after the bath Ruth would dry her. She would rub her with a towel, rub her and rub her and rub her. Marcia didn't like the feeling. It made her want to do a wee wee. Ruth was much nicer to Robert. She sang to him and carried him around with her. She said he was a nicer baby than Marcia. She said Marcia was a fat pig because Marcia liked to eat. Mummy said the same thing too. When they had afternoon tea together Marcia liked to eat the cream cakes. Chocolate éclairs were her favourites. She loved the taste of the cream and the way when she bit down into the cake the cream would gush out and get all over her mouth and her cheeks. It made her Mummy laugh. Look at her, she would say, the fat pig. And Ruth would laugh too. Even Robert would laugh although he was too young to know what he was laughing about. One day Ruth took Marcia and Robert out for a walk. They went to visit Ruth's friend Tony. He lived in a little cottage nearby. Ruth went inside and she told Marcia to look after Robert in his pushchair. Marcia pushed Robert into the garden. It was very steep and at the bottom there was a stream. Robert was crying. She tried to make him stop but he wouldn't. She wanted to pick some flowers to bring home to Mummy. She left Robert and walked away. Robert was crying and trying to get out of the pushchair. And suddenly it began to roll down the hill. Marcia stood and watched. It went faster and faster and faster. When it got to the bottom it went into the water. Marcia ran down. Robert was lying in the pushchair. He was still strapped in. She called out his name but he didn't answer. She turned around and walked back up the hill. She knocked on the door and called out for Ruth. Tony came out. His face was very red. She said, come quickly, Robert's in the water. He said, oh shit. Mummy said it was her fault. Daddy said it was Ruth's fault. They sent Ruth away and they sent Marcia to a boarding school. She was never a happy girl. Ever again.'

Silence in the room.

'Well.' Grace broke it. 'Thank you, Marcia. Thank you for taking so much trouble with your contribution to the class.'

Marcia stood. She picked up the exercise book and tore it in half. The pages scattered on the floor. She stamped on them and ground them into pieces with one foot. Then she walked out of the room. The door slammed shut behind her.

There were two rooms and a small bathroom at the top of the house. One was obviously the daughter's. The walls were covered with posters. Britney Spears and Eminem he recognized. He wasn't sure about some of the others. And there was one wall dedicated to Vincent Van Gogh. He knew the paintings. The yellow chair, the cornfield, the sunflowers, the self-portrait. There were more photographs. Amelia and her friends. Pretty girls, all of them. They reminded him of the girls he had known when he was at school. The sisters of the boys in his class. Good girls, nice girls, rich girls. He knew the type.

He walked back downstairs to Grace's bedroom. He opened the chest of drawers. Not much in the way of jewellery. A few trinkets. A gold bracelet that might be worth something. A cameo in the shape of a bunch of flowers. He put them in his pocket. He should leave her something in return. He lay down on her bed again. He undid his belt. He closed his eyes. He would leave her something sweet.

'OK, everyone. It's lunchtime. That's all for today. Tomorrow, for a change, we'll read someone else. I'll bring in some copies of Anne Frank's diary. I think you'll find it interesting.' Grace stood up. She watched them wander from the room. Time meant nothing in here, she thought. Prison time was a concept unlike any other kind of time. But she was hungry. She would stop off at the Jewish bakery on the way home and get some good bread. Sit in the garden and have a little picnic. Then take the rest of the afternoon off. She was tired now. The memory of her dream was still with her. Maybe if she slept again she'd dream some more about the baby. And maybe in the dream she could make it right for him again.

Lunchtime in the men's prison. Colm sat on his bed with his tray beside him. He had let the shepherd's pie go cold. Now it lay, a congealed mess of grey, in the middle of the plastic plate. The tea that invariably accompanied the meal was also cold. A scum of milk floated on its yellow surface. Just the look of it made him feel ill. He dumped the tray on the floor, swung his legs up and stretched himself out. It had taken a while to get used to eating on his own, locked into his cell. He had lost his appetite. Not that the food was bad. It was indifferent, but edible. Better than the stuff they served up in Manchester. But it was just so depressing being left alone with nothing but a plastic plate, knife, fork and spoon. And the bitter-sweet smell of urine that hung in the stale air and clung to the inside of his nose.

The only thing that had made him feel good was the news from Adam. Colm had phoned him yesterday evening. Used a combination of cocaine and clout to get hold of a mobile. And Adam had told him. He had found Grace. He had found her house. He had seen her.

'What is she like now?'

'Now? As compared to when?'

'Don't play fucking games with me, Adam. What is she like? Does she look good? Does she look old? Does she look the way she used to look when she was a girl?'

'Can't answer that, but I can say that she looks very good. The photo in the magazine doesn't do her justice. She looks fucking gorgeous.'

Colm lay back and stared up at the ceiling of his cell. It was curved, barrel-shaped. Low enough at the highest point in the middle and even lower at the sides where it met the walls. It made him feel trapped, claustrophobic. He'd had a meeting with the governor this morning. They'd discussed what the governor called his future. He had explained. Colm had to serve fifteen years before he could be considered eligible for parole. He had done twelve of those years.

'So next year you'll be up before the board. But you won't get out immediately. They'll knock you back for another while, a year if you're lucky, if you impress them.'

'And how do I do that?'

'Well, apart from showing due remorse, accepting responsibility for what you did, acknowledging your guilt. You know what I mean.' Colm nodded. 'Well, apart from all that, you'll need a plan: you'll need to think where you want to be in, say, five years' time. Do you want to be living back at home with your family? Do you want to be working on the farm again, or maybe fishing? How do you intend earning a living? And what about some education?' The governor dropped his eyes to Colm's file. 'I see you never got involved in anything like that when you were in Manchester. Pity really. They have great facilities over there. Much better than we have.' He looked up at Colm. 'Well, perhaps now's the time to start. It's never too late.'

Colm didn't reply.

'You do want to get out of here, don't you?'

Again Colm made no response.

'Because, we will let you out. We've a more humane approach than the Brits, we reckon. But we're not fools, Colm. Nor are we a pushover. Anyone who thinks that had better think again. You know, prisoners like you are intrinsically political. All it takes is for a change in the Minister. We could get a "hang 'em, flog 'em" type, and the release of a man who had murdered his wife would be set back years. Now,' he smiled at him, 'the current guy is a good guy, but there's a bad bollocks snapping at his heels. So, if I was you, I'd start to think very seriously about where I want to spend my next few years. OK?'

The problem was, he didn't know what he wanted to do. He rolled over on his side, folding his arms across his body and jamming his hands under his armpits. Inside prison he had a function and a purpose. He had a way of life. He had dreams and fears. But most of all he had power. Outside, what was he? A middle-aged man who had killed his wife. Penniless, despised, rejected. He could go back to the island. He could become a curiosity for the summer visitors. He could see them now. All those arseholes who came into the harbour in their big boats, covered from head to toe in rain gear that cost as much as a week's wages. When he was a kid, he and the others would sit around and watch them. How they loved to swank their way from the pier to the pub. Loved to be known and recognized, to be on first-name terms with all the islanders. Loved to show off to their city friends. He could never understand it. Why it should matter so much to these big shots. Whether Jimmy or Pat or Mary or Bridie or whoever remembered who they were. But it did. He could see them now, walking up the hill. See Cáit going by in her old banger. Hear the braying comments.

'Do you see her? There in the old Cortina. That's Cáit Ni Laoire, Brid and Conn's youngest. Don't see any sign of the prodigal. You know the story, don't you? Colm the eldest, went off to England under something of a cloud. Got himself married, then went to the bad. Killed his wife. Ended up in prison. Got life for it. They've let him out now. We hear he's come back to the island. We're bound to see him in the pub tonight. Dangerous? Not at all. He's not dangerous. A nice lad really, just a bit hot-tempered.'

No, he didn't need that. Nor did he need his mother whingeing and his sister whining. What he needed was the kind of thing that Adam could give him. Sweet revenge. The dish best eaten cold. Revenge for the way that Lydia accused him of fathering Grace's baby. Sneered at him. Humiliated him in front of Grace. He had wanted to be able to say that it was him. That he and Grace had been lovers. That he, the lad from the islands, had fucked the girl from the big house. That she had wanted him. More than any of the rich kids, with their surnames from the Planters and the followers of Cromwell, who came on the sailing course. That he, who had spoken nothing but Irish until he was eight, whose family had lived along the river and on the islands since before records were kept, was the one she had chosen. But she hadn't chosen him. She wouldn't say who it was. And Lydia had decided not to believe her.

'There's no way that child will be brought up in this house,' she had shouted, so everyone could hear her. And then she had gone into his room above the garage and thrown all his belongings out into the yard. And told him to go.

He lay back and stared up at the ceiling. At the hourglass stain. It was like the hourglass he had tattooed on his shoulder. Like the fob from the pocket watch in the shape of the hourglass that Grace had given him. He leaned over and pulled open the door to the bedside locker. He reached into it. His fingers felt the smooth grain of a small wooden box. It had been made for him by the boy who had preceded Adam in Manchester. He had come back from woodwork class one afternoon and presented it to Colm.

'It's a treasure box,' he said. 'For all your special things. It's made of elm. Look. See how the lid slides backwards and forwards.'

He had kept the hourglass fob in it. It was a sweet little thing. The gold shone with a dull glow. And the fine sand ran smoothly from one end to the other. He didn't have many things of his own after fourteen years in prison. But he had hung on to the hourglass. Fought to protect it. He wondered now. What might be the value of the hourglass in this prison economy? How many calls on the mobile phone would he get for it? How many cigarettes? How many joints? How many lines of coke? How many armfuls of heroin? How many blow jobs?

But it had been worth more than any of that to him. Because he owned it and Lydia Beauchamp didn't. He owned something beautiful that had once belonged to the Chamberlain family. Something with their Latin motto engraved on its base. *Veritatem dies aperit.* He repeated it over and over again out loud. Times reveals the truth. He wanted to see her face when he held the hourglass in front of her.

'Look,' he wanted to say. 'Look what I have. I know all about you, you fucking bitch. I know all about you and your daughter. And I'm going to make you suffer for what you did to me.'

And how much he wished that he could witness what would happen when she found out about the cuckoo he had sent to her nest. Such a handsome creature. So nice and charming. No one would ever guess that he was ruthless, heartless, without any conscience.

Now he put the little box back into the bedside locker. He lay down again and closed his eyes. He

236

pushed his right hand up the sleeve of his left arm and felt for the rough edges of his tattoo. Adam had done it for him. And he had done the same for Adam. He closed his eyes. He let out his breath in a long, slow expulsion of air. And heard the keys rattle in the lock as his door swung open.

'Wakey, wakey, rise and shine. Let's be having your tray.' The screw's voice was loud in the confines of the cell. He sat up, yawned and stretched. Grace would have left the women's prison by now. Her class would be over. He'd asked around, asked some of the men who had girlfriends, sisters, wives inside. They all knew her. They liked her. She was popular.

'And a fuckin' ride, man. Have you seen her?' one guy said, a grin stretching from ear to ear.

He got up. He'd go the gym. He'd run on the treadmill. Miles and miles and miles. As far as Trawbawn. He'd lift weights. He'd make himself strong. As strong as Adam. And afterwards he'd phone Adam. And he was sure that he would have news for him. Good news.

Adam woke. He sat up. He had heard something from downstairs. He listened. He heard voices. He swung his legs over the side of the bed and stood up. He moved carefully to the door. He tiptoed to the top of the stairs.

Grace closed the door behind her. She walked through into the kitchen. She reached out and switched on the radio. She dropped her bag on the floor. She opened the fridge and pulled out a carton of orange juice. She opened the cupboard and picked up a glass. Then she turned back.

237

Something was different. Something wasn't right. There were photographs, pictures of Amelia that she had taken last summer, lying on the kitchen table. She hadn't left them there. She was sure of it. She looked at the door of the fridge again. The magnets were still stuck onto its shiny white surface. But the photographs had been removed. She poured juice into the glass and sipped it. Then she walked to the French windows and tried the handles. They were locked. The outside door had been locked too when she opened it. She walked into the sitting room. The petals from the vase of roses on the mantelpiece had fallen onto the floor. They lay like a piece of pale pink chiffon on the boards. The still air of the room was scented.

She walked back into the kitchen and moved to the stairs. She listened. All she could hear was the radio. She switched it off. She walked up the stairs.

'Hello,' she called out. 'Who's there?'

There was no reply. She looked into the drawing room. It was empty, undisturbed. She walked back out into the hall. She tried the front door. It was double-locked. She turned away. She stood still for a moment. Then she walked back down into the kitchen again.

Adam heard her footsteps in the hall. He hugged the wall in the stairwell. He could see the top of her head below him. Then she was gone. He waited. He moved slowly down. He held the bunch of keys in his hand. He walked to the heavy front door. He slipped the Chubb key into the lock. It turned smoothly. He opened the door with

238

the upper latch. He stepped outside. He pulled the door to behind him and locked it again. Then he took the steps two at a time. He didn't look back. He got into the car. He drove away.

It must be Jack, Grace thought. He must have let himself into the house. She had told him before he wasn't to do it. She had told him he no longer had rights over the house. She had said she would change the locks. He had promised that he wouldn't presume again. That he respected her privacy. She sat at the table and looked at the photographs. She picked them up and stuck them back on the fridge door. She lifted the phone and punched in his number. She heard his voice. Pleasant, friendly, sympathetic.

'Can't take your call at the moment. Leave a message and I'll get back to you as soon as possible.'

'Jack,' her voice was cold and hostile, 'I've told you before. I don't want you coming into the house when I'm not here. This time you've really pissed me off. Enough's enough. OK?'

She hung up the phone and moved upstairs to her bedroom. He'd even been in here. The quilt was disturbed, the pillows heaped into a pile. She pushed them onto the floor and stripped the bed. Then she turned away and walked up to Amelia's room. She stood in the doorway and looked around. At least this room looked untouched. She lay down on the bed and closed her eyes. She turned her head into the pillow. She was so tired now. She'd sleep and then she'd phone him again.

TWENTY

So now Johnny had a name, and he had a place. He sat in front of his computer screen. He put in Grace Beauchamp and Skibbereen, County Cork. He pressed enter. He waited. There was a page of responses. He read the first entry out loud. 'Trawbawn House, home of the garden designer Lydia Beauchamp, two miles outside the picturesque West Cork town of Skibbereen...'

He double-clicked on the highlighted words. He waited. He watched the hourglass. It hung immobile. Then changed shape and became an arrow. And behind it the computer screen changed too. A picture began to reveal itself, slowly, so slowly. He could see blue sky, the slated roof of a house shining in bright sunshine. Tall trees flanking it. And then suddenly, in a rush, the whole scene was in front of him. He pushed back his chair and picked up his cup of coffee. A beautiful house. Early nineteenth century, it looked. Three storeys, painted dove grey, long bay windows, a front door, dark blue with a curved fanlight above. In front, a smooth green lawn, and a monkey puzzle tree. The caption below read, 'Welcome to Trawbawn House and Gardens'.

He scrolled through the pages. Now he saw a walled garden. Row after row of vegetables. Now a large greenhouse filled with exotic plants, the datura with its orange trumpets, the bougainvillea's magenta blooms, and a vine, ripe grapes hanging in purple bunches below its serpentine tendrils. Now the river and a boathouse, tree ferns clustered around it. And a heron flapping its huge wings overhead.

He moved the mouse to the panel at the side of the screen. 'Meet Lydia Beauchamp, world-renowned garden designer,' it said. He clicked on the tiny photograph. He waited while it enlarged. The picture changed so slowly. He could hardly bear it. He wanted to pick up the computer and fling it against the wall. But he sat and waited. And watched the hourglass. And saw the woman's face as it slowly filled the screen. Thick black curly hair. A long nose. Dark brown eyes. She was sitting on a wooden bench in the middle of a beautiful garden. The sun was shining. He read the description out loud.

'Lydia Beauchamp, the internationally renowned garden designer. Author of three best-selling books. She has lived and worked in Trawbawn for nearly forty years. She has created a haven of peace and tranquillity in this beautiful setting by the Ilen River, five miles from the town of Skibbereen in West Cork.'

His hand moved quickly, clicking on each of the topics listed. But there was no mention of a family. No mention of a girl called Grace. There were garden designs, lists of plants, books to buy. There were maps showing Trawbawn's location in relation to Cork and Dublin airports. There was advice about travel. And there were products for sale. Seeds, plants, gardening equipment. And there was a section on the history of the house. He read through it quickly. Originally the home of the Chamberlain family, until the death of the last member. Lydia, her husband Alexander and daughter Grace had come to live there in 1965. Lydia had dedicated herself to maintaining the gardens and promoting the house. There were more pictures. The interior. Beautiful rooms, elegantly furnished. A staircase which curved up from the front hall. And the view from the windows. The trees, and beyond, the river and the sea.

Johnny printed it all. Then he spread the pages out on the floor. He had never imagined that there was anyone who looked like him. But here she was. His grandmother. The same hair, eyes, nose, chin. The same gap between the front teeth. He picked up his phone.

'Lucy,' he said. 'Quick. You've got to come over. You have to see what I've found. Please.'

There was no uncertainty now. There was just excitement and anticipation. He would have to do it. He would have to go to Ireland and find her. And she would lead him to his mother. He knew she would.

TWENTY-ONE

The television was on a bracket high up on the wall in the hospital waiting room. Lydia watched it. The sound boomed out. It made her head ache. She sat and waited for the nurse to beckon her into the examination room. She was exhausted. The pain had kept her awake all night. She had called a taxi to bring her to the hospital for her check-up. She had been expecting the Polish boys to come and drive her. But there had been no sign of them. She had phoned their mobile. It was switched off. Now she knew why. She lifted her head towards the television and watched them being taken from the police station. They were handcuffed. They were being questioned, so the reporter said, in connection with the disappearance of Maria Grimes.

'Mrs Beauchamp. Come with me please.' The nurse gestured impatiently. An hour later she was back in her seat. They had X-rayed her arm. They had tried to ignore her requests for increased pain medication. They had treated her as they saw her. An old, ugly, helpless woman.

'Please,' she said, 'you've no idea how bad the pain is.'

The doctor had sighed and looked at her chart.

'OK. If it's really that bad, I'll give you this.' He held out something which looked like a large bandage or dressing. 'It's that patch I was telling you about. You can stick it onto your back or your upper shoulder. Just be careful. No alcohol with it. It contains morphine. It's very strong. OK?'

The taxi driver on the way home was full of talk about the Polish boys.

'They'd been doing some gardening for your woman, Maria what's-her-name. And it turns out they'd helped themselves to a few things. Stolen her credit card and a few other bits and pieces. Well, that's what they're saying. But the guards think it's a bit more than that. They think they

243

might have got the credit card from her some other way.'

'Oh? What do you mean by that? And how do you know all this?' Her tone was hostile, dismissive.

The taxi driver wasn't put off.

'My cousin is married to one of the cops. He told her they'd searched the lads' flat. They found a penknife. Took it away and found traces of blood on it. My cousin said it was definitely the same blood group as your woman. Doesn't look good for the lads.'

She said nothing. She remembered the knife. It had been cold and heavy in her hand.

'And they found all kinds of other stuff. Bits of jewellery, money, cards. They'd even taken some old fella's war medals. From one of the big houses in Castletownsend. He'd served in the British navy. Anyway, the Polish lads had helped themselves. But my cousin says the cops reckon they might have had your woman's stuff after they'd finished her off.'

She limped slowly from the car to the house. Maybe that explained it. She'd noticed there seemed to be some small pieces of silver missing from the house. But she'd put it down to her absent-mindedness. If she'd thought about it she could have told the guards when they came and searched Trawbawn earlier that morning. Liam O'Regan had asked her permission. They came in two vans. There must have been ten of them at least. She watched them from her bedroom window. They were wearing special white overalls. And they had a dog. A big, bright-eyed

Alsatian with a long, pink tongue that flopped over its black gums. She could see them pushing through the trees down by the river. They had asked if they could go into the sheds, the greenhouses, the garage, the boathouse. She had nodded and smiled. And offered to make them tea. Liam had refused the offer.

'You're grand,' he said. 'We've a lot of ground to cover, so we'd better keep at it.' He had seen how frail she looked. How suddenly vulnerable and helpless. How her back was hunched and when he looked down at her he could see the whiteness of her skull through her hair. He winced at the sight. Once he and some of his friends had sneaked into the garden during a hot summer years ago. They had gone down to the river. It was high tide. They were going to swim from the end of the little pier which jutted out into the water. But she had beaten them to it. She was sitting with her legs dangling over the edge. Her back was to them. She stood up and prepared to dive. She was naked. She turned towards them for an instant, then turned away. They held their breath. He could still see the curve of her spine, the creamy smoothness of her skin, feel the shock as he saw, for the first time ever, the springy thickness of a woman's pubic hair. She turned back towards the water and lifted her arms. He looked away. Her nakedness was too much for him. He looked away now as the memory made him redden.

He had asked her again about Adam. He had asked her what day it was that Adam had got her prescription filled. She couldn't quite remember at first. But then it came back to her.

'I told you,' she said. 'It was first day I came out of hospital. He came to see me. He was very kind. He stayed with me all that evening.'

'I'd like to talk to him. Do you have a phone number?'

She shook her head. She wasn't going to tell him. She didn't want him to know what Adam was doing.

He had gone then. They had all gone. There was no sign of them anywhere. She pushed open the kitchen door. She slumped down at the table. Just as the phone began to ring. She reached out and picked it up.

'Hello?' she said.

'Ah, Lydia. At last. I was beginning to think I was never going to make contact with you.'

'Adam, is that you? What a relief.' She could feel a smile beginning to lift the corners of her mouth. 'Where are you? What's happening? Have you found her? Have you found Grace?'

'Hold on, hold on. One thing at a time.'

She could hear the irritation in his voice. She took a deep breath and tried to calm herself. 'OK, Adam, sorry to bombard you with questions. But I've been waiting so long. Please tell me everything.'

She listened while he explained. How difficult it had been to find her. How he found the school, but it was closed for the summer holidays. He had asked around and eventually found someone who could tell him where Grace lived. How he had finally found her house. How he had waited, sitting in his car all night until the next morning

246

when Grace had appeared with her daughter. He had wanted to go straight up to her and introduce himself. Say to her, 'I've come from your mother.' But he had decided that wasn't such a good strategy. Especially not with the daughter there.

'After all, Lydia, who knows what kind of relationship she has with her child? It might be like the one that you have with her. And then think of all the problems I might create for both of them.'

'Yes, yes, of course you're right.' She felt humbled, ashamed.

'So, the situation is this. I know where she lives. And I think what's best is if I just find a time when her daughter isn't there, before I approach her. I think that's best, don't you?'

'Yes, yes, of course, of course, Adam. Whatever you think. It's up to you.' There was silence for a moment. There were so many questions Lydia wanted to ask him.

'Lydia? Are you still there?'

'Yes, yes, I'm here. I'm wondering, I'm wondering...'

'Yes?'

'I'm wondering, what is she like? What is her child like?'

'Your granddaughter, you mean?'

'Yes.' Her tone was surprised. 'My granddaughter.'

Adam could hear her intake of breath. He waited. He wondered what she was thinking. He knew what she was thinking.

'She's very pretty, your granddaughter. But she doesn't look like her mother. She must take after her father.'

She didn't reply.

'And your daughter. She doesn't look like you, does she?'

Again she didn't reply. He could see her sitting at the kitchen table. Shrunk and shrivelled. Thinking.

'Well, that's all for now, Lydia. I'll call you when I've something else to report. OK?'

He waited for her answer. He lay back on the bed in the apartment. The remote control in his hand. He flicked from channel to channel. And saw. A group of uniformed police were standing outside what looked like a police station. Two men were being led in. They were each hand-cuffed to a cop. He recognized them. They were the Polish boys from Trawbawn. He'd know them anywhere. He picked up the remote control and increased the volume.

'...arrested last night in connection with the dis-appearance of the missing woman Maria Grimes. They have been taken to Cork for further ques-tioning.'

He watched the shots of them being driven away.

'Fine, Adam, whatever.' Lydia's voice whispered in his ear. He didn't reply. He sat up straight. There were shots now on the screen of Baltimore, scenic views of the boats and the harbour and of Skibbereen. Then, suddenly, unexpectedly, shots of Trawbawn House. The gates, the gate lodge, the drive, the slated roof above the trees. Shots of police with dogs, searching the woodland, the waters of the pond, the margins of the river. He turned up the volume again.

'Gardai have been searching houses and land locally in their investigation into the disappearance of thirty-five-year-old mother of three, Maria Grimes. Trawbawn House, well known for its award-winning garden, is just one of the many estates the guards have visited.'

He thought back. He had taken the bed linen from the old bed in the lodge. He had used the sheet to wrap her in. He had taken the pillowcases to the launderette and washed them with his work clothes. They were still in the plastic bag with the rest of his clothes in the back of Lydia's car. He had swept the floor and washed the glasses they had used. He had collected any signs of the cocaine they had snorted. He had removed the bottle of vodka too. He tried to remember, to think back. The penknife he had used on her, what had he done with it? He was pretty certain he had wrapped it into the sheet with her. Of course, if they went through the gate lodge they would find hair from her head and from his. They would find her fingerprints. They would find his DNA. But what about the van? He had left it parked at the back of the house. He picked up the phone and called her again.

'Lydia,' he said, 'the van, is it still where I left it?'

There was a pause before she spoke.

'Your van?' She sounded drowsy.

'Yes, my van, is it OK?'

'Oh, well, actually, it's not. You see.' She paused again. 'I'm sorry, Adam, I couldn't stop them.'

'Stop who? What are you talking about?'

'Pat Jordan and some other man. They came and took the van away. Pat said he needed it. He left behind your stuff. The sleeping bag, your wet gear. But don't worry. I've put it all in your bag. It's in the cupboard under the stairs.'

He let go his breath. He disconnected the call. The last thing he needed was for the van to be found at Trawbawn. He turned to the television again. The scene had changed again. He watched as the men were hustled through a small crowd of onlookers and into the building.

The reporter's voice continued. 'The men, who are being named locally as Pavel Lankiewicz and Sebastian Piwonski, have already been held for six hours. Their arrest has been extended for a further six hours with the consent of the local Garda superintendent. At the end of this time they must either be charged or released. Maria Grimes has not been seen for the last three weeks. Garda sources confirm that they are increasingly worried about her safety. The arrest of these two men is the first breakthrough in the case.'

The picture dissolved into a photograph of Maria. She was smiling, her curly dark hair blowing around her face. His heart began to pound and his palms felt damp and slippery. He got up and felt in his pockets for his wallet. She had given him the same photograph. Taken it out of her bag and flung it on the bed.

'Here,' she had said, 'here's a trophy for you. Another scalp to be added to your collection.'

He tore it into pieces. Turned on a gas burner on the stove and set fire to them. Held them until the tips of his fingers began to burn, then dropped them into the sink. Waited until there was nothing left but ash, then flushed them down the drain. Picked up his wallet again. Went through its contents. Turned out all his pockets. Tried to think. Had she given him anything else? Did he have anything anywhere that might link him into her? Began to pace the floor. Backwards and forwards, forwards and backwards. Tried to remember. No, there was just the photograph. And her keys, of course. He still had her keys. They were in his bag. Along with her lipstick.

'Calm down,' he said out loud. 'Just calm down. Take it easy. If there was anything bad happening you'd have heard about it by now. You're fine, you're in the clear. And this evening you're going to go out hunting. That's what you're going to do.'

Lydia sat motionless at the kitchen table. There was an image that she couldn't shake from her memory. Grace, naked in the bathroom. She had forgotten to lock the door. Lydia had opened it. And seen her daughter. She was about to get into the bath. She was standing in profile. Lydia looked at her. Saw her body. Her breasts, normally small and undeveloped. Now heavy with the huge dark areolae around the nipples. The swell of her belly, pushing her navel out. The dark line that ran down her stomach and into her pubic hair. Saw everything that she had not seen through her clothes. Then remembered months later. The same bathroom, the same stance. Her daughter about to get into the steaming water. Turned towards her as she opened the door. Saw her thinness, her ribs clearly visible beneath her pale skin, the flatness of her breasts, shrunken now, and the hollowness of her stomach. The dark line gone and in its stead thin silvery marks across her hips and the tops of her thighs. Saw her daughter's face. The anger in the set of her jaw, the contempt, the hatred. Heard her voice.

'Get out,' she said. 'Just get out and leave me alone.'

And the baby. What of the baby? She had never thought about the baby. All she had thought was that Grace was not to suffer the consequences of its birth. The baby would be adopted. It would be as if it had never been born. Grace would understand in time that it was for her own good. She would not be burdened with an unwanted child. It would be better in the long run.

She remembered the phone call from the home for unmarried mothers where she had sent Grace. They had said that there had been an emergency. That Grace had suddenly gone into labour. That the birth had been very difficult. That Grace had lost a lot of blood. That she was ill and the baby was weak and sickly.

'It's a boy,' the matron had volunteered. Lydia had asked no questions about the child. She had asked only after Grace.

'She will be all right,' they told her. 'But she'll need to stay in hospital for a while and then she'll need rest. Don't worry,' they had said, 'we'll look after her.'

But the baby. Suddenly she couldn't understand. Why had she not asked after the baby? Why had she not been curious about the baby? She hadn't wanted to know a single thing about him. She had never asked what had happened to him. She had never enquired as to the kind of people who had adopted him. She couldn't even remember the date on which he was born.

She got up from the table. The pain was overwhelming now. But it wasn't just the pain in her wrist and arm. It was an agony that came from deep within. She wanted to moan and cry out. Beg for forgiveness, beg for understanding. But there was no one to hear her cries. She picked up the bottle of whiskey from the dresser and a glass from the draining board. She shuffled slowly from the kitchen, up the two small steps, along the corridor and into the drawing room. It was dark here, the sun still at the back of the house. She lay down on the sofa and poured a large measure into the glass. She took a deep swallow, gagging as the alcohol bit into the soft tissue at the back of her throat. She was so tired. She rested her head on a pillow and closed her eyes. Alex had gone to England to bring Grace back. She remembered that much. She didn't remember when or how. They had never spoken of what had happened. Grace had refused to go back to boarding school. She had decided instead she would go to the local secondary school. She had gone in and out on the bus every day with the local kids. She had worked hard. Spent hours in her room. Worked at the weekends and through the holidays. Given up sailing and riding. Any of the activities of her past life. She had sat the Leaving Certificate exams just after her seventeenth birthday. Gone away that summer to be an au pair in France. Barely written. A postcard every few weeks. Lydia remembered little of that time. It had been a struggle to keep the sailing school going once Colm O Laoire had left. The weather had been bad that summer. Constant gales and rain. By the time Grace's examination results arrived, Lydia knew they were in trouble. Alex had opened the letter from the Department of Education.

'She's got As in everything,' he said. 'Look.'

When Grace phoned, he spoke to her.

'What did she say?' Lydia asked.

'Not much. Just that she won't be coming home. She's going to go straight to London to register with the university. She just wanted to know how much we'll send her every month. She says she'll get a job, but she'll need something to tide her over. I told her it was no problem. We're proud of her.'

Did he say that? She couldn't remember his words. But it was something like that. He missed her. He moped about the place. Lydia could see the signs of his depression. She suggested a trip. They would go to the south of Spain for a few weeks. To get some sun. They would go through London. They would see Grace.

'You arrange it. You arrange a time and a place.'

And he did.

'She says she'll meet us in the National Gallery. She's working near there. It's convenient,' he said. But she didn't show up. They waited and waited, long past the appointed time.

'We'll have to go,' Lydia told him. 'We'll miss our flight. We'll phone her flat from the airport. There must be an explanation.'

But there wasn't one. A man answered their call.

'She's left,' he said. 'She's moved on.' He didn't know where she had gone. He didn't know her. He hung up on them. The cheques they continued to send were never cashed. Eventually they stopped sending them.

The whiskey was working now. She felt warm and sleepy. She closed her eyes. She could hear something outside. The mewl of a cat maybe, or a seagull. Or maybe it was the choking sob of a baby. It had been a boy. A tiny, premature infant. There had been a lapse of time of, what was it? She tried to remember. A week, a few weeks, a month, a few months, between the time when Grace gave birth and the time she came home. She must have been with her baby for that time. She must have held him, maybe fed him, cuddled him, talked to him, looked down into his opaque eyes and wished for him. What must the pain have been like when they took him away from her? Lydia reached for the bottle and poured some more into her glass.

There had been a time when she and Alex had been so happy here together. Sitting in the kitchen. Cooking, talking, making plans. Grace running in and out from the garden. Daniel upstairs in the drawing room, drinking his Scotch and soda, reading the paper, the evening sunshine falling across his liver-spotted hands as he fiddled with his pocket watch. The light gleaming on the old gold, and the gold and glass of the fob. The hourglass fob. Lying in the mud at the bottom of the river. Unreachable. Irredeemable. Gone forever.

Grace phoned Jack when she left the prison. He

255

was in his office in Trinity College.

'Come and have lunch with me,' he said, his voice warm and welcoming.

They sat in the old dining room. It was half empty now that term was over. It was dark and gloomy. Grace fiddled with her plate of salad. Jack was telling her about his plans for the summer holidays with Amelia. He was going to take her on a sailing holiday in Greece.

'Why don't you come too? You're a great sailor. It would be fun. You look as if you could do with a break. I don't know why you take on that extra teaching. I know you're friends with Tanya O'Brien and all that, but really, Grace, you owe it to yourself and to Amelia to back off and have a rest.' He leaned over and put his hand on her forearm. She shrugged it off. His face fell.

'Look, Jack, I didn't come here to talk about the holidays. I came to ask you what on earth you were doing in the house yesterday morning when I was out.' Her voice sounded unnaturally loud. It bounced off the bare floorboards.

'What?' His expression was incredulous. 'What on earth are you talking about? I wasn't anywhere near the house yesterday morning. I was here, in the library.'

'I'm sorry, Jack, I don't believe you. Someone was in the house. Someone let themselves in and moved a few things around. You're the only person apart from Amelia who has a key.'

'And what about your neighbours? The O'Malleys, didn't they have one? In case of emergencies?'

'You forget, Jack. Mr O'Malley died last year and Mrs O'Malley is in a nursing home. The house is in flats now.' She sipped from her glass of water. 'Look, I know the separation has been hard for you. I know that. But really, it's over. It's time you moved on.' She held out her hand. 'Please, give me back the keys. You've no need for them any longer.'

He pulled them from his jacket pocket and slammed them down on the wooden table.

'You're wrong, you know. It wasn't me.' He stood up. 'You've a nerve, Grace. Who do you think I am? Some kind of lovelorn teenager? Forget it.'

She watched him walk away. People greeted him as he threaded his way through the tables. He was popular, well liked. No one could understand why they had separated. All her friends had told her she was mad.

'He's a great guy, Grace. You're lucky to have him. He's a fantastic father. He's honest and reliable. You'll never find anyone like him again.'

But she didn't want to. She didn't want another relationship. It was easier on her own. She had plenty in her life. She had her work. She had Amelia. That was enough.

She stood up and followed him out into the bright sunshine. She didn't believe that he hadn't been in the house. He had been too defensive, too angry. She put the keys away in her bag. She'd have to change the locks. Just to be on the safe side. She walked down the wide stone steps into the cobbled square. She unlocked her bike and wheeled it through College Park. It was so lovely here, all this open space in the middle of the city. So different from the prison. All the women had turned up today. They'd read some of Anne Frank's diary and discussed it. Would Anne have written it differently if she'd known that millions of strangers would read it, she had asked. They had been intrigued by Anne's imprisonment. They had understood her.

'What happened to her in the end?' Lisa asked. Grace told them. How she had died of typhus in Bergen-Belsen. There was silence. Then tears.

She wheeled her bike through the university's back gate into Lincoln Place. She locked it to the railings and crossed the road towards the National Gallery.

She pushed through the heavy doors into the modern entrance. Inside, it was cool, the sunlight filtering down from the roof lights high above her head. On one side was the shop, on the other, the restaurant. She peered through the windows into the shop's darkened interior. There were posters and cards for sale. Paul Henry's landscapes, Jack Yeats's swimmers in the Liffey, Nathaniel Hone's conjuror. Paintings she had loved for as long as she could remember. Her own face gazed back at her. She looked suddenly old, her eyes hollowed, a shadow beneath her chin, making it seem heavy and slack. She lifted her hand to push back her hair and saw another face in the glass. It was a young man. Light-coloured hair falling forward over his face. He was standing behind her, just to her right. She felt as if he was looking over her shoulder. She turned quickly. He was close to her. He smiled. She noticed his eyes. One was a light greeny blue, the other was almost yellow with hazel flecks through it.

'Can you tell me?' he asked. 'The Caravaggio, *The Taking of Christ*, do you know where it is?'

She hesitated and looked around.

'I'm not sure. You need to find one of the guides. They'd be able to help you.'

'Oh, of course.' He smiled again. 'Of course, that's what I need. A guide. Silly of me. Sorry to bother you. Thanks.'

His accent was English. His manner was pleasant, polite. She watched him walk away, then lost sight of him as a busload of Japanese tourists pushed past her. She turned towards the restaurant. She was hungry suddenly. She queued at the counter for coffee and a chocolate muffin. Then she saw him again. He was waiting at the information desk. He turned towards her. His mobile phone was to his ear. His expression was uneasy. She suddenly felt annoyed with herself. She should have helped him. She shouldn't have fobbed him off like that. She knew perfectly well where to find the Caravaggio. She and Amelia had often come to the gallery to look at it. She put down her tray and she walked towards him.

'Hey, Colm, listen,' Adam whispered. 'I have good news for you, lots of good news.'

'Tell me. Tell me everything.' Colm lay back on his bed.

'I've been in her house. I've seen pictures of her daughter.'

'Oh?'

'Oh is right.'

'Tell me.'

'Very tasty. Small, cute, long hair. Bare belly. Stud in the tummy button.'

259

'Been in her house, you say?'

'Yes, I left her a little present in her bed.'

'A present?'

'Yeah. You know the kind of thing. Warm and wet.'

There was silence for a moment. Then Colm spoke again.

'Where are you now?'

'I'm in the National Gallery. Do you know it?'

'Been there once. School trip. Years ago.'

'Well, she's here. I've just spoken to her. I asked her for directions.'

'And?'

'And nothing. She was polite, that was all.'

'Polite?'

'Yeah, polite. You know the way. Hey, hold on a minute.'

'What?'

'I've just seen her again. She's walking towards me. Hang on, Colm.'

Grace held out her hand to him. She smiled.

'Hi,' she said. 'Sorry, listen, don't bother with the queue for the guides. I'll show you myself. If you'd like me to.'

He took the phone from his ear.

'Are you sure?' he said. 'That would be really nice of you. If it's no trouble.'

'No.' She shook her head. 'No, really, I'd be pleased to do it. If I'm not interrupting anything.'

'No, you're not. Just a minute.' He held up one hand and turned away from her. 'Got to go,' he said loudly. 'Talk to you later.'

He put the phone away in his pocket.

'Now,' he said. 'I'm all yours.'

She was really glad she'd made the effort. He was nice. He was on holiday in Dublin. A week or so, he said. She asked him where he was from. He told her. He lived in Falmouth.

'Oh, that's a lovely place.'

'You've been there?' He sounded surprised.

'Well, no, I haven't actually. But I've heard a lot about it. I'm from West Cork originally. And a lot of people there have friends in Falmouth. It's the sailing connection, you know?'

'Yeah, I know. Traditional boats, gaffers, all that kind of thing.'

'Mm, that's right.' She stopped in front of the painting. 'They've become really popular in the last few years.' She turned to face the Caravaggio. 'Now, what do you think of that?'

He didn't reply. He just stared at it.

'It's amazing really.' She stepped back from it. 'You know it was hanging for decades in a house that belonged to the Jesuits, and they had no idea what it was. My daughter loves it. It used to be hard to drag her away from the TV, but she's always ready to come here now and have a look at it.'

'You have a daughter?' He half-turned towards her. 'How old?'

'She's fifteen.'

'You're kidding. You don't look old enough to be the mother of a teenager.' He smiled at her. She laughed.

'You're the one who's kidding. I'm plenty old enough.'

'Well, you could have fooled me,' he said. He suddenly seemed awkward. There was silence for

261

a moment. She looked at her watch.

'I'd better go. I've a few things to do.' She fiddled with her bag. 'I hope you enjoy the rest of your time here.'

'Yeah, I'm sure I will.' They turned away from the painting and his arm brushed against her.

'Sorry,' he said. 'Sorry.'

'No, don't you be sorry.' Her face had reddened. 'Take care, won't you?' She moved quickly towards the door. He pulled his phone from his pocket. He pushed the redial button.

'Colm,' he said. 'What do you want me to do to her?'

Later, a gentle breeze stirred the branches of the silver birches which clustered against the back wall of Grace's garden. It stirred the lock of hair that hung down over Adam's forehead. He shivered. He looked up at the sky. It was cloudy tonight, the half-moon partially obscured. He stood in the lane behind the house. He pulled himself up onto the wall and slipped down into the garden. He waited. For the sudden glare of a security light. But there was none. He eased himself out of the protection of the trees and moved slowly down the lawn towards the house. Lights were on throughout. The kitchen was brightly lit. The table left with the remains of dinner. Pots and pans stacked in the sink. Beside it, in the sitting room, he could see the coloured flicker of the television set. A lamp cast a golden glow over a sofa which was at right angles to his view. Grace was lying down, her head on a cushion. As he watched, she stood up and stretched. Her shirt lifted and he saw a pale strip of skin. She bent down and switched off the TV. He watched her walk into the kitchen. She poured herself a glass of water. She moved towards the stairs. The lights went off. He watched her progress up through the house. She switched off the lights as she passed each room. She stood at her bedroom window, looking down. Then she pulled the curtains together. And she was gone. He began to walk back across the lawn. He slipped through the trees.

Scrambled over the wall and dropped down into the lane on the other side. The clouds parted and moonlight poured down over him. He waited for a moment, then he turned and walked away.

TWENTY-TWO

There had been congratulations all round about the arrest of the Polish lads, but Liam O'Regan wasn't convinced. The tiny traces of blood found on the penknife matched Maria Grimes's blood group. When the guards searched the boys' flat, they had found some items of jewellery which Maria's husband had identified. And her credit cards had been used. The boys had admitted the theft, and that they had sold on the cards. But they had categorically denied that they had anything to do with Maria's disappearance.

And Liam was inclined to believe them. But the Super wanted a result. It was summertime. Tourist time. It was a bit like the film *Jaws*, Liam thought. The mayor had pressured the police chief to keep the beaches open so the summer season wouldn't be ruined. But the result was more free dinners for the great white shark. The Super wanted the pictures on the TV news. The two foreigners in handcuffs, the leaked stories to the press about the penknife and the credit cards. He had wanted to remand them in custody, but there was no point. The Director of Public Prosecutions would have to make a decision about whether to charge them or not and in the meantime they'd be out on bail. Their passports would be confiscated and they'd have to sign on in the Garda station every day. And Liam would go on looking.

He sat down at his desk and went through the list of everyone they'd questioned. He looked back at the statements taken from the women with whom Maria had been drinking the last day she'd been seen. They'd all said the same thing about her. She'd been in great form at lunchtime. Then sometime round mid-afternoon, when they'd been in O'Brien's bar in town, she'd said she wasn't feeling well. They'd tried to jolly her along, but she had said she had a headache and she was going home.

'No one went with her, no?'

'No, we all offered. But we'd all been drinking, so none of us were driving. I would have got a taxi for her, but she just got up, said she'd find her own way back to the cottage. And off she went. Isn't that right, Dee?' Trish, the small blonde with the Dublin accent, appealed to her friend.

'Yeah, that's right. Anyway, you know the way it

264

is. We were all doing nicely. Having great crack. And, anyway, that was Maria all over. Changeable, you know? One minute she'd be the life and soul of the party and the next, she'd be well, sort of sulky. Aren't I right, girls?'

Four heads nodded.

'And are you sure she wasn't seeing anyone?'

'You mean a fella?' The woman called Dee giggled.

Liam looked at her, then down at his sheet of paper.

'Well, she never said anything, but to be honest she wouldn't have talked about it. Not if she had any sense. If Brian had got a sniff of it, you'd be locking him up.'

'He's the jealous type, is he?'

'Jealous? Jesus, you've no idea.'

Liam went back to the questionnaires. God how much he hated all this boring, slow, detailed work. It had been a busy Friday. Height of the summer. God knows how many tourists and visitors from all over the world and from all over Ireland had been crammed into the town that afternoon. No one had seen Maria after she had left the pub. No one had seen anything. He had made a note of all the places she had gone regularly. There were a number of pubs and restaurants where she and her husband were well known. There was Field's supermarket, where she did her shopping. And she had been a regular visitor to the boatyard too. Her husband kept his small boat there during the winter, and she'd organized getting it back into the water for the summer holidays. There were always people hanging around. Guys with an interest in boats. Fishermen from the trawlers that tied up at the pier. Casual labourers working on a daily rate. Pat Jordan had been very organized and given him a list of them all. Liam ran his eye down it. He knew most of them by sight. Some he knew even better. He had gone to school with them. There was one name that he couldn't put a face to. It was the English guy, Adam Smyth. The same guy who had got Mrs Beauchamp's prescription filled. They hadn't managed to talk to him yet. Everyone said he'd gone to Dublin. But he might be back. Liam supposed he should give him another try. He pulled out his phone and punched in Pat's number. He left him a message.

'Hey, Pat, Liam here. Any word about your man, Adam whatever? Seen him around at all? Give us a call when you get this, if you wouldn't mind.'

Meantime he'd go back and talk to Brian Grimes again. He still reckoned the husband was their prime suspect. He'd heard he'd been out and about. Socializing around town. Not behaving like a grieving husband. Maybe it was time to give him a bit of a fright.

Grace was late. She had overslept. It wasn't like her. Usually she woke early and dozed until it was time to get up. But she had slept so badly last night. She had woken at two, then at three and it had been getting light when she at last closed her eyes. And then she had dreamed. About the baby. And when she opened her eyes and saw the clock she couldn't believe that it was 9.30 already.

No time for breakfast. Just a quick cup of tea

and a shower. It was drizzling when she left the house. The first rain for weeks. She had to go back inside and look for her rain gear. And when she came out, pulling on her coat, she saw that her front tyre was flat.

'Shit.' She swore out loud and looked at her watch. There was no point taking the car. The cross-town traffic was chaotic. She'd be better off on the bus.

She began to walk quickly away from the house and turned left for the main road and the bus stop. And bumped into a man who had stopped suddenly in front of her.

'Hey, watch it,' she shouted.

'Sorry, sorry.' He turned to look at her. He smiled. He held out his hand.

'Oh, it's you.' She could feel herself redden.

'Yeah, and you. Sorry for stopping like that. It's just, I think I'm lost. I'm looking for the canal. Is it near here?'

'Yes, it is. You're nearly there.' She turned and pointed. 'Turn left here and go straight along Mount Pleasant Avenue. The canal is just at the end. You can't miss it.' She paused and pushed her hair back out of her face. 'Can I ask you? What on earth do you want with the canal?'

He smiled again.

'Well, I have this map.' He took it out of his pocket. 'And it has all these references to poets and writers, and apparently there's a bench dedicated to one of them on the bank somewhere.'

'Yes, of course, Patrick Kavanagh. Well, when you get to the canal, just turn right and keep walking. It's a couple of bridges down, but you can't miss it.'

'Thanks. Someone should be paying you for all this. You're the best guide in town.'

She smiled and made a little curtsey.

'You're too kind. Look, I have to go, I'm sorry. I'm late for work. But if you're passing again, I actually live on Mount Pleasant Avenue. Number 120. I'm usually home in the late afternoon. Call in. Do.'

'Thanks, that's very kind of you.' He smiled again. 'By the way, my name is Adam.'

'Adam, well, hello, Adam. I'm Grace.' She suddenly felt light-hearted, happy.

'Well, hello, Grace,' he replied and inclined his head. Then he paused and looked away for a moment, then looked back at her. 'But I wouldn't want to impose on you and your daughter,' he said.

'Oh, you wouldn't be. My daughter's away. She's gone to Irish college in County Galway. It's kind of obligatory for kids of her age. She hates it. But it's good for her.' She turned to leave. 'Look, I have to go, I really am late now.' She began to walk backwards away from him. 'But if you're passing, drop in. OK?'

He watched her for a few moments. Then he began to walk quickly in the direction of her house. He stopped outside it and looked around. The street was empty. He pushed open the front gate. He unlocked the door and let himself in. He was sweating. He'd been lucky. A few minutes earlier and he'd have walked right in on her. And then he would have had to act. Too soon, far too soon.

He was hungry now. Breakfast first, he thought. He opened the fridge and took out some rashers of bacon and two eggs. He put them in the pan and began to fry them. He found bread and made toast, made coffee in a glass jug. Sat at the kitchen table and looked out at the garden as he ate. This was a nice house. Worth a lot of money, he reckoned. He finished his meal and washed up the dishes.

He walked into the small sitting room next door and lay down on the sofa. He picked up the remote control and turned on the television. And felt from beneath the cushion the vibration of a mobile phone. He pulled it out. A text message had been received. He opened it and read it out aloud.

'HATE THIS PLACE. WANT TO COME HOME. PLEASE PLEASE PLEASE XXXX'

He opened up the message-in box and read through all the recent texts. They were all from Amelia. She was not a happy bunny. She was complaining about everything. The food, the other kids, the teachers. He opened up the latest message again and pressed the reply button. Now, what would he say? Would he be tough or tender? His father would have told him to get a grip, be a man. His mother would have told him to come home. He began to spell out his message.

POOR YOU. DON'T WORRY, I'M THINKING OF YOU ALL THE TIME XXX

He pressed the send button. He leaned back on the sofa and smiled. Well, it was true. He was thinking about her all the time. He stood up. He felt dirty. He walked upstairs and into the bathroom. Grace had left wet towels on the floor. He stepped over them and leaned into the bath. He fitted the plug and turned on the taps. He stripped off his clothes and sank into the steaming water. He leaned back and covered his face with her face cloth. This was good. This was nice.

The women were all in the classroom when she arrived. There was a strange air of excitement in the room. They were talking loudly, interrupting each other, laughing hysterically.

'What's up?' she asked as she dumped her bag on the floor and sat down.

'You're late, that's what's up.' Marcia's face was sullen and hostile.

'Yeah, sorry. Slept in.' She looked from face to face. 'But I'm here now. So what's wrong?'

No one spoke. Then Lyuba broke the silence.

'We have a death last night. One of our girls.'

'Who? What happened?'

'She kill herself. Her name is Rosa. She is from Brazil.'

Lisa was crying. Honey put her arms around her and hugged her.

'She hung herself with her bed sheet. She tore it into strips with her nail scissors and she hung herself from the door. Lisa found her. They took her to the Mater hospital, but she was dead on arrival.' Honey's voice was high-pitched.

Grace said nothing.

'She got a letter from her husband. He told her he was divorcing her and getting married to another woman. The bastard.' Marcia was shouting now.

'I'm sorry. I can understand how you all must feel.' Grace held out her hand, but Marcia just pushed her away.

'No you fucking can't. You spoiled fucking bitch. You come in here with your books and your platitudes and your "Let's write our little stories and then we'll feel better" shit. You know fuck all about fuck all.' She stood up. She towered above Grace. Grace could smell her sweat, see the slick of moisture on her face. She sat very still. She said nothing.

'Marcie, girl, cool it.' Honey's voice was gentle. 'Just cool it, babe. It ain't Grace's fault. It ain't nothin' to do with her. Sit down here beside me and maybe we'll just have a cup of coffee and a cigarette and take it nice and easy.'

Adam opened his eyes. He must have dozed off. The water was cool now. His hands were white and ridged. He pulled himself upright and stepped out onto the mat. He took the towelling bathrobe from the back of the door. He slipped his arms into it and tied the cord around his waist. He opened the bathroom cabinet. He ran her brush through his hair. He hunted through her make-up. Mascara was nice. He stroked his eyelashes with it. They looked really good. There was one lipstick he fancied. He unscrewed the barrel. It was the colour of an old French rose. The kind his gran used to grow. There was one that was her favourite. Zephirine Drouhin it was called. He remembered because he always had difficulty saying the name. He carefully outlined his lips, then filled them in. He smacked his lips together. Just the way gran always did it. He stood back and looked at himself. He picked up her phone. Pity it wasn't the kind that could send pictures. Colm would like to see him like this. There was another message. He opened it up.

THANKS MUM, LOVE YOU TOO XXX

Aah, so sweet. He walked upstairs to Amelia's room and lay on her bed. He reached under her pillow. His fingers felt the cover of a notebook. He pulled it out. 'Dear Diary' was written in gold italics across the cover. He flicked open the pages. Nothing like a little bit of light reading to pass the time. He was sure he would enjoy this. This was good. This was fun. This could only get better.

More tears and more anger. Eventually the women became quiet. They sat in silence in a circle.

'OK,' Grace asked, 'anyone anything to read?'

Honey pulled a wad of paper from her pocket.

'I guess it's my turn,' she said.

'Go ahead.' Grace nodded and leaned back in her chair.

'I was born in Trinidad but I lived most my life in New Orleans. People say it's a beautiful city and it is. But not for me. Not any longer. You know, I'm a sucker for men. I loved my daddy very much and he went away and left me when I was just a little girl. I think I've always been looking for him ever since. I got pregnant when I was a teenager. I gave my baby away. She went to a good home with some good people. I knew it was the right thing to do but it broke my heart. I tried to forget all about her but it was always there at the back of my mind. Anyway, I got a few jobs here and there. Then I was offered a job in a club. I thought it would be something good, like a cashier or a manager. But it turned out to be doing what I do best. Dancing and stripping. Still, the money was OK and I didn't mind the guys too much. And then I met Vince. He was cool. Very handsome, very rich, very smooth. Smooth as silk. He had a beautiful apartment in the French Quarter. Wooden floors, high ceilings, antique furniture. A patio and a pool with a sauna built in the old slave quarters. He used to have amazing parties around the pool. The coolest people in town came to Vince's parties. And I was one of them. I told my momma and she said, "Be careful, girl, be careful who you wind up swimming with. Watch Out for the sharks and the barracudas." But I told her this was different. Vince was different. And for a while he was. He was real sympathetic. He told me he loved me. I told him about my baby girl and he said he could find out where she was, that he had contacts and maybe I could get to see her and maybe he'd help me get her back. We could be a family together. And then he said he needed me to do something for him. That he had business contacts in Amsterdam and would I go there and pick up some documents. I said why didn't he use a courier company, but he said it was real important and he needed someone he could trust. So I went. And it was cool. I stayed in a cute little hotel right by a canal and I picked up letters and parcels and a couple of times a bag, and I brought them back with me. Then he asked me to do it again and he said this time I would have to stop off in Ireland for a couple of days. I was real excited. I thought, wow, the emerald isle and all that shit. So I got on a plane to Shannon. I didn't know where Shannon was. But that didn't matter. And I remember when we were coming in to land I looked down and everything was so green and so pretty. All these little white houses and the river. When I got off the plane I picked up my bag and I was walking through customs and suddenly I was stopped. They searched me. They searched my bag. They told me there was cocaine in my suitcase. I laughed at them. I said they were crazy. But they showed me where it was hidden. They told me if I gave them the names of the people I worked for they would let me off lightly. But I wouldn't talk. So they charged me, sent me to Limerick gaol. Then I went to trial and I got fifteen years. I tried to make contact with Vince, but I never heard from him again. My mom came over to see me. I asked her to find him. She told me she went to the house and it was sold and he was gone. You know what hurts most is that I believed him when he said he'd find my baby for me. I believed him when he said he'd help me get to see her. I believed him when he said he'd help me get her back. I believed it all. As the song says, I was a fool for love. Now all I can hope is that one day my little girl will have grown up and she will come looking for me. And I will be out of here. And I will have a home of my own and a job and something that I can offer her.'

Adam stretched and yawned. He liked it here. He

rolled over on his side. The phone beeped. Another message from Amelia.

I WANT TO COME HOME. I HATE IT HERE. PLEASE PLEASE PLEASE.

He pressed reply.

OK, COME HOME TODAY, he wrote and pressed send. The response was immediate.

DAD WILL BE MAD WITH ME.

He pressed reply.

WE WON'T TELL HIM, he wrote and pressed send again. Again the response.

YIPPEE. LOVE YOU MUM. SEE YOU THIS EVENING.

He sat up. So now he'd have the two of them here in this house. Just what Colm wanted. He swung his legs off the bed and stood. He walked downstairs and into the bathroom. He wiped off the lipstick and hung the robe on the hook on the door. He got dressed and walked down into the kitchen again. He put Grace's phone in his pocket. Then he moved to the front door and opened it. He looked outside. There was no one around. He locked the door behind him. He'd be back later on. Back to finish what he'd started.

Grace walked slowly away from the prison. She felt weak and ill. Honey's words replayed themselves in her head. She walked slowly through the city towards home. All she could think about was the baby, her baby, the baby she had given away. He would be twenty-eight now, she thought. He would be an adult. Would she know him if she saw him? Who would he look like? She scanned the faces of the young men that passed her by. She couldn't bear to think that she would not recognize him. Surely she would know who he was. Surely it would be obvious to her. She stood on the island in the middle of O'Connell Bridge. The lights changed from green to orange to red. But she couldn't move. Which way should she turn? There were so many young men of her son's age all around her. Which should she follow? She felt dizzy and sick. Her stomach heaved and she felt bile in her mouth. There was a pain in her head. She closed her eyes. She sank down in a squat, reaching out to the filthy pavement for support. People were staring at her, pointing at her. A policeman in a high-visibility jacket came towards her. She looked up at him. His young face was friendly. He reached down and took her arm.

'Are you all right, love?' he said and helped her up to standing. 'Are you not feeling well? Would you like me to call an ambulance?'

She tried to shake her head but the pain was too powerful. It held her tightly in its grip.

'No, I'm fine. I just felt a bit faint,' she said and pulled herself free. She picked up her bag. 'I'm OK, really I am.'

She turned towards the road. The traffic had stopped. She took a deep breath and stepped off the pavement. She'd be home in ten minutes. Home was where she needed to be. Home was safe. Home was secure. She'd be fine once she got home.

TWENTY-THREE

The phone was ringing. The noise was loud in her ears. Grace stirred, twisted around, opened her eyes. She tried to sit up, but her legs felt weak and her body uncoordinated. She lay still. The phone had stopped ringing. She pushed herself to sitting. Her mouth was dry and her eyes were gritty.

She stood up and walked into the kitchen. She filled a glass with cold water and drank it all down. It was getting dark. The birch trees at the end of the garden were casting their long shadows across the grass. Like the monkey puzzle tree in Trawbawn, she thought. She turned away from the glass doors. As the phone began to ring again. This time she got to it before it stopped.

'Hello?' Her voice was still husky with sleep.

'Mum, where have you been? I've been ringing you all evening. I wanted you to come and pick me up.'

'Amelia, is that you?'

'Of course it's me. Who else would it be? What's going on with you? You tell me to come home and then you're not here at the station. Didn't you get the text I sent you?'

Grace sat down. She felt so sleepy still. She had come home, taken some painkillers for the migraine, then collapsed and slept. She had dreamt. About the baby again and also about Trawbawn and her mother. It had all been so

277

clear and vivid. She still felt as if she were there.

'Mum, are you listening to me? I'm starving and I've so much stuff. How am I going to get home?' Amelia's voice cut through her lethargy.

'Just a minute, love. Where did you say you were?'

A taxi brought Amelia home. Grace stood in the doorway and watched her daughter unload her bags. Amelia walked past her into the house. She dumped them all in the hall and turned away.

'Hold on.' Grace's voice was sharp. 'Hold it right there, missy. Perhaps you'd like to explain to me exactly what has been going on.'

They sat in an angry silence at the table. Amelia fiddled with her phone and Grace with her fork. She refilled her glass with wine and sipped from it.

'You shouldn't be drinking if you've had one of your headaches. You know that.' Amelia glared at her.

Grace ignored the reproach and drank some more. She looked past Amelia towards the garden. The dark outside threw back their reflection. Mother and daughter sitting opposite each other. The kitchen, bright and welcoming. Silver and glasses shining.

'OK, start again. You sent me a text saying you were unhappy and wanted to come home. And I replied telling you it was OK. Do you really expect me to believe that?'

'I don't give a fuck what you believe. It's the truth.' Amelia pushed away her plate. 'You know I didn't want to go to that stupid place. My Irish is perfectly good. It's better than most of the other girls there. In fact, if you must know, it's better than most of the so-called teachers. And as for it being a Gaeltacht. That's a joke. No one speaks Irish there any longer. It's just a scam to get those extra government grants. The kids are all watching MTV and the soaps, just like the kids everywhere else in the country.' She stood up.

'Where do you think you're going?' Grace raised her voice. 'If you think you're going out, you can think again. You're not leaving this house until you tell me the truth.'

'It is the truth. I hate you. You're a fucking bitch. You don't care about me. All you care about are people like those women in prison, or the kids who go to your school. They qualify for your love and attention because they're all helpless and pathetic. Just because I'm not, you don't give a damn.' Amelia was screaming at her now, her small heart-shaped face white with fury. 'I've had it with you, Mum. I don't want to live here any longer. I've rung Daddy. He's coming to pick me up.'

She turned away. Grace listened to her footsteps, light and quick as she rushed up the stairs to her bedroom. Another tantrum. Amelia's way of dealing with frustration. Ever since she was a small child it had been like this. She couldn't bear to be challenged or controlled. But she had gone too far this time. She had lied.

Grace stood up and opened the French windows. It was still warm outside. She stepped out onto the terrace. The smell of night-scented stock filled the air. She sat down on the low stone wall. It had been like this in Trawbawn too. Summer evenings in the twilight, the scent of the night flowers, the stars and the moon flooding the gardens with light. The distant sound of the river and the sea. It should have been perfection. But it wasn't. She stood up and began to walk through the garden. She turned around and looked back at the house. The lights were on throughout. Trawbawn had always been lit up at night. Daniel didn't like the dark. Not the inside dark, he'd say. Inside dark was dangerous and threatening. You never knew what was hiding in the corners, he'd say. But he liked the outside dark. Outside dark was velvety and beautiful. Outside dark was silent footsteps across the grass and the feeling of the breeze on your face. And the smell of the mud in the river, and the sudden cry of a gull on its way to its nighttime roost. She suddenly missed it all so much. She missed Daniel and the way it once had been. She remembered his funeral. Everyone had come. They had crammed into the small Church of Ireland church. They had sung his favourite hymn, 'Oh hear us when we cry to thee, for those in peril on the sea'. And they had stood around his open grave while his coffin was lowered in. And all the men of the Trawbawn townland had helped fill the grave with dark earth. Afterwards the house had seemed so empty. She had walked from room to room, looking at all the beautiful furniture and paintings. Half-expecting Daniel to appear. To say to her, 'Now, Grace, I want you to look at this chair, or this rug, or this picture.' As he explained to her its origins, its provenance, how it was that it came all the way from Istanbul, or Peking, or Naples, all the way to Trawbawn.

She turned back to the house again. And saw Amelia on the stairs. And Jack with her. This was all she needed. He always took Amelia's side. Now he waved and beckoned to her to come inside. She took a deep breath and straightened her shoulders. Best get it all over with.

Adam sat on the back wall. He could see Grace in the garden. He looked past her to the house. No worries about the electricity bill, he thought. A pity, really, a pity they didn't turn some of the lights off. It would be easier for him if it was darker. Not too dark. But dark enough so he could slip from shadow to shadow. He eased himself down into the shrubbery. She was walking away from him. And now he saw why. The doors to the kitchen had opened. A man was standing there. And beside him the girl, Amelia. He had his arm around her. She was hiding her face against his shoulder. This must be Dad, Adam thought. The dad who would be mad with her. He stopped and crouched down. He waited. He watched Grace walk inside the house. She closed the doors behind her. He moved closer. It was hard to tell what was going on. A lot of shouting, he reckoned. Then tears. Hugs, kisses. He stood and walked out onto the lawn. He looked up at the sky, but the moon was safely hidden behind the clouds. They were sitting down now at the table. Grace was filling glasses with wine. The man stood and opened the fridge. He was bringing out food. A large tub of ice cream. Amelia was handing around bowls. She was very pretty. She reminded him of Lydia. He had a sudden over-

281

whelming desire to burst in. He wanted to take hold of her and hurt her. His heart was pounding and he felt dizzy. He watched them. They were moving into the sitting room next to the kitchen. They looked comfortable and happy. Playing happy fucking families. He moved back and away. He scrambled over the wall and dropped down into the lane. He walked around to the road and got into his car. Not far from here to the parts of the city where he would find a woman. Not far from here to find someone who would do everything he wanted. He drove slowly. There were crowds of girls around the canal. He scrutinized them as he passed them by. He saw the one he wanted. She was small and cute. She looked like Amelia. He leaned over and rolled down his window. He jerked his head at her. She flung her cigarette on the ground. She opened the door and sat in beside him.

'How are you?' he said.

'Grand, couldn't be better,' she replied. She smelt of smoke and alcohol.

'Let's go somewhere quiet,' he said and put the car in gear. He reached into the side pocket and pulled out a bottle of vodka. He handed it to her. She unscrewed the cap.

'*Slainte,*' she said and giggled.

'Your health,' he responded automatically.

He drove out along the coast. She sat quietly beside him. Her eyes were closed. She breathed slowly. She was fast asleep by the time he found the place he wanted. He dragged her from the car and laid her on the ground. He put his hands around her throat and squeezed tightly. She didn't move. He put his finger on her neck. There was no pulse. He stripped her clothes from her small body. He picked up her bag and rummaged inside it. His fingers slipped over the smooth barrel of her lipstick. He unscrewed it and smeared the dark purple over his mouth. Then he lay down on top of her. She wasn't as pretty as Amelia. But she would do. She would do for now.

It was late when Jack left. Amelia had fallen asleep on the sofa beside him. Grace sat in the armchair and watched them. Amelia's head was on his lap and she was holding his hand. He stroked her hair and every now and then he would lean down and kiss the top of her head.

'What do you think, Jack? Do you believe her?' Grace asked quietly.

He turned to look at her.

'Well, someone sent her those texts. You saw them for yourself. They came from your phone. You said yourself you'd lost it. Whatever you say about Amelia, and I know she can be headstrong and selfish, she's not a liar. And she's not devious. It's impossible to believe that she would set up something as elaborate as stealing your phone and sending the messages herself just to be able to come home. It seems to me, Grace, that someone's been playing some kind of a practical joke. Anyway, she's probably right about the Gaeltacht and all that. She can come and do some work for me for the next couple of weeks until term starts. I could do with a hand with my research project. There's a lot of routine office stuff involved and you know what the university is like. It's all cutbacks. There's practically no secretarial staff any longer.'

'Well, I don't know. I just can't remember when I had my phone last.' She sighed. 'If you're sure, about the job and all that. I just worry about her getting her own way all the time.' She shifted in her seat and uncurled her legs.

Jack looked at her and smiled.

'You're a puritan aren't you, Grace? Where does that come from, I wonder?'

He carried Amelia up to her room and together they tucked her into bed. Then they walked downstairs. He paused as they passed Grace's bedroom.

'This is a lovely house,' he said. 'My memories of living here are all happy.' He reached out and touched her face. 'You look tired. You need a break before your term starts. Why don't you go to the sun for a couple of weeks? I'll look after madam upstairs.'

She smiled.

'Maybe, we'll see. When I finish in the prison. Maybe.'

Sometime in the night Grace heard Amelia cry out. She sat up and listened. She heard the sound of her bare feet on the stairs and the squeak as she pushed open the door.

'Are you all right, love?' Grace reached out for her. Amelia snuggled in beside her.

'Yes, Mummy,' she said. Grace heard the sound of Amelia's thumb slipping into her mouth.

'It's all right, sweetheart,' Grace whispered. 'It's all right. Mummy's here.'

She pulled her close and breathed in the sweet smell of her daughter's hair.

It was morning when she woke again. She lay on her side, savouring the remains of sleep. She could hear the radio was on downstairs. Loud music drifted up to her. She rolled over and closed her eyes again. She hoped Amelia was making tea. And then she heard the sudden shrillness of the doorbell. She turned onto her back and opened her eyes. Who on earth could it be on a Saturday morning?

'Mum.' She heard Amelia call up to her.

'What is it?'

'It's some bloke. He says his name is Adam. He says you told him to call in.' Amelia's head appeared around the door.

'Oh God, Adam. That's right. Tell him I'll be down in a minute. Make him some coffee or something, will you? And be nice to him, love.'

'Sure thing.' Amelia giggled. 'He's kind of cute, isn't he?'

Grace watched them from the landing window. They were on the terrace. Amelia was showing off. Grace could see it in the way she was moving. The sun shone down on Adam's pale blond hair. He stretched, one arm up straight, the other bent around his head, his hand taking hold just above his elbow. He reminded her so much of someone. She couldn't quite put her finger on it. Someone from years ago. It was his stance, his posture, his long fingers and his thumbs with the prominent joint where they met the palm. It was the fine stubble on his chin, that gleamed golden in the

285

light. And the pale skin of his chest that showed where his shirt was unbuttoned. It was his narrow hips and his way of standing with his legs crossed at the knees and one hand at the back of his neck. It was everything about him.

He turned around towards the house and he saw her. He waved and smiled. And she suddenly saw him, as if for the first time. Saw him for who he was. Knew who he must be. She began to cry. She covered her face with her hands and turned away. He was standing looking up at her. He must have been waiting for the opportunity to tell her. She hurried into the bathroom and washed her face. She opened the cabinet and found some make-up. It wouldn't do to frighten him off. She must be looking her best. She walked downstairs and out into the garden.

'Adam,' she said, 'how lovely to see you. I'm so glad you've come. You've met my daughter, Amelia, haven't you?'

He nodded.

'Yes, she's been very sweet. She's made me tea.'

'Good. I'm so glad.' She put her hand on his shoulder. She could feel the bones beneath the soft cotton of his shirt.

'Listen, Adam,' she said, 'you were talking about Kavanagh and the canal seat when I met you the other day. Did you find it?'

He looked surprised and suddenly uneasy.

'No, actually I didn't.'

'Well, why don't I take you to see it? It's a lovely day for a walk by the canal.'

'Great,' Amelia joined in. 'We could go for brunch somewhere on the way back.'

'No, love. I want to talk to Adam by myself. We'll all do something together later maybe.' Grace's tone was firm.

'That's not fair.' Amelia screwed up her face in an exaggerated frown.

'We won't be long.' Grace picked up her bag. 'And anyway, aren't you supposed to be talking to your dad about that work he wants you to do. You said you'd call him today.'

'Oh, all right.' Amelia's sigh was long and drawn out. 'If you insist.'

They walked along the canal bank. The water gleamed like burnished metal in the summer sun. Two swans swam slowly by. They stopped and entwined their long white necks in a perfect heart shape. Grace's mouth was dry. Sweat prickled on her forehead and between her breasts. She wasn't sure she would be able to find the words to say to him. He was humming a tune. It was familiar. She could heard the words running through her memory.

Whenever I feel afraid,
I hold my head erect,
And whistle a happy tune,
So no one will suspect,
I'm afraid.

She turned to him.

'Adam,' she said. 'It's OK. I know all about you. I know who you are.'

'What?' He looked shocked and apprehensive. He stopped. He gazed around him, as if he was looking for a way to escape her.

'Yes,' she continued. She put out her hand as if to hold on to him. 'I've figured it out. I couldn't understand why I kept on bumping into you over the past few days. But it's because of who you are, and who I am and all that happened in the past, isn't it? All that we share from that time. That's what's brought us together now. That's it, isn't it?'

He turned away from her. She put out her other hand and touched his face. She took hold of his chin and tried to turn him towards her. He remembered the way her mother had done the same thing, that afternoon in the kitchen in Trawbawn. He wanted to jerk away from her, as he had jerked away from Lydia.

'Sorry, I'm sorry, I shouldn't do that.' She let go of him. 'Forgive me, Adam, please forgive me. And look at me now, and tell me what you see.'

He slowly lifted his eyes to her face. Her expression was joyful, almost ecstatic.

'I've been waiting so long for you to come,' she said. 'You've no idea what it's been like for all these years. But I knew you would come. I knew you would want to find me. I couldn't find you, no matter how much I wanted to. It had to be your decision. You had to find it in your heart to forgive me for what I had done. And now you must have, because now you're here.'

Adam stared at her for a moment, then turned away and looked down at the water. Grace felt as if her heart would burst from her breast. She wanted to grab hold of him and draw him close to her. Stare into his eyes and see what lay beneath. But he wouldn't look at her. His gaze was downcast. And for a moment she doubted what she had done. She had made a bad mistake. She should never have said anything to him. She should have waited for him to speak.

And then he took a deep breath and turned back to her. He smiled and put his arm around her. She began to cry. Tears streamed down her face.

'Don't cry,' he said. 'Don't cry.' And he pulled her close and rested his head on her shoulder.

TWENTY-FOUR

'Say that to me again, slowly.'

'In words of one syllable?'

'If that will make it clear.'

'OK, here goes. Grace thinks I am her son. How's that?'

There was silence.

'Colm, did you hear what I said?'

Silence, then a long, slow sigh.

'I heard what you said. It's better than I ever imagined. Oh, there is a god and he is good.'

'So what will I do now?'

'Be her son. Be nice to her. Give her all the love and affection a son could have for a mother he's never met before.'

'Love and affection? Closeness? Intimacy?'

'Yeah, that's it. Intimacy. I think that's the word for it.'

'And what about my sister, the sweet little Amelia?'

'Ah, there's a thought.'

'Yes, there's a thought. But you're going to have to help me, Colm. I'm having dinner with her tonight. Some restaurant in Dun Laoghaire. I need to know a few details. For example, tell me, how did I find her? What do I know about her? All that stuff. Otherwise I'll blow it. And it's too good an opportunity to miss, isn't it?'

'Too good an opportunity. You've no idea where this could get you.'

'So come on, Colm. Talk to me. Tell me all that stuff you told me before. About the baby clothes and the place she was in. Tell me everything you can remember.'

Adam lay on the bed in the apartment. As Colm spoke he rolled himself a joint. He tucked the phone between his shoulder and his ear and listened. He drew the smoke deep into his lungs.

It was what was called then a mother and baby home. It had the look of a convent, but it was run by the Church of England. It was outside Birmingham somewhere. A big, rambling, red-brick house. The hospital where she'd had the baby was a fifteen-minute walk away. Colm had gone there with her a few times, while the baby was still weak and ill. He remembered the way the nurses in the hospital had treated them. With a mixture of pity and contempt. They'd assumed that he was her brother or some relation. The hospital was called St Bartholomew's. And the home was the Fannin Institute. It had once been called the Fannin Institute for Fallen Girls. Its full name was written across the front, partly hidden by the dense Virginia creeper which covered the brickwork with a dark red sheen. He remembered Grace standing and looking up at it, then giggling and half-collapsing on the gravel.

'See that, Colm. Fallen, that's what I am.'

And he had grabbed hold of her, and pulled her up and said,

'You're a fallen angel, that's what you are.'

The Fannin Institute, St Bartholomew's, and she had called the baby Daniel.

'He's my Daniel,' she had said, rocking him. 'Named after a good man.'

And Colm had looked down at the baby's screwed-up face and tried to see. Who did he resemble? Which of the boys with the cars and the boats and the bullshit had fathered him? And Grace had watched and said nothing.

And then she had given Colm the hourglass fob.

'Because you're a good man too, Colm,' she had said that day when the social worker from the adoption society came to take the baby away. He had thought she would die from weeping. He had never seen such tears. They had dripped down onto the baby's face making him wriggle and pull away from her when she had changed his nappy for the last time and dressed him again. She had put on his going-away clothes. That's what she had called them. She had knitted the cardigan herself. It had little sailing boats around the bottom and she had made a matching hat and little boots. He had slagged her about it. Said she didn't seem like the knitting type. That it was only ould biddies sitting over the fire who knitted ganseys like that.

And afterwards, what had they done afterwards? They had gone out and got drunk. They had walked away from the hospital and walked and walked until they found a pub. And they had drunk for the rest of that day and that night. Until Grace had fallen over, crashed from her seat onto the filthy floor and the landlord had shouted abuse at them, told them they were drunken Micks and they were to get out of his pub. And Colm had dragged her to standing and half-carried her out into the cold. Got a taxi to his digs in town and put her to bed. And when she woke the next morning she had cried out in despair.

'I thought I was dead,' she had sobbed. 'I wanted to be dead. Why didn't you let me die last night? Why didn't you kill me?'

And then, when she had had some tea, she had got dressed and left him. Gone back to the Fannin Institute. To wait for them to take her back to Trawbawn.

'But how did I find her?' Adam's voice sounded loud in his ears.

'It's not so difficult these days. There was a guy in Manchester. You know the guy who made me the little box? Well, he was adopted. Really hung up about it. One of the social workers in the prison had a soft spot for him. She showed him what to do. There's a government department that will give you the information about your birth mother. If you were adopted after 1975 that is. And he was.'

'And what about me? Was I?'

Silence, then a snort of laughter, 'Yes you were.

I remember the date well. It was 20 October 1977. That was the date that they took you away from your mother. So, you know what you did, Adam? You got onto the government department and you filled in the form and they gave you your original birth certificate and they let you look at your adoption file. And guess what was in it? Your mother's name and her last-known address. So you took yourself over to Trawbawn and somehow or another you tracked her down in Dublin. How does that sound?'

Adam sucked hard on the joint. The end glowed bright red.

'Pretty good. Sounds pretty good to me. Just one thing.'

'Yeah? Make it quick, there's a queue for this phone and I'm running out of credit, if you know what I mean. I'll be wanting some more soon.'

'OK, no problem. But listen, I want to ask you the big question. Who's my father? Is it you?'

Another snort of laughter.

'You are kidding, aren't you? She would never let me within an ass's roar of her pussy. I wasn't good enough for little Miss Muffet.'

'But you helped her when she was in England. You helped her when the baby was taken away.'

'Yeah I was good enough for that. But not for the other.'

'So, if it wasn't you, who was it then?'

'You can sort that one out for yourself, Adam. There's not that many candidates, are there?'

'I don't know. The whole of fucking west Cork I would say, if she was as much a ride when she was a kid as she is now.'

'Think about it, Adam. Use your head. Anyway, I've got to go. Phone me later. Enjoy your dinner. And I want all the details. All of them. And we're not talking about the menu. Do you hear me? And just one more thing. Don't do anything to her yet. Let's knock a bit more fun out of this before we pull the plug. OK? And just one other thing. I need you to visit me. I need some more stuff. It's the only way to keep your head above the scum. Do you hear me, Adam? One good turn and all that? Don't let me down, will you?'

Adam lay back and stared up at the ceiling. Grace had said that he was just the way she had always imagined him. She had always thought he'd be fair. And tall. And slim.

'Your eyes are a bit of a surprise, though.' She smiled up at him. 'They're very beautiful. The one on the left is like the colour of the sea, and the other is like the yellowy brown of autumn leaves.'

She had given him the name and address of the restaurant where they were to meet.

'Do you know where Dun Laoghaire is?' she asked. 'It's not far from here. It's the ferry port.'

'Sure I know it. I've been there before,' he replied. He smiled. It was where he had taken the girl last night. To the car park, at the back of the West Pier. It was deserted at night.

He lay now, half asleep. The television was on with the sound turned down. He'd been keeping an eye on it. Just to see. If the girl had been found yet. If there'd been any more news about Maria. But there was nothing. No need to worry on either score. He closed his eyes. He'd sleep for an hour or so. Then he'd go out and meet her. And see what would happen next.

Lydia woke. She had no idea what time of day it was. The sun was edging around the curtains. But that gave her no hint or clue. It was summer. And in the summer the sun barely set at all. She sat up slowly and pushed aside the bedclothes. She was still dressed. She moved gingerly, reaching with her feet for the floor. The pain in her arm was dormant. As long as she was careful not to bang it, or disturb it in any way. She stood up and walked carefully towards the windows. She grasped one of the long, cream brocade curtains and pulled it back. Light streamed into the room, hurting her eyes, so she winced and almost lost her balance. She reached out for the other curtain and drew it back too. Then she moved into the bay of the window and looked out across the tops of the trees. The sky was a bright periwinkle blue. It was cloudless. She stood still and gazed out at it, then let her eyes drift down to the garden below. And saw movement, the sudden shuddering of the shrubbery. And saw someone among the greenery. A someone with dark hair. Something familiar about it. And she saw at the same time her own reflection in her dressing-table mirror. Her hair that was still dark, despite the thick streaks of white. And the particular tilt of her head, the way she held it on the column of her neck. She stepped forward again and picked up the binoculars from their place on the window sill. It was awkward holding them to her eyes with just the one hand, difficult to focus them properly.

295

She had to do it by guesswork, taking them down from her eyes, fiddling with them, then putting them back again to see whether the image was sharper. And this time it was. And she saw the man in the garden, as he turned around to look at the house. Saw him as if she could reach out and touch him. Put her hand to his sharp cheekbones and chin. Put her hand on the top of his head and feel his springy black curls. Put her hand on his shoulder and feel his bones beneath her fingers. She stepped back from the window and put the binoculars down on the sill. She raised her good arm and patted her own black curls, feeling their sparseness, their rough brittleness. Knew that they would no longer lift in the breeze which funnelled through the trees from the river. Then held the binoculars again, and again trained them on the young man below. As he turned to look at the house, she found herself staring right into his eyes. She stepped back quickly, felt the plaster cast catch on the edge of the wall, the pain begin, and saw the young man turn away, turn towards the river, turn his eyes from hers.

Grace was early. She had booked the table for eight o'clock, but it was just after seven-thirty when she got to the restaurant. She parked the car along the sea road. It was another hot evening. The streets gave back the warmth of the day. But she was shivering as she walked past the ferry terminal and up the incline towards the Victoria fountain at the bottom of Marine Road. Sweat was cooling on her skin, her palms damp, her stomach in a knot of tension. She felt as if at any moment she would get sick. She looked up at the clock on the Town Hall. Its hands seemed to be stuck at twenty-five to eight. She would walk for a few minutes, down the East Pier, past the bandstand, past the strolling couples, the family groups, the children running and playing, the dogs straining at their leads, the elderly men and women who walked with sticks and stopped every few paces to catch their breath. She turned and looked back at the town. At the steeples. The Mariner's Church now a museum and further west the spire of St Michael's. She turned towards the sea. The evening breeze sent small shivers across its silken turquoise surface. She sat down on a wrought-iron bench and tried to calm herself. It would be all right. They liked each other already. She would explain to him why she had given him up for adoption. She would find a way to do it without burdening him with the dirty reality of the circumstances of his birth. She got up and walked to the edge of the pier. Steep granite steps dropped to the water's edge. She took them slowly and carefully. They were wet and slippery. The slop from a passing motorboat washed up against them in a frill of white. Close up the water was the colour of fresh spring grass. She breathed in deeply, breathed the smell of salt. The smell of her childhood.

She looked across the harbour to the clock on the Town Hall. It was five to eight. Time to go. She walked back up the steps and turned towards the town. A band had set up in the stand. They were playing Viennese waltzes. She stopped to listen and watch. An elderly couple had begun to dance. Their movements were stately, precise, elegant. Around and around they twirled and swirled. The crowd began to clap in accompaniment. Grace moved from foot to foot, her body responding to the rhythm of the music. Alex had loved to waltz. He had taught her that summer. Tried to teach Colm O Laoire. But he hadn't taken to it. Complained there wasn't enough beat to the music. Showed them how to dance the jig and the reel instead. Battered his feet on the kitchen's flagged floor. And laughed at Alex's feeble attempts to copy him. Then took hold of her and held her close as he whistled a polka, one hand in the small of her back, the other squashing her fingers into his palm as he danced her out into the garden. And she had been embarrassed by his clumsiness and rushed to free herself.

Now she raised her hand to push her hair back from her face, and saw Adam. He was standing on the edge of the crowd. He was watching the dancers too. She felt a strange sense of pride as she looked at him. He was very good-looking. Tall and slender. His hair was paler than hers, more the way hers had been when she was a child. His cheekbones were high and sharp, and his mouth was full. As she watched, he took his phone from his inside jacket pocket. She watched him as he made a call. Who was he speaking to? She felt suddenly jealous. He was laughing, happy. Careless with his happiness. It spilled from him, infecting the people around him. They were all smiling too, looking at him as if for approval. He glanced down at his watch and turned away from the band and the dancers. She had better hurry. She didn't want him to arrive first. She wanted to be able to greet him, welcome him, show him his seat, hand him his menu, offer him wine, make him feel welcome. She slipped away through the crowd, and around behind the pier's high granite wall. She could do it if she hurried. The sweat was beading her forehead and running in a delicate cold trickle down between her breasts. For a sudden moment she wondered if she should just walk away. Did she want to know him? She had a child, she had a life. She had made a decision all those years ago.

'But it wasn't you,' she said out loud. 'It was your mother. She made the decision. You didn't.'

But still, even though that was so, did she want him now? She slowed down. Across the road was the restaurant. A couple of waiters in their black and white uniforms were lounging against its granite walls. Taking a breather, she thought, before it really gets busy. Its doors were open. She could see inside. It was light and airy. Half empty. She could phone now and say there had been a family emergency, that she wanted to cancel the booking. They would tell him when he arrived. Or she could just not show up. He would wait and wait. Eventually he would realize that she had made a decision about it. No, she couldn't do that. It would be too cruel. She had to go through with this. One way or another she had to face him. She took a deep breath and looked to right and to left. The road was clear. She could see him now. He was walking briskly up to the door. She could see him at the reception desk. She had better hurry. She didn't want to disappoint him.

She straightened herself up, smoothed back her hair and began to walk quickly towards him. As she crossed the road he turned towards her. He smiled and waved. And she smiled and waved too. My son, she thought, my only son.

It was late when they left the restaurant. They were the last to go. She had cried and laughed. And cried some more. She had cried first when he told her he had gone to the Fannin Institute to see what it was like.

'It's closed now,' he said. 'It's almost derelict.'

'And the hospital? Did you go to the hospital?'

He nodded.

'Yeah, but it's changed. It's a geriatric hospital now.'

She had asked him about his adoptive parents. And he had asked her. What did she know about them?

'Nothing,' she said. 'At the time they didn't tell you anything. It's not like that now. Now you know everything. One of the teachers in my school adopted last year. She and her husband met the girl who was having the baby. Before the baby was even born. They told her all about themselves. And after they were given the baby, they sent her photos and wrote to her regularly telling her how the baby was doing. But I knew nothing. It wasn't encouraged. Any kind of contact. In fact, it was unusual for a mother to have so much time with her baby then. It was only because you were premature and you were ill and I was pretty weak and we were in the same place together. And then, I don't know, I think they all felt sorry for me.

They let me hold you and feed you and change you and bath you. I think I almost forgot that I wasn't going to take you home.'

'And could you have changed your mind? Could you have walked out with me?'

She looked down at her plate. She didn't speak for a while.

'I suppose I could, if it came to it. I suppose I could have been very brave and very independent. But,' she took a sip from her glass, 'but it wasn't easy.'

'You had no one to help you; you were there on your own?'

'Well.' She drank some more. 'Yes and no. My mother didn't come with me. She didn't really want to get involved. But there was a friend. A friend from where we lived. Well.' She paused and drank some more. He noticed that her cheeks were flushed, and her voice was slightly slurred. 'He was living near where I was staying. He used to come and see me all the time. Especially after you were born. He was very kind to me when I was in a bad way. But you know.' She fiddled with her napkin, dabbing her lips carefully. 'He did say he'd help me, but I couldn't do it. I knew I had to finish my education. I had to be able to work, get a good job, get on with my life.'

'And was he, was he, well,' he spread his hands out on the table, 'you know, was he?'

She took a deep breath and picked up her glass.

'Was he your father? Is that what you want to know? Well.' Again the pause, again the dabbing of the lips, the fingers clutching the napkin. 'No, he wasn't.'

'So, who was?' He watched how she responded to the bluntness of his question. She sank back into her chair, her eyes flickering as she scanned the room. Her hand reached for the glass of wine and raised it. As she drank, a small dribble of red trickled from the corner of her mouth. He leaned forward. He was tempted to lick it from her chin.

'Your father, who was your father?' She repeated the question, looked down, looked away, then looked back at him. 'I don't want to tell you that just now. I will one day, but it's very painful for me.'

'But, I have a right to know, don't I?'

She nodded.

'Yes you do, but please, let's leave it for now. Isn't it enough that you have found me? Won't I do for the time being?'

He was enjoying this. He shrugged.

'But you said I looked like him. So, of course, I'm curious. And I wonder. What about me looks like him? My hair, my eyes, my body? What?'

She was really squirming now. She finished her wine and held out her glass for more.

'Please don't ask me, Adam. I just can't face it at the moment. I will tell you, I will tell you everything. I promise you. But just not yet.'

'And will you tell your daughter about me? Will you do that?'

Again he could see the indecision in her face and in her body.

'I will, but I have to find the right moment. Do you understand?'

He shrugged.

'I suppose I'll have to, won't I?'

She covered her face with her hands. He noticed that her fingers were long, her palms were broad. She wore no rings. Her nails were short and unpainted. He picked up the bottle of wine. It was empty. He gestured to the waiter to bring another. Then he reached out and unpeeled her fingers from her eyes.

'It's OK, Grace, I understand. I know it's difficult for you. It will take time. Here.' The waiter put the opened bottle on the table. Adam picked it up and poured a generous measure into her glass. 'Let's make a toast. Let's drink to us, and then I have a suggestion to make. And here, you could do with this.' He took a clean tissue from his pocket and handed it to her. She smiled her thanks and wiped her eyes. She blew her nose.

'I'm sorry. I guess that even though I've been thinking about this happening for years, well, the reality is very different from the fantasy.'

'And the fantasy? How did that play?'

'Oh,' she smiled ruefully, 'it was all very soft focus. No concrete details. Just a sense of warmth, of belonging, of loving, but none of the awkwardness of a real relationship.' She picked up her glass. 'Thanks, just what I needed.' Her shoulders shuddered as tension flowed from her. 'Anyway, what was that you said? A suggestion to make? About what?'

He suggested then that they go away together, just for a weekend, or a few days. Spend some time on their own.

'Would you like that?' he asked. He could see she wasn't sure. He was beginning to be able to read her. He watched the confusion of desires flit

303

across her face.

'Yes, but, well, of course.' She smiled as if to reassure him.

'Do you remember the gansey with the blue boats?' He sat back in his chair. She looked puzzled for a moment, then her eyes filled with tears again.

'The gansey with the blue boats, and the little knitted hat and the mittens and the bootees to match. They are called bootees, aren't they? The little sock things that babies wear?'

She nodded.

'And you put them on me the day the social worker came to take me away.'

She nodded.

'And I've always kept them. I found them in a cupboard in my adopted parents' house. And they told me where they had come from. And I found it so sad and sweet. That you went to all that trouble to make those clothes. That you made the gansey with the blue boats and the hat and the mittens and the little bootees, you made them for me. For your baby Daniel. Wasn't that what you called me?'

'Yes, I wanted you to have something that had come from your mother. That was special. I can't believe that you knew about them.' She reached out and touched his hand. 'I thought that they would have been abandoned. Thrown away. Discarded. You know, when I had Amelia, I couldn't bring myself to make anything for her. Every time I picked up the knitting needles I thought of you.'

They finished their wine. She called for the bill. He watched her pay for it. She was drunk. Her handwriting was uneven and careless. He helped her to her feet. He wrapped her linen shawl around her shoulders. They stood outside the restaurant. It was still warm.

'You can't drive,' he said. 'You've had far too much to drink.'

She nodded and giggled. She slipped her hand into the crook of his arm and leaned against him.

'You drive.' She handed him the keys. 'My big grown-up son can drive his silly mother home.' She giggled again and nearly tripped as they walked down the wide steps to the footpath. He felt her body against his. Her breasts pushed into his chest as he held her upright. He could smell the scent of her hair.

'Come on, where are you parked?' He turned her around and she pointed vaguely, giggling and swaying gently from side to side.

He settled her into the passenger seat. She leaned back and closed her eyes.

'Take me home, Adam,' she said. Her face turned towards him and her body drooped over the gear lever. He pushed her back into place and pulled her seat belt across her chest. The back of his hand brushed against her breasts. She sighed and moved. He touched her again. Then he leaned over and unbuttoned her blouse. He slipped his index finger down into her cleavage, then cupped her breast with his hand. She breathed deeply. He kissed her neck and touched her skin with his tongue. Then he pulled back and looked at her. It would be so easy. He would drive away from the street lights. He would find a dark place. He would ease back her seat so she was lying flat. Then he would pull up her skirt. And she would be his.

A sudden loud noise. A knuckle rapping the window. A policeman, his high-visibility jacket gleaming with an unnatural iridescence in the street lights. Adam rolled down the window.

'You're illegally parked here, sir. You'd best be on your way.' The guard leaned down to have a look at Grace. 'Is she all right?'

'Yes, she's fine. Just a few glasses of wine too many.'

'You're taking her home, I assume?'

'That's right, officer. Bed's what she needs.'

He drove slowly towards the main road. He was lucky. He'd got away with that. He drove carefully back to the city. Beside him, Grace slept. As they approached the house, he leaned over and shook her. He said her name loudly and she stirred and groaned. He parked as close to the house as he could.

'Grace, wake up. You're home,' he said as he undid his seat belt. He reached over and shook her shoulder. Her eyes flickered and opened.

'What time is it? Where are we?' Her voice was hoarse and breathy.

'It's late. And you're home. But don't worry, everything's fine.'

'Oh God.' She sat up, pushing her hair back from her face. 'What did I do? What happened?'

'Nothing. You did nothing. You just had a bit too much to drink, that's all. But you're home now, safe and sound. Here.' He undid her seat belt and reached across to open the passenger door. 'Get out and I'll give you a hand to get into the house.' He bent down and picked up her bag from beside her feet. He handed her the car keys.

'Come on now, it's time for bed.'

He walked her to the door and waited as she opened it.

'Thanks.' She turned back to him. 'Thanks for being so understanding. It's just, you know.'

'I know, I understand. For me too. You get a good night's sleep and I'll call you tomorrow. OK?'

She nodded, then turned back to him. She reached forward and kissed him on the cheek. Her touch was soft and gentle. She stroked his hair and rested her hand on his shoulder.

'Thank you, Adam. Thank you.'

He waited outside for a moment, then hurried down the road, turning into the lane that ran behind the house. He pulled himself up onto the wall. He could see her walking up through the house. See her reach her bedroom. See her standing looking out into the garden as she began to undress. Drawing the curtains, then switching off the light. He could imagine the mattress sinking beneath the weight of her body. The indentation in the pillow as her head nuzzled into it. The sighing of her breath as she sank into a deep sleep. He could imagine it as clearly as if he were there in the room, in the bed, inside her. As if his body were pushing down on her. The fingers of his hand gripping her neck, her throat, her larynx, her cervical vertebrae. Crushing them until she could no longer move or breathe. Until she could no longer be anything but his.

TWENTY-FIVE

'You've got to go back. You can't leave it like that. You've gone all that way. You found the house. You went into the gardens. You've got to go and see her. Find out if she is your grandmother and where your mother is.' Lucy's voice was shrill with frustration. Johnny could imagine her sitting cross-legged on their bed, the phone in one hand, a cup of black coffee in the other. Lucy never did just one thing. She would be brushing her hair, or putting on her make-up, or drawing up a shopping list. She would have a book open, a newspaper spread out beside her. She would be going through the small ads, looking for cheap holiday deals, or car boot sales. She was so full of energy. Sometimes she made him feel like shutting himself in a darkened room.

He took a deep breath and tried to cut across her.

'Look, Lucy, it's not as easy as all that. You don't know what it's like.' But she wasn't having any of it.

'I should have come with you,' she said. 'I knew this would happen. I knew you'd try and chicken out. Honestly, Johnny, what am I going to do with you?'

Johnny lowered his voice. The hotel dining room was full.

'Will you stop?' he said as loudly as he could.

'You're not being fair, Lucy. It's easy for you to say all this. You're at home. You're safe. You don't have something, oh, I don't know what, ahead of you.'

He stopped and sipped his tea.

'OK, OK, I'm sorry. I shouldn't be yelling at you. Here, here's a little something sweet.' He heard the sound of a kiss. He smiled. 'But I just can't believe you only went and had a look at the place and you didn't speak to anyone. So, you'd better tell me what it's like. I'm dying to know. Is it as lovely as it looks on the website?'

He didn't answer immediately. He could see the lawn sloping down to the river and the huge monkey puzzle tree. He could see the walled garden filled with ripening vegetables and flowers. And he could see the house, its long sash windows shining in the afternoon sunshine.

'Yes it is. It's lovely. I couldn't believe it. I don't think I've ever seen anything as nice.' He wiped his mouth with his heavy linen napkin. 'Listen, Lucy, you're right, I know you are. I'm going to go back. I've just finished my breakfast. I'll go now. OK?'

He pushed back his chair and stood up.

'Well, if you're sure. I wouldn't want you to do anything you don't feel OK about. But after all...'

'Yes, I know. I've started so I should finish, isn't that right?'

He heard her giggle.

'Exactly. Call me when you can. I'll be dying to hear how you get on.'

He walked through the lobby and stepped outside into the sunshine. He wished he hadn't had such a big breakfast. The bacon and eggs were lodged in his stomach, a heavy undigested lump of food. He unlocked the door of his hire car and got in. He put his hands on the steering wheel. They were damp and sticky. He took a packet of tissues from the glove compartment and dried them off.

'Here goes,' he said out loud. 'Here goes.'

Adam drove slowly towards Grace's house. He had slept well. He had spoken to Colm. He was ready. He turned off the canal and stopped the car. And saw Amelia. She was walking quickly towards him. He opened his window.

'Hey,' he shouted. 'How goes it?'

She stopped and looked around.

'Amelia, over here.' He waved his arm and beckoned. She smiled and broke into a jog. He reached over and opened the passenger door. 'Get in,' he said.

She was on her way into Grafton Street to meet some friends. The ones who hadn't been packed off to Irish college. The really cool ones she hung out with all year round, she said.

'But what on earth did you and my mum get up to last night?' she turned towards him, her expression one of mock outrage. 'The state of her this morning. She could hardly move.'

'The demon drink, I think.' He smiled. 'You know what the old folks are like. They get a whiff of it and they're unstoppable. Me, now, I prefer a whiff of the other.'

She giggled.

'Yeah, me too. That's what I'm going to do this

afternoon. We're all going into the Green to get wrecked. Do you want to come?'

'Oh, I don't know. Wouldn't want to impose.'

'You wouldn't be.' She leaned towards him. He could smell her perfume and the tang of tooth-paste. 'You wouldn't be. Although,' she pulled away, 'who are you exactly? I mean, what's going on with you and my mother?'

'Ah,' he glanced sideways at her, 'now that'd be telling, wouldn't it? But I can assure you, Amelia, it's all very innocent. I have a friend in England who used to know her years ago and when I told him I was coming to Dublin on holiday he said I should look her up.'

'A friend, eh? A mystery man. That's Mum all over. She's full of secrets. She never really opens up.' She leaned back in her seat. 'This is a really neat car. I like the old ones. Much more funky than the shiny new models.' She reached out and turned on the radio. She began to flick through the stations. The newsreader's voice was sud-denly loud in his ears.

'Gardai are looking for witnesses to the abduc-tion and murder of nineteen-year-old Bernie Gallagher. Gallagher was last seen getting into a car in the Fitzwilliam Square area of Dublin around midnight on Thursday night. The man is described as being between the ages of twenty-five and thirty, with light-coloured hair...' Adam reached down and flicked over to the tape. Deborah Kerr's voice filled the car.

'Where are we going?' Amelia sat up. The trees of Fitzwilliam Square blocked off the sun. 'This is a funny way to get to Grafton Street. It's certainly not the shortest.'

'Really?' He smiled at her. 'Is that so?'

'Yeah, you shouldn't have turned off back there at the bridge. You should have just kept going.'

He was watching her mouth. He wasn't listening to what she was saying. Her lipstick was pale pink and frosted. He'd never tasted one like that before.

She looked down at her phone, which was lying in her lap.

'Don't worry.' He reached over and stroked the back of her hand with his index finger. 'We'll be there soon.'

And then a phone rang. It wasn't his. It wasn't his ring. It wasn't hers either.

'Where's that coming from?' Amelia looked around. 'Funny ring tone. Sounds like Mum's. She got a weird kind of African drum beat one from some refugee kid in her school.' She reached towards the glove compartment. 'Sounds like it's coming from in here.' She fiddled with the catch. He stopped the car quickly and put his hand out. He pulled down the flap. His fingers grabbed hold of the phone. He shut it off.

'It's nothing,' he said. 'This car is borrowed. The phone belongs to the guy who owns it. That's all.' He put it in his pocket.

'Well, listen.' She reached for the handle. 'I might as well walk the rest of the way. But thanks. It was nice talking to you.'

He smiled.

'Yeah, it was. What's your mum up to today?'

'Apart from curing her hangover? Not much I wouldn't think. I'm sure she'll call you later.' She opened the door and stepped out. Then she leaned down. He could see her breasts and the pale pink of her bra. Just like her lipstick. 'See you round, Adam. Have a nice day. If you change your mind, you know where to find me.' She stepped back and waved her fingers, then turned and began to walk quickly.

'Missing you already, you little cunt,' he muttered. He waited until she was out of sight. Then he got out of the car. There was a grating in the gutter by the front wheel. He looked around, then squatted down. He dropped Grace's phone into it. He got back into the car and put it in gear.

Grace sat in the kitchen. She had tried phoning her mobile from the landline. So silly, she thought. So middle-aged. She had punched in the number, then stepped away, straining to hear the sound of the ring tone. But there was silence throughout the house. She couldn't understand what she had done with it. She still didn't quite believe Amelia's story about the texts. Even though she had shown her the record on her own phone. And it was irritating. All the numbers that were stored in its memory. It would take ages to gather them together again.

'Stupid woman,' she said out loud as she poured herself yet another cup of tea and took two more paracetamol. Stupid woman in more than one way. She had drunk far too much with Adam last night. Made a real fool of herself. She would ring him and apologize. And make an arrangement to meet him. She couldn't wait to find out more about him. She had talked too much. Poured out all those painful memories about her pregnancy, the place in England where she'd given birth. And she had been so touched. That he knew about the baby clothes. The gansey, he'd called it, with the little blue boats and the hat and the bootees to match. She'd knitted them in the last few days before he was born. The matron, Miss Briggs, had given her the wool and the pattern. Had offered to help her. But she didn't need any help. She'd always knitted. Daniel had taught her. It seemed strange now, looking back. But at the time it was just one of those things that Daniel did.

She got up from the kitchen table and went into the sitting room next door. She lay down on the sofa and turned on the TV. A luxury to while away a Sunday with a hangover. She lay back on the cushions and closed her eyes. She had been so proud of the little cardigan. They called them matinee jackets in those days, she remembered. And she had especially loved the tiny little bootees. She had threaded narrow blue ribbon through them to tie at the ankles. None of the other girls could be bothered to make anything for their babies. 'What's the point?' they had said to her. But she had wanted to give her baby something special. Matron had been surprised that she'd chosen to knit them in blue wool. But Grace had been certain. Her baby would be a boy. She turned over on her side. It was so quiet here today. She would sleep for a while. And when she woke, she would feel better.

He had come back. The young man who had

been in the garden had come back. Lydia heard the car on the gravel, and watched from the drawing-room window as he got out and stood looking up at the house. She stayed very still. She thought he might go away. She didn't want to talk to anyone. She had barely slept all night, the pain had been so bad. But he kept on ringing the bell, insistently, so she couldn't ignore it. She opened the door. He said nothing. Until eventually she spoke. Asked him what he wanted. Asked him who he was. He didn't reply immediately. He just stared at her, then his words came out in a rush.

'I think I might be your grandson. You are Lydia Beauchamp, aren't you? And your daughter is Grace? Well, my understanding is that Grace is my mother.'

She stared back at him. He wasn't very tall. His eyes were dark, like hers. She couldn't think what to say. So she just stood back and gestured to him.

'Well,' she said. 'You'd better come in.'

They sat at the kitchen table. He opened the small rucksack he was carrying and took out an envelope.

'Do you want to look?' he asked.

She nodded.

'Well this, here, this is my file from the adoption agency. And my original birth certificate. Look at this.' He picked up a piece of paper. She turned it around with the tips of her fingers. Mother's name, mother's address. Name and date of birth of the baby. She called him Daniel. In the space for the father's details there was a thick black line. There were other forms, too, that Grace had filled

315

out when she entered the home. Block capitals. Neat. Precise. Name, name of next of kin. Date of birth, her home address. Physical details. Height, weight, previous illnesses. Measles, chicken pox, mumps. Broken collar bone. Lydia tapped her finger on the stiff paper.

'She fell off her pony when she was twelve or thirteen. Jumping stone walls,' she said quietly.

'And here. This is me.' He put his hand in his denim jacket. 'John Bradshaw is my name. See here, on my driving licence, and on my identity card for the school where I teach.'

He dropped them on the table. Lydia put out her good hand and touched the card's shiny laminated surface.

'And here, look what I have here.' Again his hand went into the rucksack. And brought out a plastic bag. 'Look at these. These are what I was wearing when I left the hospital. Look.'

He laid the baby clothes out on the table. A hand-knitted white cardigan decorated with blue sailing boats around the waist. A matching blue hat and mittens and tiny blue bootees. Lydia picked them up and stroked the soft wool. Grace had always loved knitting. It was one of the few indoor activities that she enjoyed. Daniel had shown her how. He had shown Grace how to cast on stitches, knit plain and purl, cast off. Wet days when the trees sagged with water and the clouds scraped the roof. And Daniel and Grace sat in front of the fire, their heads together as they examined her knitting.

'So.' He pushed back his chair. 'You don't seem very surprised.'

She smiled at him.

'Have a look at yourself in the mirror over there. Then have a look at me. My hair isn't as black as yours now. It's not as curly either. But I don't think that makes much difference, do you?' She reached out and took his hand. 'Put the kettle on and make us some tea. And then tell me all about yourself.'

'I just want to know where my mother is. Is she here?'

Lydia shook her head.

'No, she isn't. She lives in Dublin. It's a long story. Make the tea and I'll tell you.'

They sat in the kitchen. The hours passed. He told her about his life. He was a teacher in a grammar school in Chichester. His parents had owned a second-hand book shop. He told her about Lucy, how she had organized the trip for him. Booked him into the local hotel, fixed up his car hire. Made it all possible. He wanted to know everything about Grace, about her life. Lydia sent him up to the drawing room, to open the bottom drawer in the desk, to pull out all the photo albums. She watched him as he pored over the pictures.

'Look.' He picked up a small black-and-white photo which had become freed from its sticky backing. 'Who's that?'

She took it from him. It had been taken when she was at school. She was wearing her uniform. She must have been about twelve, she thought.

'It's me, when I was a child.'

'It's me, too, isn't it?'

She nodded.

'But my mother isn't like you at all.'

'No, she takes after her father. He was Swedish. That's where she gets the hair and the eyes.'

'He's not your husband, though, is he? The man who's named on the website, who you started the garden with?'

'No, he isn't. That was my husband, Alex, Grace's stepfather. I was what was called back in the sixties an unmarried mother. Believe me, it wasn't an enviable state. Despite what people say about the sixties, women on their own with babies had a very tough time. I wanted to come home with Grace, back to my parents' house outside Dublin. But they didn't want to know. They wouldn't even let me come and visit them with Grace. They didn't want the neighbours to see the pram. So I got a job in a hospital in the city. And I managed to find someone to mind her. But it was very hard and very lonely. Until I met Alex and we came here.'

'And my father? Who was he?'

She closed her eyes tightly then opened them. He was staring straight at her.

'That's the difficult part, John. I'm not sure I can tell you. I think it should be Grace who makes the decision.'

'Why?'

She didn't reply for a moment.

'It's not my secret to tell. It's Grace's. You know, I haven't seen or spoken to her for many years. It was me who insisted that she put you up for adoption. I didn't want her to suffer the way I had. I didn't want her choices in life to be determined by her baby. She never forgave me. She

318

wouldn't tell me who your father was. I only found out years later. I don't know how to tell you, John. I think you need to hear it all from your mother.'

He stood up. His face was very pale. He stuffed the baby clothes back into his bag.

'It was my girlfriend's idea that I come over here. I didn't really want to know. I had a bad feeling about all this. I think I was right. I should have stayed away.'

'I'm sorry, John, I really am. Look.' She reached out and took hold of his hand. 'You've told me that your parents are dead. You have a family here now.'

'Do I? I don't think so.' He moved towards the door.

'No.' She pulled herself upright. 'No, don't go. Please. Grace would never forgive me if she knew I'd let you go now. Please stay. I can contact her. I know I can find her. Please wait.'

But he had already opened the back door. She cried out again, but he slammed it shut behind him.

'John, come back, please come back,' she called. But it was too late. She shuffled out into the corridor and up the stairs to the drawing room. She sat down on the sofa and picked up the phone. She would have to phone Adam. He had to go to Grace. He had to tell Grace what had happened. He would be able to make it all right. She was sure of that.

Grace woke. Her mouth was dry but her headache was gone. She stretched and straightened out her legs. She looked at her watch. It was five o'clock. She had been asleep for hours. She got up and went into the kitchen. She opened the fridge and took out a carton of orange juice. It tasted good. Cold and sweet. Just what she needed. She walked upstairs and into the bathroom. She turned on the taps and undressed. She stepped into the bath and sank down into the water. She watched as the water foamed up around and in between her legs, until it was deep enough just about to float. She leaned back and closed her eyes. She felt like a boat in dry dock. A boat on the cradle. Funny, she thought as she opened her eyes and looked down at her body. That was a phrase she hadn't heard for years and years. It was a phrase that Cape Clear islanders used. They described pregnant women as 'on the cradle'. And Adam had said it last night. She couldn't remember how or why it had come up. But he had said those words. And he had called the little cardigan she had knitted a gansey. It had struck her at the time that it wasn't a word English people employed. She had meant to ask him about it, but somehow the moment had passed. Oh well, she thought as she soaped herself. These days language knows no boundaries. Amelia speaks a version of English with words from all over the world. And it isn't just a one-way traffic. Maybe he had Irish friends. Perhaps the people who had adopted him had Irish connections. It was probably that. She would ask him when she saw him again.

She got out of the bath. She wrapped herself in a big towel and walked into her bedroom. The clothes she had worn last night were dumped on the floor. She picked them up. They smelt of smoke. Adam had smoked through the meal. In between courses he had taken out a plastic pouch of tobacco and a packet of cigarette papers. She hadn't seen anyone smoking roll-ups for years. When she was a student in London all her friends had smoked them. And, of course, she remembered that Colm O Laoire had too. He had made the most perfect cigarettes. Thin, neat, with a little twist of cardboard for a mouthpiece. And he had blown the most perfect smoke rings. Adam had blown them too. It had seemed funny. Not the kind of thing that was commonplace in a smart restaurant. She had laughed when he did it. An indulgent sound.

She dressed quickly and walked downstairs, carrying an armload of dirty washing. Might as well do something useful with the rest of the day. She filled the machine and turned it on. Then she walked back into the sitting room, sat down and turned on the television. She flicked around from channel to channel. The early evening news was on. There had been another murder. A girl had been found dead in a car park in Dun Laoghaire. The guards were looking for a man who had picked her up from the corner of Fitzwilliam Square. He was described as between twenty-five and thirty-five years old with light-coloured hair. There was a photo of the girl. Grace recognized her. Bernie Gallagher had been a pupil of St Bridget's until a couple of years ago. Then heroin had taken over her life and she had dropped out. Grace picked up the phone book and flicked through the pages. She found the Gallaghers' number. She would ring Bernie's mother and commiserate with her. See if there was anything she could do. But as she waited for her call to be answered she saw, suddenly, a house she recognized. Beautiful, stately, the slate roof gleaming in the sunshine. She put down the phone and reached for the remote control. She turned up the volume. She listened.

'...continuing their search for the missing mother of three, Maria Grimes. Gardai have searched many local properties. Among them is Trawbawn House and gardens. Their owner, Lydia Beauchamp, is one of Ireland's foremost garden designers.'

Lydia walked into view. She looked old and stooped. One arm was in a plaster cast. She moved slowly into the greenhouse and sat down on a stool at the propagating bench. The reporter stood beside her.

'Mrs Beauchamp, you must be very concerned about the disappearance of Mrs Grimes.' The camera focused on Lydia's face. Her skin was lined. There were deep circles beneath her eyes.

'Of course,' she said, 'of course, everyone who lives in the area is horrified and shocked that someone could just vanish without trace. We all extend our sympathy to her family and we trust that she will soon be found safe and well.'

Grace watched her. Lydia's mouth trembled as she spoke. She wasn't wearing any make-up. She looked frail and vulnerable. She looked old. The report ended and the newsreader introduced the next item. Grace reached out and turned off the television. Her hands were shaking. Lydia must have broken her arm. How was she managing all by herself in that big house? She would be all right, she thought. Lydia was a survivor. She never asked for help. She never showed weakness. Not in the past anyway. In all the years since Grace had seen her, she had never thought how her mother would have aged. Whenever she imagined her, it was always as a beautiful, strong, healthy woman. The woman whom she hated and resented. She had never thought she could become the old woman that she had seen on the screen.

She sat in front of the television. She was still sitting there when she heard the front door bang and Amelia's voice calling out.

'I'm in here, sweetheart,' she shouted. She stood up and walked into the kitchen. Amelia had the fridge open.

'Hey, Mum, how are you? Feeling better? Would you like something to eat?' She waved a large chunk of cheese and some slices of ham in greaseproof paper in her direction.

'Yes, that looks good.' Grace took the bread from the bin and began to cut thick slices. 'Have you had a good day? You met all your friends, did you?'

Amelia nodded, her mouth full of food.

'Yeah,' she said, chewing noisily. 'Yeah, it was great. So great to be home.'

'Mm.' Grace eyed her speculatively. 'I bet. Just hope you don't regret it when it comes to exam time.'

'I won't, silly Mummy.' Amelia leaned over and planted a kiss on her cheek. 'Oh, by the way I met that Adam guy. He's a bit of a hunk, isn't he?'

'Is he? Where did you meet him?'

'Just down the road. He gave me a lift into town. He told me a few things about you.' Amelia looked at her with a knowing expression on her face.

'Really?' Grace's heart began to speed up. 'What kinds of things?'

'Secrets, that's what.' Amelia filled a glass with wine. 'Just a few secrets.' She giggled. 'I told him you were a very secretive person.'

Relief flooded through Grace.

'That's not true,' she said and held out her glass for more juice. 'You know I've always been honest with you.'

'Have you?' Amelia's expression was suddenly very sober.

'I have. Of course I have.' Grace's voice was suddenly loud.

'OK, I believe you.' Amelia smiled. 'Silly Mummy, of course you're honest with me. You're the honestest person in the whole wide world.' She reached over and kissed her on the cheek. 'Will you wake me in the morning before you go to the prison? I told Dad I'd meet him in college so we can sort out what he wants me to do.'

Grace put her arms around her daughter and held her tight.

'Of course I will, sweetheart. And hey, it's good to have you home.' She kissed her forehead. 'I love you, darling. Always remember, no matter what, how much I love you.'

She lay in bed. There was a wind tonight. It

rattled the sash windows and made the curtains shiver. Nothing like the wind in Trawbawn. The wind there made the whole house shake and sounded as if it was going to burst through the glass. She could see Lydia lying in her bed on her own. She could see the paintings on the walls, the long pier glass by the bay window, the huge mahogany wardrobe where Grace had often hidden herself away. She suddenly wanted to speak to her mother. She wanted to tell her about Adam. She wanted to share the news with her. After all, her mother was one of the few people who knew about him, Maybe, after so many years, she would be curious. She would want to know about her grandson. She sat up in bed and switched on the light. She reached over for the phone. She began to punch in the number for Trawbawn. Quickly, before she might change her mind. But all she heard was the engaged tone. She put her finger down and disconnected the call. Then she punched in Adam's number. She heard his voice, his voicemail message.

'Adam, it's me,' she said. 'It's Grace. I really want to see you again. I'm sorry I got rather drunk last night. It was all the tension, I think. I don't usually behave like that. But thanks for bringing me home. I hear you met Amelia today. Thanks for not telling her, you know, who you are. I will tell her, but I need to find the right time. But listen, I'll phone you tomorrow. Perhaps you'd come around for dinner. Or we could meet for a drink or something. Oh, maybe not a drink, but you know what I mean. Anyway, I can't wait to see you again. Bye.'

325

She hung up the phone and lay down. If Lydia wanted her help, she was sure she could find her. But Lydia wouldn't want her help. That wasn't her way. She switched off the light and turned over on her side. She closed her eyes. But sleep did not come.

Adam lay back on his bed. He picked up his phone. There were two voice messages. One was from Grace. He listened to it and deleted it. The next was from Lydia.

'Adam, you've got to get in touch. Something incredible has happened. I never told you why Grace and I fell out. It was because she had a baby boy who was adopted in England. And now this young man, Grace's son, has found us. He just turned up today, out of the blue. He wants to see her. I don't know what to say to him. You have to find her and speak to her. You have to tell her. Please, Adam. Please phone me as soon as you get this. Please.'

Adam played the message over and over again. Then he got up and went into the bathroom. He opened the cabinet. He took out his lipsticks. There was the one he had taken from Lydia's house. He unscrewed it. He pressed the dark red to his upper lip. He opened his mouth. He covered half his bottom lip with Maria's scarlet and the other half with the little slag's purple. He ran his tongue over them and tasted them all. They tasted good. He walked back into the bedroom and lay down. He had begun to enjoy being Grace's son. He had it all planned. She and her daughter trusted him already. They would invite him to come and stay. Grace would tell him the whole story. She would explain to him about his father, her stepfather, her mother, the house in Cork. He would suggest that they go and see it. Of course, she wouldn't have that. So he would go on their behalf. Lydia would have an accident. A woman of her age, living on her own, hardly surprising. The house and gardens would pass to Grace. He would persuade her to sell. It was worth a fortune. Somehow a large chunk of that money would make its way into his hands. And then, well, whatever.

He laughed out loud. What a thought. It would never have worked. He'd never have been able to hold it together for that long. He picked up a hand mirror from the bedside table and looked at himself. He wasn't sure which of the lipsticks suited him best. He still had to claim two more. Grace's dark rose and Amelia's frosted pink. But even if he might have been able to pull it off, he definitely couldn't now. Now there was the small problem of the real son. But who, he wondered, knew about this man? Lydia did. But who else?

He got off the bed and opened the cupboard. He pulled out his bag and put his hand inside it. He had more treasures here. His first lipstick. The one he had got from his gran's bathroom. It was called Burnt Orange and it was worn down to a stub. He had taken it the day she fell and broke her hip. He had stood and looked down at her. She was lying naked on the cold tiles. She was shaking with shock. He'd seen her naked before, many times. But not since he had grown up and she had grown old. She was fat and white, and her flesh hung in heavy folds. She had hardly any pubic hair and, for an instant, she reminded him of one of those big plastic dolls that his sister used to play with. They all had folds that suggested a pubic bone and when you turned them over they had big round bottoms with a split between the buttocks. Her white scalp showed clearly through her thin hair. She was so ugly. And yet she was beautiful too. When he looked at her, he could remember the way it felt to sit on her knee and be enfolded in her embrace. She always smelt the same. Of Johnson's Baby Powder with a slight hint of sweat. And he felt tears come into his eyes as he watched her struggle to sit up. That had been the end of her. And he had been sorry.

He reached further into the bag. He felt the smooth gold of the hourglass fob. He lay back on the bed. He swung it on its long gold chain. Backwards and forwards, backwards and forwards. It shone in the light. It was such a pretty little thing. Colm had given it to Adam when he was leaving the prison.

'Take it with you wherever you go. It will remind you of me,' he had said. He had kissed it, then pressed it into Adam's hand. Adam held it up in front of his face. The light twinkled on the glass. He wrapped the chain around his hand. He rolled over on his side. He closed his eyes. He slept.

TWENTY-SIX

Lydia had woken at dawn. It was the pain again that had dragged her from her sleep. She got up and shuffled to the bathroom. She opened the cabinet and took out the patch that the doctor in the hospital had given her. She tore at the shiny paper covering it with her teeth. She managed to pull it free with her good hand. She shrugged her right shoulder from her nightgown and pressed it hard down onto her skin. Then she walked slowly downstairs. She went into the drawing room and opened the desk. She searched through piles of old letters. And found the envelope she wanted. She clutched it tightly and moved down the corridor, down to the kitchen. She made herself tea, added whiskey to it and sat down at the table. She looked at the envelope and lifted the cup to her lips. She sipped the hot drink. Then she put it down. She slid the pages from the envelope and began to read.

My dearest Lydia,

I know what you will think when you get this letter. You will think that I am a coward. That I am weak and useless. You will think all the thoughts that you have always had about me. Ever since we met so many years ago when I came into the hospital. I was a wreck then and I'm a wreck now. A wreck of a man. Broken and shattered like the boats that founder on the Stags rocks.

Forgive me, Lydia, if you can, for what I am about to tell you. Or not tell you. I am going to write the words to you because for the past twenty years or so I have kept these words locked inside me. But now I can no longer contain them. And they must destroy me. They should have destroyed me then. I knew they would eventually.

By this stage you will have that familiar expression of impatience and irritation on your face. Get on with it, Alex, you'll be thinking, even saying out loud. For Christ's sake just get on with it.

So, deep breath, here goes. I have to tell you that I am the father of Grace's child. There. I've written it now. There, it's out in the open. It doesn't look so bad when I read back over the words, but that's because I'm not with you, feeling what you will be feeling as you read this letter. How can I explain to you what happened? How can I make you understand what it was like all those years ago in that summer that we all remember so well? I suppose the best thing is to go back to the beginning. You remember how it was between Grace and me. She was three when I came into your life. She hated me from the start. She was jealous. I don't blame her. I took you away from her. She didn't gain a father when you and I got married. She lost part of her mother. At least that was the way she saw it. She told me all about it that summer when we worked together on the boats. She made me feel all those three-year-old's emotions. Everything that stubborn, bossy, curly-haired little girl felt then. You know that was the first time I'd ever really spent alone with Grace. After Daniel died and you inherited the house and every-

thing else, and we sent Grace to boarding school, I hardly ever saw her. And when I did, it was all hostility and anger. I didn't want her to be part of the sailing school. But you insisted. And you were right. Grace was a wonderful sailor and a wonderful teacher. And I fell in love with her. That was it. Plain and simple. You see, I'd never experienced her as a daughter. She was always a stranger to me. Beautiful, intelligent, gifted in many ways. But a stranger. And then somehow she wasn't a stranger any longer. She was just my Grace. And I loved her with all my heart.

She told me about the money that my mother had paid you to stay with me. You cannot imagine how humiliated, belittled, worthless I felt. And I was so angry with you. I wanted to hurt you too. But I didn't set out to use Grace to hurt you. I knew what I was doing was wrong, but I justified it to myself. We weren't blood relations. It wasn't incest in the technical sense. But, of course, it was. When she told me she was five months pregnant I nearly died. I panicked. I made her promise she would keep it a secret. I told her it would kill you if you found out. I told her you would take my side. And she believed me. That was, I think, the worst thing I did. But you never suspected that I might be involved with her. You immediately assumed that Colm O Laoire was the father of the baby. And you went your own headstrong way. I tried to dissuade you, but I couldn't do anything that would draw attention to me. So I let you go ahead. You ruined his life. I ruined Grace's life. Between us, we destroyed so much.

And now I can't stand it any longer. I don't want to go on living. I know you're having an affair with someone in America. I know he's not the first. And he

331

won't be the last. I have some small glimmer of hope that you might meet someone and love them truly, the way you once loved me. That you might be able to find happiness again. You have a great talent for happiness, Lydia. You're a lucky person. You'd dismiss that notion. You'd say that you make your own luck. Well maybe you do. Or maybe, as I would see it, you were born under a lucky star.

Goodbye, Lydia. I'm going now. I love the river. I want it to be my resting place. Leave me there. Don't look for me. You'll get this letter when you come back from America. I'll be long gone by then.

Whatever love I have to give, I give it to you.

She folded the pages again and put them back in the envelope. She sipped her tea. She would phone John Bradshaw at the hotel and tell him she had something she wanted to show him. She would try Adam's phone again, but if he did not answer, she would tell John where Grace was living. And it would be up to him after that.

She finished her cup of tea. She was feeling a little better now. The tea and the whiskey had helped. Her wrist felt numb. She walked slowly upstairs. She would get dressed. It was a nice day. Sunny and warm. She looked out of her bedroom window. A Garda car was coming towards the house. She quickly pulled on a pair of trousers and a blouse and pushed her feet into her slippers. The bell was ringing. She hurried downstairs, clutching the banister for support. She opened the door. Liam O'Regan stood outside.

'Mrs Beauchamp, how are you?' he said. 'Can I come in for a minute?'

332

She nodded and gestured towards the drawing room.

Liam hesitated. He tried to control his expression. She looked like a different woman. Her face was without make-up. In the bright sunlight, he could see how her skin was pitted and wrinkled. Her hair was a matted frizz and her clothes were crumpled.

'Mrs Beauchamp, are you all right?' He put out his hand to support her as she moved, but she shook it away.

'What do you want?' she asked. Her voice was cold.

He drew back from her. He cleared his throat.

'It's your car, Mrs Beauchamp. Your Saab. Where is it?'

She opened her mouth to speak, but somehow she couldn't find the words. She shuffled into the room and sat down heavily on the sofa.

'It's, um... I lent it to someone. That young man, the one from England,' she mumbled.

'You didn't tell us that before, Mrs Beauchamp.' Liam sat down beside her.

'Didn't I?' She looked at him. 'Are you sure?'

'Quite sure. Do you know where he is?'

'He's gone to Dublin. I told you that. But he should be back soon.' Her eyes closed, then opened again. 'Why do you ask?'

'Oh, just some routine enquiries. Nothing for you to worry about. The guards in Dublin are trying to track down a car that was seen on some CCTV footage. They have the make and a partial number plate, and when they put it into the computer your name came up. So they were just wondering if it was you who was driving it.' He turned towards her. 'Are you sure you're feeling all right? Would you like me to get the doctor for you?'

She smiled. He suddenly seemed very far away.

'No, I don't want anyone. I'm fine, a bit sleepy. It's the stuff they've given me for the pain in my arm. It makes me feel kind of woozy.' She stood up. 'I think I'll go back to bed, if you don't mind.'

'Of course not.' He took her by the arm. 'Do you want a hand?' He led her to the stairs.

'No, I can manage. Was there anything else you wanted?'

'No, that's all for the time being. If you see him, the guy you lent the car to, will you let me know?'

She nodded.

'Of course, Liam, of course I will.'

He stood at the bottom of the stairs and watched her progress. It was slow, but she seemed steady enough. He'd call in again later and see how she was. She shouldn't be on her own really, the poor old thing, he thought. He got back into the car.

'Well?' Bill McCarthy lifted his head from the newspaper.

'It's her car all right. She says she lent it to that English bloke. Adam Smyth, the one who was working for Pat Jordan.'

'And?'

'And she says he's still in Dublin. That's about it really. I'd better ring Harcourt Square and let them know. It could be that it was the car that the girl got into in Fitzwilliam Square. And if it was, there could be a connection with Maria Grimes. What do you think?'

'Here.' Bill handed him a phone. 'Give them a

334

call now. And see if anyone knows anything about our lad.'

Grace was up early too. She had slept badly and woken thinking about Lydia. She tiptoed into Amelia's room. She bent down and kissed her.

'Wake up, sweetheart,' she whispered.

Amelia opened her eyes. She smiled and pulled Grace down to her.

'I love you, Mummy,' she said.

'You too, sweetheart. I'm going now. I'll be home this afternoon. I'll phone you later and see what you're doing. Be good.' She kissed her again. She tried Adam's mobile before she left the house. She got his voicemail. Maybe he didn't want to talk to her. Perhaps he felt he had said too much to her in the restaurant. He had talked about himself. How he had this strange phobia about rats. She had been sympathetic, but maybe he was embarrassed now. Or maybe it was something she had said. She must have upset him. Or something Amelia said to him when he gave her the lift into town. Something thoughtless and flippant. She couldn't bear to think that he had been hurt in some way. She owed him so much. Would she ever be able to make it up to him, she wondered. And if she couldn't, how would she bear the pain?

She cycled across the city to the prison. Her legs moved rhythmically, calming her down. She breathed slowly and deeply. She would put him out of her mind for the next few hours. Today it would be Mags Kelly's turn to read. If she bothered to turn up, that is. Mags had contributed little to the class. She had sat, chewing gum, and fid-

335

dling with her blonde hair. It was braided into tiny plaits. Each was decorated with a coloured ribbon.

'Nice,' Grace had commented. Mags hadn't replied. Grace didn't know much about her. She was a pretty girl, early twenties, big, round, blue eyes and a soft, round body. She was chewing gum this morning too, her hands resting on the pile of paper and pens on the table in front of her.

'So.' Grace sat down and looked from face to face. 'How are you all today? Have a nice weekend?'

No one replied.

'OK, well, Mags, do you have something to read for us?'

Mags nodded.

'Great, good for you. In your own time.' Grace sat back in her chair and crossed her legs. Mags pulled the piece of gum from her mouth and carefully wrapped it in a piece of silver foil. She cleared her throat.

'Well, the way it is, I like robbing. I'm good at it. I've always been doing it. Ever since I was a small kid. My big brother, Jason, he was an addict. He needed money for his habit. He used take me into town, into O'Connell Street, and I used go dipping for him. Dipping is fun. You'd be amazed the number of women out there who have handbags that are open. It's the easiest thing in the world to put your hand in and help yourself to a purse or a wallet. Nothing to it. Then I started robbing cars. Joyriding. We were all doing it. We'd go out, any time of the day or night. Pick up a Merc or a Beamer. I loved driving. I was good at it. We'd rob the car in some rich street and then we'd drive it back to the estate. Everyone would be out watching us. We'd be doing wheelies and handbrake turns all around the green. It was great. The cops couldn't catch us. They didn't have the balls for it. My ma tried to stop me. She even locked me in the house. But I could climb out the window and down the drainpipe. She never knew where I was. But then one day it all went wrong. I was out with Kevin, my boyfriend. We'd robbed a car in Stillorgan and we were heading back home. But these cops had spotted us and they were following us. We turned onto the dual carriageway. Kevin was driving. He was getting freaked out by it all. He went onto the wrong side of the road. It was early in the morning, four or five or something, so there wasn't much traffic and for a while it was all OK. He was going to drive the car across the green bit in the middle, but suddenly there was this other car. Right in front of us. He tried to swerve, but it was no use. We smacked right into them. He went through the windscreen and he died on the spot. I was wearing my seat belt. I was pretty banged up, broken pelvis, ruptured spleen, broke both my legs, but I survived. But the people in the other car didn't. It was a man and a woman and their baby. I remember when I was waiting for the fire brigade and the ambulance to come. I could hear the baby crying. It was screaming and screaming. It was still strapped into its little seat. Anyway, they got me for that. They put me away in here. I got five years. I couldn't go to Kev's funeral because I was in hospital. When I get out of here

I'm going to visit his grave every day. I miss him all the time. I wish I'd been driving that day. If I'd been at the wheel we'd never have had the crash. And I feel very sorry about the couple. Their name was O'Doherty. Patrick and Carmel O'Doherty and the baby's name is Sinead. I heard that she's living somewhere near Bray with her granny. I'd like to go and see her too when I get out of here. I'd like to go and say sorry to her for what happened. That's what I'd like to do.'

Silence again. Mags put her hand in her pocket and pulled out another stick of chewing gum. She unwrapped it and put it in her mouth. She began to chew. Tears slid down her round, pink cheeks.

Grace stared out of the window. She cleared her throat. But she had no words to say. Mags shifted on her chair. Marcia broke the silence. She reached across and picked up the piece of paper.

'Call this writing? Look at the spelling.' She began to go through it with her pen. 'That's wrong and that's wrong and that's wrong.' She scored out the words with thick, red lines.

'Hey, you fucking bitch.' Mags grabbed the paper from her. 'You're a crazy cow, do you know that? I'll get you for this.'

She stood up. Her cheeks had turned from pink to scarlet.

'Hold on a minute.' Grace reached out. 'Marcia, you've no right to correct her like that. At least she was honest with us.'

'Honest?' Marcia's expression was incredulous. 'Honest? You are joking, aren't you? It wasn't the boyfriend who was driving that car. It was her.

She killed that couple. She caused all the injuries to that kid. She's a fucking little liar.'

'It's not true. It's not what happened.' Mags launched herself at Marcia. 'You're an evil witch. I'll get you.' The two women fell to the floor. They were wrapped around each other, kicking, biting, tearing at each other's hair. Honey opened the classroom door and screamed for help. Two prison officers ran in. They separated the fighting women and dragged them outside into the corridor.

'Well.' Grace's voice was trembling. 'Well, what do we do now?' She tried to smile.

'We have a nice cup of tea.' Honey smiled. 'What do you say, girls? And I have some chocolate biscuits. They do say that chocolate is a natural sedative.'

They sipped their tea appreciatively.

'Tomorrow is our last day,' Grace said. 'What would you like to do?'

'You know what I'd like?' Lisa looked up. 'It's my baby's anniversary next week. I'd like to make him something. I'd like to write him a story. What about you, Honey? Why don't you write something for your baby too?'

'Yeah, that sounds good.' Honey licked her fingers.

'And you, Lyuba, what would you like to do?' Grace looked at her.

'I write to my momma. She doesn't know where I am. I'd like to do that.'

Grace waited at reception for the steel door to slide back. The prison officer at the desk looked sympathetically at her.

'Bad day, eh? Don't know what's wrong with them all. Must be a full moon. There was a big fight in the men's prison earlier. One of the lads was taken to the Mater.'

'Will he be all right?'

The officer shrugged.

'Don't know yet. He got a very bad beating. Poor bloke. He's only been here a couple of weeks. He was transferred back from England.'

'Oh? And the fight? What was it about?'

'The usual. Drugs. Access to phones. Someone stepping on someone else's toes. Sometimes the atmosphere over there is really strange. You think I'm joking about the moon? I wish.' She looked over Grace's head to a group of women who were waiting to come in. 'You know what, I think he's from your part of the country. One of the islands. Cape Clear, I think. I've been there a couple of times. Hard to imagine someone from such a lovely place ending up over there.' She jerked her head in the direction of the high granite wall topped with razor wire.

The steel door rumbled open. Grace walked through into the sunshine. She unlocked her bike and wheeled it down towards the main road. The Mater hospital cast a deep shadow over the traffic. Could it be Colm? she wondered. It sounded like him all right. She walked around to the entrance hall. Uniformed Gardai were standing beside the desk.

'Excuse me,' she said. 'The prisoner from Mountjoy, is he OK?'

'Are you family?' The clerk looked at her.

She shook her head.

'Sorry, we can't give any information to anyone who isn't a relative.'

She backed away. She looked around her. The hall was crowded. People hurrying in and out. Lift doors opening and closing. She stood still. The strong smell of disinfectant was making her feel ill. She turned away and walked towards the sign for the toilets. She pushed open the door. She stood, looking at herself in the dirty mirror above the wash-hand basins. She opened her bag and took out a pair of sunglasses. She put them on and walked back into the lobby. She scanned the noticeboard quickly, then began to walk up the stairs. Up, up, up to the fourth floor. She followed the signs for intensive care. Again she saw the guards. They were standing in a group, talking among themselves. She walked straight past them and into the ward. A man was lying in the bed by the far wall. His face was covered with an oxygen mask. She moved towards him. His eyes were closed. Tubes ran into his arms. Monitors beeped and lights flashed. She stood beside him. She reached down and touched his hand. He was cold. She twisted her fingers around his. He didn't respond. His hair was shaved close to his skull. There was heavy bruising on his forehead and cheeks, and his eyes were purple and swollen. He looked much smaller than she had remembered, lying there, covered with a pale blue blanket. And then she noticed the tattoo on his shoulder. It was crude. It looked as if someone had smeared the ink before it had dried. But the shape was unmistakable. It was an hourglass. She reached out to touch it. The hourglass fob had been so pretty. And it worked. Turn it up and the sand would run down; turn it up again and the sand would run back. It had the Chamberlain motto engraved in tiny letters on the base. *Veritatem dies aperit.* Time reveals the truth. It was the only thing of value that she had owned. And she had given it to Colm. To thank him for helping her.

She stared down at his face. And felt suddenly as if he were looking at her. His eyes were shut, the lids stretched tightly over them, but she could feel his gaze. It was as angry and as bitter as that last time she had seen him. In the pub in London when he had attacked Jack. And it was as if she could hear his voice. There was a whispering in her head. *Grace,* the voice was saying, *Grace, I haven't forgotten you. I haven't forgotten all I know of you. Remember that. Remember me.*

'Hey, no visitors allowed in the ICU. Who on earth let you in?' A nurse bustled in. She reached down and felt for Colm's pulse. 'Out, now. You can wait outside. He's in no fit state for visitors.'

'Sorry.' Grace picked up her bag. 'I'm sorry. I'm going now. But can you tell me what's wrong with him?'

'Just about everything. Lacerated liver, ruptured spleen, swelling of the brain. He's been in surgery. The next few hours are crucial. If you want to know anything else you'll have to speak to the guards.'

'Thanks, I will.' Grace backed away from the bed. Then turned and hurried out into the corridor. She took the stairs at a run. She pushed through the swing doors and out into the bright

342

afternoon. She mounted her bike and began to freewheel down the hill towards the city. There was a phone call she had to make. When she got home, before she could change her mind. She had to phone her mother. More than anything else, she needed to talk to her.

Liam O'Regan stood over the fax machine. He pulled out the sheets of paper. They were still warm.

'Well, what do you know?' he said. 'Come and have a look at this, Bill.'

They'd got a phone call from the police in Utrecht in Holland. A woman who had been on holiday in Skibbereen had made a complaint. She said she had been raped. The police were faxing a copy of her statement to them. She named her attacker. She said his name was Adam. She didn't have a surname. And his description matched the description that they had of Adam Smyth.

'Why didn't she come to us at the time?' Bill peered over his shoulder at the fax from the Dutch police.

'Well, they say she was deeply shocked by her experience. She went to hospital here and had her injuries treated. The hospital suggested she contact us, but she wouldn't. But now she's had time to think about it and she wants the whole thing investigated.'

'Do you believe her? It's a bit late, isn't it? A bit like shutting the stable door after the horse has bolted.' Bill's expression was cynical.

'I wouldn't say that too loudly if I was you. Not the attitude we're supposed to take to sex crime.

And you'd better have a look at this before you start dismissing her claims.' He handed him another sheet from the fax machine. It was from the British police's database.

'Ah, I see. He has a record. Assault, credit-card fraud. Nothing of a sexual nature though.'

'Nothing proven, but off the record they told me that he was charged with rape in 1998. Found not guilty. The victim's evidence collapsed under cross-examination. He's actually on probation for the fraud charges. He got permission from his probation officer to come to Ireland on holiday. He phoned her and said he'd been offered a job here and she told him to take it.'

'So, where is he?' Bill asked.

'So far no one has a clue. But he can't disappear. Now we've got the car to look for, we'll find him soon.' Liam put on his jacket.

'Well, he's hardly likely to come here, is he? Much more likely to head back to England or even further afield.' Bill picked up the phone. 'I presume the lads in Dublin have put out the alert. Maybe we should be thinking about going public with the car.'

'Maybe. Maybe I should call on the old lady again.'

'What for?' Bill looked dismissive. 'She's told you everything she knows. He's not going to come back to her. He'll know it's only a matter of time before we spot the car. No, I reckon he's already gone. Look, why don't you go to the hospital and ask them for whatever evidence they have. Make yourself useful. The old lady can wait.'

The house was empty when Grace got home. She dumped her bag in the hall. She walked into the kitchen. She picked up the phone. She punched, in the number for Trawbawn. She felt sick and light-headed. The phone rang and rang. She could see it. On the table in the drawing room by the sofa. The light angled in through the French windows. Dust hung in shimmering bars. The afternoon light would shine in the same way through the windows in Trawbawn. It would glance off the bevelled edges of the mirror above the mantelpiece. It would splinter into little rainbows.

The phone kept on ringing and ringing. She could feel the vibrations against her cheek. She wouldn't wait much longer. She would hang up soon. But suddenly there was a voice in her ear.

'Hello?' The voice was slow and hesitant.

Grace opened her mouth to speak. Her tongue and lips were dry. She swallowed.

'Mum, is that you?'

Grace leaned against the wall. She began to cry.

TWENTY-SEVEN

Grace hadn't forgotten the road to Cork, even though it was years since she had driven it. The sun was setting in front of her. Getting lower and lower in the western sky. Soon it would be dark, and driving would be more difficult. But she had no choice. She had to go home.

She ran through the conversation with Lydia.

345

Over and over again. None of it made sense.

'Darling Grace, at last you've phoned me. Thank you, thank you.' Lydia sounded half asleep.

'Mum, I saw you on TV. You've hurt yourself. Are you all right?'

'Saw me on TV? What are you talking about? I'm fine, darling, I'm fine. I have new painkillers. I can't feel a thing now. But I don't want to talk about me. You have to come home, Grace. There's someone you have to meet. Your son is here. Your son has come to find you.'

'Adam. You've met Adam? He didn't tell me.'

'Of course I've met Adam. I sent Adam to Dublin to look for you. But that was before, before all this happened.'

'Mum, I don't understand what you're saying. You don't sound well. Have you been drinking?'

'No, darling, I haven't been drinking. It's the pain-patch thing they gave me in the hospital. It's got morphine in it or something. It makes me very sleepy. But the pain was so bad I had to use it. But, Grace, listen to me, listen to me. Your son is here. His name is John Bradshaw. He was brought up in Chichester in England. He wants to meet you. You have to come and see him. I'm worried that he will leave unless I can tell him that you are coming. Please, please, you must do this. Forget about me and all that has happened in the past. You must come. You will, won't you?'

'Mum, you're not making sense.' Grace couldn't work out what she was saying. 'Adam is my son. It's Adam.'

But now there was silence. And a soft hiss. Like the sound from the inside of a seashell held

346

against the ear.

'Mum, are you there? Mum,' Grace shouted. 'Mum, Lydia, where are you?' She hung up the phone, then tried again. It was engaged. She tried again and again and again. It was still engaged. She sat down at the kitchen table. Adam had said he was her son. He had told her about himself. He had told her about the baby clothes. He had told her about the Fannin Institute. He had known all about that. But what else had he told her? Not much. He was from Falmouth. His parents were dead. He had traced her through the government information service. He had been vague. She hadn't pushed him. She didn't want him to feel under pressure. She had taken him at face value. What was it he had said? He had used the words the Cape people use. He had said she was 'on the cradle'. He had called the little cardigan a gansey.

She thought back to that time by the canal. She had said to Adam, 'I know who you are.' She remembered the expression on his face. He was surprised, defensive. She had felt so sorry about him. She had felt his pain, his sadness. But she remembered. She had said to him, 'I know who you are. You are my son.' It was she who had said it. It wasn't Adam. It was only later when they had met for dinner that he had spoken about his birth, his adoption, that he had told her what he knew. She felt suddenly sick. If he wasn't her son, then who was he? What did he want with her? And how did he know Lydia? And if Lydia had asked him to come to Dublin to find her, why had he not told her this when they met? When they met – she thought back to the first time in the gallery. He was talking to someone on his phone. Was it Lydia? she thought. And if it wasn't Lydia, then who could it be? Someone else who knew her? And the next time they had met was in the street near her house. It had seemed at the time like a lucky coincidence. And he had explained it to her. He knew where she lived because he had come to Dublin to find her. Because I'm his mother, she had thought. And we are linked forever.

But what if there was another reason why he had wanted to find her? She had opened herself up to him. She had given him access to her world. And now she was afraid of what she had done. She picked up the phone again. She tried Amelia's mobile. There was no reply. She phoned Jack.

'Where is Amelia?' she asked.

'She went out for lunch hours ago. She's skiving.' He sounded irritated.

'Where are you?' She tried to keep the fear from her voice.

'I'm walking through College Park. I'm just going to the library. I'm doing the kind of tedious jobs I was hoping she'd do.' He paused. 'Hold on, Grace, I see her. Oh right, that's typical.' She could hear the exasperation in his voice.

'What, what?' Grace's voice rose.

'She's with a bloke, wouldn't you know?'

'What does he look like?'

'He's tall, slim, blond, good-looking. They're actually walking away. What is she at?'

'Go after her, Jack. Get her, bring her back.'

Grace could feel tears in her eyes.

'Oh, she's seen me. The little brat. Now she's waving. Caught in the act. Brazen as anything. She's coming over now.'

'And the guy? What about the guy?'

'Well, here, you can talk to her yourself.' Grace heard the sound of the phone changing hands.

'Hey, Mum, how you doing?' Amelia's voice was happy, excited.

'Who are you with? Who is the man you're with?' Grace tried not to shout, but there was hysteria in her tone.

'Hey, cool it, calm down. He's Lotte's brother. You know, from school? What's wrong?'

'Lotte's brother. Oh, right. So you know him?'

'Of course I know him. Who do you take me for? A complete idiot?' Amelia's voice dripped disdain.

'OK, sorry, love, sorry. But listen, have you seen Adam today?'

'Adam, your Adam? No, of course I haven't. Dad's kept me locked in his office getting hay fever from the dust.'

'OK, sorry, love. Look, I need to speak to your father. I'm going away for a couple of days. He'll explain.'

She hadn't told Jack everything. She couldn't tell him everything. Not like this. Not about Adam and what had been going on. She told him she was going to see her mother. She was worried about her. She was going to try to make it better between them.

'Amelia's to stay with you. Not in the house and not with her friends. OK?'

'Of course, Grace, of course. Look, don't worry. Would you like me to come with you? It might be easier with me there.'

'No.' She tried not to shout at him. 'No, really, it's better if I go on my own. If it works out, of course, next time I'd love you to come. Explain to Amelia, will you? And you know I've no mobile. So I'll have to phone you. I'll call when I get there.'

'Of course, I know you will. Grace?'

'Yes?'

'Grace, I love you. Even if it doesn't work out with your mother, you still have me.'

She couldn't reply. Her throat was tight. She ran upstairs and packed quickly. It was getting late. She had a long drive ahead. And she didn't know what would be waiting for her.

Liam O'Regan drove down the drive to Trawbawn House. There was a young man walking quickly just ahead of him. Liam stopped the car and got out.

'Hey,' he said. 'Can I ask you for some ID?'

The man looked surprised.

'ID? Why?'

'We're investigating a disappearance. It's a young woman who's gone missing in this area. We're checking on everyone. Where are you from?'

The man put his hand in his pocket and pulled out a passport.

'I'm from England. I'm over here on a few days' holiday.'

Liam looked down at the picture and looked back at his face.

'And what are you doing here, in Trawbawn?'

'I'm interested in the gardens. I came to speak to Mrs Beauchamp yesterday and she asked me to call back.' He looked ill at ease. Liam took out his notebook and copied down the name, date of birth and passport number.

'Hold on a minute. I'm just going to call that in.' He reached back into the car and pulled out the radio. 'Won't be long.'

They waited in silence until he got the call back.

'OK, fine. Thanks.' Liam gestured to the car. 'Sorry about that. We just have to check, you know. I'll give you a lift the rest of the way. You're not driving, are you?'

'No, I thought I'd get a bit of exercise. I'm staying in Skibbereen, in the West Cork Hotel. I walked out here along the river. It's lovely.' He settled into the passenger seat. Liam put the car in gear.

'She's not too good, the old lady,' Liam said. 'I'll just check up on her, make sure she's OK.' They moved slowly towards the house. A light breeze stirred the leaves of the ash trees. The bunches of ash keys rattled. Autumn was on its way, Liam thought.

'So, I'm not a suspect, then?'

'No, here.' Liam handed him the passport. He stopped the car outside the front door. It was standing open. They both got out. Liam looked in through the window. Lydia was sitting on the sofa. Her eyes were closed. Liam knocked on the glass. She lifted her head. She looked tired. She smiled and raised a hand. She waved.

351

'She looks OK. I'll leave you to it.' Liam moved back towards the car. 'If you've any problems you can give us a call. Here.' He took his card from his pocket.

Johnny smiled.

'Thanks,' he said, and took it from him. 'And thanks for the lift.' Then he turned and walked inside.

Colm lay with his eyes closed. He had tried to open them. He had tried to move his arms and his legs, lift his hands, open his mouth, but he couldn't move a muscle. He couldn't work out whether he was awake or asleep. He could hear perfectly well. The beep of electronic machines, the voices of the nurses and doctors, the rattle of some kind of trolley on wheels that squeaked on the floor. And he could smell too. Mostly it was disinfectant, that horrible hospital smell, but there were other scents. The nurses who lifted him and washed him and prodded him all had their own distinctive smells. And earlier he had had the strangest experience. He seemed to have been sleeping and then he seemed to have woken and he had the sense that Grace was standing by the bed. He could feel her fingers on his hand. And when she moved he could smell her. He tried so hard to open his eyes, but it was as if they were nailed shut. He wanted to speak to her but it was as if his lips were stapled together. *Grace*, he thought. *Grace, I haven't forgotten you. I haven't forgotten all I know of you. Remember that. Remember me.* And then he heard the nurse's voice. Telling her to leave. And Grace replying.

Asking what was wrong with him. And then she was gone.

He hadn't started the fight in the prison. But he'd had to defend himself. They had tried to take back the mobile phone. He wasn't having that. It was his lifeline. He had called Adam time after time. But Adam wasn't listening. Adam was gone. He had left him behind. He had taken all his knowledge, all his memories, all his anger and his rage. And he was going to use it. And what would Colm have left? What would Colm have to dream about if Adam had taken it all? Colm could see Grace so clearly. And he could see Adam too. And suddenly he could see what Adam was and what Adam would do. And he knew that Adam had finished with him. He didn't need Colm any longer. He had left him alone. When the heavies from the landing came to get the phone, Colm went for them. But he hadn't expected the response he got. They were all over him. Kicking him, punching him, smashing his head onto the concrete floor. And it took forever for the screws to come. He had known this place was dangerous. Behind the smiling faces and the use of his first name, and the banter and the jokes, there was nothing but danger. And he had been right.

He was going to die. He knew it. He could feel the strength leaving his body. It was like the ebb tide on the river. It was going, slipping and sliding towards the sea, and there was nothing he could do to stop it. Nothing at all.

Grace was getting closer to Trawbawn all the

time. Once she got through Cork city it was all so familiar. She counted off the towns as she passed through them. Innishannon, Bandon, Clonakilty with its brightly coloured shop fronts and hanging baskets. And just outside Clon on the long hill, there was the point near Owenahincha where she always got first sight of the Atlantic Ocean.

She could hear Daniel's voice, saying, 'Look, Grace, look. The sea, the sea, the beautiful sea.'

And she would jump up and down in the back seat of his old car, and clap her hands and whoop and holler at the joy of it. There was a moon tonight. It was beginning to rise. There was light on the water as she came down into Ross Carbery. Light on the old convent and the new hotel. But dark then as she turned inland again. Then light just beyond Leap, shining on the estuary of the river. The twin towns of Glandore and Unionhall out of sight behind the lime-covered hill. And she was nearly there now. Only Skibbereen left between herself and Trawbawn. She slowed for the town. There was some kind of festival. The streets were decorated with bunting and there was a jazz band up on the back of a truck in the middle of the square. She opened her window. They were playing Dixieland music, all saxophones and trumpets, and a man wearing a boater and a striped blazer standing up at the piano. People everywhere, wandering in and out of the pubs with glasses in their hands. And everywhere noise, gaiety, excitement. She was sure she would recognize faces in the crowd. And they would recognize her too. But she kept on going, increasing her speed as she left the town behind. Swung over the bridge by the old boatyard and the pub, saw the river meandering parallel to the road, appearing and disappearing from view, behind fields and trees and small, rounded hills. And saw, at last, the gate lodge and the gates and the sign which said 'Trawbawn House and Gardens. Open to the public.' Stopped the car. Got out. Pushed the gates open. Got back into the car. Drove through. Stopped. Got out. Closed the gates. Turned and looked down the drive. So beautiful in the twilight. The ash and the oak and the arbutus on either side. The long herbaceous border. The cattle chewing the cud in the far field. And just visible above the trees, the roof of the house. Shining now in the light from the moon, which hung, huge and round and mottled and marked, silver and grey. She got back into the car. She put her hand on the gear lever. Which would it be? First gear or reverse? She put her foot on the clutch and shifted into first. She moved slowly forward.

Light spilling out from the open door. A shaft of yellow that lit up the front steps and the path. Light in the drawing room, the curtains open. Above the house a scattering of stars, heads of pins hammered into the navy blue sky. Grace stood still and looked in. It was all so familiar. The polished wooden floor. The faded rug. The walnut table with the gilt mirror above it. She took a step forward. She could just about smell the house. Dust, beeswax, Lydia's perfume, Daniel's pipe, the meal that Alex was cooking. And always the smell of the sea. She turned and looked through the drawing-room windows. It was exactly as she remembered. The baby grand with its collection of silver-framed photographs. The painting above the fireplace. One of the Chamberlain ancestors, she thought, with his elegant whiskers and monocle. The glass-fronted bookcases and the glass chandelier which tinkled gently when the windows were open and the breeze came up from the river. She could hear music coming from somewhere. The kitchen perhaps. The radio might be on. Lydia might have forgotten about it. Forgotten to turn it off before she went to bed. She took a step hesitantly, slowly towards the door. She had sworn that she would never come back. That it meant nothing to her. That she didn't want to have anything to do with the house, the gardens, any of it. But now as she stood and looked around, and smelt the mud of the river, mixed with the night-scented stock which pushed its modest straggling flowers through the cracks in the paving, she wondered why.

She looked at her watch. It was just after ten. She looked back over her shoulder. The lawn behind her stretched down towards the band of trees along the riverbank. It was dark, almost black. She had a sudden desire to feel the grass beneath her feet. She bent down and took off her sandals. She walked across the gravel. Her toes softened into the turf. And she began to cry.

Adam stood back from the first-floor window and watched her. Behind him, on the bed, Lydia lay sprawled on her back. She was sleeping. She had been so upset that he had made her take some more of her pills. He had come into the drawing room and found her with the man she called John. Grace's son, she had explained. She had thought Adam would be pleased and welcoming. But he had grasped John by the arm and pulled him from the room, into the hall, out into the garden. She had tried to follow them, but her balance was bad and she fell over. So she hadn't seen him hit John on the head – just a little tap really, just to stop him from shouting and running away. She hadn't seen him push him ahead, down the path to the river. It was such a lovely day. John had said he wanted to go for a swim. It was a perfect day for a swim. John had swum away. Swum far away. He wouldn't be back. He seemed like a nice boy. But there couldn't be two of them, could there? Grace could only have one son. And it was going to be Adam. That was why he had to take the phone away from Lydia. It wouldn't be right for her to speak to Grace about John. It would just upset her. And Grace had enough upset in her life. And that was why he had to get rid of John. Grace would only have one son. And his name was Adam.

Now Adam moved closer to the window and pressed his face and hands against the glass. Pressed his hands so hard that his palms became bloodless. Grace was standing below. She looked up. Her face was washed white by the pearly light. He lifted his hand and waved to her. Then he stepped back. He took the stairs two at a time. He landed with a small jump on the rug in the hall. He walked to the front door. He leaned against the jamb, his legs crossed, his arms folded.

'Welcome home, Mother,' he said. 'Welcome home.'

TWENTY-EIGHT

The passport lay on the floor where Adam had dropped it. Grace reached out and picked it up.

'Go on, open it. See what your son really looks like.' Adam sat back in his chair. He smiled at her. 'He's a bit of a disappointment really. He's not what you'd expect. He doesn't look anything like you.'

'Where is he?' Grace said. 'What have you done with him?'

Adam shrugged.

'Well now, where do I begin? I invited him down to the river for a swim. He wasn't too happy about it to begin with. He said the water was cold. But I persuaded him. I said he wasn't to be such a wimp. I said it wouldn't be too bad once he got wet all over. And do you know something? I was right.'

Grace flicked open the stiff cover and looked down. A solemn face looked back at her. Short, dark hair and a pointed chin. An expression that told her nothing.

'Here.' Adam threw something else to her. 'This is a better likeness.'

She picked it up. It was a laminated ID card. He said he was a teacher at Chichester Grammar School. It gave his name, date of birth and address. He was smiling in this photo. His hair was longer. It was curly. He was wearing a dark

358

blue, open-necked shirt. He looked happy.

'A teacher,' she said. 'Like me.'

'Was a teacher.' Adam reached forward and grabbed it from her. 'Not any longer.'

He walked over to the fireplace. He flung it into the grate, then turned back for the passport. He took the box of matches from the mantelpiece. He bent down and set fire to them both. Then he stood back and watched them burn. Grace lay on her side. It hurt to breathe. He had kicked her in the ribs. It hurt to speak. He had punched her in the mouth. She closed her eyes. She wept.

It had been so easy to subdue her. He had thought she would fight harder. But one well-aimed blow had done it. He had walked her into the drawing room and as she turned to speak, he had hit her. She went down like a house of cards. And she didn't get up again. Colm had told him how to do it. Surprise, first of all, then unreasonable force. Surprise again. They never expected that.

He had picked up her bag and emptied its contents onto the polished lid of the grand piano. He had selected the lipstick he favoured. The one that was the colour of an old French rose. He stood in front of the mirror. He unscrewed the barrel. He pressed the point to the middle of his upper lip. He outlined his mouth. He looked at her in the mirror. She wasn't moving. He filled in the outline with the dusky pink. He smacked his lips together. He could smell the cloying sweetness. And taste it too. She raised her head. She was watching him. She began to crawl towards the door. He hummed quietly to himself.

Whenever I feel afraid,
I hold my head erect,
And whistle a happy tune,
So no one will suspect,
I'm afraid.

She was inching slowly, very slowly. He watched her. He smacked his lips together loudly. She paused and looked towards the mirror.

'Naughty, naughty,' he said and shook his finger. Then he turned and, before she could defend herself, he took hold of her hair and dragged her back into the room.

'Why?' she screamed. 'Why are you doing this to me?'

'Because I can, that's why. And because of this.' He put his hand in his pocket and pulled out the hourglass. He swung it to and fro in front of her face. 'Remember this?'

'Colm,' she whispered. 'He gave it to you. You know him.'

'Indeed I do. I know him very well. He gave it to me. And he told me to go and find your mother.'

'But he didn't tell you to do this. Colm would never have wanted you to hurt me. Colm was good to me. Colm looked after me after I had the baby. He was my friend. He stood by me. I know he wouldn't have wanted it to be like this.'

'But look how you repaid his friendship.' Adam smiled at her. 'Look how you rewarded his kindness. You turned your back on him. You were too good for him, weren't you? You were going places where a man like Colm wouldn't be fit to polish the brass handles on the door.'

'That's not true.' She tried to sit up but he held her down. 'I was never like that. My mother was. But I wasn't, and Colm knew that. There's no justification for this. None at all. You're pathetic.'

'Pathetic,' he screamed the word back at her. 'Pathetic, is that what I am?' He pulled her to her feet again. And hit her. So hard that she spun backwards and landed again on the floor.

He knelt down beside her and put his face close to her.

'Do you see what I'm wearing, Grace? I'm wearing your lipstick. It tastes good. But not half as good as the pale pink frosted one that your lovely daughter Amelia wears. And when I'm finished with you I'm going after her. I know all about you and your family. I have the keys to your house. And nothing will keep me away from Amelia. But first, we've a bit of business to attend to.'

He stood up and locked the drawing-room door. Then he took a long, black, plastic strap from the pocket of his jacket.

'See this, little Gracey. I took the trouble of doing a raid on the shed in the vegetable garden. They've all these really useful bits and pieces there. This is a tree tie. But it makes a very useful form of handcuff. Won't mark your skin. But will stop you from waving around too much.' He pulled her hands behind her back and strapped them together.

'I would do your ankles too. But that would stop me from pulling your legs apart. And that would sort of defeat the purpose, wouldn't it?' He

361

straddled her body and undid his belt. 'But you're not going to make a fuss, are you? Your mother is asleep upstairs and we wouldn't want to wake her. An old woman like that. Because if we woke her and she came downstairs and saw what I was doing, she might want some of it herself. And I wouldn't want to disappoint her, would I?' He rolled her over onto her back with her arms trapped beneath her. 'Now, that's better isn't it? Wouldn't do not to be able to see your face. Take all the fun out of it. So now, are you ready? Are you lying comfortably? Then let's begin.'

Lydia opened her eyes. She couldn't understand what was happening. She seemed to have been sleeping forever. But was she sleeping? Was she awake? She could hear noises coming from somewhere in the house. But such strange noises. Screams and shouts that sounded like the cry of an animal in pain. She struggled to sit up. Her mouth was dry and foul. She pulled herself off the bed and staggered. Her legs were unable to hold her upright. She waited, then tried again. She moved slowly towards the bathroom, holding onto the wall. She switched on the light and re-coiled at the image she saw in the mirror. Her skin was yellow. Her eyes were bloodshot. Her hair was in a matted frizz. She turned on the tap and filled a glass with water. Her hand was shaking so much that she spilt it all over her blouse. She sat down on the closed lid of the lavatory and tried to steady herself. What had happened to her? There was a prickly irritation on the skin of her shoulder. She remembered. She had stuck the pain patch there. She pulled at her sleeve and pushed it up. She grasped hold of the sticky strip and ripped it free. She dropped it on the floor.

Adam had been with her. She remembered. And the other boy, the boy who said he was Grace's son.

'Oh no,' she cried out loud. Adam had come into the drawing room. He had taken hold of John and pulled him out of the room. John had protested, tried to shake him off, looked to her for help. But Adam wouldn't listen, wouldn't pay any heed. She had followed them out into the hall, but then she had lost her balance and fallen. The last thing she had seen before Adam slammed the front door was the look on John's face. He was frightened. And a few minutes later Adam had come back, locked her into the drawing room, left her there. And then later, she didn't know how much later, he had returned. This time he had made her take some more of her painkillers, given her a glass of whiskey to drink. And after that she remembered nothing.

Except the voices. And there was something else. There was the hourglass fob. She had asked him where he got it. And he had told her. He had got it from Colm. She couldn't work out how he could have known Colm. And then he had told her all about Colm, the prison, everything.

But she still didn't understand.

'But how did Colm get it?' she asked.

'Grace, of course. Grace gave it to him,' he replied.

And she realized. Alex had given it to Grace. *Veritatem dies aperit.* Times reveals the truth.

She stood up and shuffled to the door. She moved out onto the landing. She could hear the terrible cries coming from below. She grasped the banister with her good hand and began to inch slowly down. The cries were loud now. They frightened her. She stopped. Perhaps she should go back to her room. She was safe there. But she heard the voice from downstairs and she recognized it. She moved again. Step by step down to the hall. The door to the drawing room was shut. She tried the doorknob. It was locked. She opened the drawer in the small table under the mirror in the hall. Daniel always kept a spare key. Just in case, he used to say. Just in case. She fitted it into the lock. It clicked smoothly into place. She opened it. She saw Adam and a woman. She didn't know her at first. Her face was covered in blood. But then she saw her hair.

'Grace,' she said 'Grace.'

Adam looked up at her.

'Lydia, just in time. So glad you decided to join us. Do come in.'

Her legs refused to move. He stepped forward and took her by the hand. Tears were slipping down her face.

'Oh,' he said, 'isn't that sweet? So pleased to see your daughter.' He led her to the sofa and pushed her to sit.

'Now, I'll tell you what we're going to do. We're going to wait until it begins to get light. And then we're going for a walk down to the river. But first.' He moved towards Lydia. 'I think it's time, don't you?' He held the hourglass fob in front of her face. 'Time for you and me.'

'No, please don't do that. Leave her alone. Don't hurt her.' Grace raised herself up on her elbow. 'She's an old woman. She's no use to you.'

He looked at her. Then he looked at Lydia.

'Oh, I think you're wrong there. I think you're very wrong.' He bent down to check on the tie on her wrists. Then he fastened her ankles together. He held open the door and gestured with his head towards the stairs. 'After you, Lydia,' he said. 'After you.'

He pulled the drawing-room door closed behind them and locked it.

'Now,' he prodded her in the back, so she moved forward quickly, 'where were we?'

TWENTY-NINE

With the dawn came the light. And with the light came the pain. The light shone into the house. The pain throbbed through her body. The light brightened the dried blood on her hands and her face. It glanced across her swollen eyes so she winced and her eyelids closed of their own volition. She tried to sit up, to move towards the window, to draw the curtains to keep out the light, but she couldn't lift her legs. Not even to crawl on her hands and knees over the polished floorboards. She could do nothing. Nothing to protect herself. Nothing to save herself. Nothing except lie as still and as quietly as she could. And hope that he had satisfied himself. And that he was gone.

She wrapped her arms around her body. And she listened. The house was quiet. Perhaps she could sleep for a few minutes. And when she woke she would feel better. Stronger. Braver. And she could pick herself up and tiptoe to the door. And open it. And creep out onto the landing. And listen. Always listen. For the sound of his footsteps in the hall below. For the sound of his fist. For the sound of his voice. And if she waited quietly and heard nothing she could put one hand on the banister and begin to walk downstairs. And maybe then he would not be there any longer. He would have decided that enough was enough for one day. That he had got everything that he could. And he would leave her and her daughter in peace.

But as she lay on the floor she heard him. Not his fist, not his footsteps. Just his voice. He was shouting. She lifted her head and held it up. She tried to twist around towards the door but her neck was stiff and so sore that she could not move it. She laid her head down again. Tears dribbled from the corners of her swollen eyes. They stung as they slid down into the cuts on her face. She could hear what he was saying.

'I have the hourglass, Lydia. And you know what that means. I have all the time in the world. Time means nothing any longer, nothing for you, and everything for me.'

But it didn't matter what he said. All that mattered was how he said it. And what he was going to do. And she knew from the tremors that rose up through the house. She knew what he was going to do. He was coming back for her.

And this time there would be no way out.

Liam O'Regan was awake too. He had slept fitfully. He couldn't stop thinking about Maria Grimes. The more he thought about her, the more he wanted to find Adam Smyth. But so far there had been no sightings of the car or Adam. It was just a matter of time, Liam was sure. He'd show up, sooner or later. Guys like him always showed up.

He got out of bed and walked downstairs to the kitchen. He put on the kettle. It was still dark. He'd have his cup of tea, listen to the early morning news, and then maybe he'd sleep for an hour or so before the alarm went off. But just as he was pouring the boiling water into the pot, his phone rang. He picked it up and looked at the display. It was Peter Finnegan from the traffic police in Cork city. And the news was good. There'd been an accident in the Jack Lynch tunnel yesterday. A three-car pile-up. Peter had been going back through the CCTV tapes looking for a probable cause and he'd seen the Saab on the southbound lane.

'We have it here, Liam, the car you and the lads in Dublin are suddenly so interested in.'

'And the driver, do you get a good look at the driver?'

'Yeah, male, fair hair, thin face, aged late twenties, I'd say.'

'And he's heading south, is he?'

'Isn't that what I said, Liam?'

'Sorry, Peter, sorry. A bit early to be on the ball. For me anyway, not for you, obviously.'

'End of my shift. Been here all night. I'm just

off home to bed. Anyway, hope you can do something with the info. Will I phone Dublin or will you?'

'I'll do it. I've a couple of other things I want to ask them. See you round, Peter, and thanks again, mate.'

He got dressed quickly. Why would Adam Smyth be coming back here? He didn't get it. He didn't believe all those old wives' tales about people returning to the scene of the crime. But perhaps he had forgotten something. Perhaps there was something he needed to get, something that would be incriminating for him. There was the van, of course. Pat Jordan's van. They had given it a cursory search and found nothing. But they needed to take it in and do a proper job. They had also gone over the room in Pat's house where Adam Smyth had been staying. Again they had found nothing. And they had searched Trawbawn. But maybe they hadn't looked hard enough. Maybe that was where they should have started.

He left the house and got into his car. A thin line of pale grey was showing just above the trees. He'd phone Bill McCarthy and drag him out of bed. And by that time it would be daylight. And who knows what they'd find down there by the river.

Adam stood in the bedroom doorway. Lydia was sitting in the chair by the dressing table. She had washed the blood from her mouth and nose. She was staring at the floor. Her face was expressionless.

'Come on,' he said, 'it's time to go.'

She stood up. She didn't look at him. He opened the door for her. As she passed him, she flinched away.

'Don't worry, sweetheart,' he said. 'I wouldn't dream of touching you again. Once was plenty.'

They walked in line towards the river, Adam at the front. He was carrying a sports bag in one hand. Grace was behind him, a rope tied around her neck. He had undone the strap on her ankles. She had begged him to undo her hands. The pressure on her shoulders was excruciating. So he had unfastened them, then tied them again, but this time in front of her.

'See,' he said. 'I do care about you, Grace my sweet. In a filial kind of way. I'm not so bad, am I?' And he leaned forward and kissed her on the cheek. Lydia limped behind. He hadn't bothered to disable her. She wasn't going anywhere on her own. Every now and then he jerked the rope and Grace stumbled, fell forward.

'Just to remind you,' he said, turning around and walking backwards in front of her. 'Just to remind you who's the boss.'

Grace didn't respond. She was trying to keep calm. She could hear Lydia mumbling something. It sounded like a prayer. Grace wanted to turn around and touch her, reassure her in some way, that everything would be all right. She had been so shocked when she first saw her. So unprepared for the reality of what her mother had become. Who was this small, stooped creature with the wrinkled face and the hair in a matted frizz? Her clothes were filthy. She smelt of urine. Her fingernails were long and ragged. Her hands were ingrained with dirt. She didn't seem to know who Grace was. She had stared at her when she had first seen her. Then her eyes had become blank and glazed, and she had not responded any more. Grace tried to look back at her, but Adam tugged at the rope and she fell forward again. She put out her hands to save herself. The path was damp underfoot. Even though there had been no water for days the ground was still soft beneath her bare feet. There'll be footprints, she thought. When they come to look for us, there'll be footprints here.

'Come on.' Adam tugged at the rope again and her head snapped forward. She looked down. And saw. A dead rat was lying in the grass. Its mouth was open, its teeth exposed. There was the shimmer of flies' wings over its dark back. She stopped and, before Adam could respond, she had bent down and picked it up by its tail.

'Look,' she shouted, and swung it in an arc over her head. Adam screamed. His eyes widened and his face turned white.

'Look,' she shouted again and swung it out towards him.

'No, get it way from me.' His voice was a hysterical shriek. He dropped the rope. He turned and ran. She flung the rat towards him and it hit him between the shoulder blades. He screamed again. He looked back over his shoulder.

'I'll get you, you fucking bitch, I'll get you for that.' He plunged into the undergrowth, pulling his shirt from his back.

'Quick,' Grace whispered. 'Come on, quick. The boathouse.'

She could see its corrugated roof through the trees. She pushed Lydia in front of her.

'Hurry, before he follows us. Quick.'

Liam heard the ambulance before he saw it. The sing-song siren was coming from over the hill beyond the gate to Trawbawn. He slowed and waited for it to pass. It was travelling as fast as it possibly could on the narrow, twisting road.

'Check that out, Bill, will you?' He gestured toward the radio.

Bill picked it up. Liam waited and listened. Bill's conversation with the dispatcher was short and to the point.

'OK,' he said. 'Got it.' He turned to Liam. 'A drowning. Tim O'Connor from Church Strand was out early checking on a heifer that was in trouble down by the beach. He found a body on the mud. Just about alive. They're taking him into Skib, but it's touch and go, they say.'

'Him, not her?'

'Male, young, no other details.'

Liam flicked on his indicator and began to turn towards Trawbawn.

'Shit,' he said, 'for a minute there I thought it might have been Maria. And this whole thing might have been over.'

It was dark inside the boathouse. Grace leaned against the wall. She reached up and felt for the knotted rope around her neck. She couldn't see it beneath her chin. But she knew what it was. It

371

was a bowline. A fisherman's knot. She knew what to do. She remembered. How Alex had taught her. To tie and untie by feel and not by sight. It was difficult with her hands constricted by the tree tie. But she could do it. She pulled off the rope and dropped it down into the bottom of the nearest boat.

'Free my hands, quickly. Get this thing off me.' She held out her wrists. Lydia gazed vacantly at her. She moistened her lips but no words would come.

'Mum, come on; you can do it. You have to do it. He'll find us soon. You know what he said. He said we would die together. In the river. We can't let that happen. Please, Mum, just take hold of one end and unthread it. Then we can get help.'

Lydia looked at her. Her body was floppy and uncoordinated.

'Grace,' she said, 'tell me. Did you come here with Alex? Was it here that he used to take you?'

'Not now, Mum. We can't talk about this now. It was a long time ago. It's in the past.'

'No, it isn't, darling.' Lydia reached out and stroked her face. 'It's why this is happening. None of this would have happened if I hadn't treated you the way I did. If I had loved you more, and cared less about this place and my own vanity, you would have stayed here. You would have had your son here. He would have grown up with us. We would have been happy. You would have told me that Alex was his father. I would have got rid of him. It would have been all right.'

'Don't,' Grace said, 'don't talk about it now. It wasn't your fault. I could have told you. But I didn't. I thought Alex would leave you and come to England and rescue me. I hated you because he loved you still. I didn't want the baby without him. At least I thought I didn't. But it doesn't matter now. We can make it better in the future. We can be together again. But you must help me. You have to take this off my hands so I can defend us. Please, Mummy, please try.'

Lydia lifted her hand and grasped the end of the plastic tongue. She tugged. But it wouldn't budge.

'I can't. With one hand I can't do it,' she said. Her voice was plaintive and tearful, like the voice of a child.

'OK.' Grace moved towards the boat. 'We'll just have to manage as best we can. If we can get into this punt here and out onto the river, we can drift. Someone will see us.' She bent down and began to untie the painter.

'Grace?' Lydia looked at her.

'Yes?'

'You do forgive me, don't you? I've done some very bad things in my life. Daniel wanted you to have this place. He wanted it to go to you. But I–' Her voice faltered. 'I–'

'It doesn't matter, Mum. Nothing matters now. All that matters is that we get away from here. You've got to stay strong, you've got to fight. OK?' Grace leaned forward and kissed her on the cheek. She held out her hands and steadied her mother.

'But I just want you to know. When I die, all this goes to you. The way it should have been when Daniel died. Do you understand?' Lydia stepped awkwardly onto the boat's slatted floor.

Grace nodded.

'Don't worry, no one's going to die,' she said. She began to push the boat away towards the river. Then she heard her mother scream.

Grace turned around. Adam was behind her. He hit her so she fell backwards into the boat. He pulled down one of the oars that was stored in the rafters above their heads. He jumped in beside her.

'Good girl,' he said, 'making my life easy.' He slotted the oar into the rowlock on the stern. 'Now,' he said. 'Just sit back and enjoy the trip.'

The front door was open. Liam walked in.

'Hello,' he called out. There was no response. He moved into the drawing room. It was a mess. Silver-framed photographs lay on the carpet, their glass smashed. Chairs had been overturned. There were dark smears on the wall and across the floorboards. Liam squatted and touched them with his fingers. Bill made for the stairs. Liam could hear his footsteps up above.

'No one up here,' he called out, 'but something's been going on all right. There's more blood in the front bedroom,' he called out.

Liam walked through the house and down into the kitchen. It was a mess too. Piles of unwashed dishes and food, covered with flies, left on the table. He opened the back door and stepped outside. He walked quickly towards the walled garden. The Saab was neatly tucked behind a sheltering canopy of huge rhododendrons. He turned back towards the house.

'Bill,' he shouted. 'The car, we've found the car.'

Adam sat in the stern of the boat. He sculled quickly with one oar.

'Not much further now. Nearly there.'

Grace looked around her. She opened her mouth to shout but no sound would come. She could hear Lydia's breathing. It was laboured and harsh.

'Are you all right?' She turned to look at her. Her mother's face was grey. Her eyes were dull and unfocused.

'Of course she's all right.' Adam sniggered. 'She's never been better. Reunited with her daughter. Met her grandson. So many treats for a woman of her age.'

'Why are you doing this, Adam?' Grace leaned forward. 'Why? What did we ever do to you? Don't you think you've done enough? What do you have to gain by killing us? They'll find you, you know. You won't get away with it. And they'll send you back to prison. And Colm won't be there this time. Because Colm is dying. Did you know that?'

Adam stopped sculling.

'What do you mean? How do you know?'

'He was in a fight in the prison. I saw him in hospital. He's in a coma. He's not expected to survive.'

'You're lying.' Adam picked up the oar again. 'You're making it up. You're just saying this to upset me. Well, it won't work. I'd know if Colm was hurt. I'd just know.'

'No, you wouldn't. Why would you? Colm

doesn't love you. He was just using you to get at us. You're an instrument, a tool for him. You're not a person.' She tried to keep her voice calm. 'He never cared about you, Adam. And he cares even less now. Stop now. Turn back. Leave us at the boathouse. Go away. Go as far away from this place as you can. We won't say anything. We'll let you go. That's all we want.' She tried to smile.

'Go as far away from this place as I can. How far, I wonder? As far as Cork? As far as Dublin? How far will I go? As far as Amelia's bedroom up at the top of your lovely house? Will that do?' He smiled now.

'You're mad. You're a psychopath. That's what you are.' Grace tried to stand up. The boat rocked from side to side. Adam reached out and grabbed her around the neck.

'That's what they all say. That's what my father said. He said I was mad. He sent me out into the world. My grandmother said I was mad too. She cried when she said it. I cried when I pushed her and she fell. She never walked again. She died. They all die. Just the way you and your mother and your daughter will die. Now.' He began to ship the oar. 'This is it.'

He leaned forward and made as if to take hold of Grace. But she stood up. The rope that had been around her neck was now in her hands. It was looped in a coil. She hit him across the face, lashing him, backwards and forwards. He pulled away. He was off balance. He reached out for her, but she hit him again, catching his eyes.

'Quick, Lydia, help me,' she screamed. Lydia stumbled forward. She took hold of the sports bag. She recognized it. It was the bag she had taken from the back of Pat Jordan's van. She hit Adam with it, just below the knees. He lurched and lost his balance. The boat rocked violently. He reached out and tried to wrench it from Lydia's grasp, but she hung on as best she could. Grace leaned towards him, trying to slip the rope over his neck, but he pushed her hard and she fell back.

'I've got you now, you old bitch,' he screamed at Lydia as he flung himself onto her. But she stepped back and he fell heavily. The boat lurched to one side. The gunwales dipped beneath the water.

'Watch out, watch out,' Grace cried. Adam struggled to get up. The boat lurched again. He fell heavily on his knees. One hand was holding Lydia's legs. She dragged herself forward. He pulled himself up onto her, but before he could regain his balance, Lydia had turned, grasped hold of his hair, then turned back and pushed herself into the river, dragging him with her.

Grace leaned over the side of the boat. The current was carrying them away from her. She managed to pick up the oar, but she couldn't slot it into the rowlock. She turned back to the river. She could see them, both their heads, their hair slicked to their skulls, their arms flailing.

'Mum, hold on, Mum. I'll help, hold on,' she screamed. But Lydia was failing. Grace could see that she couldn't keep herself afloat. She kept on disappearing beneath the river's rippled surface.

Lydia couldn't breathe. Her lungs were filling with water. This is it, she thought. This is how it will end. She had tried to hold onto Adam's hair, to drag him down with her, but he was too strong. He had freed himself from her grasp. His expression was triumphant.

'You stupid old woman. You thought you could hurt me? It's you who's mad, not me.' He pushed her away and began to swim to the boat. Grace leaned out. She was trailing the piece of rope in the water. She shouted to her mother.

'Here, Lydia, grab hold of this. Quick.'

'No.' Lydia could barely speak. Every time she opened her mouth, water slopped in. 'No, you save yourself. Leave me, just leave me.'

And it was Adam who took hold of the rope, Adam whose fingers, whitening with the effort, were grasping the side of the boat, Adam who was beginning to pull himself up. Grace reached down and, with her two hands, clumsily took the oar again. She swung around with it just as Adam's upper body began to fall forward into the boat. She missed his head but the oar grazed his shoulders. He cried out and began to slip slowly back. She kicked him then. In the face, again and again. Blood ran from his nose and, as his head dipped beneath the water, it spread out, an iridescent sheen that gleamed in the early morning sunshine.

'Mum,' Grace shouted. 'Where are you?' But there was no sign of her mother.

Adam pushed down with his feet, treading water frantically. He flailed with his arms, trying to keep afloat. But he was tired. And he was scared. The river was full of rats. He had seen them from the safety of the trawler. Scurrying across the mudflats at low tide, their bright red eyes gleaming, their small, neat paws busy. He could feel something gently touching his legs, tickling his ankles. He was sure it was them.

'Help me, help me, Colm,' he screamed. He looked around. Lydia had come to the surface. Her skin was white. Her eyes were closed. He grabbed hold of her arm. She didn't respond. She rolled over and began to slip beneath the surface.

'Lydia!' Grace's voice was despairing. 'Come back. I need you.'

'Help me,' Adam shouted and waved his arms. 'Here, over here; help me.'

Water filled his mouth as he tried to call out, but now there was something dragging at his legs. He could see dark fronds of weed, thick, luxuriant, terrifying. He kicked out, but they coiled around him, clinging. His head dipped beneath the water. He kicked down with his feet and pushed himself out into the sunshine again. He gasped for breath, then felt his strength waning. The river closed over his head again. Again he pushed himself up. He tried to speak, to say something, but now there were no words.

Grace leaned over the side of the boat. Her hands flopped uselessly in front of her. She called out her mother's name, over and over again. But there was no response. She sank down onto the seat. She bowed her head. She wept.

The last time Adam saw the house it was from the river. It seemed to float above the thick green frill of trees along the shore. The grey slate roof shone in the early morning sunshine. The long bay windows were dark. It was the last thing he saw before the salt and the fresh filled his lungs, dragged him down, down, down to the black mud below. The sun filtered through the water and the weed, and shone for an instant on the gold of the hourglass before it too sank beneath the ooze.

Colm tried to open his eyes. They would not respond to his will. Nothing would respond. He was getting weaker all the time. The sounds in the room were more and more distant, more and more faint. He couldn't feel the touch of the nurses. Or smell their scent any longer. The only thing he could smell was the salt tang of the mudflats in the river. The smell filled his nostrils. He could feel the cold water lapping around his shoulders, around his neck. He could taste the water. It filled his mouth. He tried to swallow but he couldn't. The water was choking him now. It was making him retch. It was slipping down into his lungs. It was pushing out all the air. It was stopping him breathe. He began to gasp. He wanted to call out for help. But he could do nothing to save himself. Nothing at all.

THIRTY

They found Maria Grimes' body just near where Adam and Lydia had gone into the river. The police divers went down time after time. Grace watched them from the bank. She had come back from the hospital. Liam O'Regan and the other guard, who had rowed out and brought her into the shore, had told her about the young man who had been found further downriver. She asked to see him. She recognized him from the photographs in the passport and the school ID card.

'It's a miracle he survived,' the doctor said. 'He has acute hypothermia, but that's all. He'll be fine in a couple of days' time.'

Grace sat by his bed and watched him sleep. Adam had been right. He wasn't what she expected. He was very like Lydia and in a strange kind of way he reminded her of Amelia. When she was sure that he was going to recover, she phoned Jack and told him everything. Then she went home to Trawbawn.

The gate lodge and the house were sealed off for technical examination so she walked down the same path that she and Lydia and Adam has walked early that morning. She stood on the bank near the boathouse and watched the divers at work. She saw them bring in Maria's body, and then an hour later they found Lydia. Grace went down to the little slip. Lydia was already encased in a black plastic body bag, but she asked them if they would unzip it for a moment. She knelt beside her mother. Lydia was very pale and very cold and there was weed in her hair. Grace picked it out and kissed her on the cheeks and on the mouth. Then she stood up and let them take her away.

They searched the riverbed for the rest of that day and for the next and the next. But they found nothing of Adam. Not his shoes, nor his clothes, nor any part of his body. After a week they abandoned the search. The bag that he had brought down to the boat, with his sleeping bag and his wet gear and fleece, contained enough DNA evidence to convict him of the murder of Maria Grimes. And the Saab contained plenty of evidence that Bernie Gallagher had been in it the night that she was murdered. Liam O'Regan wondered why they hadn't found his body. But he was sure that some day they would. Some day it would appear on one of the little islands in Roaring Water Bay. Washed out of the river by the fresh water pouring down from the land.

They buried Lydia next to Alex in the Chamberlain family graveyard. People came from miles around for the funeral. Her daughter and her grandchildren were the chief mourners. It was a beautiful day, bright and sunny. But just as Grace took hold of the shovel to scatter the earth on the coffin, it began to rain. She turned her face to the sky. The fresh water coursed down her cheeks. It washed clean her salt tears. The drops on her eyelashes refracted the light into tiny little rainbows. She brushed them away and looked down into the grave.

'Goodbye,' she said. 'Goodbye.'

The publishers hope that this book has given you enjoyable reading. Large Print Books are especially designed to be as easy to see and hold as possible. If you wish a complete list of our books please ask at your local library or write directly to:

Magna Large Print Books
Magna House, Long Preston,
Skipton, North Yorkshire.
BD23 4ND

This Large Print Book for the partially sighted, who cannot read normal print, is published under the auspices of

THE ULVERSCROFT FOUNDATION